BLOOD SHOT

Also by Sara Paretsky

BITTER MEDICINE
KILLING ORDERS
DEADLOCK
INDEMNITY ONLY

BLOOD SHOT

SARA PARETSKY

Delacorte
Press

For Dominick

Published by
Delacorte Press
The Bantam Doubleday Dell Publishing Group, Inc.
666 Fifth Avenue
New York, New York 10103

ISBN 0-440-50035-4

Acknowledgments

A writer working on a project that includes much technical material incurs many debts. As with the Bill of Rights, the enumeration of some does not mean that others are not considered equally important.

Judy Freeman and Rennie Heath, environmental specialists with the South Chicago Development Commission, gave freely of their time and expertise on both the geography and the economic issues facing South Chicago. Jeffrey S. Brown, Environmental Manager of Velsicol Corporation, and John Thompson, Executive Director of the Central States Education Center, both provided valuable insights into the corporate and technical problems that might arise in the situation I envisioned. Doctors Sarah Neely and Susan S. Riter were most helpful in diagnosing the problems besetting Louisa Djiak. And Sergeant Michael Black of the Matteson Police Department has been unfailingly helpful throughout V.I.'s career with advice on police procedure, handgun use, and other matters.

Because this is a work of fiction, all companies, persons, chemicals, manufacturing processes, medical side effects, and political or community organizations are totally the creation of my unaided—and unfettered—imagination. While some major corporations are mentioned by name, it is only where their plants form a well-known part of the Chicago landscape —to omit them would mean too much tampering with geography. For the same reason, existing ward boundaries were used, without in any way referring to real politicians who serve the citizens of those wards.

For those who are fanatics about geographical details, some minor ones have been deliberately altered to facilitate the story. However, South Chicago does contain some of Illinois's last wetlands for migratory birds, and a part of that marsh is really known as Dead Stick Pond.

CONTENTS

1. Highway 41 Revisited 1
2. Bringing Up Baby 7
3. My Sister's Keeper 13
4. The Old Folks at Home 20
5. The Simple Joys of Childhood 27
6. The Mill on the Calumet 34
7. The Boys in the Back Room 39
8. The Good Doctor 47
9. Lifestyles of the Rich and Famous 54
10. Fire When Ready 62
11. The Brat's Tale 69
12. Common Sense 78
13. Dead Stick Pond 83
14. Muddy Waters 88
15. Chemistry Lesson 93
16. House Call 100
17. Tombstone Blues 106
18. In His Father's Shadow 115
19. You Can't Go Home Again 120
20. White Elephant 126
21. Mama's Boy 133
22. The Doctor's Dilemma 138

23.	End Run	142
24.	In Grimpen Mire	147
25.	Visiting Hours	154
26.	Back to Home Base	160
27.	The Game's Afoot	165
28.	The Golden Notebooks	171
29.	Night Crawlers	177
30.	Fence Mending	182
31.	Old Fireball	188
32.	Flushed Out of the Pocket	194
33.	A Family Affair	200
34.	Bank Shot	205
35.	Changing Words at Buckingham Fountain	213
36.	Bad Blood	221
37.	The Shark Puts Out Bait	228
38.	Toxic Shock	235
39.	Plant Clean-Up	243
40.	Night Shakes	250
41.	A Wise Child	257
42.	Humboldt's Gift	263
43.	Bringing It All Back Home	273

1

Highway 41 Revisited

I had forgotten the smell. Even with the South Works on strike and Wisconsin Steel padlocked and rusting away, a pungent mix of chemicals streamed in through the engine vents. I turned off the car heater, but the stench—you couldn't call it air—slid through minute cracks in the Chevy's windows, burning my eyes and sinuses.

I followed Route 41 south. A couple of miles back it had been Lake Shore Drive, with Lake Michigan spewing foam against the rocks on my left, expensive high rises haughtily looking on from the right. At Seventy-ninth Street the lake disappeared abruptly. The weed-choked yards surrounding the giant USX South Works stretched away to the east, filling the mile or so of land between road and water. In the distance, pylons, gantries, and towers loomed through the smoke-hung February air. Not the land of high rises and beaches anymore, but landfill and worn-out factories.

Decaying bungalows looked on the South Works from the right side of the street. Some were missing pieces of siding, or shamefacedly showing stretches of peeling paint. In others the concrete in the front steps cracked and sagged. But the windows were all whole, tightly sealed, and not a scrap of debris lay in the yards. Poverty might have overtaken the area, but my old neighbors gallantly refused to give in to it.

I could remember when eighteen thousand men poured from those tidy little homes every day into the South Works, Wisconsin Steel, the Ford assembly plant, or the Xerxes solvent factory. I remembered when each piece of trim was painted fresh every second spring and new Buicks or Oldsmobiles were an autumn commonplace. But that was in a different life, for me as well as South Chicago.

At Eighty-ninth Street I turned west, flipping down the sun visor to shield my eyes from the waning winter sun. Beyond the tangle of deadwood, rusty cars, and collapsed houses on my left lay the Calumet River. My friends and I used to flout our parents by swimming there; my stomach turned now at the thought of sticking my face into the filthy water.

The high school stood across from the river. It was an enormous structure, sprawling over several acres, but its dark red brick somehow looked homey, like a nineteenth-century girls' college. Light pouring from the windows and streams of young people going through the vast double doors on the west end added to the effect of quaintness. I turned off the engine, reached for my gym bag, and joined the crowd.

The high, vaulted ceilings were built when heat was cheap and education respected enough for people to want schools to look like cathedrals. The cavernous hallways served as perfect echo chambers for the laughing, shouting crowd. Noise hurled from the ceiling, the walls, and the metal lockers. I wondered why I never noticed the din when I was a student.

They say you don't forget the things you learn young. I'd last been here twenty years ago, but at the gym entrance I turned left without thinking to follow the hall down to the women's locker room. Caroline Djiak was waiting at the door, clipboard in hand.

"Vic! I thought maybe you'd chickened out. Everyone else got here half an hour ago. They're suited up, at least the ones who can still get into their uniforms. You did bring yours, didn't you? Joan Lacey's here from the *Herald-Star* and she'd like to talk to you. After all, you were tournament MVP, weren't you?"

Caroline hadn't changed. The copper pigtails were cut into a curly halo around her freckled face, but that seemed to be the only difference. She was still short, energetic, and tactless.

I followed her into the locker room. The din there rivaled the noise level in the hall outside. Ten young women in various stages of undress were screaming at each other—for a nail file, a tampon, who stole my fucking deodorant. In bras and panties they looked muscular and trim, much fitter than my friends and I had been at that age. Certainly fitter than we were now.

In a corner of the locker room, making almost as much noise, were seven of the ten Lady Tigers with whom I'd won the state Class AA championship twenty years ago. Five of the seven had on their old black-and-gold uniforms. On some the T-shirts stretched tight across their breasts, and the shorts looked as though they might split if the wearer tried a fast breakaway.

The one packed tightest into her uniform might have been Lily Goldring, our leading free-throw shooter, but the permed hair and extra chin made it hard to be sure. I thought Alma Lowell was the black woman who had spread far beyond the capacity of her uniform and had her letter jacket perched uneasily on her massive shoulders.

The only two I recognized for certain were Diane Logan and Nancy Cleghorn. Diane's strong slender legs could still do for a *Vogue* cover. She'd been our star forward, co-captain, honors student. Caroline had told me Diane now ran a successful Loop PR agency, specializing in promoting black companies and personalities.

Nancy Cleghorn and I had stayed in touch through college; even so, her strong square face and frizzy blond hair were so unchanged, I would have known her anyplace. She was responsible for my being here tonight. She directed environmental affairs for SCRAP—the South Chicago Reawakening Project where Caroline Djiak was the deputy director. When the two of them realized the Lady Tigers were going into the regional championships for the first time in twenty years, they decided to get the old team together for a pregame ceremony. Publicity for the neighborhood, publicity for SCRAP, support for the team—good for everyone.

Nancy grinned when she saw me. "Yo, Warshawski—get your ass moving. We gotta be on the floor in ten minutes."

"Hi, Nancy. I ought to have my head examined for letting you get me down here. Don't you know you can't go home again?"

I found four square inches of bench to dump my gym bag on and quickly stripped, stuffing my jeans into the bag and putting on my faded uniform. I adjusted the socks and tied the high-lacing shoes.

Diane put an arm around me. "You're looking good, Whitey, like you still could move around if you had to."

We looked into the mirror. While some of the current Tigers topped six feet, at five-eight I'd been the tallest one on our team. Diane's afro was about level with my nose. Black and white, we'd both wanted to play basketball when race fights were a daily disruption in hall and locker room. We hadn't liked each other, but junior year we'd forced a truce on the rest of the team and the next February we'd taken them to the first statewide girls tournament.

She grinned, sharing the memory. "All that garbage we used to put ourselves through seems mighty trivial now, Warshawski. Come over and meet the reporter. Say something nice about the old neighborhood."

The *Herald-Star'*s Joan Lacey was the city's only woman sports columnist. When I said I read her stuff regularly she smiled with pleasure. "Tell my editor. Better still, write a letter. So how do you feel putting on your uniform after all these years?"

"Like an idiot. I haven't held a basketball since I left college." I'd gone to the University of Chicago on an athletic scholarship. The U of C offered them long before the rest of the country knew that women played sports.

We talked for a few minutes, about the past, about aging athletes, about the fifty percent unemployed in the neighborhood, about the current team's prospects.

"We're rooting for them, of course," I said. "I'm anxious to see them on the court. In here they look as though they take conditioning much more seriously than we did twenty years ago."

"Yeah, they keep hoping the women's pro league will revive. There're some top-notch women players in high school and college with no place to go."

Joan put her notebook away and told a photographer to get us out on the court for some shots. We eight old-timers straggled out to the gym floor, Caroline worrying around us like an overzealous terrier.

Diane picked up a ball and dribbled it behind her, under her legs, then bounced it to me. I turned and shot. The ball caromed from the backboard and I ran in to get it and dunk it. My old teammates gave me a ragged hand.

The photographer took some pictures of us together, then of Diane and me playing one-on-one under the net. The crowd got into it a little, but their real interest was on the current team. When the Lady Tigers took the floor in their warm-up suits, they got a big round. We worked out a little with them, but turned the floor over to them as soon as possible: this was their big night.

When the girls from visiting St. Sophia came out in their red-and-white sweats, I slid back to the locker room and started to change back to my civvies. Caroline found me as I finished tying my neck scarf.

"Vic! Where are you going? You know you promised to come over to see Ma after the game!"

"I said I'd try, if I could stay down here."

"She's counting on seeing you. She can hardly get out of bed she's in such bad shape. This really matters to her."

In the mirror I could see her face flush and her blue eyes darken with the same hurt look she used to give me when she was five and I wouldn't let her tag along with my friends. I felt my temper rise with twenty-year-old irritation.

"Did you arrange this basketball farce to manipulate me into visiting Louisa? Or did that only come to you later?"

The flush deepened to scarlet. "What do you mean, farce? I'm trying to do something for this community. I'm not a la-di-da snot going off to the North Side and abandoning people to their fate!"

"What, you think if I'd stayed down here I could've saved Wisconsin Steel? Or stopped the assholes at USX from striking one of the last operating plants around here?" I grabbed my peajacket from the bench and angrily thrust my arms into it.

"Vic! Where are you going?"

"Home. I have a dinner date. I want to change clothes."

"You can't. I need you," she wailed loudly. The big eyes were swimming with tears now, a prelude to a squawk to her mother or mine that I was being mean to her. It brought back all the times Gabriella had come to the door—saying "What difference can it make to you, Victoria? Take the child with you"—so forcibly it was all I could do not to slap Caroline's wide trembling mouth.

"What do you need me for? To make good on a promise you made without consulting me?"

"Ma isn't going to live much longer," she shouted. "Isn't that more important than some stupid-ass date?"

"Certainly. If this were a social occasion, I would call and say excuse me, the little brat next door committed me to something I can't get out of. But this is dinner with a client. He's temperamental but he pays on time and I like to keep him happy."

Tears were streaming across the freckles now. "Vic, you never take me seriously. I told you when we were discussing this how important it would be for Ma if you came to visit. And you completely forgot. You still think I'm five years old and nothing I say or think matters."

That shut me up. She had a point. And if Louisa was that sick, I really ought to see her.

"Oh, all right. I'll phone and change my plans. One last time."

The tears disappeared instantly. "Thanks, Vic. I won't forget it. I knew I could count on you."

"You mean you knew you could make another end run around me," I said disagreeably.

She laughed. "Let me show you where the phones are."

"I'm not senile yet—I can still find them. And no, I won't sneak off while you're not looking," I added, seeing her uneasy look.

She grinned. "As God is your witness?"

It was an old pledge, picked up from her mother's drunk Uncle Stan, who used it to prove he was sober.

"As God is my witness," I agreed solemnly. "I just hope Graham's feelings aren't so hurt, he decides not to pay his bill."

I found the pay phones near the front entrance and wasted several quarters before running Darrough Graham down at the Forty-Nine Club. He wasn't happy—he had made reservations at the Filagree—but I managed to end the conversation on a friendly note. Slinging my bag over my shoulder, I made my way back to the gym.

2

Bringing Up Baby

St. Sophia gave the Lady Tigers a tough ride, leading through much of the second half. The play was intense, much faster paced than in my basketball years. Two starters for the Lady Tigers fouled out with seven minutes left, and things looked bad. Then the toughest Saint guard went out with three minutes left. The Tigers' star forward, who'd been penned in all evening, came to life, scoring eight unanswered points. The home team won 54–51.

I found myself cheering as eagerly as anyone. I even felt a nostalgic warmth for my own high school team, which surprised me: my adolescent memories are so dominated by my mother's illness and death, I guess I've forgotten having any good times.

Nancy Cleghorn had left to attend a meeting, but Diane Logan and I joined the rest of our old team in the locker room to congratulate our successors and wish them well in the regional semifinals. We didn't stay long: they clearly thought we were too old to understand basketball, let alone have played it.

Diane came over to say good-bye to me. "You couldn't pay me enough to relive my adolescence," she said, brushing my cheek with her own. "I'm going back to the Gold Coast. And I'm definitely staying there. Take it easy, Warshawski." She was gone in a shimmer of silver fox and Opium.

Caroline hovered anxiously around the locker-room door, worried I would leave without her. She was so tense I began to feel uneasy about what I was going to find at her house. She'd acted just this way when she'd dragged me home from college one weekend, ostensibly because Louisa had hurt her back and needed help replacing a broken window. After I got there I found she expected me to explain why she'd given Louisa's little pearl ring to the St. Wenceslaus Lenten fund drive.

"Is Louisa really sick?" I demanded as we finally left the locker room.

She looked at me soberly. "Very sick, Vic. You're not going to like seeing her."

"What's the rest of your agenda, then?"

The ready color flooded her cheeks. "I don't know what you're talking about."

She flounced out the school door. I followed slowly, in time to see her get into a battered car parked with its nose well into the street. She rolled down the window as I walked by to yell that she'd see me at the house and took off in a squeal of rubber. My shoulders were sagging a little as I unlocked the Chevy door and slid in.

My gloom increased when I made the turn onto Houston Street. I'd last been on the block in 1976 when my father died and I came back down to sell the house. I'd seen Louisa then, and Caroline, who was fourteen and following determinedly in my steps—she even tried playing basketball, but at five feet even her tireless energy couldn't get her onto the first squad.

That was the last time I had talked to any of the other neighbors who had known my parents. There was genuine grief for my gentle, good-humored father. Grudging respect for Gabriella, dead ten years at the time. After all, the other women on the block had shared her scraping, saving, cutting each penny five ways to feed and shelter their families.

Now she was dead, they glossed over the eccentricities that used to make them shake their heads—taking the girl to the opera with an extra ten dollars instead of buying her a new winter coat. Not baptizing her or giving her to the sisters at St. Wenceslaus for schooling. That disturbed them enough that they sent the principal, Mother Joseph Something, around one day for a memorable confrontation.

Maybe the biggest folly of all to them was her insisting on college for me, and demanding that it be the University of Chicago. Only the best did for Gabriella, and she'd decided that was Chicago's best when I was two. Not, perhaps, comparing in her mind with the University of Pisa. Just as the shoes she bought herself at Callabrano's on Morgan Street didn't compare to Milan. But one did what one could. So two years after my mother's death I'd left on a scholarship for what my neighbors called Red University, half scared, half excited to meet the demons up there. And after that, I'd never really gone home again.

Louisa Djiak was the one woman on the block who always stood up for Gabriella, dead or alive. But then, she owed Gabriella. And me, too, I thought with a flash of bitterness that startled me. I realized I was still pissed at spending all those glorious summer days baby-sitting, at doing my homework with Louisa's baby howling in the background.

Well, the baby was grown up now, but she was still howling exigently in my ear. I pulled up behind her Capri and turned off the engine.

The house was smaller than I remembered, and dingier. Louisa wasn't well enough to wash and starch the curtains every six months and Caroline belonged to a generation that emphatically avoided such tasks. I should know—I was part of it myself.

Caroline was waiting in the doorway for me, still edgy. She gave a brief, tense smile. "Ma's really excited you're here, Vic. She's waited all day to have her coffee so she could drink it with you."

She took me through the small, cluttered dining room to the kitchen, saying over her shoulder, "She's not supposed to drink coffee anymore. But it was too hard for her to give it up—along with everything else that's changed for her. So we compromise on one cup a day."

She busied herself at the stove, tackling the coffee with energetic inefficiency. Despite a trail of spilled water and coffee grounds on the stove, she carefully arranged a TV tray with china, cloth napkins, and a geranium cut from a coffee can in the window. Finally she set out a little dish of ice cream with a geranium leaf in it. When she picked up the tray I stood up from my perch on the kitchen stool to follow her.

Louisa's bedroom lay to the right of the dining room. As soon as Caroline opened the door the smell of sickness hit me like a physical force, bringing back the odor of medicine and decaying flesh that had hung around Gabriella the last year of her life. I dug the nails into the palm of my right hand and willed myself into the room.

My first reaction was shock, even though I thought I'd prepared myself. Louisa sat propped in bed, her face gaunt and tinged a queer greenish gray under her wispy hair. Her twisted hands emerged from the loose sleeves of a worn pink cardigan. When she held them out to me with a smile, though, I caught a glimpse of the beautiful young woman who'd rented the house next to ours when she was pregnant with Caroline.

"Good to see you, Victoria. Knew you'd come by. You're like your ma that way. Look like her, too, even though you have your daddy's gray eyes."

I knelt by the bed and hugged her. Underneath the cardigan her bones felt tiny and brittle.

She gave a racking cough that shook her frame. "Excuse me. Too many damned cigarettes for too many years. Little missy here hides 'em from me —as if they could hurt me any worse now."

Caroline bit her lips and moved over next to the bed. "I brought you your coffee, Ma. Maybe it'll take your mind off your cigs."

"Yeah, my one cup. Damned doctors. First they pump you so full of shit you don't know whether you're coming or going. Then when they got you tied by the hind legs they take away anything that'd make the time pass easier. I'm telling you, girl, don't ever get yourself in this spot."

I took the thick china mug from Caroline and handed it to Louisa. Her hands shook slightly and she pressed the mug against her breast to steady it. I slid off my heels into a straight-backed chair near the bed.

"You want to spend some time alone with Vic, Ma?" Caroline asked.

"Yeah, sure. You go on, girl. I know you got work to do."

When the door shut behind Caroline I said, "I'm really sorry to see you like this."

She made a throwaway gesture. "Ah—what the hell. I'm sick of thinking about it, and I talk about it to the damned docs often enough. I want to hear about you. I follow all your cases when they make it to the papers. Your ma'd be real proud of you."

I laughed. "I'm not so sure. She hoped I'd be a concert singer. Or maybe a high-priced lawyer. I can just imagine her if she saw the way I live."

Louisa laid a bony hand on my arm. "Don't you think so, Victoria. Don't you think so for one minute. You know Gabriella—she'd of gave her last shirt to a beggar. Look how she stood up for me when people came by and threw eggs and shit at my windows. No. Maybe she'd of liked to see you living better than you do. Heck—I feel that way about Caroline. Her brains, her education and all, she could do better than hanging around this dump. But I'm real proud of her. She's honest and hardworking and she sticks up for what she believes in. And you're just the same. No, sir. Gabriella could see you now she'd be as proud as can be."

"Well, we couldn't have managed without your help when she was so sick," I muttered, uncomfortable.

"Oh, shit, girl. My one chance to pay her back for everything she did? I can still see her when the righteous ladies from St. Wenceslaus were out parading around my front door. Gabriella come out with a head of steam that damn near drove 'em into the Calumet."

She gave a shout of hoarse laughter that changed to a coughing fit which left her breathless and slightly purple. She lay quietly for a few minutes, panting in short, gasping breaths.

"Hard to believe folks cared so much about one pregnant unmarried teenager, ain't it," she said finally. "Here we got half the people outa work in the community—that's life and death, girl. But back then I guess it seemed like the end of the world to folks. I mean, my own ma and pa, even, throwing me out like they did." Her face worked for a minute. "Like it was all my fault or something. Your ma was the only one stood up for me. Even when my folks come around and decided to admit Caroline was alive, they never really forgave her for being born or me for doing it."

Gabriella never did anything by half measures: I helped her look after the baby so Louisa could work the night shift at Xerxes. The days when I had to take Caroline to her grandparents' were my worst torment. Rigid, humorless, they wouldn't let me into the house unless I took my shoes off. A couple of times they even bathed Caroline outside before they'd admit her to their pristine portals.

Louisa's parents were only in their sixties—same age as Gabriella and Tony would be if they were still alive. Because Louisa had a baby and lived by herself, I'd always thought of her as part of my parents' generation, but she was only five or six years older than me.

"When did you stop working?" I asked. I called Louisa occasionally, when my guilty imagination conjured up Gabriella's image, but it had been awhile. South Chicago hovered too uneasily at the base of my mind for me to willingly court its return to my life, and it had been over two years since I'd spoken to Louisa. She hadn't said anything then about feeling bad.

"Oh, it got so I couldn't stand anymore about—must be just over a year. So they put me on disability then. It's only been the last six months or so I couldn't get around at all."

She flicked the covers back from her legs. They were twigs, thin bones a bird might use but mottled greeny-gray like her face. Livid patches on her feet and ankles showed where her veins had given up carting blood around.

"It's my kidneys," she said. "Darned things don't want me to pee properly. Caroline takes me over two, three times a week and they stick me on that damned machine, supposed to clean me out, but between you and me, girl, I'd just as soon they'd let me go in peace." She held up a thin hand. "Don't you go telling Caroline that, now—she's doing everything to see I get the best. And the company pays for it, so it's not like I feel she's digging into her own savings. I don't want her to think I ain't grateful."

"No, no," I said soothingly, pulling the cover up gently.

She reverted to the old days on the block, to the days when her legs were slim and muscular, when she used to go dancing after getting off work at midnight. To Steve Ferraro, who wanted to marry her, and Joey Pankowski, who didn't, and how if she had to do it over, she'd do it the same, because she had Caroline, but for Caroline she wanted something different, something better than staying on in South Chicago working herself to an early old age.

At last I took the bony fingers and squeezed them gently. "I've got to go, Louisa—it's twenty miles to my place. But I'll come back."

"Well, it's been real good to see you again, girl." She cocked her head on one side and gave a naughty smile. "Don't suppose you could find a way to slip me a pack of cigarettes, do you?"

I laughed. "I'm not touching that with a barge pole, Louisa—you work it out with Caroline."

I shook out her pillows and turned on the TV for her before going off to find Caroline. Louisa had never been much given to kissing, but she squeezed my hand tightly for a few seconds.

3

My Sister's Keeper

Caroline was sitting at the dining-room table, eating fried chicken and making notes on a colored graph. Chaotic stacks of paper—reports, magazines, flyers—covered all of the small surface. A large pile near her left elbow teetered uncertainly on the table edge. She put down her pencil when she heard me come into the room.

"I went out for some Kentucky Fried while you were in with Ma. Want some? What did you think—kind of a shock, huh?"

I shook my head in dismay. "It's terrible to see her like this. How are you holding up?"

She grimaced. "It wasn't so bad until her legs wouldn't support her anymore. She show 'em to you? I knew she would. It's really tough on her not being able to get around. The hard part for me was realizing how long she'd been sick before I noticed anything. You know Ma—she'd never complain in a million years, especially about anything as private as her kidneys."

She rubbed a greasy hand through her unruly curls. "It was only three years ago, when I suddenly noticed how much weight she'd been losing, that I even knew anything was wrong. Then it came out she'd been feeling off for a long time—dizzy and stuff, her feet numb—but she didn't want to say anything that might jeopardize her job."

The story sounded depressingly familiar. People on the hip North Side went to the doctor every time they stubbed their toes, but in South Chicago you expected life to be tough. Dizziness and weight loss happened to lots of people; it was the kind of thing grown-ups kept to themselves.

"You satisfied with the doctors she's seeing?"

Caroline finished gnawing on the chicken thigh and licked her fingers. "They're okay. We go to Help of Christians because that's where Xerxes has their medical plan, and they do as much as anyone could. I mean, her kidneys just aren't working at all—they call it acute renal failure—and it looks like she may have some bone marrow problems and maybe starting with emphysema. That's our only real problem—she keeps going on about her damned cigarettes. Hell, they may have helped get her into this fix to begin with."

I said awkwardly, "If she's in that bad shape, the cigarettes aren't going to make her any worse, you know."

"Vic! You didn't say that to her, did you? I have to fight her about them ten times a day as it is. If she thinks you're backing her up, I might as well quit on the spot." She slapped the table emphatically; the teetering pile of papers flew across the floor. "I was sure you of all people would support me on this."

"You know how I feel about smoking," I said, annoyed. "I expect Tony would be alive today if he hadn't had a two-pack-a-day habit—I still hear him wheezing and coughing in my nightmares. But how much time is smoking going to shave from Louisa's life at this point? She's in there by herself, got nothing but the tube to keep her company. I'm just saying it'd make her feel better mentally and won't make her any worse physically."

Caroline set her mouth in an uncompromising line. "No. I don't even want to talk about it."

I sighed and got down on the floor to help her with the loose papers. When we had them all collated again I looked at her suspiciously: she had reverted to her tense abstracted mood.

"Well, I think it's time for me to push off. I hope the Lady Tigers go all the way again."

"I—Vic. I need to talk to you. I need your help."

"Caroline, I came down and pranced around in my basketball uniform for you. I saw Louisa. Not that I grudge the time with her, but how many items you got on your agenda tonight?"

"I want to hire you. Professionally. I need your help as a detective," she said defiantly.

"What for? You give SCRAP's money to the church Lenten fund and now you want me to find it for you again?"

"Goddamn you, Vic! Could you stop acting like I'm still five years old and treat me seriously for a minute?"

"If you wanted to hire me, why couldn't you have said something about it on the phone?" I asked. "Your step-by-step approach to me isn't exactly designed to make me feel serious about you."

"I wanted you to see Ma before I talked to you about it," she muttered, looking at her graph. "I thought if you saw how bad off she is, you'd think it was more important."

I sat at the end of the table. "Caroline, lay it out for me. I promise I'll listen as seriously to you as to any other potential client. But tell me the whole story, front, middle, and end. Then we can decide if you really need a detective, if it should be me, and so on."

She took a breath and said quickly, "I want you to find my father for me."

I was quiet for a minute.

"Isn't that a job for a detective?" she demanded.

"Do you know who he is?" I asked gently.

"No, that's partly what I need you to find out for me. You see how bad Ma is, Vic. She's going to die soon." She tried to keep her voice matter-of-fact, but it quavered a little. "Her folks always treated me like—I don't know—not the same way they are to my cousins. Second-class, I guess. When she dies I'd like to have some kind of family. I mean, maybe my old man will turn out to be an asshole jerk. The kind of guy who lets a girl go through what Ma did when she was pregnant might be. But maybe he'd have folks who'd like me. And if he didn't, at least I'd know."

"What does Louisa say? Have you asked her?"

"She practically killed me. Practically killed herself—she got so upset she almost choked to death. Screaming how I was ungrateful, she'd worked herself to the bone for me, I never wanted for anything, why'd I have to go nosing around in something that wasn't any of my damned business. So I knew I couldn't go on about it with her. But I have to find out. I know you could do it for me."

"Caroline, maybe you're better off not knowing. Even if I knew how to go about it—missing persons aren't a big part of my business—if it's that painful to Louisa, you might prefer not to find out."

"You know who he is, don't you!" she cried.

I shook my head. "I have no idea, honestly. Why did you think I do?"

She looked down. "I'm sure she told Gabriella. I thought maybe Gabriella told you."

I moved over to sit down next to her. "Maybe Louisa told my mother, but if so, it wasn't the kind of thing Gabriella thought I ought to know about. As God is my witness, I don't know."

She gave a little smile at that. "So will you find him for me?"

If I hadn't known her all her life, it would have been easier to say no. I specialize in financial crime. Missing persons takes a certain kind of skill, and certain kinds of contacts I've never bothered cultivating. And this guy'd been gone more than a quarter of a century.

But in addition to whining and teasing and tagging along when I didn't want her, Caroline used to adore me. When I went off to college she'd race to meet my train if I came home for the weekend, copper pigtails flying around her head, plump legs pumping as hard as they could. She even went out for basketball because I did. She almost drowned following me into Lake Michigan when she was four. The memories were endless. Her blue eyes still looked at me with total trust. I didn't want to, but I couldn't keep from responding.

"You got any idea where to start this search?"

"Well, you know. It had to be someone who lived in East Side. She never went anyplace else. I mean, she'd never even been to the Loop until your mother took us there to look at the Christmas decorations when I was three."

East Side was an all-white neighborhood to the east of South Chicago. It was cut off from the city by the Calumet River, and its residents tended to lead parochial, inbred lives. Louisa's parents still lived there in the house she'd grown up in.

"That's helpful," I said encouragingly. "What do you figure the population was in 1960? Twenty thousand? And only half of them were men. And many of those were children. You got any other ideas?"

"No," she said doggedly. "That's why I need a detective."

Before I could say anything else the doorbell rang. Caroline looked at her watch. "That might be Aunt Connie. She sometimes comes this late. Be back in a minute."

She trotted out to the entryway. While she dealt with the caller I flipped through a magazine devoted to the solid-waste-disposal industry, wondering if I was really insane enough to look for Caroline's father. I was staring at a picture of a giant incinerator when she came back into the room. Nancy Cleghorn, my old basketball pal who now worked for SCRAP, was trailing behind her.

"Hi, Vic. Sorry to barge in, but I wanted to fill Caroline in on a problem."

Caroline looked at me apologetically and asked if I'd mind waiting a few minutes to finish up.

"Not at all," I said politely, wondering if I was doomed to spend the night in South Chicago. "Want me to go to the other room?"

Nancy shook her head. "It's not private. Just annoying."

She sat down and unbuttoned her coat. She'd changed from her basketball uniform to a tan dress with a red scarf, and she'd put on makeup, but she still managed to appear disheveled.

"I got to the meeting in plenty of time. Ron was waiting for me—Ron Kappelman, our lawyer"—she put in an aside to me—"and we found we weren't on the agenda. So Ron went up to talk to that fat moron Martin O'Gara, saying we'd filed our material in plenty of time and talked to the secretary this morning to make sure she included us. So O'Gara makes this big show of not knowing what the hell is going on, and calls the board secretary and disappears for a while. Then he comes back and says there were so many legal problems with our submission, they'd decided not to consider it this evening."

"We want to build a solvent recycling plant here," Caroline explained to me. "We've got funding, we have a site, we have specs that have passed every EPA test we can think of, and we have some customers right on our doorstep—Xerxes and Glow-Rite. It means a good hundred jobs down here, and a chance to make a dent in the crap going into the ground."

She turned back to Nancy. "So what can the problem be? What did Ron say?"

"I was so mad I couldn't speak. He was so mad I was afraid he'd break O'Gara's neck—if he could find it underneath the fat rolls. But he called Dan Zimring, the EPA lawyer, you know. Dan said we could come by his place, so we went over there and he looked through everything and said it couldn't be in better shape."

Nancy fluffed out her frizzy hair so that it stood up wildly around her head. She helped herself absently to a piece of chicken.

"I'll tell you what I think the problem is," Caroline snapped, cheeks flushed. "They probably showed the submission to Art Jurshak—you know, professional courtesy or some shit. I think he blocked it."

"Art Jurshak," I echoed. "Is he still alderman down here? He must be a hundred and fifty by now."

"No, no," Caroline said impatiently. "He's only in his sixties somewhere. Don't you agree, Nancy?"

"I think he's sixty-two," she answered through a mouthful of chicken.

"Not about his age," Caroline said impatiently. "That Jurshak must be trying to block the plant."

Nancy licked her fingers. She looked around for a place to put the bone and finally laid it back on the plate with the rest of the chicken. "I don't see how you figure that, Caroline. There could be a lot of people who don't want to see a recycling center down here."

Caroline looked at her through narrowed eyes. "What did O'Gara say? I mean, he must have given some reason for not giving us a hearing."

Nancy frowned. "He said we shouldn't try to make proposals like this without community backing. I told him the community was a hundred percent behind us, and got ready to show him copies of petitions and crap, when he gave this jolly laugh and said, not a hundred percent. He'd heard from people who weren't behind it at all."

"But why Jurshak?" I asked, interested in spite of myself. "Why not Xerxes, or the Mob, or some rival solvent recycler?"

"Just the political tie-in," Caroline answered. "O'Gara's chairman of the zoning board because he's good buddies with all the old hack Dems."

"But, Caroline—Art's got no reason to oppose us. Our last meeting he even acted like he would support us."

"He never put it in so many words," Caroline said grimly. "And all it would take is someone willing to wave a big enough campaign contribution in front of him for him to change his mind."

"I suppose," Nancy agreed reluctantly. "I just don't like to think it."

"Why are you so pally with Jurshak all of a sudden?" Caroline demanded.

It was Nancy's turn to flush. "I'm not. But if he's against us, it'll be damned near impossible to get O'Gara to give us a hearing. Unless we could come up with a bribe big enough to make Jurshak respond to us. So how do I find who's against the plant, Vic? Aren't you a detective or something these days?"

I frowned at her and said hurriedly, "Or something. Trouble is, you've got too many possibilities in a political mess like this. The Mob. They're into a lot of waste-disposal projects in Chicago. Maybe they figure you'd be cutting into their turf. Or Return to Eden. I know they're supposed to be foursquare for the environment, but they've been raising a lot of money lately based on dramatic gestures they're making here in South Chicago. Maybe they don't want something that cuts off their fund-raising tactics. Or the Sanitary District—maybe they're taking kickbacks to look the other way on local pollution and they don't want to lose the revenues. Or Xerxes doesn't—"

"Enough!" she protested. "You're right, of course. It could be all of them or any of them. But in my place, where would you look first?"

"I don't know," I said thoughtfully. "Probably nuzzle up to someone on Jurshak's staff. See if the pressure came from there to begin with. And if it did, why. It'd save you the trouble of making the rounds of an infinite number of possibilities. Plus you wouldn't rub against someone who might want to put you in cement booties just for asking."

"You know some of the people who work for Art, don't you?" Caroline asked Nancy.

"Yes, yes I do." She fiddled with another piece of chicken. "It's just I haven't wanted . . . Oh, well. Anything for the cause of right and justice, I guess."

She picked up her coat and headed for the door. She stood looking at us for a moment, then set her lips firmly and left.

"I thought you might want to help her find out who's against the plant," Caroline said.

"I know you did, sweet pea. And even though it would be lots of fun, working for one poor customer in South Chicago is about all my budget can take at a time."

"You mean you'll help me? You'll find my father?" The blue eyes turned dark with excitement. "I can pay you, Vic. Really. I'm not asking you to do it for nothing. I've got a thousand dollars saved."

My usual rate is two-fifty a day, plus expenses. Even with a twenty percent family discount, I had a feeling she was going to run out of money before I ran out of detecting. But no one had forced me to agree. I was a free agent, governed only by my own whims, and guilt.

"I'll send you a contract to sign tomorrow," I told her. "And you can't be on the phone to me every half hour demanding results. This is going to take a long time."

"No, Vic. I won't." She smiled tremulously. "I can't tell you how much it means to me to know you're helping me out."

4

The Old Folks at Home

In my sleep that night I saw Caroline again as a baby, her face pink and blotchy from crying. My mother stood behind me telling me to look after the child. When I woke at nine the dream lay heavy in my head, cloaking me in lethargy. The job I'd agreed to do filled me with distaste.

Find Caroline's father for a thousand dollars. Find Caroline's father against Louisa's strongly voiced opposition. If she felt that violently about the guy after all this time, he was probably better left unfound. Assuming he was still alive. Assuming he'd lived in Chicago and hadn't been an itinerant journeyman amusing himself on his way through town.

At last I stuck a leaden foot out from under the bedclothes. The room was cold. We'd had such a mild winter I'd turned off the radiator to keep the place from becoming stuffy, but the temperature had apparently dropped during the night. I pulled my leg back under the blanket for a minute, but moving cracked my shell of indolence. I swung the covers back and got up.

Grabbing a sweatshirt from a pile on a chair, I trotted into the kitchen to start coffee. Maybe it was too cold out to go running. I parted the curtain overlooking the backyard. The sky was gray and an east wind was blowing debris against the back fence. I was dropping the curtain when a black nose and two paws appeared against the window, followed by a sharp bark. It was Peppy, the golden retriever I shared with my downstairs neighbor.

I opened the door, but she wouldn't come in. Instead she danced around on the little porch, indicating that the weather was perfect for running and would I please get a move on?

"Oh, all right," I grumbled. I turned off the water and went into the living room to do my stretches. Peppy didn't understand why I wasn't limber and ready to go as soon as I got out of bed. Every few minutes she'd give a minatory bark from the back. When I finally appeared in my sweats and running shoes, she raced down the stairs, turning at every half landing to make sure I was still coming. She gave little grunts of ecstasy when I opened the gate to the alley, even though we make the trip together three or four times a week.

I like to run about five miles. Since that's beyond Peppy's range, she stops at the lagoon when we get to the lake. She spends the time nosing out ducks and muskrats, rolling in mud or rotted fish when she can find them, and bounds out at me with her tongue hanging out in a self-satisfied grin when I make my way back west. We do the last mile home at a mild jog and I hand her over to my downstairs neighbor. Mr. Contreras shakes his head, chews us both out for letting her get dirty, then spends a pleasurable half hour grooming her coat back to its gleaming golden-red.

He was waiting as usual this morning when we got back. "You two have a good run, doll? You keep the dog out of the water, I hope? This cold weather it isn't good for her to get wet, you know."

He hung in the doorway prepared to talk indefinitely. He's a retired machinist, and the dog, his cooking, and I make up the bulk of his entertainment. I extricated myself as quickly as I could, but it was still close to eleven by the time I'd showered. I ate breakfast in my bedroom while I dressed, knowing if I sat down with coffee and the paper I would keep making excuses for lingering. Leaving the dishes on the dresser, I wrapped a wool scarf around my neck, picked up my bag and car coat from the hall where I'd dumped them the night before, and headed south.

The wind was whipping up the lake. Ten-foot waves crashed against the rocky barrier and spewed fingers of water onto the road. The display of nature, angry, contemptuous, made me feel small.

Every detail of decay struck me as the road wound southward. The white paint was peeling and the gates sagging at the old South Shore Country Club, once a symbol of that area's wealth and exclusivity. As a child I used to imagine I would grow up to ride a horse along its private bridle paths. The memory of such fantasies embarrasses me slightly now—the trappings of caste don't sit well on my adult conscience. But I would have wished a better fate for the club than to rot slowly under the hands of the Park District, its indifferent current masters.

South Chicago itself looked moribund, its life frozen somewhere around the time of World War II. When I drove past the main business area I saw that most of the stores had Spanish names now. Other than that they looked much as they had when I was a little girl. Their grimy concrete walls still framed tawdry window displays of white nylon communion dresses, vinyl shoes, plastic furniture. Women wrapped in threadbare wool coats still wore cotton babushkas as they bent their heads into the wind. On the corners, near the ubiquitous storefront taverns, stood vacant-eyed, shabbily clad men. They had always been a presence, but the massive unemployment in the mills swelled their numbers now.

I had forgotten the trick to getting into East Side and had to double back to Ninety-fifth Street, where an old-fashioned drawbridge crosses the Calumet River. If South Chicago hadn't changed since 1945, East Side stuck itself in formaldehyde when Woodrow Wilson was President. Five bridges form the neighborhood's only link to the rest of the city. Its members live in a stubborn isolation, trying to recreate the Eastern European villages of their grandparents. They don't like people from across the river, and anyone north of Seventy-first Street might as well have rolled in on a Soviet tank for the reception they get.

I drove under the massive concrete legs of the interstate to 106th Street. Louisa's parents lived south of 106th on Ewing. I thought her mother would be home and hoped her father wouldn't be. He'd retired some years ago from the little printshop he'd managed, but he was active in the Knights of Columbus and his VFW lodge and he might be out having lunch with the boys.

The street was crammed with well-kept bungalows set on obsessively tidy lots. Not a scrap of paper lay on the street. Art Jurshak tended this part of his ward with loving hands. Street-cleaning and repair crews came through regularly. All along the southeast side, sidewalks had been built three or four feet above the original ground level. South Chicago held numerous gaping pits where the newer paving had collapsed, but in East Side not a crack showed between sidewalk and house. As I got out of my car I felt as though I should have undergone a surgical scrubdown before visiting the neighborhood.

The Djiak house lay halfway down the block. Its curtained front windows gleamed in the dull air, and the stoop shone from much scouring. I rang the bell, trying to build up enough mental energy to talk to Louisa's parents.

Martha Djiak came to the door. Her square, lined face was set in a frown suitable for dismissing door-to-door salesmen. After a moment she recognized me and the frown lightened a little. She opened the inner door. I could see she had an apron covering the crisply ironed front of her dress: I'd never seen her at home without an apron on.

"Well, Victoria. It's been a long time since you brought little Caroline over for a visit, hasn't it?"

"Yeah, it has," I agreed unenthusiastically.

Louisa would not let Caroline go to her grandparents' alone. If she or Gabriella couldn't take her, they gave me two quarters for the bus and careful instructions to stay with Caroline until it was time to return home again. I never understood why Mrs. Djiak couldn't come and fetch Caroline herself. Maybe Louisa was afraid her mother would try to keep the baby so she wouldn't grow up with an unwed single parent.

"Since you're down here, maybe you'd like a cup of coffee."

It wasn't effusive, but she'd never been demonstrative. I accepted with as much good cheer as I could muster and she opened the storm door for me. She was careful not to touch the glass panel with her hands. I slid through as unobtrusively as I could, remembering to take my shoes off in the tiny entryway before following her to the kitchen.

As I'd hoped, she was alone. The ironing board stood open in front of the stove, a shirt draped across it. She folded the shirt, laid it on the clothes basket, and collapsed the ironing board with quick silent motions. When everything was stowed in the tiny pantry behind the refrigerator, she put on water to boil.

"I talked to Louisa this morning. She said you'd been down there yesterday."

"Yes," I acknowledged. "It's tough to see someone that lively laid up the way she is."

Mrs. Djiak spooned coffee into the pot. "Lots of people suffer more with less cause."

"And lots of people carry on like Attila the Hun and never get a pimple. It just goes to show, doesn't it?"

She took two cups from a shelf and stood them primly on the table. "I hear you're a detective now. Doesn't really seem like a woman's job, does it? Kind of like Caroline, working on community development, or whatever she calls it. I don't know why you two girls couldn't get married, settle down, raise a family."

"I guess we're waiting for men as good as Mr. Djiak to come along," I said.

She looked at me seriously. "That's the trouble with you girls. You think life is romantic, like they show in the movies. A good steady man who brings his pay home every Friday is worth a lot more than fancy dinners and flowers."

"Was that Louisa's problem too?" I asked gently.

She set her lips in a thin line and turned back to the coffee. "Louisa had other problems," she said shortly.

"Like what?"

She carefully took a covered sugar bowl down from the cupboard over the stove and placed it with a little pitcher of cream in the middle of the table. She didn't say anything until she'd finished pouring the coffee.

"Louisa's problems are old now. And they never were any of your business."

"And what about Caroline? Are they any concern of hers?" I sipped the rich coffee, which Louisa still infused in the old European style.

"They don't have anything to do with her. She'd be a good deal better off if she learned not to poke around in other people's closets."

"Louisa's past matters a lot to Caroline. Louisa is dying and Caroline is feeling very lonely. She'd like to know who her father was."

"And that's why you came down here? To help her dig up all that trash? She should be ashamed she doesn't have any father, instead of talking about it with everyone she knows."

"What's she supposed to do?" I asked impatiently. "Kill herself because Louisa never married the man who got her pregnant? You act like it was all Louisa and Caroline's fault. Louisa was sixteen years old—fifteen when she got pregnant. Don't you think the man had any responsibility in this?"

She clenched the coffee cup so tightly, I was afraid the ceramic might shatter. "Men—have difficulty controlling themselves. We all know that," she said thickly. "Louisa must have led him on. But she would never admit it."

"All I want to know is his name," I said as quietly as I could. "I think Caroline has a right to know if she really wants to. And a right to see if her father's family would give her a little warmth."

"Rights!" she said bitterly. "Caroline's rights. Louisa's! What about my right to a life of peace and decency? You're as bad as your mother was."

"Yeah," I said. "In my book that's a compliment."

Behind me someone turned a key in the back door. Martha paled slightly and set down her coffee cup.

"You must not mention any of this in front of him," she said urgently. "Tell him you were just visiting Louisa and stopped by. Promise, Victoria."

I made a sour face. "Yeah, sure, I suppose."

As Ed Djiak came into the room Martha said brightly, "See who's come to visit us? You'll never recognize her from the little Victoria she used to be!"

Ed Djiak was tall. All the lines in his face and body were elongated, like a Modigliani painting, from his long, cavernous face to his long, dangling fingers. Caroline and Louisa inherited their short, square good looks from Martha. Who knows where their lively tempers came from.

"So, Victoria. You went off to the University of Chicago and got too good for the old neighborhood, huh?" He grunted and shifted a sack of groceries onto the table. "I got the apples and pork chops, but the beans didn't look right so I didn't buy any."

Martha quickly unpacked the groceries and stowed them and the bag in their appointed cells. "Victoria and I were just having some coffee, Ed. You want a cup?"

"You think I'm some old lady to drink coffee in the middle of the day? Get me a beer."

He sat down at the end of the small table. Martha moved to the refrigerator, which stood immediately to his side, and took a Pabst from the bottom shelf. She poured it carefully into a glass mug and put the can in the trash.

"I've been visiting Louisa," I said to him. "I'm sorry she's in such bad shape. But her spirits are impressive."

"We suffered for her for twenty-five years. Now it's her turn to suffer a little, huh?" He stared at me with sneering, angry eyes.

"Spell it out for me, Mr. Djiak," I said offensively. "What'd she do to make you suffer so?"

Martha made a little noise in her throat. "Victoria is working as a detective now, Ed. Isn't that nice?"

He ignored her. "You're just like your mother, you know. She used to carry on like Louisa was some kind of saint, instead of the whore she really was. You're just as bad. What did she do to me? Got herself pregnant. Used my name. Stayed in the neighborhood flaunting her baby instead of going off to the sisters the way we arranged for her to do."

"Louisa got herself pregnant?" I echoed. "With a turkey baster in the basement, you mean? There wasn't a man involved?"

Martha sucked in a nervous breath. "Victoria. We don't like to talk about these things."

"No, we don't," Ed agreed nastily, turning to her. "Your daughter. You couldn't control her. For twenty-five years the neighbors whispered behind my back, and now I have to be insulted in my own house by that Italian bitch's daughter."

My face turned hot. "You're disgusting, Djiak. You're terrified of women. You hate your own wife and daughter. No wonder Louisa turned to someone else for a little affection. Who was it to get you so exercised? Your local priest?"

He sprang up from the table, knocking over his beer stein, and hit me in the mouth. "Get out of my house, you mongrel bitch! Don't ever come back with your filthy mind, your vile tongue!"

I got up slowly and went over to stand in front of him, my face close enough to smell the beer on his breath. "You may *not* insult my mother, Djiak. Any other garbage from the cesspool you call a mind I'll tolerate. But you ever insult my mother again in my hearing I will break your neck."

I stared at him fiercely until he turned his head uneasily away.

"Good-bye, Mrs. Djiak. Thanks for the coffee."

She was on her knees mopping the floor by the time I got to the kitchen door. The beer had soaked through my socks. In the entryway I paused to take them off, slipping my bare feet into my running shoes. Mrs. Djiak came up behind me, cleaning my beery footprints.

"I begged you not to talk to him about it, Victoria."

"Mrs. Djiak, all I want is Caroline's father's name. Tell me and I won't bother you anymore."

"You mustn't come back. He will call the police. Or perhaps even shoot you himself."

"Yeah, well, I'll bring my gun the next time I come." I fished a card from my handbag. "Call me if you change your mind."

She didn't say anything, but she took the card and tucked it into her apron pocket. I pulled the gleaming door open and left her frowning in the entryway.

5

The Simple Joys of Childhood

I sat in the car for a long time before my anger cooled and my breathing returned to normal. "How she made us suffer!" I mimicked savagely. Poor scared, spunky teenager. What courage it must have taken even to tell the Djiaks she was pregnant, let alone not to go to the home for unwed mothers they'd picked out for her. Girls in my high school class who hadn't been as resilient returned with horrifying tales of backbreaking work, spartan rooms, poor nourishment as a nine-month punishment meted out by the nuns.

I felt fiercely proud of my mother for standing up to her righteous neighbors. I remembered the night they marched in front of Louisa's house, throwing eggs and yelling insults. Gabriella came out on the front stoop and stared them down. "Yes, you are Christians, aren't you?" she told them in her heavily accented English. "Your Christ will be very proud of you tonight."

My bare feet were beginning to freeze inside my shoes. The cold slowly brought me back to myself. I started the car and turned on the heater. When my toes were warm again I drove down to 112th Street and turned west to Avenue L. Louisa's sister Connie lived there with her husband, Mike, and their five children. While I was churning up the South Side I might as well include her.

Connie was five years older than Louisa, but she'd still been living at home when her sister got pregnant. On the South Side you lived with your parents until you got married yourself. In Connie's case, she lived with her parents even after she married while she and her husband saved money for a house of their own. When they finally bought their three-bedroom place she quit her job to become a mother—another South Side tradition.

Compared to her mother, Connie was quite a slattern. A basketball lay on the tiny front lawn, and even my untutored eye could tell that no one had washed the front stoop in recent memory. The glass in the storm door and front windows gleamed without a streak, however, and no fingerprints marred the wood on the frame.

Connie came to the door when I rang the bell. She smiled when she saw me, but nervously, as if her parents had called to warn her I would be stopping by.

"Oh. Oh, it's you, Vic. I—I was just going to the store, actually."

Her long, bony face wasn't suited to lying. The skin, pink and freckled like her niece's, turned crimson as she spoke.

"What a pity," I said dryly. "It's been over ten years since we last saw each other. I was hoping to catch up on the kids and Mike and so on."

She stood with the door open. "Oh. You've been to see Louisa, haven't you? Ma—Ma told me. She's not very well."

"Louisa's in terrible shape. I gather from Caroline there's nothing they can do for her except try to keep her comfortable. I wish someone had told me sooner—I'd have been down months ago."

"I'm sorry—we didn't think—Louisa didn't want to bother you, and Ma didn't want—didn't think—" She broke off, blushing more furiously than ever.

"Your mother didn't want me coming down here and stirring the pot. I understand. But here I am, and I'm doing it anyway, so why don't you put off your trip to the store for five minutes and talk to me."

I pulled the storm door toward me as I spoke and moved closer to her in what I hoped was a nonthreatening, persuasive manner. She backed away uncertainly. I followed her into the house.

"I—uh, would you like a cup of coffee?" She stood twisting her hands like a schoolgirl in front of a hostile teacher, not a woman pushing fifty with a life of her own.

"Coffee would be great," I said bravely, hoping my kidneys could handle another cup.

"The house is really a mess," Connie said apologetically, picking up a pair of gym shoes that stood in the little entryway.

I never say that to visitors—it's obvious that I haven't hung up my clothes or carried out the papers or vacuumed in two weeks. In Connie's case, it was hard to see anything she might be talking about, other than the gym shoes. The floors were scoured, chairs stood at right angles to each other, and not a book or paper marred the shelves or tables as we went through the living room into the back of the house.

I sat at the green Formica table while she filled an electric coffee maker. This small deviation from her mother cheered me slightly: if she could make the switch from boiling water to percolator, who knows how far she might go.

"You and Louisa were never much alike, were you?" I asked abruptly.

She blushed again. "She was always the pretty one. People don't expect so much of you if you're pretty."

The poignant gaucherie of her reply seemed almost unbearable. "What, didn't your mother expect her to help out around the house?"

"Well, she was younger, you know—she didn't have to do as much as I did. But you know Ma. Everything got cleaned every day whether you'd used it or not. When she got mad at us we had to scrub the underside of the sinks and the toilets. I swore my girls would never do any of that kind of thing." Her mouth set in the hard line of remembered grievance.

"It sounds rough," I said, appalled. "Do you feel Louisa left you holding the bag too often?"

She shook her head. "It wasn't really her fault as much as the way they treated her. I can see that now. You know, Louisa could talk back and Pa'd think it was kind of cute. At least when she was little. He wouldn't take it even from her when she got older.

"And Ma's brother liked Louisa to sing and dance for him when he came over. She was so little and pretty, you know, it was like having a doll around. Then when she got older it was too late, of course. Too late to discipline her, I mean."

"Seems like they did a pretty good job," I commented. "Throwing her out of the house and all. That must have been scary for you too."

"Oh, it was." She was rubbing her hands over and over in the towel she'd taken out to wipe up a little spot of water left from filling the coffeepot. "They didn't even tell me what was going on at first."

"You mean you didn't know she was pregnant?" I asked, incredulous.

She turned so red I thought blood might actually start oozing through her skin. "I know you won't understand," she said in a voice that was little more than a whisper. "You led such a different life. You had boyfriends before you got married. I know. Ma—Ma kind of follows your life.

"But when Mike and I were married, I didn't even know—I didn't know—I—the nuns never talked about things like that at school. Ma, of course, she couldn't—couldn't begin to say anything. If Louisa was missing her—her period—she wouldn't have said anything to me. She probably didn't know what it meant, anyway."

Tears spurted from her eyes against her will. Her shoulders shook as she tried controlling her sobbing. She wound the towel so tightly around her hands that the veins in her arms stood out. I got up from my chair to put a hand on one heaving shoulder. She didn't move or say anything, but after a few minutes the spasms calmed down and her breathing grew more normal.

"So Louisa got pregnant because she didn't know what she was doing, or that she might start a baby?"

She nodded mutely, her eyes on the floor.

"Do you know who the father might have been?" I asked gently, keeping my hand on her shoulder.

She shook her head. "Pa—Pa wouldn't let us date. He said he hadn't paid all that money to send us to Catholic school to see—see us chasing after boys. Of course lots of boys liked Louisa, but she—she wouldn't have been going out with any of them."

"Can you remember any of their names?"

She shook her head again. "Not after all this time. I know the boy at the grocery store used to buy her pop when she'd go in. I think his name was Ralph. Ralph Sow-something. Sower or Sowling or something."

She turned to the coffeepot. "Vic, the terrible thing is—I was so jealous of her, at first I was glad to see her in trouble."

"God, Connie, I hope so. If I had a sister who everyone said was prettier than me, and was petted and fussed over while they sent me off to Mass, I'd put an ax through her head instead of waiting for her to get pregnant and be kicked out of the house."

She turned to look up at me, astonished. "But, Vic! You're so—so cool. Nothing ever bothered you. Not even when you were fifteen years old. When your mother died Ma said God gave you a stone instead of a heart, you were so cool." She put her hand over her mouth, mortified, and started to protest.

"Well, I was fucked if I was going to sob in public in front of all those women like your mother, who never had a good word to say about Gabriella," I said, stung. "But you'd better believe I cried plenty in private. And anyway, Connie, that's the whole point. My parents loved me. They thought I could succeed at anything I wanted to do. So even though I lose my temper a hundred times a week or so, it's not like I had to spend my life listening to my folks tell me how my baby sister was wonderful and I was garbage. Loosen up, Connie. Give yourself a break."

She looked at me doubtfully. "Do you really mean it? After what I said and everything?"

I took her shoulders between my hands and turned her to face me. "I really mean it, Connie. Now how about some coffee?"

After that we talked about Mike and his job at the waste-management plant, and young Mike and his football playing, and her three daughters, and her youngest, who was eight and so bright she really thought they'd have to try to get him to go to college, although Mike was nervous, he thought it gave people ideas that they were better than their parents or their neighborhood. The last comment made me grin to myself—I could hear Ed Djiak warning Connie: You don't want the kid turning out like Victoria, do you?—but I listened patiently for forty-five minutes before moving my chair back and getting to my feet.

"It was really good to see you again, Vic. I—I'm glad you came by," she said at the door.

"Thanks, Connie. Take it easy. And say hi to Mike for me."

I walked slowly back to my car. The heel of my left shoe was rubbing on the back of my foot. I savored the pain the way you do when you're feeling like crap. A little pain: the gods letting you expiate the damage you caused.

How had I learned the facts of life? A little in the locker room, a little from Gabriella, a little from our basketball coach, a relaxed, sensible woman except on the court. How could Connie have made it through junior high without one of her friends tipping her off? I pictured her at fourteen, tall, gawky, timid. Maybe she hadn't had any friends.

It was only two o'clock. I felt as though I had spent a whole day loading bales on the levee instead of a few hours drinking coffee with the old folks at home. I felt as though I'd already earned a thousand dollars, and I didn't even know where to start looking. I put the car into gear and headed back to the mainland.

My socks were still damp. They filled the car with the smell of beer and sweat, but when I opened a window the cold air was too much for my bare toes. My irritation rose with my discomfort: I wanted to stop at a service station and call Caroline at SCRAP to tell her the deal was off. Whatever her mother had done a quarter century ago should decently be left to rest there. Unfortunately, I found myself making the turn to Houston Street when I should have been heading north to Lake Shore Drive and freedom.

The block looked worse in daylight than it had at night. Cars were parked at all angles. One was abandoned in the street, black showing around the hood and windshield where a fire had burned the engine block. I left the Chevy in front of a hydrant. If the traffic patrols were as assiduous down here as the street cleaners, I could probably stay until Labor Day without getting a ticket.

I went around to the back, where Louisa always used to leave a spare key on the ledge above the little porch. It was still there. As I let myself in a curtain twitched in the house next door. Within minutes everyone on the block would know a strange woman was going into the Djiaks'.

I heard voices inside the house and called out to let people know I was there. When I got to Louisa's bedroom I realized she had the television on at top volume—what I thought were visitors was only *General Hospital*. I knocked as hard as I could. The volume went down and her scratchy voice called out, "That you, Connie?"

I opened the door. "Me, Louisa. How're you doing?"

Her thin face lighted in a smile. "Well, well, girl. Come right in. Make yourself at home. How's it going?"

I pulled the straight-backed chair next to the bed. "I just went down to see Connie and your folks."

"Did you now?" She looked at me warily. "Ma never was one of your biggest fans. What're you up to, young Warshawski?"

"Spreading joy and truth. Why did your mother hate Gabriella so much, Louisa?"

She shrugged bony shoulders under her cardigan. "Gabriella never went in much for hypocrisy. She didn't keep to herself how she felt about Ma and Pa kicking me out."

"Why did they?" I asked. "Were they mad at you just for getting pregnant, or did they have something special against the boy—the father?"

She didn't say anything for a few minutes, but lay with her eyes on the television. Finally she turned back to me.

"I could kick your ass right out the back door for poking around in this." Her voice was calm. "But I know what happened. I know Caroline and how she always twisted you around her little finger. She called you down here, didn't she—wants to know who her old man was. Spoiled stubborn little bitch. When I blew up at her she called you in. Isn't that right?"

My face was hot with embarrassment, but I said gently, "Don't you think she has a right to know?"

Her mouth set in a tight line. "Twenty-six years ago a goddamn bastard tried to ruin my life. I don't want Caroline anywhere near him. And if you're your ma's daughter, Victoria, you'll do your best to keep Caroline from prying into it instead of helping her out."

Tears smarted in her eyes. "I love that girl. You'd think I was trying to beat her, or kick *her* out on the street instead of protecting her. I did my best to see she got a different shot at life than I did and I'm not watching that go down a sewer now."

"You did a great job, Louisa. But she's grown up now. She doesn't need protecting. Can't you let her make her own decision on this?"

"Goddamn you, no, Victoria! And if you're going to keep on about it, get your ass out of here and don't come back!"

Her face turned red under its greenish sheen and she started coughing. I was batting a thousand with the Djiak women today, getting them furious in descending order of age. All I needed to do was tell Caroline I was quitting and I could make it four for four.

I waited for the paroxysm to subside, then led the conversation gently back to topics Louisa enjoyed, to her young days after Caroline was born. After talking to Connie I could see why Louisa had relished that time as one of freedom and gaiety.

I finally left around four. All during the long drive home through the evening rush hour I listened to Caroline's and Louisa's voices debating in my head. I could understand Louisa's strong wish to protect her privacy. She was dying, too, which gave her desires more weight.

At the same time I could empathize with Caroline's fear of isolation and loneliness. And after seeing the Djiaks close up, I understood why she'd like to find other relatives. Even if her father turned out to be a real jerk, he couldn't have a crazier family than the one she already knew about.

In the end I decided to look for the two men Louisa had talked about last night and this afternoon—Steve Ferraro and Joey Pankowski. They'd worked together at the Xerxes plant, and it was possible she'd gotten the job through her lover. I'd also try to track down the grocery clerk Connie had mentioned—Ron Sowling or whoever. East Side was such a stable, unchanging neighborhood, it was possible that the same people still owned the store and that they would remember Ron and Louisa. If Ed Djiak had come around playing the heavy father, it might have made an indelible memory.

Making a decision, even one to compromise, brings a certain amount of relief. I called up an old friend and spent a pleasant evening on Lincoln Avenue. The blister on my left heel didn't stop my dancing until past midnight.

6

The Mill on the Calumet

In the morning I was ready early, at least early for me. By nine I had done my exercises. Skipping a run, I dressed for the corporate world in a tailored navy suit that was supposed to make me look imposing and competent. I steeled my heart against Peppy's importunate cries and headed for the South Side for the third day in a row. Instead of following the lake down, this morning I went west to an expressway that would spew me into the heart of the Calumet Industrial District.

It's been over a century since the Army Corps of Engineers and George Pullman decided to turn the sprawling marshes between Lake Calumet and Lake Michigan into an industrial center. It wasn't just Pullman, of course—Andrew Carnegie, Judge Gary, and a host of lesser barons all played a part, working on it for sixty or seventy years. They took an area about four miles square and filled it with dirt, with clay dredged from Lake Calumet, with phenols, oils, ferrous sulfide, and thousands of other substances you not only never heard of, you never want to.

When I got off the expressway at a 103rd Street, I had the familiar sensation of landing on the moon, or returning to earth after a nuclear decimation. Life probably exists in the oily mud around Lake Calumet. It's just not anything you'd recognize outside a microscope or a Steven Spielberg movie. You don't see trees or grass or birds. Only the occasional feral dog, ribs protruding, eyes red with madness and hunger.

The Xerxes plant lay in the heart of the ex-swamp, at 110th Street east of Torrence. The building was an old one, put up in the early fifties. From the road I could see their sign, "Xerxes, King of Solvents." The royal purple had faded to an indeterminate pink, while the logo, a crown with double X's in it, had almost disappeared.

Made of concrete blocks, the plant was shaped like a giant U whose arms backed onto the Calumet River. That way the solvents manufactured there could flow easily onto barges and the waste products into the river. They don't dump into the river anymore, of course—when the Clean Water Act was passed Xerxes built giant lagoons to hold their wastes, with clay walls providing a precarious barrier between the river and the toxins.

I parked my car in the gravel yard and gingerly picked my way through the oily ruts to a side entrance. The strong smell, reminiscent of a darkroom, hadn't changed from the times I used to drive down with my dad to drop off Louisa if she'd missed her bus.

I had never been inside the plant. Instead of the crowded noisy cauldron of my imagination, I found myself in an empty hall. It was long and dimly lit, with a concrete floor and cinder-block walls that went the height of the building, making me feel as though I were at the bottom of a mine shaft.

Following the arm of the U in the direction of the river, I came at length to a series of cubbyholes cut into the interior wall. Their walls were made of that grainy glass used for shower doors; I could see light and movement through them but couldn't distinguish shapes. I knocked at the middle door. When no one answered I turned the knob and went in.

I entered a time warp, a long narrow room whose furnishings apparently hadn't changed since the building had gone up thirty-five years ago. Olive-drab filing cabinets and gunmetal desks lined the wall across from the doors. Fluorescent lights hung from an old acoustic-tile ceiling. The outer doors all opened into the room, but two had been blocked shut by filing cabinets.

Four middle-aged women in purple smocks sat at the row of desks. They were working on vast bales of paper with Sisyphus-like doggedness, making entries, shifting invoices, using old-fashioned adding machines with experienced stubby fingers. Two were smoking. The smell of cigarettes mingled with the darkroom chemical scent in acrid harmony.

"Sorry to interrupt," I said. "I was trying to find the personnel office."

The woman nearest the door turned heavy, uninterested eyes to me. "They're not hiring." She went back to her papers.

"I'm not looking for a job," I said patiently. "I just want to talk to the personnel manager."

All four of them looked up at that, weighing my suit, my relative youth, trying to decide if I was OSHA or EPA, state or federal. The woman who'd spoken jerked her faded brown hair toward a door facing the one I'd entered by.

"Across the plant," she said laconically.

"Can I get there from inside or should I go around?"

One of the smokers reluctantly put down her cigarette and got up. "I'll take her," she said hoarsely.

The others looked at the old-fashioned electric clock over their desks. "You going on break then?" a flabby woman in the back asked.

My guide shrugged. "Might as well."

The others looked chagrined: she'd been faster than they to think how to squeeze five extra minutes from the system. One of them pushed her chair back in a hopeful way, but the first speaker said sternly, "One's enough to go," and the would-be rebel scooted back to her station.

My guide took me out the far door. Beyond it lay the inferno I'd been expecting when I first entered the plant. We were in a dimly lit room that stretched the length of the building. Stainless-steel pipes ran along the ceiling and at intervals below, so that you felt suspended in a steel maze that had flipped up on its side. Steam hissed from the overhead pipes in little puffs, filling the maze with vapor. Large red "No Smoking" signs hung every thirty feet along the walls. Enormous cauldrons were hooked to the pipes at intervals, huge vats designed for a coven of giant witches. The white-suited figures tending the place might have been their familiars.

Although the air in here actually smelled better than it did outside, a number of the workers wore respirators. I wondered about the majority who didn't, as well as how smart it was for my guide and me to be taking the shortcut through the plant. I tried asking her over the hissing and clatter of the pipes, but she apparently had decided I must be an OSHA spy or something and refused to answer. When an overhead valve let out a belch so loud that I jumped, she gave a small smile but said nothing.

Skirting the maze expertly, she led me to a door diagonally across the plant from the one we'd entered by. We were in another narrow, cinder-block hallway, this one forming the base of the U. She took me down it, turning left to follow the second arm toward the river. Halfway along, she stopped at a door labeled "Canteen—Employees Only."

"Mr. Joiner's on down there—third door on your right. Door marked 'Administration.' "

"Well, thanks for your help," I said, but she had already disappeared into the canteen.

The door marked "Administration" was also made of grainy glass but the rooms beyond it looked a little classier than the Tartarus where I'd visited the four clerks. Carpeting, not linoleum, covered the concrete floor. Wallboard ceiling and wall covering created an illusion of an intimate space within the cinder-block tunnel.

A woman in street clothes sat behind a desk with a modern phone bank and a not-so-modern electric typewriter. Like the clerks I'd stumbled on, she was middle-aged. But her skin was firm under a generous layer of makeup, and she'd dressed with care, if not style, in a crisp pink shirtwaist with large plastic pearls at her neck and clipped to her ears.

"You need something, honey?" she asked.

"I'd like to see Mr. Joiner. I don't have an appointment, but it shouldn't take more than five minutes." I dug in my handbag for a business card and handed it to her.

She gave a little laugh. "Ooh, honey, don't expect me to pronounce that one."

This wasn't a Loop office where receptionists give you a KGB-style interrogation before grudgingly agreeing to find out if Mr. So-and-so can see you. She picked up a phone and told Mr. Joiner there was a girl out here asking for him. She gave another little laugh and said she didn't know and hung up.

"He's back there," she said brightly, pointing over her shoulder. "Middle door."

Three little offices were carved into the wall behind her, each about eight feet square. The door to the first one was open and I glanced in curiously. No one was there, but an array of papers and a wall covered with production charts showed it was a working office. A little sign next to the open middle door announced it was home to "Gary Joiner, Accounting, Safety, and Personnel." I knocked briefly and went in.

Joiner was a young man, maybe thirty years old, with sandy hair cut so short it merged with his pink skin. He was frowning over a stack of ledger printouts but looked up when I came in. His face was blotchy and he smiled at me with worried, innocent eyes.

"Thanks for taking the time to see me," I said briskly, shaking his hand. I explained who I was. "For personal reasons—nothing to do with Xerxes —I'm trying to find two men who worked here in the early sixties."

I pulled a slip of paper with Joey Pankowski and Steve Ferraro's names on it from my purse and handed it to him. I had a story about why I wanted to find them, something dull about being witnesses to an accident, but I didn't want to volunteer a reason unless he asked for it. Unlike Goebbels's belief in the big lie, I believe in the dull lie—make your story boring enough and no one will question it.

Joiner studied the paper. "I don't think those guys work here. We only employ a hundred and twenty people, so I'd know their names. But I've only been here two years, so if they go back to the sixties . . ."

He turned to a filing cabinet and riffled through some files. I was struck suddenly by the absence of any computer terminals, either here or elsewhere in the plant. Most personnel or accounting officers would be able to look up employees on a screen.

"Nope. Of course, you can see we barely have room for current files." He swept an arm in an arc that knocked part of the ledger sheets to the floor. He blushed vividly as he bent to pick them up. "If someone leaves or retires or whatever and we don't have activity on them—you know, like an ongoing comp claim—we ship the files out to our warehouse in Stickney. Want me to check for you?"

"That'd be great." I got up. "When can I call back? Monday too soon?"

He assured me Monday would be fine—he lived out west and could stop off at the warehouse on his way home tonight. He conscientiously scribbled a note in his pocket diary, inserting the scrap of paper with the names on it. By the time I left the room he had already returned to his printouts.

7

The Boys in the Back Room

I'd had enough of the city, of pollution and cramped, painful lives. When I got home I changed into jeans, packed an overnight bag, and took off with the dog to spend the weekend in Michigan. Although the water was too cold and wild for swimming, we spent two invigorating days on the beach, running, chasing sticks, or reading, depending on individual temperament. When I got back to Chicago late Sunday I felt as though my head had been thoroughly aired out. I turned the dog over to a jealous Mr. Contreras and headed upstairs to bed.

I'd told the personnel guy at Xerxes I'd call him in the morning, but when I woke up I decided to go visit him in person. If he had addresses for Pankowski and Ferraro, I could go see them and maybe get the whole mess cleared up in one morning. And if he'd forgotten to stop at the Stickney warehouse, a personal visit would make him more responsive than a phone call.

It had rained overnight, turning Xerxes's gravel yard into an oily mud puddle. I parked as close to the side entrance as I could and picked my way through the sludge. Inside, the cavernous hallway was cold; I was shivering slightly by the time I reached the pebbly glass entrance to the administrative suite.

Joiner wasn't in his office, but the incurious secretary cheerfully directed me to a loading bay where he was managing a shipment. I followed the hall down to the river end of the long building. Heavy steel doors, difficult to open, led to the bay. Beyond lay a world of dirt and clamor.

Sliding steel doors enclosing the loading bay had been rolled open on two sides. At the far end, facing me, the Calumet lapped against the walls, its brackish waters green and roiling from the downpour. A cement barge lay motionless in the turbulent water. A gang of dockhands was removing large barrels from it, rolling them along the concrete floor with a clatter echoed and intensified by the steel walls.

The other door opened on a truck bay. A phalanx of silver tankers was lined up there, looking like menacing cows attached to a high-tech milking machine as they received solvents from an overhead pipe rack. Their diesels vibrated, filling the air with an urgent racket, making it impossible to understand the shouts of the men who were moving around them.

I spied a group in conference around a man with a clipboard. The light was too dim to make out faces but I assumed the man was Joiner and headed toward him. Someone darted from behind a vat and seized my arm.

"Hard-hat area," he bellowed in my ear. "What are you doing here?"

"Gary Joiner!" I bawled back at him. "I need to talk to him."

He escorted me back to the entrance to wait. I watched him go over to the confabbing group and tap one of the figures on the arm. He jerked his head to where I was standing. Joiner stuck his clipboard on a barrel and trotted over to me.

"Oh," he said. "It's you."

"Yeah," I agreed. "I was in the neighborhood and thought I'd stop by instead of phoning. I can tell this is a bad time to talk to you—want me to wait in your office?"

"No, no. I—uh, I couldn't find anything about those men. I don't think they ever worked here."

Even in the dim light I could tell his splotchy skin was flushing.

"I bet that warehouse is a mess," I said sympathetically. "No one has time to look after records when you're running a manufacturing plant."

"Yes," he agreed eagerly. "Yes, that's for sure."

"I'm a trained investigator. If you gave me some kind of authorization, I could have a look through there. You know, see if their records were misplaced or something."

He flickered his eyes nervously around the room. "No. No. Things aren't that big a mess. The guys never worked here. I gotta go now."

He hurried away before I could say anything else. I started after him, but even if I could get past the foreman, I couldn't think of a way to get Joiner to tell me the truth. I didn't know him, didn't know the plant, didn't have a clue as to why he would lie to me.

I walked slowly back down the long hall to my car, absentmindedly stepping in an oozy patch that plastered sludge firmly to my right shoe. I cursed loudly—I'd paid over a hundred dollars for those pumps. As I sat in the car trying to scrape it clean, I got oily sludge on my skirt. Feeling outraged with the world, I threw the shoe petulantly into the backseat and changed back into my running gear. Even though Caroline hadn't sent me to the plant, I blamed my problems on her.

As I drove up Torrence, passing rusted-out factories that looked dingier than ever from the rain, I wondered if Louisa had called Joiner, asking him not to help me if I turned up. I didn't think her mind worked that way, though: she'd told me to mind my own business, and as far as she was concerned, I was doing just that. Maybe the Djiaks had fumed self-righteously to Xerxes, but I thought they were too myopic to analyze how I might conduct an investigation. They could only see how Louisa had hurt them.

On the other hand, if Joiner didn't want to talk to me about the men because of some problem the company was having with them—say a lawsuit—he would have known when I came in on Friday. But the first time I spoke to him he'd obviously never heard of them.

I couldn't figure it out, but the thought of lawsuits made me realize another place to look for the men. Neither Pankowski nor Ferraro was in the phone book, but the old ward voter registration records might still be around. I turned right on Ninety-fifth Street and headed into East Side.

The ward offices were still in the tidy brick two-flat on Avenue M. A variety of errands may take you to your committeeman's office, from help with parking tickets to ways of getting on the city payroll. The local cops are in and out a lot what with one thing and another, and even though my dad's beat had been North Milwaukee Avenue, I'd come here with him more than once. The sign proclaiming Art Jurshak alderman and Freddy Parma ward committeeman, which covered all of the building's exposed north wall, hadn't changed. And the storefront next door still housed the insurance agency that had given Art his toehold in the community.

I knocked most of the sludge from my right shoe and put my pumps back on. Brushing my skirt as best I could with a Kleenex, I went into the building. I didn't recognize any of the men lounging in the first-floor office, but judging from their age and their air of being as one with the furnishings, I thought they probably went back to my childhood.

There were three of them. One, a graying man smoking the fat little cigar that used to be a Democratic pol's badge of office, was huddled in the sports pages. The other two, one bald-headed, the other with a white Tip O'Neill-style mop, were talking earnestly. Despite their differing hairdos, they looked remarkably alike, their shaved faces red and jowly, their forty extra pounds hanging casually over the belts of their shiny pants.

They glanced sidelong at me when I came in but didn't say anything: I was a woman and a stranger. If I was from the mayor's office, it would do me good to cool my heels. If I was anyone else, I couldn't do anything for them.

The two speakers were going over the rival merits of their pickup trucks, Chevy versus Ford. No one down here buys foreign—bad form with three quarters of the steel industry unemployed.

"Hi," I said loudly.

They looked up reluctantly. The newspaper reader didn't stir, but I saw him move the pages expectantly.

I pulled up a rollaway chair. "I'm a lawyer," I said, taking a business card from my purse. "I'm looking for two men who used to live down here, maybe twenty years ago."

"You oughta try the police, cookie—this isn't the lost-and-found," the bald-headed one said.

The newspaper rattled appreciatively.

I slapped my forehead. "Damn! You're so right. When I lived down here Art used to like to help out the community. Shows you how times have changed, I guess."

"Yeah, ain't nothing like it used to be." Baldy seemed to be the designated spokesman.

"Except the money it takes to run a campaign," I said mournfully. "That's still pretty expensive, what I hear."

Baldy and Whitey exchanged wary glances: Was I trying to do the honorable thing and slip them a little cash, or was I part of the latest round of federal entrapment artists hoping to catch Jurshak putting the squeeze on the citizenry? Whitey nodded fractionally.

Baldy spoke. "Why you looking for these guys?"

I shrugged. "The usual. Old car accident they were in in '80. Finally settled. It's not a lot of money, twenty-five hundred each is all. Not worth a lot of effort to hunt them down, and if they're retired, they've got pensions anyway."

I stood up, but I could see the little calculators moving in their brains; the newspaper reader had let Michael Jordan's exploits drop to his knees to join in the telepathic exercise. If they arranged a meeting, how much could they reasonably skim? Make it six hundred and that'd be two apiece.

The other two nodded and Baldy spoke again. "What did you say their names were?"

"I didn't. And you're probably right—I should have taken this to the cops to begin with." I started slowly for the door.

"Hey, just a minute, sister. Can't you take a little kidding?"

I turned around and looked uncertain. "Well, if you're sure . . . It's Joey Pankowski and Steve Ferraro."

Whitey got up and ambled over to a row of filing cabinets. He asked me to spell the names, letter by painful letter. Moving his lips as he read the names on old voter registration forms, he finally brightened.

"Here we are—1985 was the last year Pankowski was registered, '83 for Ferraro. Why don't you bring their drafts in here? We can get them cashed through Art's agency and see that the boys get their money. We should get 'em to reregister and it'd save you another trip down here."

"Gee, thanks," I said earnestly. "Trouble is, I have to get them to personally sign a release." I thought for a minute and smiled. "Tell you what —give me their addresses and I'll go see them this afternoon, make sure they still live down here. Then next month when the claim drafts are issued I can just mail them both to you here."

They thought it over slowly. They finally agreed, again silently, that there was nothing wrong with the idea. Whitey wrote Pankowski's and Ferraro's addresses down in a large, round hand. I thanked him graciously and headed for the door again.

Just as I was opening it a young man came in, hesitantly, as if unsure of his welcome. He had curly auburn hair and wore a navy wool suit that enhanced the staggering beauty of his pale face. I couldn't remember ever seeing a man with such perfect good looks—he might have posed for Michelangelo's *David*. When he gave a diffident smile it made him look vaguely familiar.

"Hiya, Art," Baldy said. "Your old man's downtown."

Young Art Jurshak. Big Art had never looked this good, but the smile must have made the kid resemble his old man's campaign posters.

He flushed. "That's okay. I just wanted to look at some ward files. You don't mind, do you?"

Baldy hunched an impatient shoulder. "You're a partner in the old man's firm. You do what you want, Art. Think I'm going for a bite, anyway. Coming, Fred?"

The white-haired man and the newspaper reader both got up. Food sounded like a swell idea to me. Even a detective looking at a meager fee has to eat some of the time. The four of us left young Art alone in the middle of the room.

Fratesi's Restaurant was still where I remembered it, on the corner of Ninety-seventh and Ewing. Gabriella had disapproved of them because they cooked southern Italian instead of her familiar dishes of the Piedmont, but the food was good and it used to be a place to go for special occasions.

Today there wasn't much of a lunchtime crowd. The decorations around the fountain in the middle of the floor, which used to enchant me as a child, had been allowed to decay. I recognized old Mrs. Fratesi behind the counter, but felt the place had grown too sad for me to identify myself to her. I ate a salad made of iceberg lettuce and an old tomato and a frittata that was surprisingly light and carefully seasoned.

In the little ladies' room at the back I got the most noticeable chunks of dirt off my skirt. I didn't look fabulous, but maybe that suited the neighborhood better. I paid the tab, a modest four dollars, and left. I didn't know you could get bread and butter in Chicago for under four dollars anymore.

All during lunch I'd turned over various approaches to Pankowski and Ferraro in my mind. If they were married, wives at home, children, they wouldn't want to hear about Louisa Djiak. Or maybe they would. Maybe it would bring back the happy days of yore. I finally decided I'd have to play it by ear.

Steve Ferraro's home was nearer to the restaurant, so I went there first. It was another of the endless array of East Side bungalows, but a little seedier than most of its neighbors. The porch hadn't been swept recently, my critical housekeeping eye noted, and the glass on the storm door could have done with a washing.

A long interval passed after I rang the bell. I pushed it again and was about to leave when I heard the inner door being unlocked. An old woman stood there, short, wispy-haired, and menacing.

"Yes," she said in one harsh, heavily accented syllable.

"Scusi," I said. *"Cerco il signor Ferraro."*

Her face lightened marginally and she answered in Italian. What did I want him for? An old lawsuit that might finally be going to pay out? To him only, or to his heirs?

"To him only," I said firmly in Italian, but my heart sank. Her next words confirmed my misgivings: *il signor Ferraro* was her son, her only child, and he had died in 1984. No, he had never married. He had talked once about a girl in the place where he worked, but *madre de dio,* the girl already had a baby; she was relieved when nothing came of it.

I gave her my card, with a request to call me if she thought of anything else, and set out for Green Bay Avenue without any high expectations.

Again a woman answered the door, a younger one this time, perhaps even my age, but too heavy and worn out for me to be certain. She gave me the cold fish eye reserved for life insurance salesmen and Jehovah's Witnesses and prepared to shut the door on me.

"I'm a lawyer," I said quickly. "I'm looking for Joey Pankowski."

"Some lawyer," she said contemptuously. "You'd better ask in Queen of Angels Cemetery—that's where he's spent the last two years. At least, that's his story. Knowing that bastard, he probably pretended to die so he could go off with his latest little chickadee."

I blinked a little under her fire. "I'm sorry, Mrs. Pankowski. It's an old case that's been settled rather slowly. A matter of some twenty-five hundred dollars, not really worth bothering you about."

Her blue eyes almost disappeared into her cheeks. "Not so fast, lady. You got twenty-five hundred, I deserve that money. I suffered enough with that bastard, God knows. And then when he died there wasn't even any insurance."

"I don't know," I said fussily. "His oldest child—"

"Little Joey," she said promptly. "Born August 1963. In the Army now. I could hold it for him till he gets home next January."

"I was told there was another child. A girl born in 1962. Know anything about her?"

"That bastard!" she screamed. "That lying, cheating bastard. He screwed me when he was alive and now he's dead he's screwing me still!"

"So you know about the girl?" I asked, startled at the thought that my search might be over so easily.

She shook her head. "I know Joey, though. He could of had a dozen kids before he got me pregnant with little Joey. If this girl thinks she's the first, all I can say is you better run an ad in the *Little Calumet Times.*"

I took a twenty from my purse and held it casually. "We could probably advance something from the settlement. Do you know anyone who could tell me for certain if he had any children before little Joey? A brother, maybe? Or his priest?"

"Priest?" she cackled. "I had to pay extra just to get his bones into Queen of Angels."

She was thinking hard, though, trying not to look directly at the money. At last she said, "You know who might know? Doc at the plant. He talked to them every spring, took their blood, their histories. Knew more about them than God, Joey once said."

She couldn't tell me his name; if Joey ever mentioned it, she couldn't be expected to remember it after all this time, could she? But she took the money with dignity and told me to come back if I was in the neighborhood.

"I don't expect to see any more of it," she added with unexpected cheerfulness. "Not from what I know of that bastard. If my old man hadn't made him, he wouldn't of married me. And between you and me, I'd of been better off."

8

The Good Doctor

Louisa and Caroline were returning from the dialysis center when I stopped by. I helped Caroline maneuver Louisa into a wheelchair for the short ride up the front walk. Getting her up the five steep steps took ten minutes of patient labor while she leaned heavily on my shoulder to hoist herself up each rise, then rested until she had enough wind for the next one.

By the time we had her settled in her bed, her breathing had turned to shallow, stertorous gasps. I panicked a little at the sound and at the purplish tinge beneath her waxy green skin, but Caroline treated her with cheerful efficiency, giving her oxygen and massaging her bony shoulders until she could breathe on her own again. However much Caroline might irritate me, I could only admire her unflagging goodwill in looking after her mother.

She left me alone with Louisa while she went off to make herself a snack. Louisa was drifting into sleep, but she remembered the Xerxes doctor with a hoarse little chuckle: Chigwell. They called him Chigwell the Chigger because he was always sucking their blood. I waited until she was sleeping soundly before releasing my hand from the grasp of her bony fingers.

Caroline was hovering in the dining room, her little body vibrating with anxiety. "I've wanted to call you every day, but I've forced myself not to. Especially last week when Ma told me you'd been by and she'd ordered you not to look for him." She was eating a peanut-butter sandwich and the words came through thickly. "Have you found out anything?"

I shook my head. "I tracked down the two guys she remembers best, but they're both dead. It's possible one of them might have been your father, but I don't have any real way of knowing. My only hope is the company doctor. He apparently used to compile copious records on the employees, and people tell their doctor things they might not say to anyone else. There's also a clerk who worked at the corner grocery twenty-five years ago, but Connie couldn't remember his name."

She caught my doubtful tone. "You don't think any of these guys might have been the one?"

I pursed my lips, trying to put my doubts into words. Steve Ferraro had wanted to marry Louisa, baby and all. That sounded as though he knew her after Caroline's birth, not before. Joey Pankowski did seem like the kind of person who could have gotten Louisa pregnant and gone off unconcerned. Which would fit. That repressive household, Connie's and her total ignorance of sex—she might well have turned to some happy-go-lucky type. But in that case why be so upset about it now? Unless she'd absorbed so much of the Djiak's fundamental fear of sex that the very memory of it terrified her. But that didn't fit my memories of Louisa as a young woman.

"I don't know," I finally said helplessly. "It just has the wrong kind of feel to it."

I debated with myself a minute, then added, "I think you need to prepare yourself for failure. My failure, I mean. If I can't learn anything from the doctor or track down this clerk, I'm going to have to throw it in."

She scowled fiercely. "I'm *counting* on you, Vic."

"Let's not play that record again right now, Caroline. I'm beat. I'll call you in a day or two and we'll take it from there."

It was almost four, time for the evening rush hour to congeal the traffic. It was close to five-thirty before I'd oozed the twenty-some miles home. When I got there Mr. Contreras stopped me to ask about the burrs I'd allowed the sacred dog to collect in her golden tail. The dog herself came out and expressed herself ready for a run. I listened to both with such patience as I could muster, but after five minutes of his nonstop flow I left abruptly in mid-sentence and headed for my place on the third floor.

I took off my suit and left it on the entryway floor where I'd be sure to remember it for the cleaners in the morning. I didn't know what to do about the shoe, so I left it with the suit—maybe the cleaners would know a place that could resurrect it.

While I ran a bath I pulled my stack of city and suburban directories from the floor under the piano. No Chigwell was listed in the metropolitan area. Naturally. He'd probably died himself. Or retired to Majorca.

I poured an inch of whiskey and stomped into the bathroom. While lying half submerged in the old-fashioned tub, it occurred to me that he might be in the medical directories. I hoisted myself out of the tub and went into the bedroom to call Lotty Herschel. She was just getting ready to leave the clinic she runs near the corner of Irving Park and Damen.

"Can't it wait until the morning, Victoria?"

"Yeah, it can wait. I just want to get this monster out of my life as fast as possible." I sketched Caroline and Louisa's story as quickly as I could. "If I can run this Chigwell down, I only have one other lead I need to look into and then I can get back to the real world."

"Wherever that is," she said dryly. "You don't know this man's first name or his speciality, do you? Of course not. Industrial medicine probably, hmm?"

I could hear her rustling through the pages of a book. "Chan, Chessick, Childress. No Chigwell. I don't have a complete directory, though. Max probably does—why don't you give him a call? And why do you let this Caroline run you through hoops? You are manipulated by people only when you allow yourself to be, my dear."

On that cheering note she hung up. I tried Max Loewenthal, who was executive director of Beth Israel Hospital, but he had gone home for the day. As any rational person would have. Only Lotty stayed at her clinic until six, and of course a detective's work is never done. Even if you're only willingly responding to the manipulations of an old neighbor.

I poured the rest of the whiskey down the sink and changed into my sweats. When I'm in a febrile mood the best thing to do is exercise. I picked up Peppy from Mr. Contreras—neither he nor the dog was capable of harboring a grievance. By the time Peppy and I returned home, panting, I'd run the discontent out of my system. The old man fried some pork chops for me and we sat drinking his foul grappa and talking until eleven.

I reached Max easily in the morning. He listened with his usual courteous urbanity to my saga, put me on hold for five minutes, and came back with the news that Chigwell was retired but living in suburban Hinsdale. Max even had his address and his first name, which was Curtis.

"He's seventy-nine, V.I. If he doesn't talk willingly, go easy on him," he finished, only half joking.

"Thanks a whole bunch, Max. I'll try to restrain my more animal impulses, but old men and children generally bring out the worst in me."

He laughed and hung up.

Hinsdale is an old town about twenty miles west of the Loop whose tall oaks and gracious homes were gradually being accreted by urban sprawl. It's not Chicagoland's trendiest address, but there's an aura of established self-assurance about the place. Hoping to fit into its genteel atmosphere, I put on a black dress with a full skirt and gold buttons. A leather portfolio completed the ensemble. I looked at my navy suit on the entryway floor as I left, but decided it would keep another day.

When you go from the city to the north or west suburbs, the first thing you notice is the quiet cleanness. After a day in South Chicago I felt I'd stepped into paradise. Even though the trees were barren of leaves and the grass matted and brown, everything was raked and tidied for spring. I had total faith that the brown mats would turn to green, but couldn't imagine what it would take to create life in the sludge around the Xerxes plant.

Chigwell lived on an older street near the center of town. The house was a two-story, neo-Georgian structure whose wood siding gleamed white in the dull day. Its well-kept yellow shutters and a sprinkling of old trees and bushes created an air of stately harmony. A screened porch faced the street. I followed flagstones through the shrubs around the side to the entrance and rang the bell.

After a few minutes the door opened. That's the second thing you notice in the burbs—when you ring the bell people open the doors, they don't peer through peepholes and undo bolts.

An old woman in a severe navy dress stood frowning in the doorway. The scowl seemed to be a habitual expression, not aimed at me personally. I gave a brisk, no-nonsense smile.

"Mrs. Chigwell?"

"*Miss* Chigwell. Do I know you?"

"No, ma'am. I'm a professional investigator and I'd like to speak with Dr. Chigwell."

"He didn't tell me he was expecting anyone."

"Well, ma'am, we like to make our inquiries unannounced. If people have too much time to think about them, their answers often seem forced."

I took a card from my bag and handed it to her, moving forward a few steps. "V. I. Warshawski. Financial investigative services. Just tell the doctor I'm here. I won't keep him more than half an hour."

She didn't invite me in, but grudgingly took the card and moved off into the interior of the house. I looked around at the blank-windowed houses next door and across the street. The third thing you notice in the suburbs is, you might as well be on the moon. In a city or small-town neighborhood, curtains would flutter as the neighbors tried to see what strange woman was visiting the Chigwells. Then telephone calls or exchanges in the Laundromat. Yes, their niece. You know, the one whose mother moved to Arizona all those years ago. Here, not a curtain stirred. No shrill voices betokened preschoolers recreating war and peace. I had an uneasy feeling that with all its noise and grime, I preferred city life.

Miss Chigwell rematerialized in the doorway. "Dr. Chigwell has gone out."

"That's very sudden, isn't it? When do you expect him back?"

"I—he didn't say. It will be a long while."

"Then I'll wait a long while," I said peaceably. "Would you like to invite me inside, or would you prefer me to wait in my car?"

"You should leave," she said, her frown deepening. "He doesn't want to talk to you."

"How can you know that, ma'am? If he's away, you haven't spoken to him about me."

"I know who my brother does and does not wish to see. And he would have told me if he wanted to see you." She shut the door as forcefully as she could, given both their ages and the thick carpeting underneath.

I returned to my car and moved it to where it was clearly visible from the front door. WNIV was playing a cycle of Hugo Wolf songs. I leaned back in the seat, my eyes half closed, listening to Kathleen Battle's golden voice, wondering what there was about talking to an investigator that would fluster Curtis Chigwell.

In the half hour I waited I saw one person go down the street. I began feeling as though I were on a movie set, not part of a human community at all, when Miss Chigwell appeared on the flagstone walk. She moved determinedly to the car, her thin body as rigid as an umbrella frame, and as bony. I courteously got out.

"I must ask you to leave, young woman."

I shook my head. "Public property, ma'am. There's no law against my being here. I'm not playing loud music or selling dope or doing anything else that the law might construe as a nuisance."

"If you don't drive away now, I'm going to call the police as soon as I'm back inside."

I admired her courage: to be seventy-something and confront a young stranger takes a lot of guts. I could see the fear mingling with the determination in her pale eyes.

"I'm an officer of the court, ma'am. I would be happy to explain to the police why I want to speak to your—brother, is it?"

That was only partially true. Any licensed attorney is an officer of the court, but I much prefer never talking to the police, especially suburban cops, who hate urban detectives on principle. Fortunately, Miss Chigwell, impressed (I hoped) by my professional demeanor, didn't demand a badge or a certificate. She compressed her lips until they almost disappeared into her angular face and went back to the house.

I had barely settled back in my car when she returned to the walk and beckoned me vigorously. When I joined her at the side of the house she said abruptly:

"He'll see you. He was here all along, of course. I don't like telling his lies for him, but after all these years it's hard to start saying no. He's my brother. My twin, so I got into too many bad habits too long ago. But you don't want to hear all that."

My admiration for her increased, but I didn't know how to express it without sounding patronizing. I followed her silently into the house. We went through a passageway that looked onto the garage. A dinghy was leaned neatly on its side next to the open door. Beyond it was a tidy array of gardening tools.

Ms. Chigwell whisked me along to the living room. It was not large, but gracefully proportioned, with chintz furniture facing a rose-marble fireplace. While she went for her brother I prowled around a bit.

A handsome old clock stood in the center of the mantel, the kind that has an enamel face and brass pendulum. On either side of it were porcelain figures, shepherd girls, lute players. A few old family photos stood in the recessed shelves in the corner, one showing a little girl in a starched sailor dress standing proudly with her father in front of a sailboat.

When Ms. Chigwell returned with her brother, it was obvious they'd been arguing. His cheeks, softer than her angular face, were flushed and his lips were compressed. She started to introduce me, but he cut her off sharply.

"I don't need you to oversee my affairs, Clio. I'm perfectly able to look after myself."

"I'd like to see you do so, then," she said bitterly. "If you're in some kind of trouble with the law, I want to hear what it is now, not next month or whenever you feel brave enough to tell me about it."

"I'm sorry," I said. "I seem to have caused a problem, most inadvertently. There's no trouble with the law that I know of, Miss Chigwell. Merely, I need some information on some people who used to work at the Xerxes plant in South Chicago."

I turned to her brother. "My name is V. I. Warshawski, Dr. Chigwell. I'm a lawyer and a private investigator. And I've been retained as the result of a lawsuit whose settlement leaves some money to the estate of Joey Pankowski."

When he ignored my outstretched hand I looked around and chose a comfortable armchair to sit in. Dr. Chigwell remained standing. In his ramrod posture he resembled his sister.

"Joey Pankowski used to work at the Xerxes plant," I continued, "but he died in 1985. Now there's some question that Louisa Djiak, who also worked there, has a child whose father he may have been. That child is also entitled to a share of the settlement, but Ms. Djiak is very ill and her mind wanders—we can't get a clear answer from her as to who the father is."

"I can't help you, young lady. I have no recollection of any of these names."

"Well, I understand you took blood and medical histories from all the employees every spring for a number of years. If you would just go back and look at your records, you might find that—"

He cut me off with a violence that surprised me. "I don't know who you've been talking to, but that's an absolute lie. I won't stand to be harassed and harangued in my own house. Now you get out right now, or I'll call the police. And if you're an officer of the court, you can explain that to them in jail." He turned without waiting for a reply and marched from the room.

Clio Chigwell watched him leave, her scowl deeper than ever. "You'll have to go."

"He did the tests," I said. "Why is he so upset?"

"I don't know anything about it. But you can't ask him to violate his patients' confidentiality. Now you'd better leave, unless you do want to speak with the police."

I got up as nonchalantly as I could under the circumstances. "You have my card," I said to her at the door. "If something occurs to you, give me a call."

9

Lifestyles of the Rich and Famous

A light drizzle had started to fall. I sat in the car staring at the windshield, watching the rain break up on the greasy glass. After a while I turned on the engine, hoping to coax a little heat from the noisy motor.

Was it the Pankowski name that had rattled Chigwell so? Or was it me? Had Joiner phoned him telling him to beware Polish detectives and the questions they bring? No, that couldn't be right. If that was the case, Chigwell would never have agreed to see me at all. And anyway, Joiner wouldn't know Chigwell. The doctor was almost eighty; he must have been long retired when Joiner started at the plant two years ago. So it had to have been the mention either of Pankowski or Louisa. But why?

I wondered with growing uneasiness what Caroline knew that she hadn't bothered to tell me. I remembered in vivid detail the winter she had asked me to fight an eviction notice served on Louisa. After a week of running between courts and landlord, I saw an article in the *Sun-Times* on "Teens Who Make a Difference." It featured a glowing sixteen-year-old Caroline and the soup kitchen she'd used the rent money to set up. That was the last cry for help I'd answered from her for ten years, and I was beginning to think I should have let it go for twenty.

I fished around on the backseat for a Kleenex and found a towel I'd used at the beach last summer. After wiping a peephole in the windshield I finally put the car into gear and headed for the expressway. I was torn between calling Caroline to tell her the deal was off and the elephant child's 'satiable curiosity to find out what had rattled Chigwell so badly.

In the end I did nothing. When I had fought my way through the noontime Loop traffic to my office, messages from several clients awaited me—inquiries I'd let slide while I mucked around in Caroline's problem. One was from an old customer who wanted help with computer security. I referred him to a friend of mine who's a computer expert and tackled the other two. These were routine financial investigations, my bread and butter. It felt good to work on something where I could identify both problem and solution, and I spent the afternoon burrowing through files in the State of Illinois Building.

I returned to my office around seven to type the reports. They were worth five hundred dollars to me; since both clients paid promptly, I wanted to get the invoices into the mail.

I was rattling along on my old standard Olympia when the phone rang. I looked at my watch. Almost eight. Wrong number. Caroline. Maybe Lotty. I picked up the phone on the third ring, right before the answering service kicked in.

"Ms. Warshawski?" It was an old man's voice, fragile and quavering.

"Yes," I said.

"I want to speak to Ms. Warshawski, please." For all its quavering, the voice was confident, used to managing people on the phone.

"Speaking," I said as patiently as I could. I had missed lunch and was dreaming of a steak and whiskey.

"Mr. Gustav Humboldt would like to see you. When would it be convenient to schedule an appointment?"

"Can you tell me what he wants to see me about?" I backspaced and used white-out to cover a typo. It's getting harder to find correction fluid and typewriter ribbons in these days of word processors, so I capped the bottle carefully to save it.

"I understand it's a confidential matter, miss. If you're free this evening, he could see you now. Or tomorrow afternoon at three."

"Just a minute while I check my schedule." I put the phone down and got *Who's Who in Chicago Commerce* from the top of my filing cabinet. Gustav Humboldt's listing covered a column and a half of six-point type. Born in Bremerhaven in 1904. Emigrated in 1930. Chairman and chief stockholder of Humboldt Chemical, founded in 1937, with plants in forty countries, 1986 sales of $8 billion, assets of $10 billion, director of this, member of that. Headquarters in Chicago. Of course. I'd passed the Humboldt Building a million times walking down Madison Street, an old nononsense structure without the attention-getting lobbies of the modern giants.

I picked up the phone. "I could make it around nine-thirty tonight," I offered.

"That will be fine, Ms. Warshawski. The address is the Roanoke Building, twelfth floor. I'll tell the doorman to look out for your car."

The Roanoke was an old dowager on Oak Street, one of six or seven buildings bordering the strip between the lake and Michigan Avenue. All had gone up in the early decades of this century, providing housing for the McCormicks and Swifts and other riffraff. Nowadays if you had a million dollars to invest in housing and were related to the British royal family, they might let you in after a year or two of intensive checking.

I set a speed record for two-finger typing and got reports and invoices into their envelopes by eight-thirty. I'd have to forgo whiskey and steak—I didn't want to be logy for an encounter with someone who could set me up for life—but there was time for soup and a salad at the little Italian restaurant up Wabash from my office. Especially if I didn't have to worry about parking at the other end.

In the restaurant bathroom I saw that my hair was frizzing around my head from this morning's drizzle, but at least the black dress still looked tidy and professional. I put on a little light makeup and retrieved my car from the underground garage.

It was just nine-thirty when I pulled into the semicircle under the Roanoke's green awning. The doorman, resplendent in matching green livery, bent his head courteously while I gave him my name.

"Ah, yes, Ms. Warshawski." His voice was fruity, his tone avuncular. "Mr. Humboldt is expecting you. If you'll just give me your keys?"

He led me into the lobby. Most modern buildings going up for the rich these days feature glass and chrome lobbies with monstrous plants and hangings, but the Roanoke had been built when labor was cheaper and more skillful. The floor was an intricate mosaic of geometric shapes and the wood-paneled walls were festooned with Egyptian figurines.

An old man, also in green livery, was sitting on a chair next to some wooden double doors. He got up when the doorman and I came in.

"Young lady for Mr. Humboldt, Fred. I'll let them know she's here if you'll take her on up."

Fred unlocked the door—no remote-control clicks here—and took me to the elevator at a stately tread. I followed him into a roomy cage with a floral carpet on the floor and a plush-upholstered bench against the back wall. I sat casually on the bench, crossing my legs, as though personal elevator service were an everyday occurrence with me.

The elevator opened onto what might have been the foyer of a mansion. Gray-white marble tiles showing streaks of pink were covered here and there by throw rugs that had probably been made in Persia when the Ayatollah's grandfather was a baby. The hall seemed to form an atrium, with the elevator at its center, but before I could tiptoe down to a marble statue in the left corner to explore, the carved wooden door in front of me opened.

An old man stood there in morning dress. His scalp showed pink through wisps of fine white hair. He inclined his head briefly, a token bow, but his blue eyes were frosty and remote. Rising to the solemnity of the occasion, I fished in my bag and handed him a card without speaking.

"Very good, miss. Mr. Humboldt will see you now. If you'll follow me . . ."

He walked slowly, either from age or from some concept of a butler's proper gait, giving me time to gawk in what I trusted was a discreet fashion. About halfway along the length of the building he opened a door on the left and held it for me to enter. Looking at the books lining three walls and the opulent red-leather furniture in front of a fireplace in the fourth, my keen intuition told me we were in the library. A florid man, heavy without being corpulent, sat in front of the fire with a newspaper. As the door opened he put the paper down and got to his feet.

"Ms. Warshawski. How good of you to come on such short notice." He held out a firm hand.

"Not at all, Mr. Humboldt."

He motioned me to a leather armchair on the other side of the fire from him. I knew from the *Who's Who* entry that he was eighty-four, but he could have said sixty without anyone raising an eyebrow. His thick hair still showed a touch of pale yellow, and his blue eyes were sharp and clear in a face almost free of wrinkles.

"Anton, bring us some cognac—you drink cognac, Ms. Warshawski?—and then we'll be fine on our own."

The butler disappeared for perhaps two minutes, during which my host courteously made sure the fire wasn't too hot for me. Anton returned with a decanter and snifters, poured, carefully placed the decanter in the center of a small table at Humboldt's right hand, fiddled with the fire tongs. I realized he was as curious as I about what Humboldt wanted and was trying to think of ways to linger, but Humboldt dismissed him briskly.

"Ms. Warshawski, I have an awkward matter to discuss, and I beg your indulgence if I don't do so with maximum grace. I'm an industrialist, after all, an engineer more at home with chemicals than beautiful young women." He had come to America as a grown man; even after close to sixty years a mild accent remained.

I smiled sardonically. When the owner of a ten-billion-dollar empire starts apologizing for his style, it's time to hold tightly to your purse and count all your fingers.

"I'm sure you underestimate yourself, sir."

He gave me a quick, sidelong glance and decided that warranted a barking laugh. "I see you are a careful woman, Ms. Warshawski."

I sipped the cognac. It was staggeringly smooth. Please let him call me for frequent consultations, I begged the golden liquid. "I can be reckless when I have to, Mr. Humboldt."

"Good. That's very good. So you're a private investigator. And do you find it a job that allows you to be both careful and reckless?"

"I like being my own boss. And I don't have the desire to do it on the scale you've achieved."

"Your clients speak very highly of you. I was talking to Gordon Firth just today and he mentioned how grateful the Ajax board was for your efforts there."

"I'm delighted to hear it," I said, sinking back in the chair and sipping some more.

"Gordon does a lot of my insurance, of course."

Of course. Gustav calls Gordon and tells him he needs a thousand tons of insurance and Gordon says sure and thirty young men and women work eighty-hour weeks for a month putting it all together and then the two shake hands genially at the Standard Club and thank each other for their trouble.

"So I thought I might be able to help you out with one of your inquiries. After listening to Gordon's glowing report I knew you were intelligent and discreet and not likely to abuse information given you in confidence."

With enormous effort I kept myself from bolting up in the chair and spilling cognac all over my skirt. "It's hard for me to imagine where our spheres of activity intersect, sir. By the way, this is most excellent cognac. It's like drinking a fine single malt."

At that Humboldt roared with genuine laughter. "Beautiful, my dear Ms. Warshawski. Beautiful. To take my news so calmly and then praise my liquor with the most subtle of insults! I wish I could persuade you to cease being your own boss."

I smiled and put the snifter down. "I love compliments as much as the next person, and it's been a tough day—I can use them. But I'm beginning to wonder who is meant to be helping whom. Not that it wouldn't be a privilege to be of service to you."

He nodded. "I think we can be of service to each other. You asked where our spheres of activity intersect—a fine expression. And the answer lies in South Chicago."

I thought for a minute. Of course. I should have known. Xerxes had to be part of Humboldt Chemical. It was just being so used to thinking of it as part of my childhood's landscape that I hadn't made the connection when Anton phoned.

I casually mentioned it and Humboldt nodded again. "Very good, Ms. Warshawski. The chemical industry made a great contribution to the war effort. The Second World War I'm talking about, of course. And the war effort in turn prompted research and development on a grand scale. Many of the products that all of us—I mean Dow, Ciba, Imperial Chemical, all of us—make our bread and butter on today can be traced to research we did then. Xerxine was one of Humboldt's great discoveries, one of the 1, 2 dichlorethanes. The last one I was able to devote time to myself."

He stopped himself with a turned-up hand. "You're not a chemist. That won't be of interest to you. But we called the product Xerxes, because of the Xerxine, of course, and opened the South Chicago plant in 1949. My wife was an artist. She designed the logo, the crown on the purple background."

He stopped to offer me the decanter. I didn't want to appear greedy. On the other hand, to refuse might have seemed rude.

"Well, that South Chicago plant was the start of Humboldt's international expansion, and it's always meant a great deal to me. So even though I no longer concern myself with the day-to-day running of the company—I have grandchildren, Ms. Warshawski, and an old man fancies himself reliving his youth with young children. But my people know I care about that plant. So when a beautiful young detective begins poking around, asking questions, they naturally tell me."

I shook my head. "I'm sorry if they needlessly alarmed you, sir. I'm not poking around in the plant. Merely trying to trace some men as part of a personal inquiry. For some reason your Mr. Joiner—the personnel manager—wanted me to believe they never worked for you."

"So you found Dr. Chigwell." His deep voice had sunk to a rumbling murmur, difficult to make out.

"Who was even more electrified by my questions than young Joiner. I couldn't help wondering if he had a personal agenda of his own. Some transactions of his youth that weigh on his old-age conscience."

Humboldt held his snifter so that he could look through it toward the fire. "How people rush to protect you when you are old and they want you to know they care about your interests." He spoke to the glass. "And what problems they needlessly cause. It's a constant issue with my daughter, one of nature's worriers."

He turned back to me. "We had a problem with these men, with

Pankowski and Ferraro. Enough of a problem that I even know their names, you see, out of fifty-some thousand employees worldwide. They engaged in an attempted sabotage of the plant. Of the product, actually. Changing the balance in the mixture so that we had highly unstable vapor and a residue that stopped up the flow pipes. We had to shut the plant down three times in 1979 to clean everything. It took a year of investigation to find out who lay behind it. They and two other men were fired, and they then sued us for wrongful dismissal. The whole thing was a nightmare. A terrible nightmare."

He grimaced and drained his glass. "So when you came around my people naturally assumed you were egged on by some unscrupulous lawyer trying to open these old wounds. But I knew from my friend Gordon Firth that that could not be so. So I have taken a risk. Invited you here. Explained the whole story to you. And I hope I am right, that you are not going to run back to some lawyer saying I tried to suborn you or whatever the expression is."

"Suborn will do admirably," I said, finishing my own glass and shaking my head at the proffered decanter. "And I can safely assure you that my inquiries have nothing to do with any suit these men might have been involved in. It is a purely personal matter."

"Well, if it involves Xerxes employees, I can see that you get whatever assistance you need."

I don't like revealing my clients' business. Especially not to strangers. But in the end I decided to tell him—it was the easiest way to get help. Not the whole story, of course. Not Gabriella and the baby-sitting and Caroline's insistent manipulativeness and the angry Djiaks. But Louisa dying and Caroline wanting to find out who her father was and Louisa not wanting to tell.

"I'm European and old-fashioned," he said when I finished. "I don't like the girl not wanting to respect her mother's wishes. But if you are committed, you are committed. And you think she might have said something to Chigwell because he was the plant doctor? I'll call and ask him. He probably won't want to talk to you himself. But my secretary will phone you in a few days with the information."

That was a dismissal. I slid forward to the edge of the chair so that I could stand without bracing my arms on the sides and was pleased to find that I moved smoothly, without the brandy affecting me. If I could make it out the front door without bumping into a priceless art object, I could easily handle the drive home.

I thanked Humboldt for the brandy and his help. He turned it aside with another chuckle.

"It's a pleasure for me, Ms. Warshawski, to talk to an attractive young woman, and one who is brave enough to stand her ground with an old lion. You must come again when you are in the neighborhood."

Anton was hovering outside the library to escort me to the door.

"I'm sorry," I said when we reached the entryway. "I promised not to tell."

He stiffly pretended not to hear me and summoned the elevator with frigid aloofness. I wasn't sure what to do about the doorman and my car, but when I tentatively displayed a five-dollar bill he caused it to vanish while tenderly helping me into the Chevy.

I devoted the drive home to thinking of reasons why I was better off as a PI than a billionaire chemist. The list was much shorter than the drive.

10

Fire When Ready

I was drowning in a sea of thick gray Xerxine. I was choking while Gustav Humboldt and Caroline stood talking earnestly on the shore, ignoring my cries for help. I woke up at four-thirty, sweaty and panting, too roused by the dream to go back to sleep.

I finally got out of bed when it started to get light. It wasn't cold in the bedroom, but I was shivering. I pulled a sweatshirt from the pile next to my bed and wandered around the apartment, trying to find something to turn my mind to. I picked out a scale on the piano, but stopped after one: it would be unfair to the neighbors to work on my rusty voice at this hour of the morning. I moved to the kitchen to make coffee, but lost interest after washing out the pot.

My four rooms normally seem open and spacious to me, but now they were making me feel cramped. The jumble of books, papers, and clothes, which usually looks homelike, began to appear shameful and squalid.

Don't tell me you've been infected by Djiakism, I scolded myself crossly. Next thing you'll be on your hands and knees in the lobby scrubbing the floor every morning.

Finally I pulled on jeans and my running shoes and went out. The dog recognized my step behind the locked first-floor door and let out a little yelping bark. I would have liked her company, but I didn't have a key to Mr. Contreras's place. I walked over to the lake alone, unable to work up energy for running.

It was another gray day. I could tell the sun was rising only by a change in the intensity behind the clouds on the eastern horizon. Under the sullen sky the lake resembled the thick gray liquid of my nightmare. I stared at it, trying to reason away my lingering unease, trying to lose myself in the changing patterns and colors of the water.

Early as it was, joggers were already on the lake path, getting in their miles before putting on pinstripe and panty hose for the day. They looked like the hollow men, each wrapped in a cocoon of sound from his private radio, their faces blank, their isolation chilling. I dug my hands deep into my pockets, shivering, and turned toward home.

I stopped on the way for breakfast at the Chesterton Hotel. It's a residential hotel for well-heeled widows. The little Hungarian restaurant where you can get cappuccino and croissants caters to their slower pace and better manners.

As I stirred the foam in my second cappuccino I kept wondering why Gustav Humboldt had summoned me to his presence. Yes, he didn't want me nosing around in his plant. No executive likes that. And yes, he had the inside dope on Pankowski and Ferraro. But the chairman of the board calling in the lowly detective to tell her in person? Despite all his talk of Gordon Firth, I'd never even seen the Ajax chairman in the course of three investigations involving the insurance company. Heads of multinational corporations, even if they're eighty-four and dote on their grandchildren, have layers and layers of underlings to do that kind of job for them.

Last night my vanity had been tickled. The invitation alone was exciting, let alone the rarefied surroundings and incredible brandy. I hadn't stopped to wonder about his comradely flow of information, but maybe I should.

And what of little Caroline? What did she know that she hadn't been telling me? That Louisa's two pals had been fired? Perhaps that Louisa herself had been involved in the efforts to sabotage the plant? Maybe Gustav Humboldt had been her lover long ago and had stepped in to protect her now. It would explain his personal involvement. Maybe he was Caroline's father and she was due a gigantic inheritance, out of which a modest fee to me would be eminently feasible.

As my speculations grew more ludicrous, my mood lightened. I headed home much faster than I'd left, passing the second-floor tenants on their way to work with a "good morning" almost cheery enough for a flight attendant.

I was getting really sick of panty hose and pumps, but I put them on again so as to make a favorable impression at the Department of Labor. A friend of mine from law school worked for their Chicago office; he might be able to tell me about the sabotage and if the men really had been suing Humboldt for wrongful dismissal. My red shoes were still in the front hallway with my navy suit. If eventually, why not eventually? I scooped them up and took off.

By the time I found a place to park near the Federal Building it was after ten. The Loop has been attacked by a development fervor the last few years that has turned the business district into a jammed, honking copy of New York. Many of the public garages have been scrapped to make way for skyscrapers taller than city code permits, so we have four times the traffic we used to vying for half as much parking.

My temper wasn't the best by the time I made it to the sixteenth floor of the Dirksen Building. It wasn't helped by the attitude of the receptionist, who looked briefly my way before returning to her typing with the curt announcement that Jonathan Michaels wasn't available.

"Is he dead?" I snapped. "Out of town? Under indictment?"

She looked at me coldly. "I said he's not available and that's all you need to know."

The door leading to the offices was kept locked. The receptionist or someone on the other side could buzz you in, but this woman clearly wasn't going to let me wander back among the cubicles to find Jonathan. I sat in one of the plastic straight-backed chairs and told her I'd wait.

"Suit yourself," she snapped, typing furiously.

When a business-suited black man came in she made a big play of friendliness with him, cooing over him and flirting a little. She flashed him a sugary smile and a wish for a nice day while releasing the lock. When I went in behind him she was too taken aback even to squawk.

My escort raised his brows at me. "You belong in here?"

"Yeah," I said. "I pay your salary. And I'm here to talk to Jonathan Michaels about it."

He looked momentarily startled, trying to figure out which Washington bureaucrat I might be. Then my meaning dawned on him and he said, "Well, maybe you'd better wait outside until Gloria tells you to go in."

"Since she never bothered to find out my name or my business, I can't imagine her interest in serving the taxpaying public is enormous."

I knew where Jonathan's office was and quickened my pace to move ahead of my attendant. I could hear him speeding up on the carpet behind me calling, "Miss—uh, miss," as I opened the corner door.

Jonathan was standing in the outer office next to his secretary's desk. When he saw me his rosy face lightened into a smile. "Oh, it's you, Vic."

I grinned at him. "Gloria call to tell you the Weather Underground was heading in to smash up your office and tear your golden hair out by the roots?"

"What's left of it," he said plaintively. He had gone partly bald, which made him look like a youthful Father William.

Jonathan Michaels had been a quiet idealist in my law school class. While students like me—locked in our liberal straitjackets, as one conservative JD put it—rushed off to become public defenders, Jonathan had surveyed social issues quietly. He had clerked in a federal circuit court for two years and then moved to the Department of Labor. He was now senior counsel for the Chicago district.

He took me into his office and shut the door. "I've got a dozen attorneys from St. Louis in the conference room. Can you do your business in thirty seconds?"

I explained fast. "I want to know if there's any trail—through OSHA, the NLRB, the Contract Compliance people, or maybe Justice—of Ferraro and Pankowski. The sabotage and the suit."

I wrote their names on one of his yellow pads and added Louisa Djiak. "She might have been a party. I don't want to tell you the whole story now —there isn't time—but I had the news personally from Gustav Humboldt. He's not anxious to have it made public."

Jonathan picked up his phone while I was still talking. "Myra, get Dutton over here, will you? I've got a research job." He spelled it out in a few words and hung up. "Vic, next time, do me a big favor and do what the ad says—phone first."

I kissed his cheek. "I will, Jonathan. But only if I can afford to spend two days playing phone tag before I talk to you. *Ciao, ciao, bambino.*"

He was back in the conference room before I had made it out the outer door. When Gloria saw me return to the reception area, she started typing furiously again. In a spirit of malice I waited outside for a minute, then peered around the door. She had picked up the *Herald-Star.*

"Get busy," I said sternly. "The taxpayers expect value for their money."

She gave me a glance of loathing. I went to the elevator laughing lightly to myself. I hope someday to outgrow such juvenile pleasures.

I walked the four blocks to my office. When I checked in with my answering service I learned that Nancy Cleghorn had been trying to reach me. Once early this morning, when I was out feeling sorry for myself along the lakefront, and again ten minutes ago. In the tiresome way that people have, she hadn't bothered to leave a phone number.

I sighed aggrievedly and pulled my city directory from under a stack of papers on the windowsill. The Wabash el runs under my windows and the directory had a fine layer of soot on it, which I smeared on the front of my green wool dress.

Nancy was the environmental affairs director for Caroline's community development group. I looked up SCRAP, which was a waste of time, since of course it was under South Chicago Reawakening Project. And that was a waste of time because Nancy wasn't in, she hadn't been in all day, and they didn't know when to expect her. And no, they wouldn't give me her home phone number, especially if I said I was her sister, because everyone knew she had four brothers, and if I didn't stop harassing them, they'd get the police.

"Can you at least take a message? Without bringing the police into it, I mean?" I spelled my name slowly, twice, not that it would make any difference—it would still probably come out as Watchski or some other hideous mutation. The secretary said she'd see Nancy got the message in that tone that tells you they're trashing the paper as soon as you hang up.

I turned back to the directory. Nancy wasn't listed, but Ellen Cleghorn was still living on Muskegon. Talking to Nancy's mother made a welcome change to the way I'd been greeted today. She remembered me perfectly, loved reading about me when my cases made the papers, wished I'd come down and have dinner with them sometime when I was in the neighborhood.

"Nancy bought herself a place in South Shore. One of those huge old mansions that's falling to bits. She's fixing it up on her own. Kind of a big place for a single woman, but she likes it." She gave me the number and hung up with repeated dinner invitations.

Nancy wasn't home. I gave it up. If she wanted me that badly, she'd call again.

I looked at the dirt on the front of my dress. My suit was still in the car. If I drove home now, I could change into jeans, dump the lot at the cleaners, and spend the rest of the afternoon on myself.

It was close to five—as I was happily working my way through the syncope of *"In dem Schatten meiner Locken,"* without Kathleen Battle's voice—that the phone rang. I left the piano unwillingly, and was even sorrier as soon as I picked up the receiver: it was Caroline.

"Vic, I need to talk to you."

"Talk away," I said resignedly.

"In person, I mean." Her husky voice was urgent, but it always was.

"You want to drive up to Lake View, be my guest. But I ain't trekking down to South Chicago this afternoon."

"Oh, fuck you, Vic. Can you ever talk to me without being a total snot?"

"Can it, Caroline. You want to talk to me, speak. Otherwise I'm going back to what I was doing when you interrupted."

There was a pause during which I could picture her gentian eyes smoldering. Then she said, so quickly I almost didn't understand, "I want you to stop."

I was confused for a minute. "Caroline, if you ever realized how upsetting I find it to have you spin me around in circles, you might understand why I sound like a snot to you."

"Not that," she said impatiently. "Stop trying to find my father, I mean."

"What!" I shouted. "Two days ago you were batting your baby blues and telling me pathetically you *counted* on me."

"That was then. I didn't see then—I didn't know—anyway, that's why I need to see you in person. You can't possibly understand over the phone if you're going to get so honked off. Just don't do any more looking until I can talk to you in person, for God's sake."

There was no denying the thread of panic in her voice. I pulled a string from the fringe where my left knee was poking through the denim. She knew about Pankowski and the plant sabotage. I pulled another. She didn't know.

"You're too late, babe," I finally said.

"You mean you've found him?"

"Nope. I mean the investigation is beyond your power to stop."

"Vic, I hired you. I can fire you," she said with terrifying ferocity.

"Nope," I repeated steadily. "You could have last week. But the investigation has moved into a new phase. You can't fire me. I don't mean that. You *can* fire me, of course. You just have. What I mean is, you may choose not to pay me but you can't stop my inquiries now. And the top one, first on the list, is why you didn't tell me about Ferraro and Pankowski."

"I don't even know who they are!" she shouted. "Ma never talks about her old lovers to me. She's like you—she thinks I'm a fucking baby."

"Not about their being her lovers. About the sabotage and their getting fired. And the lawsuit."

"I don't know what in hell you're talking about, V. I. Know-it-all Warshawski, and I don't have to listen to it. As far as I'm concerned, V.I. stands for vicious insect, which I would use Raid on if I had any." She slammed the phone in my ear.

It was the childish insult she ended on that convinced me she really didn't know about the two men. I also realized suddenly that I had no idea why she was firing me. I scowled and rang up SCRAP, but she refused to come to the phone.

"Ah, screw you, you little brat," I muttered, slamming down the phone myself.

I tried returning to Hugo Wolf, but my enthusiasm was gone. I wandered to the living-room window and watched the nine-to-fivers returning home. Suppose my speculations this morning hadn't been so far out after all. Suppose Louisa Djiak had been involved in the plant sabotage and Humboldt was protecting her. Maybe he'd called Caroline and pushed her into firing me. Although Caroline was not the kind that pushed easily. If someone Humboldt's size came for her, she'd be more inclined to sink her teeth into his calf and hang on until he got sick of the pain.

It occurred to me that whatever Nancy wanted to talk to me about might shed some light on the general problem. I tried her number again, but she still didn't answer.

"Come on, Cleghorn," I muttered. "You wanted me bad enough to leave two messages. You get run over by a train or something?"

I finally got fed up with my futile churning and called Lotty Herschel. She was free for dinner and glad to have company. We went to the Gypsy and shared a roast duck, then back to her place, where she beat me five times in a row at gin.

11

The Brat's Tale

I was skimming the paper while I made coffee the next morning when Nancy Cleghorn's name leapt out at me. The story was on the front page of *ChicagoBeat*. It explained why she hadn't been around to answer her phone yesterday. Her body had been found around eight last evening by two young boys who'd ignored both the government and their parents and gone into the posted area around Dead Stick Pond.

A small section of the original marsh remained as Illinois's last wetland for migratory birds. Dead Stick Pond had once been a great feeding and resting ground, but was now so full of PCBs that little could survive there. Even so, in the middle of the dead mills you could find herons and other unusual birds, and the occasional beaver or muskrat.

The two boys had come on a muskrat there once and hoped to see it again. At the water's edge they stumbled over a discarded boot. Since there were fifty of those for every animal—and it was dark—it had taken them a few minutes to realize it still had a body connected to it.

Nancy had been hit on the back of the head. The internal injury would have killed her eventually, but she apparently drowned when her body was dumped in the pond. The police knew of no one with a reason to kill her. She was well respected, her work at SCRAP had earned her a lot of kudos in the environmentally troubled community, and so on. She was survived by her mother and four brothers.

I slowly finished making the coffee and took the paper out to the living room, where I reread the story six or seven times. I didn't learn anything new. Nancy. My snappish thought last night, maybe she'd fallen under a train, made the little hairs prickle on the sides of my face. My thinking hadn't caused her death. My mind knew that, but my body didn't.

If only I hadn't taken that hike to the lake yesterday morning—I broke off the thought when I realized how stupid it was. If I stayed chained to my phone twenty-four hours a day, I'd be at home to needy friends or telemarketers and would have no other life. But Nancy. I'd known her since I was six years old. In my mind I thought we were still young together—that because we'd been young together we would protect each other from ever getting old.

I wandered to the window and stared out. It was raining hard again in thick sheets that made it impossible to see the street. I squinted at the water, moving my head to make patterns with it, wondering what to do. It was only eight-thirty—too early to call my friends at the papers to see if they had news that hadn't made it to the morning edition. People who go to bed at three or four in the morning are more cooperative if you let them sleep in.

She'd been found in the Fourth Police District. I didn't know anyone there—my dad had worked the Loop and northwest sides, not his own neighborhood. Besides, that's been over ten years ago.

I was chewing on my fingertip, trying to decide whom to call, when the doorbell rang. I figured it was Mr. Contreras, trying to get me to come down to take the dog out in the downpour, and scowled at the foggy window without moving. The third time the bell clamored I reluctantly left my hideout. Cup in hand, I unbolted the outer door and padded barefoot down the three flights.

Two bulky figures stood in the outer hallway. Rain glistened on their shaved faces and dripped from their navy slickers to form dirty pools on the tiled floor.

When I opened the door the older one said with heavy sarcasm, "Good morning, sunshine. I hope we didn't interrupt your beauty sleep."

"Not at all, Bobby," I said heartily. "I've been up for an hour at least. I just hoped it was a wrong number. Hi, Sergeant," I added to the younger man. "You guys want some coffee?"

As they came past me into the stairwell cold water from their slickers dripped onto my bare toes. If it had just been Bobby Mallory, I would have thought it deliberate. But Sergeant McGonnigal was always scrupulously polite to me, never participating in his lieutenant's hostility.

The truth of the matter was that Bobby had been my father's closest friend, both on and off the force. His feelings toward me were compounded of guilt at flourishing when my father had stayed in beat patrol, at living while Tony had died—and frustration at my being grown up and a professional investigator instead of a little girl he could dandle on his knee.

He looked around in the little entryway of my apartment for a place to put his dripping raincoat, finally sticking it on the floor outside the door.

His wife was a meticulous housekeeper and he had been well trained. Sergeant McGonnigal followed suit, running his fingers through his thick curly hair to squeeze some of the excess water out.

I solemnly took them into the living room and brought coffee in mugs, remembering extra sugar for Bobby.

"It's good to see you," I said politely when they were seated on the couch. "Especially on such a rotten day. How are you?"

Bobby looked at me sternly, quickly glancing away when he saw I didn't have a bra on under my T-shirt. "I didn't want to come here. The captain thought someone should talk to you and since I know you he thought it should be me. I didn't agree, but he's the captain. If you'll answer my questions seriously and try not to be a wisenheimer, the whole thing'll go faster and we'll both be happy."

"And I thought you were being social," I said mournfully. "No, no, sorry, bad start. I'm serious as—as a traffic court judge. Ask me anything."

"Nancy Cleghorn," Bobby said flatly.

"That's not a question, and I don't have an answer. I just read in this morning's paper that she was killed yesterday. I expect you know a lot more about it than I do."

"Oh, yes," he agreed heavily. "We know a great deal—that she died around six P.M. From the amount of internal bleeding, the M.E. says she was probably hit around four. We know she was thirty-six years old and had been pregnant at least once, that she ate too much high-fat food and broke her right leg as an adult. I know that a man, or a woman with size thirteen shoes and a forty-inch stride, dragged her in a green blanket to the south end of Dead Stick Pond. The blanket was sold at a Sears store somewhere in the United States sometime between 1978 when they started making them and 1984 when they discontinued that brand. Someone else, presumably also a man, came along for the stroll but didn't help with the dragging or dumping."

"The lab worked overtime last night. I didn't think they did that for your average dead citizen."

Bobby refused to let me ride him. "There's also a little bit I don't know, but it's the part that counts. I don't have any idea who wanted her to die. But I understand you two grew up together and used to be pretty good friends."

"And you want me to find her murderer? I would have thought you guys had the machinery to do that easier than me."

His look would have made an academy recruit faint. "I want you to *tell* me."

"I don't know."

"That's not what I hear." He glared at a point somewhere over my head.

I couldn't imagine what he was talking about, then the messages I'd left for Nancy at SCRAP and with her mother came back to me. Those seemed like mighty small straws to build a house from.

"Let me guess," I said brightly. "It's not even business hours and you've already rounded up everyone at SCRAP and talked to them."

McGonnigal shifted uneasily and looked at Mallory. The lieutenant nodded briefly. McGonnigal said, "I talked with a Ms. Caroline Djiak late last night. She said you advised Cleghorn on how to investigate a problem they were having with a zoning permit for a recycling plant. She said you would know who the deceased spoke to about it."

I stared at him speechlessly. Finally I choked out, "Are those her exact words?"

McGonnigal fished in his breast pocket for a notebook. He flipped through the pages, squinting at his notes. "I didn't take it down word for word, but that's pretty much it," he said at last.

"I wouldn't call Caroline Djiak a pathological liar," I remarked conversationally. "Just a manipulative little squirt. But even though I'm mad enough at her to go down and personally break in the back of *her* head, it doesn't cheer me any you coming at me this way. I mean, we go through this every time you think I'm involved in a crime, don't we, Lieutenant? You make a frontal assault that takes my guilty knowledge for granted.

"You could've started by telling me about Caroline's never-never-land remarks and asking me if they were true. Then I would've told you everything that happened, which was about five minutes of conversation in Caroline's dining room, and you could have taken off with one loose end tied up."

I got up from the floor and headed for the kitchen. Bobby came in as I was poking around the refrigerator to see if there was anything edible I might use for breakfast. The yogurt had changed to mold and sour milk. There wasn't any fruit, and the only bread I had left was hard enough to use for ammo.

Bobby unconsciously wrinkled his nose at the dirty dishes, but heroically refrained from commenting on them. Instead he said, "Seeing you near a murder always gets me in the gut. You know that."

It was as close as he was going to get to an apology. "I'm not near this one," I said impatiently. "I don't know why Caroline wants me there. She dragged me down to South Chicago last week to a basketball-team reunion. Then she manipulated me into helping her with a personal problem. Then she called to tell me to bug out of her life. Now she wants me back. Or maybe she's just trying to punish me."

I dug some crackers out of a cupboard and spread them with peanut butter. "While we were eating fried chicken Nancy Cleghorn came by to talk about a zoning problem. This would have been just a week ago. Caroline thought Jurshak—the alderman down there—was blocking the permit. She asked me what I'd do if I were investigating. I said the easiest thing to do was talk to a friend on Jurshak's staff if she or Nancy had one. Nancy left. The total of my involvement."

I poured some more coffee, angry enough that my hand shook and I spilled it across the stove. "Despite your little dig, we hadn't seen each other for more than ten years. I didn't know who her friends or enemies were. Now Caroline makes it sound as though Jurshak killed Nancy, for which there isn't an atom of evidence. And she wants to make out that I egged him on to do it. Hell!"

Bobby flinched. "Don't talk dirty, Vicki. It doesn't help anything. What are you working on for the Djiak girl?"

"Woman," I said automatically through a mouthful of peanut butter. "Or maybe brat. I'll tell you for nothing, even though it's none of your business. Her mother was one of Gabriella's charities. Now she's dying. Very unpleasantly. Caroline wanted me to find some people her mother used to work with in the hopes they'd come see her. But as she probably told you, she fired me two days ago."

Bobby's blue eyes narrowed to slits in his ruddy face. "There's some truth there. I just wish I knew how much."

"I should have known better than to speak frankly with you," I said bitterly. "Especially when you opened the conversation with an accusation."

"Oh, keep your shirt on, Vicki," Bobby said. He blushed suddenly as the image hit home with him. "And clean up your kitchen more than once a year. Place looks like the projects."

When he had stomped away with McGonnigal I went to my bedroom to change. As I scrambled back into the black dress I looked out the window —the water was forming little rivers on the walk below. I put on running shoes and carried a pair of black pumps in my bag.

Even with an extra-wide umbrella my legs and feet got soaked on my dash to the car. Most Februaries, though, this would be snow a foot or two deep, so I tried not to complain too bitterly.

The little Chevy's defroster couldn't make much headway on the fogged windshield, but at least the car hadn't died, the fate of a number of others I passed. The storm and the stalls made for a slow trek south; it was close to ten by the time I turned from Route 41 onto Ninety-second Street. By the time I found a parking space near the corner of Commercial, the rain was finally lifting—it was clear enough for me to change into my pumps.

SCRAP's offices were in the second story of a block of little shops. I trotted around the corner to the business entrance—my dentist used to have his office here and the opening on Commercial remained an indelible memory.

I stopped at the top of the uncarpeted stairs, reading the wall directory while combing my hair and straightening my skirt. Dr. Zdunek wasn't there anymore. Neither were a lot of the other tenants; I passed half a dozen or so empty offices on my way down the hall.

At the far end I walked into a room that had the unmistakable air of a poor not-for-profit agency. The scarred metal furniture and newspaper articles taped to the walls wavered under a badly winking fluorescent bulb. Papers and phone books were stacked on the floor and the electric type-writers were models IBM had abandoned when I was still in college.

A young black woman was typing while talking on the phone. She smiled at me, but held up a finger to ask me to wait. I could hear voices from an open conference room; ignoring the receptionist's urgent hissing, I went to the door to look in.

A group of five, four women and a man, sat at a rickety deal table. Caroline was in the middle, talking heatedly. When she saw me at the door she broke off and flushed to the roots of her coppery hair.

"Vic! I'm in a meeting. Can't you wait?"

"All day, if it's for you, my sweet. We need a tête-à-tête about John McGonnigal—he visited me first thing this morning."

"John McGonnigal?" Her little nose wrinkled questioningly.

"*Sergeant* McGonnigal. Chicago Police," I said helpfully.

She turned even redder. "Oh. Him. Maybe we'd better talk now. Will you all excuse me?"

She got up and took me to a cubbyhole next to the conference room. The chaos there, compounded of books, papers, graphs, old newspapers, and candy wrappers, made my office look like a convent cell. Caroline dumped a phone directory from a folding chair for me and seated herself in the rickety swivel chair behind her desk. She gripped her hands together in front of her, but stared at me defiantly.

"Caroline, I've known you twenty-six years, and you've pulled tricks that would shame Oliver North, but this one has got to head the list. After whining and snuffling you got me to agree to look for your old man. Then you called me off without any reason. Now, to top it all off, you lied to the police about my involvement with Nancy. You want to explain why? Without resorting to Hans Christian Andersen?" I was having trouble keeping my voice below a shout.

"What are you on your high horse about?" she said belligerently. "You did give Nancy advice about—"

"Shut up!" I snapped. "You're not talking to the cops, sweetie pie. I can just picture you blushing and winking away your tears with Sergeant McGonnigal. But I know what I told Nancy that night as well as you do. So cut the crap and tell me why you lied about me to the police."

"I didn't! You try and prove it! Nancy did come by that night. You did tell her to talk to someone in Jurshak's office. And she's dead now."

I shook my head like a wet dog, trying to clear my brain. "Could we start this at the beginning? Why did you tell me to stop hunting for your old man?"

She looked at the desktop. "I decided it wasn't fair to Ma. Going behind her back when it upset her so much."

"Whew boy," I said. "Hold it there. Let me get onto Cardinal Bernardin and the Pope to start beatification proceedings. When did you ever put Louisa, or anyone else, ahead of what you wanted?"

"Stop it!" she shouted, bursting into tears. "Believe me or not, I don't care. I love my mother and I don't want anyone hurting her no matter what you may think."

I looked at her warily. Caroline might bat a few tears around as part of her tragic orphan routine, but she wasn't prone to sobbing fits.

"Okay," I said slowly. "I take it back. That was cruel. Is that why you sicced the cops on me? To punish me for saying I was continuing the investigation?"

She blew her nose noisily. "It wasn't like that!"

"What was it like then?"

She caught her lower lip in her teeth. "Nancy called me Tuesday morning. She said she'd gotten threatening phone calls and she thought someone was following her."

"What were they threatening her about?"

"The plant, of course."

"Caroline, I want you to be absolutely clear on this. Did she specifically say the calls were about the plant?"

She opened her mouth, then took a breath. "No," she finally muttered. "I just assumed they were. Because it was the last thing she and I had been talking about."

"But you went ahead and told the police that she was killed because of the recycling plant. And that I told her who to talk to. Do you understand how outrageous that is?"

"But, Vic. It's not just a wild guess. I mean—"

"You mean shit!" My anger returned, making my voice husky. "Can't you tell the difference between your head games and reality? Nancy was killed. Murdered. Instead of helping the police find the murderer, you slandered me and got them on my butt."

"They don't care about Nancy, anyway. They don't care about any of us down here." She got to her feet, her eyes flashing. "They respond to political pressure, and as far as Jurshak is concerned, South Chicago might as well be the South Pole. You know that as well as I do. You know the last time he got a street repaired down here—it sure as hell was before you left the neighborhood."

"Bobby Mallory is a good, honest, thorough cop," I said doggedly. "Just because Jurshak is twenty kinds of asshole doesn't change that."

"Yeah, you don't care, either. You proved that pretty good when you moved away from here and never came back until I pushed you into it."

The pulse beside my right temple started throbbing. I pounded the desk hard enough to knock some of the papers to the floor. "I busted my ass for a week trying to find your old man for you. Your grandparents insulted me, Louisa blew up at me, and you! You couldn't be content with manipulating me into going to look for the guy and then spinning me around a few times. You had to lie to the police about me."

"And I thought you'd give a fuck," she yelled. "I thought if you didn't care about me, you'd at least do something for Nancy because you played on the same team together. I guess that proves how wrong I was."

She started for the door. I caught her arm and forced her to face me.

"Caroline, I'm mad enough to beat the shit out of you. But I'm not so mad I can't think. You fingered me to the cops because there's something you know that you're scared to talk about. I want to know what that is."

She looked at me fiercely. "I don't know anything. Just that someone had started following Nancy around over the weekend."

"And she called the police and reported it. Or you did."

"No. She talked to the state's attorney and they said they'd open a file. I guess they have something to put in it now."

She gave the smile of a triumphant martyr. I forced myself to speak calmly to her. After a few minutes she reluctantly agreed to sit back down and tell me what she knew. If she was telling the truth—a big if—it wasn't much. She didn't know whom Nancy had seen at the state's attorney's office, but she thought it could have been Hugh McInerney; he was the person they dealt with on other issues. Under further probing she admitted that McInerney had taken statements from them eighteen months ago about their problems with Steve Dresberg, a local Mob figure involved in garbage disposal.

I vaguely remembered the trial over Dresberg's PCB incinerator and his alleged sweetheart deal with the Sanitary District but didn't realize she and Nancy had been involved. When I demanded to know what role the two had played, she scowled but said she and Nancy had testified to receiving death threats for their opposition to the incinerator.

"Obviously Dresberg knew who to pay off at the Sanitary District. It didn't matter what we said. I guess he figured SCRAP was too puny to listen to so he didn't have to make good his threats."

"And you didn't tell the cops that." I rubbed my hands tiredly across my face. "Caroline, you need to call McGonnigal and make an amended statement. You need to get them looking at people you *know* threatened Nancy in the past. I'm going to phone the sergeant myself as soon as I get home to tell him about this conversation. And if you're thinking of lying to him a second time, think again—he's known me professionally for years. He may not like me, but he knows he can believe what I tell him."

She looked at me furiously. "I'm not five years old anymore. I don't have to do what you say."

I went to the door. "Just do me a favor, Caroline—the next time you're in trouble, dial 911 like the rest of the citizenry. Or talk to a shrink. Don't come hounding me."

12

Common Sense

I dragged my feet back to the Chevy, feeling as though I were a hundred years old. I was disgusted with Caroline, with myself for being stupid enough to get caught in her net once again, with Gabriella for ever befriending Louisa Djiak. If my mother had known what Louisa's damned baby would get me into . . . I could hear Gabriella's golden voice in response to the same plaint twenty-two years ago. "Of her I expect nothing but trouble, *cara*. But of you I expect rationality. Not because you are older, but because it is your nature."

I made a bitter face at the memory and started the car. Sometimes the burden of being rational and responsible while everyone around me was howling was more than I liked. Even so, instead of washing my hands of Caroline's problems and heading north toward home, I found myself driving west. Toward Nancy's childhood house on Muskegon.

But it wasn't to help out Caroline that I was making the trek. I didn't care that I'd told Nancy to talk to someone at Jurshak's office, or even that we'd shared the old school towel. I was hoping to assuage my own feeling of guilt for not having been there when Nancy called me.

Of course she might have been phoning to condole about the Lady Tigers—our successors had been eliminated in the state quarterfinals. But I didn't think so. Despite my bravura performance with Caroline, I sort of thought she was right: Nancy had learned something about the recycling plant that she needed my help to deal with.

I didn't have any trouble finding Nancy's mother's place, which didn't exactly cheer me up. I thought I'd left the South Side behind, but it seemed my unconscious had perfect recall of every house I used to spend time in down here.

Three cars were crowded into the short driveway. The curb in front was filled, too, and I had to go some way down the street before I found a parking space. I fiddled with my car keys for a moment before starting up the walk—perhaps I should postpone my visit until her mourning callers had gone. But even if it were my nature to be rational, patience isn't my leading virtue. I stuck the keys in my skirt pocket and headed up the walk.

The door was opened by a strange young woman of thirty or so, wearing jeans and a sweatshirt. She looked at me questioningly without saying anything. When a minute had stretched by without her speaking, I finally gave her my name.

"I'm an old friend of Nancy's. I'd like to talk to Mrs. Cleghorn for a few minutes if she's up to seeing me."

"I'll go ask," she muttered.

She came back again, hunched a shoulder, told me I could go on in, and returned to whatever she'd been doing when I rang the bell. I was startled by the clamor when I got into the little foyer—it was more like the noisy house of Nancy's and my childhood than a place of mourning.

As I followed the sound toward the living room, two small boys erupted from it, chasing each other with sweet rolls they were using as guns. The lead one caromed into me and bounced off without apology. I sidestepped the other and looked cautiously around the doorway before entering.

The long, homey room was packed with people. I didn't recognize any of them, but assumed the men were Nancy's four brothers grown to adulthood. The three young women were presumably their wives. What looked like a nursery school in full session was crammed around the edges, with children jabbing each other, scuffling, giggling, ignoring adult admonitions for silence.

No one paid any attention to me, but I finally spied Ellen Cleghorn at the far end of the room, holding a howling baby without much enthusiasm. When she saw me she struggled to her feet and gave the baby to one of the young women. She picked her way through her swarming grandchildren to me.

"I'm so sorry about Nancy," I said, squeezing her hand. "And I'm sorry to bother you at a time like this."

"I'm glad you came, dear," she said, giving a warm smile and kissing my cheek. "The boys mean well—they all took the day off and thought it would cheer up Grandma to see the kiddies—but the chaos is too much for me. Let's go into the dining room. There's cake in there and one of the girls is making coffee."

Ellen Cleghorn had aged well. She was a plumper edition of Nancy, with the same frizzy blond hair. It had darkened with time rather than graying and her skin was still soft and clear. She had been divorced for many years, ever since her husband ran off with another woman. She'd never gotten child support or alimony and had raised her large family on her meager earnings as a librarian, always making room for me at the dinner table after basketball practice.

Ellen had been unique on the South Side in her indifference to housekeeping. The disarray in the dining room was much as I remembered it, with dust balls in the corners and books and papers shoved to one side to make room for the food. Even so, the house had always seemed romantic to me when I was young. It was one of a handful of big homes in the neighborhood—Mr. Cleghorn had been a grade school principal before he decamped—and all five children had their own bedrooms. Unheard-of luxury on the South Side. Nancy's even had a little turreted window where we acted out *Bluebeard*.

Mrs. Cleghorn sat down behind a stack of newspapers at the head of the table and gestured me to the chair catty-corner to her.

I fiddled with the pages of the book in front of me, then said abruptly, "Nancy was trying to get in touch with me yesterday. I guess I told you that when you gave me her number. Do you know what she wanted?"

She shook her head. "I hadn't talked to her for several weeks."

"I know it's rotten of me to bug you about it today. But—I keep thinking it had something to do with—with what happened to her. I mean, we hadn't seen each other for so long. And when we did talk it was about my being a detective and what I would do in her situation. So she would have thought of me in that context, you know—something came up that she thought my special experience might help her with."

"I just don't know, dear." Her voice trembled and she struggled to control it. "Don't let it worry you. You couldn't have done anything to help her, I'm sure."

"I wish I could agree with you. Look, I'm not trying to be a ghoul, or pressure you when you're so upset. But I feel responsible. I'm an experienced investigator. I might have been able to help her if I'd been home when she called. The only thing I can do to assuage my conscience is try to find who killed her."

"Vic, I know you and Nancy were friends, and I'm sure you think you're helping by getting involved. But can't you just leave it to the police? I don't want to have to talk about it or think about it anymore. It's bad enough having to get ready for her funeral with all these children screaming through the house. If I have to worry about—about why someone wanted to kill her—I keep thinking of her in that marsh. We used to go bird-watching there when she was in Girl Scouts and she was always so scared of the water. I keep thinking of her in there being alone and afraid —" She broke off and struggled against her tears.

I knew Nancy was afraid of water. She had never joined our surreptitious swims in the Calumet and she had to get a written statement from a doctor to excuse her from the swimming requirement in college. I didn't want to think of her last minutes in the marsh. Maybe she'd never regained consciousness. It was the best I could hope for.

"That's why it matters to me to find out who put her through such torment. It makes me feel that she was a little less helpless if I can go to bat for her now. Can you understand that and tell me who Nancy might've talked to? If not to you, I mean?"

She and Nancy had always had a kind of careless camaraderie, which I'd envied. Even though I loved my mother, she was too intense for an easy relationship. If Nancy hadn't told Ellen Cleghorn what was going on with the recycling center, she'd certainly have talked to her about friends and lovers. And after a few more minutes of coaxing Mrs. Cleghorn started speaking about them.

Nancy had been in love, been pregnant, had an abortion. Since she and Charles broke up five years ago there hadn't been any special men in her life. And no close women friends down here, either.

"It wasn't really a good place for her to meet people. I hoped maybe after she bought that house—South Shore is a little livelier neighborhood and lots of university people live down there now. But there wasn't anyone in this area she would've been close enough to talk to. Except maybe Caroline Djiak, and Nancy thought she was such a hothead, she wouldn't have told her anything she wasn't dead certain about." The unconscious phrase made her wince.

I rubbed my eyes. "She talked to one of the state's attorneys. If it had something to do with SCRAP, she might've talked to their lawyer too. What's his name? She mentioned it that night she came by Caroline's and I can't remember it."

"I guess that would be Ron Kappelman, Vic. She went out with him a few times but they didn't really click together."

"When was that?" I asked, suddenly alert. Maybe it was a crime of passion after all.

"It must have been two years ago, I guess. When he first started working with SCRAP."

Maybe not. Who waits two years to revenge himself on love gone sour? Outside Agatha Christie, that is.

Mrs. Cleghorn couldn't tell me anything else. Other than the date of the funeral, set for Monday at Mount of Olives Methodist Church. I told her I'd be there and left her to the ministrations of her grandchildren.

Back at the car, I slumped dejectedly against the steering wheel. Except for the financial searches I'd done on Tuesday, I hadn't had a paying customer for three weeks. And now, if I was really going to look into Nancy's death, I'd have to talk to the state's attorney. See if Nancy had revealed anything when she told him she was being followed. Talk to Ron Kappelman. See whether he might've felt like a man scorned or, failing that, if he knew what she'd been up to the last few days.

I rubbed my head tiredly. Maybe I was getting too old for gestures of bravado. Maybe I should just call John McGonnigal, tell him about my conversation with Caroline, and go back to what I know how to do—investigate industrial fraud.

On that sensible, even rational, note, I started the car and took off. Not toward Lake Shore Drive and common sense, but to the south, where Nancy Cleghorn had died.

13

Dead Stick Pond

Dead Stick Pond lay deep in the labyrinth of marsh, landfill, and factories. I'd been there only once, as part of the Girl Scout bird-watching expedition, and wasn't sure I could find it again. At 103rd Street I headed west to Stony Island, the street that threads the maze. North of 103rd it's a major thoroughfare, but down here it turns into a gravel track of indeterminate width, worn to potholes by the giant semis chewing their way in and out of the factories.

The heavy rain had turned the track to a muddy glaze. The Chevy bounced and slid uneasily in the ruts between the high marsh grasses. Passing trucks splattered the windshield with mud. When I swerved to miss them the Chevy bucked dangerously and headed for the drainage ditches lining the road.

My arms were sore from wrestling with the steering when I finally saw the pond to my left. Parking on a patch of high ground next to the road, I donned my running shoes for my expedition. I followed the road to a posted track on the east rim of the pond, then picked my way gingerly through the marshy ground and dead grasses. Mud squelched up under my feet and slid inside my running shoes.

The pond was part of an overflow of the Calumet River. It wasn't very deep, but its murky waters covered a vast expanse of the marsh. Close up I read conflicting signs tacked to the trees, one proclaiming the area a federal clean-water project, the other warning trespassers of hazardous wastes. Some oversight agency had made a haphazard attempt to enclose the pond, but the low wire fence had fallen down in a number of places, making it easy to breach. Gathering my skirt in one hand, I stepped over one of these collapsed sections to the water's edge.

Dead Stick Pond used to be a great feeding area for migrating birds.

Now the water was a dull black, with stark tree stumps poking surreal fingers through its surface. Fish have been returning to the Calumet River and its tributaries since the passage of the Clean Water Act, but the ones that make their way into the pond show up with massive tumors and rotted fins. Even so I passed a fishing couple trying to find dinner in the dirty water. The two were shapeless, ageless, sexless in their layers of worn garments. I could feel them watching me until I disappeared around a curve in the marsh grasses.

I followed a track to the south end of the pond, where the papers said Nancy had died. I found the spot easily enough—it was still marked with yellow police tape and the big yellow signs declaring the area off limits as the site of a police investigation. They hadn't bothered to leave a patrol-man—who would have agreed to such a posting? Anyway, the rain had doubtless washed away anything the evidence team hadn't picked up last night. I ducked under the yellow tape.

The killers had parked where I left my car. Or near there. They had dragged her along the path I had just traversed. In broad daylight. They'd gone past the fishing couple, or past the place where the two stood. Just lucky that no one had seen them? Or relying on the furtive lives of those who frequent the swamps to protect them from idle curiosity?

The rain had washed away any signs of Nancy's body, but the police had marked an outline with stones. I squatted next to them. She had been dumped from the blanket and landed on her right side, head partly in the water. And had lain there in the oily water until she drowned.

I shivered in the damp air and finally pushed myself back to my feet. There was nothing to be seen here, no trace of life or death. I headed slowly back down the path, stopping every few feet to inspect the bushes and grasses. It was a futile gesture. Sherlock Holmes would no doubt have spotted the telltale cigarette butt, the gravel from another county that didn't belong here, the fragment of a missing envelope. All I saw was the endless array of bottles, potato-chip bags, old shoes, coats, proving that Nancy was only one of many discarded bundles in the swamp.

The fishing couple were standing exactly as they had on my way in. On impulse I started toward them to see if they'd been here yesterday, if they'd noticed anything. But when I stepped off the path a gaunt German shepherd got to its feet, glaring at me with wild red eyes. It braced its forelegs and bared its teeth. I muttered, "Nice doggie," and returned to the trail. Let the police interrogate the couple—they were being paid for the work and I wasn't.

Back at the road, I hunted around for the place where the killers had carried her over the fence. I finally found a few green threads snagged on the wire about twenty feet from where I'd left the car. I could see where last year's grasses still lay broken under the weight of her assailants' feet. The area was relatively untrampled, though, so I didn't think the police had bothered with a search at this end.

I moved carefully through the undergrowth, inspecting every piece of litter. I cut my hands parting the dead grasses. The skirt of my black dress grew stiff with mud and my fingers and toes were frozen when I finally decided there was nothing I could accomplish here. I turned the Chevy around and headed north to try to find Nancy's man in the state's attorney's office.

With my bedraggled dress and mud-streaked legs, I wasn't dressed for success, or even for making a good impression on public servants. It was getting close to three, though; if I went home to change, I'd never get back to Twenty-sixth and California before the end of the business day.

I'd spent my years on the county payroll as a public defender. Not only did that put me on the other side of the bench from the state's attorneys, it left me with a permanent suspicion of them. We all worked for the Cook County Board, but they earned fifty percent more than we did. And if a hot case made it to the papers, the prosecutors always got mentioned by name. We never did, even if our brilliant defense made them look like dog food. Of course I'd cultivated my share of prosecutors working out plea bargains and other deals. But there wasn't anyone on Richie Daley's staff who'd be glad to give me information for old times' sake. I'd have to do my Dick Butkus imitation and bull my way through the middle of the line.

The bailiff who searched me at the entrance remembered me. She was inclined to chaff me about my bedraggled appearance, but at least she didn't try to stop me as a dangerous abettor of criminals. I stopped in the ladies' room to wash the mud from my legs. Nothing could be done about the dress at this point, other than burning it, but with a little makeup and my hair combed, I at least didn't look like someone who'd broken out of custody.

I went up to the third floor and looked sternly at the receptionist. "My name's Warshawski; I'm a detective," I said harshly. "I want to talk to Hugh McInerney about the Cleghorn case."

Police and sheriff's deputies are a dime a dozen at the criminal courts. I figured they didn't flash a badge every time they wanted to see someone, so why should I? The receptionist responded to my bullying tone by quickly punching numbers on the house phone. Even though she was a patronage employee, like everyone else in the building, it didn't help to get a black mark with a detective.

State's attorneys are young men and women en route to big law firms or good political appointments. You never see any old people on the left side of the bench—I don't know where they ship the ones who don't move on naturally. Hugh McInerney looked to be in his late twenties. He was tall, with thick blond hair and the kind of trim muscularity that comes from a lot of racquetball.

"What can I do for you, Detective?" His deep voice, matching his build, was tailor-made for the courtroom.

"Nancy Cleghorn," I said briskly. "Can we talk in private?"

He led me through the inner door to a conference room, with the bare walls and scuffed furniture I remembered from my own county days. He left me alone for a minute to get his file on Nancy.

"You know she's dead," I said when he got back.

"I saw it in the morning paper. I've been kind of waiting for you guys to get here."

"You didn't think of using some initiative and calling us yourself?" I raised my eyebrows haughtily.

He hunched a shoulder. "I didn't have anything concrete to tell you. She came to see me Tuesday because she thought someone was following her."

"She have any idea who?"

He shook his head. "Believe me, Detective, if I'd had a name in here, I'd have been on the phone first thing this morning."

"You didn't think about Steve Dresberg?"

He shifted uncomfortably. "I—uh, I talked to Dresberg's attorney, Leon Haas. He—uh, he thought Dresberg was pretty happy with the situation down there these days."

"Yeah, he should be," I said nastily. "He made you guys look like cole slaw in court, didn't he, on that incinerator deal. You ask Haas how Dresberg felt about the recycling plant Cleghorn was working on? If he issued death threats over an incinerator, I'm not sure he'd jump for joy over a recycling center. Or did you decide that Cleghorn was imagining things, Mr. McInerney?"

"Hey, Detective—lay off. We're on the same side on this. You find who killed the Cleghorn woman and I'll prosecute hell out of him. I promise you that. I don't think it was Steve Dresberg, but hey, I'll call Haas and feel him out."

I grinned savagely and stood up. "Better leave that for the police, Mr.

McInerney. Let them investigate and find someone for you to prosecute hell out of."

I strode arrogantly from the office, but once I got on the elevator my shoulders sagged. I didn't want to mess with Steve Dresberg. If half the things they said about him were true, he could get you into the Chicago River faster than you could change your socks. But he hadn't done anything to Nancy or Caroline over the incinerator. Or maybe he figured the first time around you got a warning; the second time meant sudden death. I soberly merged the Chevy with the rush-hour jam on the Kennedy and headed for home.

14

Muddy Waters

When I got home Mr. Contreras was in front of the building with the dog. She was gnawing on a large stick while he cleaned debris from the little patch of front yard. Peppy jumped up when she saw me, but sank back down when she realized I didn't have my running clothes on.

Mr. Contreras sketched a wave. "Hiya, doll. You get caught in the rain this morning?" He straightened and looked at me. "My, my, you're certainly a sight. Look like you've been wading through a mud puddle that came up to your waist."

"Yeah. I've been down in the South Chicago swamp. It kind of stays with you."

"Oh yeah? Didn't even know there was a South Chicago swamp."

"Well, there is," I said shortly, pushing the dog away impatiently.

He looked at me closely. "You need a bath. Hot bath and a drink, doll. You go on up and rest. I'll look after her royal highness here. She don't need to go to the lake every day of her life, you know."

"Yeah, right." I collected my mail and moved slowly up the stairs to the third floor. When I saw myself in the full-length mirror on the bathroom door, I couldn't believe I'd gotten McInerney to talk to me without a struggle. I looked as though I belonged with the fishing couple out at Dead Stick Pond. My panty hose were in shreds and my legs were streaked with black where I'd tried washing the mud off down at the county building. The hem of my dress was heavy with caked dirt. Even my black pumps had gotten dusty from the dirt on my legs.

I kicked the shoes off outside the bathroom door and threw out the panty hose while turning on the bath water. I hoped the cleaners could rescue the dress—I didn't want to sacrifice my entire wardrobe to the old neighborhood.

I took the portable phone from the bedroom into the bath with me. Once I was in the tub with whiskey at close reach I checked in with the answering service. Jonathan Michaels had tried to reach me. He'd left his office number, but the switchboard was closed for the day and I didn't have his unlisted home number. I stuck the phone up on the sink and leaned back in the tub with my eyes closed.

Steve Dresberg. Also known as the Garbage King. Not because of his character, but because if you wanted to bury, burn, or ship refuse in the Chicago area, you had to cut him in on the action. Some people say that two independent haulers who disappeared after refusing to deal with him are rotting in the CID landfill. Others think the arson in a waste storage shed that caused the evacuation of six square blocks on the South Side last summer could be traced to his door—if you had enough people with paid-up life insurance to do the tracing.

Dresberg was definitely police business, if not FBI. And since the odds were against Caroline phoning McGonnigal with an amended statement, that meant I should play Cindy Citizen and tell him myself.

Holding my breath, I slid down so that the water covered my head. Suppose Dresberg wasn't involved at all, though. If I pointed the cops toward him, it would only divert their attention from more promising lines of inquiry.

I sat up and started rubbing shampoo into my hair. The water around me was turning black; I opened the drain and turned on the hot-water tap. All I had to do was find someone on Jurshak's staff who would talk to me with the same frankness he'd used with Nancy. Then, when sinister figures began following me, I would take out my trusty Smith & Wesson and blow them away. Preferably, before they could bonk me on the head and dump me in the swamp.

I wrapped myself in a terry-cloth robe and went into the kitchen to forage. The maid hadn't been shopping for some time and pickings were slim. I took the jar of peanut butter and the bottle of Black Label and went back into the living room with them.

I was on my second whiskey and my fourth spoonful of peanut butter when I heard a tentative knock on the door. I groaned in resignation; it was Mr. Contreras with a laden TV tray. The dog was at his heels.

"Hope you don't mind me barging up like this, doll, but I could see you was all in and I thought you might like some supper. Did me a little barbecue chicken in the kitchen, and even without the charcoal it tastes pretty good, if I say so. I know you try to eat healthy so I made you a big salad. Now you want to be alone, you just say the word and Peppy and me'll head back down. Won't hurt my feelings any. But you can't live on that stuff you're drinking. And peanut butter? Scotch and peanut butter? No way, doll. You're too busy to buy food, you just let me know. No trouble for me to pick up something extra when I'm buying for myself, you know that."

I thanked him lamely and invited him in. "Just let me put on some clothes."

I guess I should have sent him back downstairs—I didn't want it to become a habit with him, thinking he could come up whenever he felt like it. But the chicken smelled good and the salad looked healthy and the peanut butter was lying kind of heavily on my stomach.

I ended up telling him about Nancy's death and my trek to Dead Stick Pond. He'd never been below the Field Museum and had no inkling of life on the South Side. I got out my city map and showed him Houston Street, where I'd grown up, and then the route down to the Cal Industrial District and the wetlands, where Nancy had been found.

He shook his head. "Dead Stick Pond, huh? Guess the name says it all. It's rough losing a friend that way, one you played basketball with and all. I never even knew you was on a team, but I mighta guessed it, the way you run. But you want to be careful, doll. If this Dresburg guy is the one behind all this, he's an awful lot bigger than you. You know me, I've never backed away from a fight, but I know better than to go in single-handed against a tank division too."

He was going into an elaborate illustration based on his experiences at Anzio when Jonathan Michaels phoned. I excused myself and took the call on the bedroom extension.

"I wanted to get you before I leave town in the morning." Jonathan spoke without preamble. "I had one of my staff people look up your two guys—Pankowski and Ferraro. They did sue Humboldt. Apparently not over wrongful dismissal, but whether they could get worker's comp. It looks as though they quit due to illness and were trying to prove it was job related. They didn't get anywhere with the suit—the thing came to trial here and Humboldt didn't have any trouble winning, and then the two died and the lawyer didn't seem to want to follow up on appeal. I don't know how far you want to follow this, but the lawyer who handled it was a Frederick Manheim."

He cut short my thanks with a crisp "Gotta run."

I was hanging up when he came back on the line. "You still there? Good. I almost forgot—we didn't see anything about sabotage, but Humboldt could have kept that quiet—not wanting the idea to get popular, you know."

After he hung up I sat on the bed looking at the phone. I felt so overloaded with unconnected information that I couldn't think at all. My professional curiosity had been piqued by the reaction I'd gotten first from the Xerxes personnel manager and then the doctor. I'd wanted to find out what lay behind their jumpy behavior. Then Humboldt seemed to have a glib explanation and Nancy's death had made me shift my priorities anyway; I couldn't untangle the whole universe, and finding her killers seemed more urgent than scratching the Xerxes itch.

Now the wheel seemed to turn the other way up again. Why had Humboldt gone out of his way to lie to me? Or had he? Maybe they'd sued for worker's comp but had lost because they'd been fired for sabotage. Nancy. Humboldt. Caroline. Louisa. Chigwell. The images spun uselessly through my mind.

"You all right in there, doll?" It was Mr. Contreras hovering anxiously in the hall.

"Yeah, I'm okay. I guess." I got to my feet and went back out to him with what I hoped was a reassuring smile. "I just need to spend some time alone. Okay?"

"Yeah, sure. Fine." He was a little hurt but worked valiantly to keep it from showing. He collected the dirty dishes, waving off my offers of help, and took the tray and the dog back downstairs.

Once he'd gone I wandered moodily around the apartment. Caroline had asked me to stop looking for her father; there wasn't any reason to push matters with Humboldt. But when a ten-billion-dollar man undertakes to run me through hoops it gets my hackles up.

I hunted around for the phone book. It had somehow gotten buried under a stack of music on the piano. Naturally enough, Humboldt's number wasn't listed. Frederick Manheim, Attorney, had an office at Ninety-fifth and Halsted and a home in neighboring Beverly. Lawyers with large incomes or criminal practices don't give their home numbers. Nor do they usually hide out on the southwest side, away from the courts and the major action.

I was restless enough to want to move now, call Manheim, get the story from him, and gallop down to Oak Street to confront Humboldt. *"Festina lente,"* I muttered to myself. Get the facts, then shoot. It would be better to wait until morning and make the trek down south to see the guy in person. Which meant yet another day in nylons. Which meant I'd better get my black pumps clean.

I foraged in the hall closet for shoe polish and finally found a tin of black under a sleeping bag. I was carefully cleaning the shoes when Bobby Mallory called.

I cradled the phone under my ear and started buffing the left shoe. "Evening, Lieutenant. What can I do for you?"

"You can give me a good reason for not running you in." He spoke in the pleasant conversational tone that meant his temper was on a tight rein.

"For what?" I asked.

"It's considered a crime to impersonate a police officer. By everyone but you, I believe."

"Not guilty." I looked at the shoe. It was never going to recover the smooth finish it had when it left Florence, but it wasn't too bad.

"You aren't the woman—tall, thirtyish, short curly hair—who told Hugh McInerney you were with the police?"

"I told him I was a detective. And when I spoke of the police, I carefully used third- not first-person pronouns. As far as I know that is not a crime, but maybe the City Council blew one by me." I picked up the right shoe.

"You don't think you could leave the investigation of the Cleghorn woman's death to the police, do you?"

"Oh, I don't know. You think Steve Dresberg killed her?"

"If I told you yes, would you drop out of sight and go do the stuff you're qualified to work on?"

"If you have a warrant with the guy's name on it, I might. Without arguing over what I'm qualified to do." I capped the polish tin and laid it and the rag on a newspaper.

"Vicki, look. You're a cop's daughter. You should know better than to go stirring around in a police investigation. When you talk to someone like McInerney without telling us, it just makes our job a hundred times harder. Okay?"

"Yeah, okay, I guess," I said grudgingly. "I won't talk to the state's attorney again without clearing it with you or McGonnigal."

"Or anyone else?"

"Give me a break, Bobby. If it says POLICE BUSINESS in all caps, I'll leave it to you. That's the best you're going to get from me."

We hung up in mutual irritation. I spent the rest of the evening in front of the tube watching a badly cut version of *Rebel Without a Cause*. It did nothing to abate my ill humor.

15

Chemistry Lesson

Manheim's office lay between a beauty parlor and a florist among the little storefronts crowding Ninety-fifth Street. He had put his name on the plate glass in those black-and-gold transfers that are supposed to look old-fashioned and discreet—Frederick Manheim, Attorney-at-Law.

The front of the place, the part the little shops used as their sales floors, had been turned into a reception area. It held a couple of vinyl chairs and a desk with a typewriter and an African violet set on it. A few old copies of *Sports Illustrated* sat on a pressed-wood table in front of the vinyl chairs. I flipped through one for a few minutes to give the help a chance to make an appearance. When no one showed up I tapped on the door at the back of the room and turned the knob.

The door opened on a tiny hallway. A few pieces of wallboard had been stuck in the area where the stores held their excess inventory to create an office and a little bathroom.

I knocked on the door that had Manheim's name on it—this time in solid black Gothic—and got a thick "Just a minute." Paper rustled, a drawer slammed, and Manheim opened the door still chewing, wiping his mouth on the back of his hand. He was a young man with rosy cheeks and thick fair hair that hung over the tops of heavy glasses.

"Oh, hi. Annie didn't tell me I had an appointment this morning. Come on in."

I shook his proffered hand and told him my name. "I don't have an appointment. I'm sorry to just come barging in, but I was in the area and hoped you might have a minute or two."

He waved me in. "Sure, sure. No problem. Sorry I can't offer you any coffee—I get mine from the Dunkin' Donuts on the way over."

He'd crammed a couple of visitors' chairs in between his desk and the door. If you leaned back in the one on the left, you ran into the filing cabinet. The one on the right was jammed against the wall; a line of gray scuff marks showed where people had rubbed too hard against the pasteboard. I felt kind of bad about not being able to infuse a little cash into the operation.

He'd taken out a pad of legal paper, carefully setting the Dunkin' Donuts coffee to one side.

"Can you spell your name for me, please?"

I spelled it out. "I'm a lawyer, Mr. Manheim, but these days I work primarily as a private investigator. A case I'm involved in has brought me to two clients of yours. Former clients, I guess. Joey Pankowski and Steve Ferraro."

He'd been looking at me courteously through his thick lenses, his hands clasped loosely around his pen. At the mention of Pankowski and Ferraro he let the pen drop and looked as troubled as a man with rosy cherub's cheeks could.

"Pankowski and Ferraro? I'm not sure—"

"Employees at Humboldt Chemical's Xerxes plant in South Chicago. Died two or three years ago."

"Oh, yes. I remember now. They needed some legal advice, but I'm afraid I couldn't do much for them." He blinked unhappily behind his glasses.

"I know you don't want to talk about your clients. I don't like talking about mine, either. But if I explain what's gotten me interested in Pankowski and Ferraro, will you answer a couple of questions about them for me?"

He looked down at the desktop and fiddled with his pen. "I—I really can't—"

"What is going on with these two guys? Every time I mention their names grown men tremble in their shoes."

He looked up at me. "Who are you working for?"

"Myself." Myself, myself, it is enough, or so Medea said.

"You're not working for a company?"

"You mean like Humboldt Chemical? No. I was hired originally by the young woman who used to live next door to me to find out who her father was. It seemed remotely possible that one of those two—most likely Pankowski—could have been the guy and I started poking around trying to find someone at Xerxes who knew him. This woman fired me on Wednesday, but I've gotten piqued by the way people are reacting to me. Lying to me, basically, about what went on between Pankowski and Ferraro and Xerxes. And then a guy I know at the Department of Labor told me you used to represent them. So here I am."

He smiled unhappily. "I don't suppose there's any reason the company would send someone around after all this time. But it's kind of hard for me to believe you're on your own. Too many people got too excited over that case, and now you come in out of the blue? It's too—too strange. Too pat."

I rubbed my forehead, trying to coax some ideas into my brain. Finally I said, "I'm going to do something I've never done in my whole history as an investigator. I'm going to tell you exactly what happened. If after that you still feel you can't trust me, so be it."

I started at the very beginning, with Louisa showing up pregnant in the house next door a few months before my eleventh birthday. With Gabriella and her quixotic impulses. With Caroline's exuberant philanthropy at other people's expense and the nagging feeling I still had of being her older sister and somehow responsible for her. I didn't tell him about Nancy ending up in Dead Stick Pond, but I described everything that had happened at Xerxes, my conversation with Dr. Chigwell, and finally Humboldt's intervention. That was the only episode I muted. I couldn't bring myself to tell him the owner of the company had had me in for brandy—I felt embarrassed because I'd let myself be gulled by the trappings of wealth. So I mumbled that I'd had a call from one of the company's senior officers.

After I finished Manheim took off his glasses and went through an elaborate cleaning ritual involving his necktie. It was clearly a habitual gesture of nervousness, but his eyes looked so naked without their protective lenses that I glanced away.

At last he put the glasses back on and picked up his pen again. "I'm not a bad lawyer. I'm really a pretty decent lawyer. Just not very ambitious. I grew up on the South Side and I like it down here. I help a lot of the businesses on the street with leasing problems, employment issues, that kind of thing. So when those two guys came to me maybe I should have sent them someplace else, but I thought I could handle the case—I've done some comp claims—and it made a nice change. Pankowski's sister owns the flower shop next door—that's why they picked me—she told them I'd done a good job for her."

He started for the filing cabinet and changed his mind. "I don't know why I want the folder—nervous habit, I guess. I mean, I know the whole damned case by heart, even after all this time."

He stopped, but I didn't prompt him. Whatever he said now would be to himself more than to me and I didn't want to intrude on the flow. After a few minutes he went on.

"It's Xerxine, you know. The way they used to make it, it left these toxic residues in the air. Do you know any chemistry? I don't either, but I made quite a study of this at the time. Xerxine is a chlorinated hydrocarbon—they add chlorine to ethylene gas usually and get a solvent. You know, the kind of thing you might clean oil from sheet metal with, or paint, or anything.

"Well, if you breathe the vapors while they're manufacturing it, it doesn't do you a whole lot of good. Affects the liver and kidneys and central nervous system and all those good things. When Humboldt first started making Xerxine back in the fifties, no one knew anything about that stuff. You know, they didn't run the plants to kill the employees, but they weren't very careful about controlling how much of the chlorinated vapors got into the air."

Now that he was into his story his manner had changed. He seemed self-confident and knowledgeable; his claim to being a good lawyer didn't seem at all farfetched.

"Then in the sixties and seventies, when people started thinking seriously about the environment, guys like Irving Selikoff began looking at industrial pollution and worker health. And they started finding that chemicals like Xerxine could be toxic at pretty low concentrations—you know, a hundred molecules per million molecules of air. What they call parts per million. So Xerxes put in air scrubbers and closed up their pipes better, and got their ppm down to federal standards. That would have been in the late seventies, when the EPA issued a standard on Xerxine. Fifty parts per million."

He smiled apologetically. "Sorry to be so technical. I can't think about this case in simple terms anymore. Anyway, Pankowski and Ferraro came to me early in 1983. They were both sick as hell, one with liver cancer, the other with aplastic anemia. They'd worked at Humboldt for a long time—since '59 for Ferraro and '61 for Pankowski—but they'd quit when they got too sick to work. That would have been two years earlier. So they couldn't collect disability. I don't think they were told it was an option."

I nodded in agreement. Companies don't willingly offer information on benefits that will add to their insurance premiums. Especially looking at a case like Louisa's, where she was getting major medical payments besides her disability check.

"But what about their union?" I asked. "Wouldn't the shop steward have notified them?"

He shook his head. "It's a single-shop union and it's pretty much a mouthpiece for the company. Especially now—there's so much unemployment in the neighborhood they don't want to rock the boat."

"Unlike the Steelworkers," I interjected dryly.

He grinned for the first time, looking even younger than before. "Well, you can't blame them. The Xerxes union, I mean. But anyway, the two guys had read someplace that Xerxine could cause these health problems, and since they were both up against it financially, they thought maybe they could at least collect workers' comp for not being able to work. You know, job-related condition and all that."

"I see. So you went to Humboldt and tried to work something out? Or you went directly to litigation?"

"I had to work fast—it wasn't clear how long either of them would live. I went to the company first, but when they didn't want to play ball I didn't fool around—I filed a suit. Of course if we'd won after they died, their families would have been entitled to an indemnity payment. And that would make quite a difference to them financially. But you like your clients to be alive to see their victories."

I nodded. It would have made a big difference, especially to Mrs. Pankowski with all her children. Illinois insurers pay a quarter of a million to families of workers who die on the job, so it was worth the effort.

"So what happened?"

"Well, I saw right away the company was going to stonewall, so we sued. Then we got an early docket. Even being stuck down on the South Side, I've got a few connections." He smiled to himself, but declined to share the joke.

"Trouble was, both guys smoked, Pankowski was a heavy drinker, and they'd both lived all their lives in South Chicago. I guess if you grew up there, I don't have to tell you what the air was like. So Humboldt socked us. They said on the one hand that there wasn't any way to prove Xerxine had made these guys sick instead of their cigarettes or the general shit in the air. And they also pointed out that both of them had been working there before anyone knew how toxic the stuff was. So even if Xerxine did make them sick, it didn't count—you know, they operated the plant based on current medical knowledge. So we lost handily. I talked to a really good appellate lawyer and he felt there just wasn't anything to go on with. End of story."

I thought about it for a minute. "Yeah, but if that's all that happened, why is Xerxes jumping like a nervous rabbit when it hears those guys' names?"

He shrugged. "Probably same reason I didn't want to talk to you to begin with. They don't believe you're on your own. They don't think you're looking for a long-lost father. They think you're trying to stir the pot up again. You've got to admit your story looks pretty farfetched."

Reluctantly, I looked at it from his point of view. Given all this history I hadn't known about, I could understand, sort of. I still couldn't figure out why Humboldt felt he had to intervene. If his company had won the case fair and square, what difference did it make if his subordinates talked to me about Pankowski and Ferraro?

"And also," I added aloud, "why are you so upset? Do you think they were wrong? I mean, do you think the trial was rigged somehow?"

He shook his head unhappily. "No. Based on the evidence, I don't think we could have won. I think we should have. I mean, I think these guys deserved something for putting twenty years of their lives into the company, especially since it's probable that working there killed them. I mean, look at your friend's mother. She's dying too. Kidney failure did you say? But the law spells it out, or the precedents do—you can't fault the company for operating under the best knowledge they had available at the time."

"So that's it? You just don't like to talk about it because you feel bad that you couldn't win for them?"

He communed again with his glasses and his tie. "Oh, that would get me down. No one likes losing, and God, you couldn't help wanting these guys to win. But then, you know, the company could see that plant go belly-up if we set a successful precedent. Everyone who'd ever been sick or died there coming back for these big settlements."

He stopped. I made myself sit very quietly.

At last he said, "No. It's just that I got a threatening phone call. After the case. When we were considering the appeal."

"That would be grounds for overturning the verdict," I burst out. "Didn't you go to the state's attorney?"

He shook his head. "I just got the one phone call. And whoever called didn't mention the case by name—just a generic reference to the dangers of using the appellate system. I'm not very tough physically, but I'm not a coward either. The call made me angry, angrier than I've ever been, and I pushed and prodded every way after that to build an appeal. There just wasn't any way to."

"They didn't call you later to congratulate you for following their advice?"

"I never heard from the guy again. But when you showed up out of nowhere . . ."

I laughed. "Glad to know I could be mistaken for muscle. I may need it before the day is over."

He blushed. "No, no. You don't look—I don't mean—I mean, you're a very attractive lady. But you never know these days. . . . I wish I could tell you something about your friend's father, but we never talked about anything like that. My clients and I."

"No, I can see you wouldn't have." I thanked him for his frankness and got up.

"If you come across anything else you think I could help you with, let me know," he said, shaking my hand. "Especially if it might give me some grounds for a writ of certiorari."

I assured him I would and left. I was wiser than I'd been when I came in, but no less confused.

16

House Call

It was well past noon by the time Manheim and I finished talking. I headed for the Loop and picked up a Diet Coke and a sandwich—corned beef, which I reserve for occasions when I need special nourishment—and took them to my office.

I could see Manheim's point. Sort of. If Humboldt lost a suit like that, it could spell disaster, the kind of problem that drove Johns-Manville to seek bankruptcy protection. But Manville's situation had been different: they had known asbestos was toxic and covered up their knowledge. So when the ugly truth came out workers sued for punitive damages.

All Humboldt would have faced was a series of comp claims. Even so, that might be sticky. Say they'd had a thousand workers at the plant over a ten-year period and they all died: at a quarter of a million a pop, even if Ajax was paying for it, that was a lot of balloons.

I licked mustard from my fingers. Maybe I was looking at it wrong—maybe it was Ajax not wanting to make the payout—Gordon Firth telling his good buddy Gustav Humboldt to cool out any attempts to reopen the case. But Firth couldn't have known I was involved—the word wouldn't have run around Chicago that fast. Or maybe it would. You've never seen gossip and rumor mills until you've spent a week in a large corporation.

And then, why had someone threatened Manheim about the appeal? If Humboldt was dead to rights on the legal issues, there wasn't any percentage in going after Manheim—it would just cause a judge to vacate the decree. So it couldn't have been the company trying to brush him back.

Or maybe it was some very junior person. Someone who thought he could make a name for himself in the company by putting a little muscle on the plaintiffs. That wasn't a totally improbable scenario. You get a

corporate atmosphere where ethics are a little loose and subordinates think
that the way to management's heart is across their opponents' bodies.

But that still didn't explain why Humboldt had lied about the suit. Why
dump a charge of sabotage on the poor bastards when all they wanted was
some workers' comp money? I wondered if it would be worthwhile to try
to speak to Humboldt again. I visualized his full, jovial face with the cold
blue eyes. You have to swim carefully when your waters are shared by a
great shark. I wasn't sure I wanted to go to the big man just yet.

I groaned to myself. The problem was spreading out in front of me like
ripples in a pond. I was the stone dropped in the middle and the lines were
moving farther and farther away from me. I just couldn't handle so many
intangible waves on my own.

I tried to turn my attention to some problems that had come in the mail,
including a notice of insufficient funds to cover the check of a small hardware store whose pilfering problems I'd solved a few weeks ago. I made a
call that brought me no satisfaction and decided to pack it in for the day.
I'd just slung my mail into the wastebasket when the phone rang.

An efficient alto told me she was Clarissa Hollingsworth, Mr.
Humboldt's personal secretary.

I sat up in my chair. Time to be alert. I wasn't ready to go to him, but
the shark wanted to swim to me. "Yes, Ms. Hollingsworth. What can I do
for Mr. Humboldt?"

"I don't believe he wants you to do anything," she said coolly. "He just
asked me to pass on some information to you. About someone named—uh
—Louisa Djiak."

She stumbled over the name—she should have practiced pronouncing it
before phoning.

I repeated Louisa's name correctly. "Yes?"

"Mr. Humboldt says he talked to Dr. Chigwell about her and that it is
probable that Joey Pankowski was the child's father." She had trouble
with Pankowski too. I expected better from Humboldt's private secretary.

I took the receiver away from my ear and looked at it, as though I could
see Ms. Hollingsworth's face in it. Or Humboldt's. At last I held it back to
my mouth and asked, "Do you know who did the investigation for Mr.
Humboldt?"

"I believe he interested himself directly in the matter," she said primly.

I said slowly, "I think Dr. Chigwell may have misled Mr. Humboldt.
It's important that I see him to discuss the matter with him."

"I doubt that very much, Ms. Warshawski. Mr. Humboldt and the doctor have worked together a long time. If he gave Mr. Humboldt the information, you may certainly depend on it."

"Perhaps so." I tried to make my tone conciliatory. "But Mr. Humboldt told me himself that his staff sometimes try to protect him from unfortunate events. I suspect something like that may have been going on in this case."

"Really," she said huffily. *"You* may work in an environment where people can't trust each other. But Dr. Chigwell has been a most reliable associate of Mr. Humboldt's for fifty years. Maybe someone like you can't appreciate it, but the idea of Dr. Chigwell lying to Mr. Humboldt is totally ludicrous."

"Just one thing before you hang up in righteous indignation. Someone misled Mr. Humboldt terribly about the true nature of the suit Pankowski and Ferraro brought against Xerxes. That's why I'm not too confident about this last bit of news."

There was a pause, then she said grudgingly, "I'll mention the matter to Mr. Humboldt. But I doubt very much that he'll want to talk to you."

That was the best I could get from her. I frowned at the phone some more, wondering what I would say to Humboldt if I saw him. Fruitless. I locked up the office and drove up to the little hardware store on Diversey. They hadn't wanted to talk to me on the phone, but when they saw I was prepared to be vocal in front of their customers they took me into the back and reluctantly wrote out another check. Plus the ten dollars handling for the bad one. I paid it directly into my bank and went home.

Slipping in through the back entrance, I managed to sidestep Mr. Contreras and the dog. I stopped in the kitchen to inspect the food supply. Still grim. I fixed a bowl of popcorn and took it into the living room with me. Popcorn and corned beef—um-um good.

Four-thirty is a terrible time to find anything on TV—I flipped through game shows, *Sesame Street,* and the beaming face of *The Frugal Gourmet.* I finally turned off the set in disgust and reached for the phone.

The Chigwells were listed under Clio's name. She answered on the third ring, her voice distant, unyielding. Yes, she remembered who I was. She didn't think her brother would want to speak to me, but she went to see, anyway. He didn't.

"Look, Ms. Chigwell. I hate having to be such a pest, but there's something I want to know. Has Gustav Humboldt called him in the last few days?"

She was surprised. "How did you know?"

"I didn't. His secretary passed on some information that Humboldt supposedly got from your brother. I wondered if Humboldt made it up."

"What did he say Curtis told him?"

"That Joey Pankowski was Caroline Djiak's father."

She asked me to explain who they were, then went off to confront her brother. She was gone for a quarter of an hour. I finished the popcorn and did some leg raises, lying with the phone near my ear so I could hear her return.

She came back on the line abruptly. "He says he knew about the man, that the girl's mother had told him all about it back when they hired her."

"I see," I said weakly.

"The trouble is, you can't spend your whole life with someone without knowing when they're lying. I don't know what part of it Curtis is making up, but one thing I can tell you—he'd say anything Gustav Humboldt told him to."

While I struggled to add this news to my pickled brain, something else struck me. "Why are you telling me this, Ms. Chigwell?"

"I don't know," she said, surprised. "Maybe after seventy-nine years, I'm tired of having Curtis hide behind me. Good-bye." She hung up with an abrupt click.

I spent Saturday stewing about Humboldt and Chigwell, unable to think of any reason why they would concoct a story about Louisa and Joey, unable to think of a way to get a handle on them. When Murray Ryerson, head of the *Herald-Star'*s crime bureau, called me on Sunday because one of his gofers had dug up the news that Nancy Cleghorn and I went to high school together, I even agreed to talk to him.

Murray follows De Paul basketball. Or slobbers over it. Although I live —and die—with the Cubs every year, and maintain a wistful love for the Bears' Otis Wilson, I don't really care whether the Blue Demons ever score another basket. In Chicago that's extreme heresy—equivalent to saying you hate St. Patrick's Day parades. So I agreed to truck out to the Horizon and watch them scrap around with Indiana or Loyola or whoever.

"Anyway," Murray said, "you can sit there remembering how you and Nancy handled the same shots, only better. It will give a more intense flavor to your memories."

De Paul lost a squeaker, with Murray commenting libelously on young Joey Meyer and the entire offense during the hour wait to move from the parking lot back to the tollway. It was only when we were in Ethel's, a Lithuanian restaurant on the northwest side, filling Murray's six-four frame with a few dozen sweet-and-sour cabbage rolls, that he got down to the real business of the afternoon.

"So what's your interest in Cleghorn's death?" he asked casually. "Family call you in to investigate?"

"The cops got a tip that I sent her to her death." I calmly ate another fluffy dumpling. I'd have to run ten miles in the morning to work off all this.

"Come on. I must've heard a dozen people say you've been nosing around down there. What's going on?"

I shook my head. "I told you. I'm clearing my name."

"Yeah, and I'm the Ayatollah of Detroit."

I love it when I'm telling Murray the truth and he's convinced it's a big cover-up—it gives me terrific leverage. Unfortunately, there wasn't much to pry out of him. The police had called on Steve Dresberg, on Dresberg's mouthpiece, Leon Haas, on a few dozen other upstanding South Chicagoans—including some old lovers of Nancy's—and didn't have anything they considered a real lead.

Murray finally got tired of the game. "I guess there's enough that we could do a little human-interest story of Nancy and you in college, living on table scraps and studying the classics in between creaming the best women's teams in the region. I hate giving you print space when you're not earning it, but it'll help keep her name in front of the state's attorney."

"Thanks a whole bunch, Murray."

When he dropped me at my place on Racine, I got in my car and headed for Hinsdale. Seeing him had given me a nasty little idea on a way to pressure Chigwell.

It was close to seven when I rang the bell at the side door, not the ideal time for paying house calls. When Ms. Chigwell answered my ring I tried to make myself look earnest and trustworthy. Her stern features didn't give me any clue as to whether I was succeeding.

"Curtis won't talk to you," she said in her abrupt way, showing no surprise at my appearance.

"Try this on him," I suggested in an earnest, trustworthy manner. "His picture on the front page of the *Herald-Star* and some heartwarming stories on his medical career."

She looked at me grimly. Why she didn't just shut the door in my face I didn't understand. And why she went off to deliver the message puzzled me still further. It reminded me of some elderly cousins of my beloved ex-husband Dick, two brothers and a sister who lived together. The brothers had quarreled some thirteen years previously and refused to speak, so they would ask the sister to pass them salt, marmalade, and tea, and she obligingly did so.

However, Dr. Chigwell came to the door in person this time, not trusting his sister with the marmalade. With his thin neck bobbing forward, he looked like a harassed turkey.

"Listen here, young lady. I don't have to take these threats. If you're not away from this door in thirty seconds, I'm calling the police and you can explain to them why you've started a persecution campaign."

He had me. I could just imagine trying to tell a suburban cop—or even Bobby Mallory—that one of Chicago's ten wealthiest men was lying to me and getting his old plant doctor to collude. I bowed my head in resignation.

"Consider me gone. The reporter who'll be calling you in the morning is named Murray Ryerson. I'll explain to him about your old medical cases and so on."

"Get out of here!" His voice had turned to a hiss that chilled my blood. I left.

17

Tombstone Blues

Nancy's funeral was scheduled for eleven Monday morning in the Methodist church she had attended as a child. I seem to spend too much time at the funerals of friends—I have a navy suit associated so strongly with them that I can't bring myself to wear it anywhere else. I dawdled around in panty hose and a blouse, unable to shake a superstitious dread that putting on the suit would make Nancy's death final.

I couldn't set my mind to anything, to Chigwell or Humboldt, to organizing a plan to beat the police to Nancy's killer, or even to organizing the spreading papers in my living room. That was where I had started the morning, thinking with a few hours on my hands I could get things put away. I was too fragmented to create order.

Suddenly at ten of ten, still in my underwear, I looked up the number for Humboldt's corporate offices and phoned. An indifferent operator switched me through to his office, where I reached not Clarissa Hollingsworth but her assistant. When I asked for Mr. Humboldt, after a certain amount of dickering I got Ms. Hollingsworth.

The cool alto greeted me patronizingly. "I haven't had a chance to speak to Mr. Humboldt about seeing you, Ms. Warshawski. I'll make sure that he gets the message, but he doesn't come in every day anymore."

"Yeah, I don't suppose you call him at home for consultations, either. In case you do, you might add to my other message that I saw Dr. Chigwell last night."

She finished the conversation with a condescending speed that left me shouting into a dead phone. I finished dressing as easily as I could with my hands shaking and headed south once more.

Mount of Olives Methodist dated to the turn of the century, its high-backed dark pews and giant rose window evoking a time when it was filled with women in long dresses and children in high-buttoned shoes. Today's congregation couldn't afford to keep up the stained-glass windows showing Jesus in Calvary. Places where Jesus's brooding ascetic face had been broken were filled in with wired burglar glass, making him look like a sufferer from an acute skin disease.

While Nancy's four brothers served as ushers their children sat in the front pews, shoving and poking at each other despite the near presence of their aunt's draped casket. Their harshly whispered insults could be heard throughout the nave until drowned by some melancholy bars from the organ.

I went up to the front to let Mrs. Cleghorn know I was there. She smiled at me with tremulous warmth.

"Come over to the house after the service," she whispered. "We'll have coffee and a chance to talk."

She invited me to sit with her, glancing distastefully at her grandchildren. I disengaged myself gently—I didn't want to be a buffer between her and the wrestling monsters. Besides, I wanted to go to the back so I could see who showed up—it's a cliché, but murderers often can't resist going to their victims' funerals. Maybe part of a primitive superstition, trying to make sure the person is really dead, that she gets truly buried so her ghost doesn't walk.

After I'd settled myself near the entrance Diane Logan swept in, resplendent in her silver fox. She brushed my cheek and squeezed my hand before moving up the aisle.

"Who was that?" a voice muttered in my ear.

I gave a start and turned around. It was Sergeant McGonnigal, trying to look mournful in a dark suit. So the police were also hopeful.

"She used to play basketball with Nancy and me; she owns a Gold Coast PR firm nowadays," I muttered back. "I don't think she slugged Nancy—she could outplay her twenty years ago. Today, too, come to think of it. I don't know everyone's name—tell me which one the killer is."

He smiled a little. "When I saw you sitting here I thought my worries were over—little Polish detective is going to nab the murderer in front of the altar."

"Methodist church," I muttered. "I don't think they call it an altar."

Caroline clattered in with the group of people I'd seen in the SCRAP office with her. They had the preternatural earnestness of those who don't often find themselves at solemn functions. Caroline's copper curls were brushed into a semblance of tidiness. She wore a black suit designed for a much taller woman—the bunched clumps of material at the bottom showed where she'd hemmed it with her usual impatient inefficiency. If she saw me, she gave no sign, moving with the SCRAP contingent to a pew about halfway up the aisle.

Behind them came a handful of older women, perhaps Mrs. Cleghorn's pals at the local branch of the library. When they'd passed I saw a thin young man standing in their wake. The dim light picked out his angular silhouette. He looked around uncertainly, saw me staring at him, and looked away.

The self-deprecating embarrassment with which he turned his head brought back to me who he was: young Art Jurshak. He'd made just such an effacing move in talking to the old ward heelers at his father's office.

In the half-light from the windows I couldn't make out his beautifully chiseled features. He sidled into a seat toward the back.

McGonnigal tapped me on the shoulder. "Who's that alfalfa sprout?" he growled.

I smiled seraphically and put a finger to my lips—the organ had begun to play loudly, signaling the arrival of the minister. We went through "Abide with Me" at such a slow pace that I kept bracing myself for each succeeding chord.

The minister was a short, plump man whose remaining black hair was combed in two neat rows on either side of a wrinkled dome. He looked like the kind of TV preacher who makes your stomach turn, but as he spoke I realized I'd made the dread mistake of judging by appearances. He clearly had known Nancy well and spoke of her with eloquent forcefulness. I felt my throat tighten again and leaned back in the pew to inspect the ceiling beams. The wood had been painted in the blue and orange stencils popular in Victorian churches. By focusing on the intricate lacy patterns I was able to relax enough to join in the final hymn.

I kept glancing at young Art. He spent the service perched on the edge of his pew, gripping the back of the bench in front of him. When the last chords of "In Heavenly Love Abiding" had finally been wrenched painfully from the organ, he slid out of his seat and headed for the exit.

I caught up with him on the porch, where he was moving nervously from foot to foot, unable to free himself from a drunk panhandler. When I touched Art's arm he jumped.

"I didn't know you and Nancy were friends," I said. "She never mentioned you to me."

He mumbled something that sounded like "knew her slightly."

"I'm V. I. Warshawski. Nancy and I played high school and college basketball together. I saw you at the Tenth Ward office last week. You're Art Jurshak's son, aren't you?"

At that his chiseled-marble face turned even whiter; I was afraid he might faint. Even though he was a slender young man, I wasn't sure I could break his fall.

The drunk, who'd been listening interestedly, sidled closer. "Your friend looks pretty sick, lady. How about fifty cents for coffee—cup for him, cup for me."

I turned my back on him firmly and took Art's elbow. "I'm a private detective and I'm trying to look into Nancy's death. If you were friends with her, I'd like to talk to you. About her connections with your father's office."

He shook his head dumbly, his blue eyes dark with fear. After a long internal debate he seemed to be on the brink of forcing himself to speak. Unfortunately as he opened his mouth the other mourners began emerging from the church. As soon as people started passing us Art wrenched himself from my grip and bolted down the street.

I tried to follow, but tripped over the drunk. I cursed him roundly as I pulled myself back to my feet. He was reviling me in return, but broke off suddenly as McGonnigal appeared—years of living around the police gave him a sixth sense about them even in plainclothes.

"What's the redhead so scared of, Warshawski?" the sergeant demanded, ignoring the panhandler. We watched Art get into his car, a late-model Chrysler parked at the end of the street, and tear off.

"I have that effect on men," I said shortly. "Drives them mad. You find your murderer?"

"I don't know. Your male model here was the only person acting suspiciously. Why don't you show what a helpful citizen you are and give me his name?"

I turned to face him. "It's no secret—the name is real well known down in these parts. Art Jurshak."

McGonnigal's lips tightened. "Just because Mallory's my boss doesn't mean you have to jerk me around the way you do him. Tell me the kid's name."

I held up my right hand. "Scout's honor, Sergeant. Jurshak's his old man. Young Art just joined his agency or his office or something. If you catch up with him, don't use a rubber hose—I don't think he's got too much stamina."

McGonnigal grinned savagely. "Don't worry, Warshawski. He's got stronger protection than a thick skin. I won't mess up his curly locks.

. . .You going over to the Cleghorn place for coffee? I heard some of the ladies talking about what they were bringing. Mind if I slide in with you?"

"We little Polish detectives live to help the cops. Come along."

He grinned and held the car door open for me. "That get under your skin, Warshawski? My apologies—you're not all that little."

A handful of mourners was already at the house on Muskegon when we got there. Mrs. Cleghorn, her makeup streaked with dried tears, greeted me warmly and accepted McGonnigal politely. I stood in the little entry-way talking with her for a minute while the sergeant wandered into the back of the house.

"Kerry took the children to her house, so things will be a little calmer today," she said. "Maybe when I retire I'll move to Oregon."

I hugged her. "Go across the country to avoid being a grandmother? Maybe you could just change the locks—it'd be less drastic."

"I guess it proves how upset I am, Victoria, talking like that—I've never wanted anyone to know how I felt about my sons' children." She paused a moment, then added awkwardly, "If you want to talk to Ron Kappelman about—about Nancy or anything, he's in the living room."

The doorbell rang. While she moved to answer it I crossed the little hall to the living room. I'd never seen Ron Kappelman, but I didn't have any trouble recognizing him—he was the only man in the room. He was about my age, perhaps a bit older, stocky, with dark brown hair cut close to his head. He wore a gray tweed jacket, which was frayed at the lapels and cuffs, and corduroy pants. He was sitting by himself on a round Nauga-hyde hassock, flipping idly through the pages of an old *National Geographic.*

The four women in the room, the ones from church I'd assumed were Mrs. Cleghorn's co-workers, were murmuring together in the other corner. They glanced over at me, saw they didn't know me, and went back to their gentle buzzing.

I pulled up a straight-backed chair next to Kappelman. He glanced at me, made a bit of a face, then tossed the magazine back to the coffee table.

"I know," I said sympathetically. "It's a pain to talk to strangers at an affair like this. I wouldn't do it if I didn't think you could help me."

He raised his eyebrows. "I doubt it, but you can try me."

"My name's V. I. Warshawski. I'm an old friend of Nancy's. We played basketball together a while back. A long while back." I can't get over how fast the years started zipping by after my thirtieth birthday. It just didn't seem that long since Nancy and I had been in college.

"Sure. I know who you are. Nance talked about you a number of times

—said you kept her from going mad when the two of you were in high school. I'm Ron Kappelman, but you seemed to know that when you came in."

"Nancy tell you I'm a private investigator these days? Well, I hadn't seen her for quite some time, but we got together for a basketball reunion a week or so ago."

"Yeah, I know," he cut in. "We went to a meeting together right after. She talked about it."

A swarm of people buzzed into the room. Even though they were keeping their voices subdued, there wasn't enough space to absorb the bodies or the sound. Someone standing over me lighted a cigarette and I felt hot ash land on the round neck of my bolero jacket.

"Could we go somewhere to talk?" I asked. "Nancy's old bedroom or a bar or something? I'm trying to look into her death, but I can't seem to get a thread to pull on. I was hoping you could tell me something."

He shook his head. "Believe me, if I thought I had any hot dope, I'd've been to the cops like a rocket. But I'd be glad to get out of here."

We pushed our way through the crowd, paying affectionate respects to Mrs. Cleghorn as we left. The warmth with which she spoke to Kappelman seemed to indicate that he and Nancy had remained on good terms. I wondered vaguely what had happened to McGonnigal, but he was a big cop, he could look after himself.

Outside, Kappelman said, "Why don't you follow me down to my place in Pullman? There isn't any coffee shop nearby that's clean and quiet. As you surely know."

I trailed his decrepit Rabbit down side streets to 113th and Langley. He stopped in front of one of the tidy brick row houses that line Pullman's streets, houses with sheer fronts and stoops that make you think of pictures of Philadelphia when the Constitution was signed.

The neat, well-kept exterior didn't really prepare me for the meticulous restoration inside. The walls were papered in bright Victorian floral designs, the paneling refinished to a glow of dark walnut, the furniture and rugs beautifully maintained period pieces set on well-finished hardwood floors.

"This is gorgeous," I said, overwhelmed. "Did you fix it up yourself?"

He nodded. "Carpentry is kind of my hobby—makes a good switch from mucking about with the stunads I spend my days with. The furniture is all stuff I picked up at area flea markets."

He led me into a little kitchen with Italian tile on the floor and countertops and gleaming copper-bottomed pots on the walls. I perched on a high stool at one side of a tiled island while he made coffee at the burners on the other.

"So who asked you to investigate Nancy's death? Her mother? Not sure the cops will buck the politicos down here and see that justice runs its inexorable course?" He cocked an eye at me while deftly assembling an infusion pot.

"Nope. If you know Mrs. Cleghorn at all, you must realize her mind doesn't run to vengeance."

"So who's your client?" He turned to the refrigerator and laid out cream and a plate of muffins.

I absentmindedly watched the seat of his trousers tighten across his rear while he bent over. The seam was fraying; a few more deep bends could create an interesting situation. I nobly refrained from dropping a plate at his feet, but waited to answer until he was facing me again.

"Part of what my clients buy when they hire me is confidentiality. If I blabbed their secrets to you, I could hardly expect you to blab yours to me, could I?"

He shook his head. "I haven't got any secrets. At least not relating to Nancy Cleghorn. I'm the counsel for SCRAP. I work for a number of community groups—public interest law's my specialty. Nancy was great to work with. She was organized, clearheaded, knew when to fight and when to drop back. Unlike her boss."

"Caroline?" It was hard to picture Caroline Djiak as anyone's boss. "So all your dealings with Nancy were purely professional?"

He pointed a coffee spoon at me. "Don't try to trip me up, Warshawski. I play ball with the big boys. Cream? You ought to, you know—binds with the caffeine and keeps you from getting stomach cancer."

He set a heavy porcelain mug in front of me and stuck the plate of muffins into the microwave. "No. Nance and I had a brief fling a couple of years back. When I started at SCRAP. She was getting over a heavy thing and I'd been divorced about ten months. We cheered each other up, but we didn't have anything special to offer each other. Besides friendship, which is special enough that you don't screw it up. Certainly not by banging your friends on the head and dropping them in a swamp."

He took the muffins out of the oven and climbed onto a stool at the end of the counter on my left. I drank some of the rich coffee and took a blueberry muffin.

"I'll let the cops take you through your paces. Where were you Thursday afternoon at two P.M. and so on. What I really want to know, though, is who Nancy thought was following her. Did she think she'd got

Dresberg's back up? Or did it really have anything to do with the recycling plant?"

He grimaced. "Little Caroline's theory—which makes me want to trash it. Not a good attitude for her outfit's counsel to take. Truth is, I don't know. We were both pissed as hell after the hearing two weeks ago. When we talked on Tuesday, Nance said she'd cover the political angle, see if she could find out if and why Jurshak was blocking it. I was working on the legal stuff, wondering if we could finesse the MSD—Metropolitan Sanitary District—to get the permit. Maybe get the state and U.S. EPA departments involved."

He absentmindedly ate a second muffin and buttered a third. His bulging waistline made me shake my head when he offered me the plate.

"So you don't know who she talked to in Jurshak's office?"

He shook his head. "I had the impression, nothing concrete to go on, but I think she had a lover there. Someone she was a little ashamed of seeing and didn't want her pals to know about, or someone she thought she had to protect." He stared into the distance, trying to put his feelings into words. "Canceling dinner plans, not wanting to go to the Hawks games, which we shared season tickets to. Stuff like that. So she could've been getting information from him and not wanting me to know about it. The last time we spoke—a week ago today it must have been—she said she thought she was onto something but she needed more evidence. I never talked to her again." He stopped abruptly and busied himself with his coffee.

"Well, what about Dresberg? Based on what you know of the situation down there, would you think he might've been against this recycling center?"

"God, I wouldn't think so. Although with a guy like that you never know. Look."

He set down his coffee cup and leaned intently across the counter, sketching Dresberg's operations with sweeping gestures. The garbage empire included hauling, incinerating, storage-container and landfill operations. Within his domain Dresberg was protective of any perceived encroachments—even any questioning. Hence the threats a year before when Caroline and Nancy had tried to oppose a new PCB incinerator that didn't meet code standards.

"But the recycling center didn't have anything to do with any of his operations," he finished. "Xerxes and Glow-Rite are just dumping into their own lagoons right now. All SCRAP would do is take the wastes and recycle them."

I thought about it. "He could see expansion potential cutting into his business down the road. Or maybe he wants SCRAP to use his trucks to do the hauling."

He shook his head. "If that was the case, he'd just be putting an arm on them to use his trucks, not offing Nancy. I'm not saying it's impossible he was involved. The plant's certainly in his sphere. But it doesn't leap out at me on the surface."

We let the talk drift after that, to friends we had in common at the Illinois bar, to my cousin Boom-Boom, whom Kappelman used to watch at the Stadium when he was with the Hawks.

"There's never been another player like him," Kappelman said regretfully.

"You're telling me." I got up and put on my coat. "So if you come across something strange—anything, whether it seems to have a direct bearing on Nancy's death or not—give me a call, okay?"

"Yeah, sure." His gaze seemed a little unfocused. He seemed about to say something, then changed his mind, shook my hand, and escorted me to the door.

18

In His Father's Shadow

I didn't disbelieve Kappelman. I didn't believe him, either. I mean the guy made a living persuading judges and commissioners to support community groups instead of the industrial or political heavyweights they usually favored. Despite his frayed trousers and jacket, I suspected he was pretty convincing. And if Nancy and he were the good buddies he claimed they'd been, was it really credible that she hadn't given him the ghost of an idea about what she'd learned from the alderman's office?

Of course it was a little pat on my part looking for Dresberg to be the fall guy. Just because he had made threats in the past and had a lot of muscle and was interested in waste disposal.

I meandered across side streets and headed into East Side, to the ward offices on Avenue M. It was a little after three and the place was hopping. I passed a couple of patrol cops coming out. When I got into the main office my old pals with the paunches were hard at it with a half dozen or so favor-seekers. Another couple, maybe patronage workers through with street cleaning for the day, were playing checkers in the window.

Nobody really looked at me, but the conversations quieted down. "I'm looking for young Art," I said amiably in the direction of the bald man who'd been the spokesman on my first visit.

"Not here," he said briefly, without looking up.

"When do you expect him?"

The three office workers exchanged the silent communication I'd observed earlier and agreed that my question warranted a slight chuckle.

"We don't," Baldy said, going back to his client.

"Do you know where else I could find him?"

"We don't keep tabs on the kid," Baldy expanded, thinking perhaps of the claim drafts they were expecting from me. "Sometimes he shows up in the afternoon, sometimes he don't. He hasn't been in today so he might turn up. You never know."

"I see." I picked up the *Sun-Times* from his desk and sat in one of the chairs lining the wall. It was an old wooden one, yellow and scuffed, extremely uncomfortable. I read "Sylvia," skimmed the sports pages, and tried interesting myself in the latest Greylord trial, shifting my pelvis around on the hard surface in an unsuccessful search for a spot that wouldn't rub against my bones. After about half an hour I gave it up and put one of my cards on Baldy's desk.

"V. I. Warshawski. I'll try back in a bit. Tell him to call me if I miss him."

Except for the blueberry muffin Ron Kappelman had given me, I hadn't really eaten today. I went down to the corner of Ewing where a neighborhood bar advertised submarines and Italian beef and had a meatball sub with a draft. I'm not much of a beer drinker, but it seemed more suited to the neighborhood than diet soda.

When I got back to the ward office the visitors had pretty well cleared out except for the checker players in the corner. Baldy shook his head at me to indicate—I think—that young Art hadn't been in. I felt proud of myself—I was beginning to seem like a regular.

I pulled a little spiral notebook from my bag. To entertain myself while I waited I tried calculating the expenses I'd incurred since starting to look for Caroline Djiak's old man. I've always been a little jealous of Kinsey Milhone's immaculate record-keeping; I didn't even have receipts for meals or gas. Certainly not for cleaning up the Magli pumps, which was going to run close to thirty dollars.

I'd gotten up to two hundred and fifty when young Art came in with his usual diffident step. There was something in his face, a naked desire for acceptance from the tired old pols in the room, that made me flinch. They looked at him unblinkingly, waiting for him to speak. And finally he obliged.

"Any—anything for me from my dad?" He licked his lips reflexively.

Baldy shook his head and returned to his paper. "Lady wants to talk to you," he said from the depths of the *Sun-Times.*

Art hadn't seen me until then—he'd been too intent on the disappointment he felt bound to suffer from the men. He looked around the room then and located me. He didn't recognize me at first: his perfect forehead furrowed in a momentary question. It wasn't until he'd come over to shake my hand that he remembered where he'd seen me, and then he didn't think he could flee without achieving total humiliation.

"Where can we go to talk?" I asked briskly, taking his hand in a firm grasp in case he decided to chance the indignity.

He smiled unhappily. "Upstairs, I guess. I—I have an office. A small office."

I followed him up the linoleum-covered stairs to a suite with his father's name on it. A middle-aged woman, her brown hair neatly coiffed above a well-cut dress, was sitting in the outer office. Her desk was a little jungle of potted plants twined around family photographs. Behind her were doors to the inner offices, one with Art, Sr.'s, name repeated on it, the other blank.

"Your dad isn't here, Art," she said in a motherly way. "He's been at a Council meeting all day. I really don't expect him until Wednesday."

He flushed miserably. "Thanks, Mrs. May. I just need to use my office for a few minutes."

"Of course, Art. You don't need my permission to do that." She continued to stare at me, hoping to force me to introduce myself. It seemed to me it would be a small but important victory for Art if she didn't know whom he was seeing. I smiled at her without speaking, but I'd underestimated her tenacity.

"I'm Ida Maiercyk, but everyone calls me Mrs. May," she said as I passed her desk.

"How do you do?" I continued to smile and went on by to where Art was standing miserably in front of his office. I hoped she was scowling impotently, but didn't turn around to check.

Art flipped on a wall switch and illuminated one of the most barren cubicles I'd seen outside a monastery. It held a plain pressed-wood desk and two metal folding chairs. Nothing else. Not even a filing cabinet to give the pretense of work. A wise alderman knows better than to live above the community that's supporting him, especially when half that community is out of work, but this was downright insulting. Even the secretary had more lavish appointments.

"Why do you put up with this?" I demanded.

"With what?" he said, flushing again.

"You know—with that loathsome woman out there treating you like a submoronic two-year-old. With those ward heelers waiting to bait you like a carp. Why don't you go get a position in someone else's agency?"

He shook his head. "These things aren't as easy as they look to you. I just graduated two years ago. If—if I can prove to my dad that I can handle some of his workload . . ." His voice trailed away.

"If you're hanging around hoping for his approval, you'll be here the rest of your life," I said brutally. "If he doesn't want to give it to you, there's nothing you can do to make him. You're better off stopping the effort, because you're only making yourself miserable and you're not impressing him."

He gave an unhappy little smile that made me want to take him by the scruff of the neck and shake him. "You don't know him and you don't know me, so you don't know what you're talking about. I'm just—I've always been—just too big a disappointment. But it's nothing to do with you. If you've come around to talk to me about Nancy Cleghorn, I can't help you any more than I could this morning."

"You and she were lovers, weren't you?" I wondered if his chiseled good looks could possibly have compensated Nancy for his youth and insecurity.

He shook his head without speaking.

"Nancy had a lover here that she didn't want any of her friends to know about. It doesn't seem too likely that it was Moe, Curly, or Larry downstairs. Or even Mrs. May—Nancy had better taste than that. And anyway, why else would you go to her funeral?"

"Maybe I just respected the work she was doing here in the community," he muttered.

Mrs. May opened the door without knocking. "You two need anything? If you don't, I'm going to take off now. You want to leave any message for your father about your meeting, Art?"

He looked helplessly at me for a second, then just shook his head again without speaking.

"Thanks, Mrs. May," I said genially. "It was good to meet you."

She shot me a look of venom and snapped the door to. I could see her shadow outlined against the glass upper half of the door as she hesitated over a possible retaliatory strike, then her silhouette faded as she marched off toward home.

"If you don't want to talk about your relations with Nancy, maybe you can just give me the same information you gave her about Big Art's interest in SCRAP's recycling plant."

He gripped the front of the pressed-wood desk and looked at me imploringly. "I didn't tell her anything. I hardly knew her. And I don't know what my dad is doing about their recycling plant. Now can you please go away? I'd be as happy as—as anybody if you found her killer, but you must see I don't know anything about her."

I scowled in frustration. He was upset, but it sure wasn't because of me. He had to have been Nancy's lover. Had to. Otherwise he wouldn't have been in church this morning. But I couldn't think of any way to get him to trust me enough to talk about it.

"Yeah, I guess I'll go. One last question. How well do you know Leon Haas?"

He looked at me blankly. "I never heard of him."

"Steve Dresberg?"

His face went totally white and he fainted on me.

19

You Can't Go Home Again

By the time I got home it was past dark. I had stayed in South Chicago long enough to make sure young Art was fit to drive. It seemed unnecessarily cruel to turn him over to the ward heelers for comfort, but my display of charity didn't make him any more willing to talk. Frustrated, I finally left him at the door of the ward office.

The drive north brought me no solace. I walked wearily up the front walk, dropped my keys as I fumbled with the inner lobby door, then dropped them again as I was going upstairs. Bone-tired, I turned back down the stairs to retrieve them. Behind Mr. Contreras's door, Peppy gave a welcoming bark. As I headed back up I heard his locks scraping back behind me. I stiffened, waiting for the flow.

"That you, doll? You just getting back? Your friend's funeral was today, huh? You haven't been out drinking, have you? People think it's a way to drown their sorrows, but believe me, it only causes you more grief than you started with. I should know—I tried it more than once. But then when Clara died I took one drink and remembered how it used to get her down, me coming home from a funeral with a good one tied on. I said I wouldn't do it, not for her, not after all the times she told me how stupid I was, crying over some friend when I was too drunk to get his name out straight."

"No," I said, forcing a smile, holding my hand out for the dog to lick. "I haven't been drinking. I had to see a whole bunch of people. Not a lot of fun."

"Well, you go on upstairs and take a hot bath, doll. By the time you've done that and had a chance to rest, I'll have some dinner ready. I have me a nice steak I've been saving for sometime special, and that's what you need when you're feeling this low. A little red meat, get your blood flowing again, and life'll look a whole lot better to you."

"Thanks," I said. "It's very good of you, but I really don't—"

"Nope. You think you want to be alone, but believe me, cookie, that's the worst thing for you when you're feeling like this. Her royal highness and I'll get you fed, and then if you're ready to be on your own again, you say the word and we'll be back down here on the double."

I just couldn't bring myself to bring the cloud of hurt to his faded brown eyes by insisting on being alone. Cursing myself for my soft heart, I trudged up the stairs to my apartment. Despite my neighbor's dire words, I headed straight for the Black Label bottle, kicking off my pumps and pulling off my panty hose while I unscrewed the cap. I drank from the bottle, a long swallow that sent a glow of warmth to my weary shoulders.

Filling a glass, I took it into the bathroom with me. I dumped my funeral suit on the floor and climbed into the tub. By the time Mr. Contreras showed up with the steak, I was a little drunk and much more relaxed than I'd have thought possible a half hour before.

He had already had dinner; he brought his grappa bottle to keep me company while I ate. After a few bites I grudgingly admitted—only to myself—that he'd been right about the food: life did start to look better. The steak was done to a turn, crisply brown on the outside, red within. He'd cooked up some pan fries with garlic and brought his conscientious nod to my diet, a plate of lettuce. He was a good plain cook, self-taught as a hobby during his widowhood—he'd never done more in the kitchen than fetch beer when his wife was still alive.

I was finishing off the fries with the rest of the meat juice when the phone rang. I handed Peppy the bone she'd been eyeing—not begging for, just keeping an eye on in case someone broke in and tried to steal it—and went over to the piano, where I'd left the living-room extension.

"Warshawski?" It was a man's voice, cold and harsh. Not one I knew.

"Yes."

"Maybe it's time you butted out of South Chicago, Warshawski. You don't live there anymore, you don't have any business there."

I wished I hadn't had the third whiskey and desperately tried assembling my scrambled brain. "And you do?" I asked insolently.

He ignored me. "I hear you can swim pretty good, Warshawski. But the swimmer hasn't been born that can float through a swamp."

"You calling on Art Jurshak's behalf? Or Steve Dresberg's?"

"It doesn't matter to you, Warshawski. Because if you're smart, you're butting out, and if you're not, you won't be around to worry about it."

He hung up. My knees felt slightly weak. I sat on the piano bench to steady myself.

"Bad news, cookie?"

Mr. Contreras's weather-beaten face showed kindly concern. On second thought, it wasn't such a bad idea to have him with me tonight.

"Just an old-style thug. Reminding me that Chicago's the world float-fish capital." I tried keeping my tone airy, but the words came out heavier than I wanted.

"He threaten you?"

"Sort of." I tried to grin, but to my annoyance my lips were trembling. The image of the rank marsh grasses, the mud, the shapeless fishing couple and their wild red-eyed dog made me shiver uncontrollably.

Mr. Contreras hovered over me solicitously: Shouldn't I get out my Smith & Wesson? Call the police? Barricade the doors? Check into a hotel under an assumed name? When I turned down those offers he suggested I call Murray Ryerson at the *Herald-Star*—an act of true nobility because he had a fierce jealousy of Murray. Peppy, sensing his tension, dropped her bone and came over with a little bark.

"It's okay, guys," I assured them. "It's just talk. No one's going to shoot me. At least not tonight."

Mr. Contreras, unable to do anything else, offered me his grappa bottle. I waved it aside. The threat had cleared out my brain; I didn't see any point in fogging it up again with my neighbor's repellent booze.

On the other hand, I wasn't quite ready to be on my own again. Amid the stack of old notebooks and school papers in the back closet I dug out a worn checker set my dad and Bobby Mallory used to linger over.

We played four or five games, the dog contentedly returning to her bone in the corner behind the piano. Mr. Contreras was just getting reluctantly to his feet when the doorbell rang. The dog let out a deep bark. The old man became extremely excited, urging me to get out my gun, to let him go downstairs, telling me to go down the back way and summon help.

"Oh, nonsense," I said. "No one's going to shoot me in my own home two hours after a phone call—they'll at least wait until morning to see if I've listened to them."

I went to the intercom by the front door.

"Vic! Let me in! I need to see you." It was Caroline Djiak.

I pressed the button releasing the lobby door and went out to wait in the upper hallway for her. Peppy stood next to me, her golden tail lowered and moving gently to show she was on the alert. Caroline ran up the stairs, her feet clattering on the uncarpeted risers like an ancient el rounding the curve at Thirty-fifth Street.

"Vic!" she shrieked when she saw me. "What are you doing? I thought I told you to stop looking for my father. Why can't you just once do what I ask you to!"

Peppy, taking exception to her ferocity, began to bark. One of the second-floor tenants came to his door and yelled up at us to shut up. "Some people have to work, you know!"

Before Mr. Contreras could leap to my defense, I took Caroline firmly by the arm and dragged her into my apartment. Mr. Contreras looked at her critically. Deciding she wasn't dangerous—at least not an immediate physical threat—he stuck a calloused hand at her and introduced himself.

Caroline was in no mood for ordinary civility. "Vic, I'm begging you. I came all this way since you wouldn't listen to me on the phone. You've got to leave my affairs alone."

"Caroline Djiak," I informed Mr. Contreras. "She's pretty upset. Maybe you should leave me to talk to her."

He started getting the dinner dishes together. I pulled Caroline to the couch.

"What is going on with you, Caroline? What is frightening you so much?"

"I'm not frightened," she yelled. "I'm angry. Angry with you for not leaving me alone when I asked you to."

"Look, kiddo, I'm not a television you turn on and off. I could overlook my conversation with your grandparents—they're so sick nothing I could do would make any difference to them anyway. But everyone at Humboldt Chemical is lying to me about the men your mother used to work with, the ones who had the best chance of being your father. I just can't let that go. And it's not trivial, what they're saying—they're completely reinventing the last years of these guys' lives."

"Vic, you don't understand." She grabbed my right hand in her intensity, squeezing it hard. "You can't keep crossing these people. They're totally ruthless. You don't know what they might do."

"Such as what?"

She looked wildly around the room, seeking inspiration. "They might kill you, Vic. They might see you end up in the swamp the way Nancy did, or in the river!"

Mr. Contreras had stopped all pretense of getting ready to leave. I removed my hand from Caroline's grasp and stared at her coldly.

"Okay. I want the truth now. Not your embellished version. What do you know about the people who killed Nancy?"

"Nothing, Vic. Nothing. Honestly. You have to believe me. It's just . . . just . . ."

"Just what?" I grabbed her shoulders and shook her. "Who threatened Nancy? You've been saying for the last week that it was Art Jurshak because he didn't want her starting the recycling plant. Now you want it to be the people down at Xerxes because I'm hunting for your old man there? Goddamnit, Caroline, can't you see how important this is? Can't you see that this is life and death?"

"That's what I've been telling you, Vic!" She shouted so loudly that the dog started barking again. "That's why I'm telling you to mind your own business!"

"Caroline!" I felt my voice go into an upper register and tried to get a grip on myself before I broke her neck. I moved to the easy chair next to the sofa.

"Caroline. Who called you? Dr. Chigwell? Art Jurshak? Steve Dresberg? Gustav Humboldt himself?"

"No one, Vic." The gentian eyes were awash with tears. "No one. You just don't understand anything about life in South Chicago anymore, you've been away so long. Can't you just take my word for it, take my word that you should quit already?"

I ignored her. "Ron Kappelman? Did he call you this afternoon?"

"People talk to me," she said. "You know how it is down there. At least you would if—"

"If I hadn't been a chicken shit and run away," I finished for her. "You've been hearing little rumblings around the office that someone—you don't know who—has it in for me, and you're here to save my butt. Thanks a bundle. You're scared out of your little mind, Caroline. I want to know who's been frightening you, and don't tell me it's some street snitch with tales of drowning me because I just won't buy it. You wouldn't be beside yourself if it was just that. Lay it out for me. Now."

Caroline jerked herself to her feet. "What do I have to do to get you to listen to me?" she screamed. "Someone called me today from the Xerxes plant and said they were sorry I'd gone to all the expense of hiring you. They said that they had proof that Joey Pankowski was my father. They told me to get you to believe me and get off the case."

"And did they offer to show you this remarkable evidence?"

"I didn't need to see it! I'm not as untrusting as you are."

I put a restraining hand on Peppy, who was starting to growl. "And did they threaten you with mayhem if you didn't force me to withdraw?"

"I wouldn't care what anyone threatened me with. Can't you believe that?"

I looked at her as calmly as I could. She was wild, manipulative, unscrupulous in getting her own way. But I would never in my remotest imagination think of her as a coward.

"I can believe it," I said slowly. "But I want to hear the truth. Did they really tell you they'd hurt me if I didn't stop looking?"

The gentian eyes turned away. "Yes," she muttered.

"Not good enough, Caroline."

"Believe what you want to. If they kill you, don't expect me to show up at your funeral because I won't care." She burst into tears and stormed out of the apartment.

20

White Elephant

Mr. Contreras finally left around one. I slept fitfully, my mind thrashing over Caroline's visit. Caroline didn't fear anything. That's why she confidently followed me into Lake Michigan's pounding surf when she was four years old. Even a near-drowning hadn't scared her—she'd been ready to go right back again when I'd gotten her lungs cleaned out. If someone had told her my life was on the line, it might've made her mad, but it wouldn't terrify her.

Someone had called to tell her Joey Pankowski was her father. She couldn't have pulled that out of the blue. But had they added a rider about hurting me, or was that an inspired guess? I hadn't seen her for a decade, but you don't forget the mannerisms of the people you grow up with: that sidelong glance when I asked her directly made me think she was lying.

The only reason I believed her at all—about the threat, that is—was because I'd gotten my own call. Until Caroline showed up I'd been assuming my threat came from Art Jurshak because I'd accosted his son. Or because I'd talked to Ron Kappelman. But what if it came from Humboldt?

When the orange clock readout glowed three-fifteen I turned on the light and sat up in bed to use the phone. Murray Ryerson had left the paper forty-five minutes earlier. He wasn't home yet. On the chance, I tried the Golden Glow—Sal shuts down at four. Third time lucky.

"Vic! I'm overwhelmed. You had insomnia and you thought of me. I can see the headline now—'Girl Detective Can't Sleep for Love.'"

"And I thought it was the onions I had for dinner. Must've been what was wrong with me the day I agreed to marry Dick. You know our little conversation yesterday?"

"What little conversation?" he snorted. "I told you stuff about Nancy Cleghorn and you sat with Velcro on your mouth."

"Something came back to me," I said limpidly.

"Better make it good, Warshawski."

"Curtis Chigwell," I said. "He's a doctor who lives in Hinsdale. Used to work at a plant down in South Chicago."

"He killed Nancy Cleghorn?"

"As far as I know he never met Nancy Cleghorn."

I felt rather than heard Murray sputter. "It's been a tough day, V.I. Don't make me play Twenty Questions with you."

I reached down next to the bed for a T-shirt. Somehow the night was making me feel too exposed in my nakedness. As I leaned over the lamplight highlighted dust in the corner of the bedroom. If I lived past next week, I'd vacuum.

"That's what I've got for you," I said slowly. "Twenty questions. No answers. Curtis Chigwell knows something that he doesn't want to tell. Twenty-four hours ago I didn't think it had the remotest possible connection to Nancy. But I got a threatening phone call tonight telling me to bug out of South Chicago."

"From Chigwell?" I could almost feel Murray's breath through the phone line.

"No. I thought it had to come from Jurshak or Dresberg. Only thing, a couple of hours later I heard the same thing from someone who knows me only through the Xerxes side—the plant that Chigwell used to work for."

I explained the discrepancies I'd gotten between Manheim and Humboldt's version of Pankowski and Ferraro's suit—without telling him about hearing it from Gustav Humboldt himself. "Chigwell knows what the truth is and why. He just doesn't want to say. And if the Xerxes people are threatening me, he'll know why."

Murray tried a thousand different ways to get me to tell him more about it. I just couldn't give him Caroline and Louisa—Louisa didn't deserve to have her unhappy past spinning around the streets of Chicago. And I didn't know anything else. Anything about what possible connection there could be between Nancy's death and Joey Pankowski.

Murray finally said, "You're not trying to help me, you're getting me to do your legwork. I can feel it. But it's not a bad story—I'll send someone out to talk to the guy."

When he hung up I managed to sleep a little, but I woke again for good around six-thirty. It was another gray February day. Sharp cold with snow would have been preferable to this unending misty chill. I pulled on my sweats, did my stretches, and ruthlessly roused Mr. Contreras by knocking on his door until the dog barked him awake. I took her to the lake and back, stopping now and then to tie my shoes, to blow my nose, to throw her a stick—gestures that let me subtly check my rear. I didn't think anyone was on it.

After depositing the dog I went to the corner diner for pancakes. Back home to change, I'd just about made up my mind to visit Louisa, see if she could shed any light on Caroline's panic, when Ellen Cleghorn called. She was most upset: she'd gone over to Nancy's house in South Chicago to collect her financial records and found the place ransacked.

"Ransacked?" I repeated foolishly. "How do you know?"

"The way you always do, Victoria—the place had been ripped to shreds. Nancy didn't have much and she'd only been able to fix up a couple of rooms. The furniture was pulled apart and her papers strewn all over the place."

I shuddered involuntarily. "Sounds like housebreakers gone mad. Could you tell if anything was missing?"

"I didn't try to see." Her voice caught a little on a nervous sob. "I looked at her bedroom and ran out of there as fast as I could. I—I was hoping you might come down and go through the house with me. I can't bear to be alone there with this—this ravaging of Nancy."

I promised to meet her in front of her house within the hour. I'd wanted to go directly to Nancy's, but Mrs. Cleghorn was too nervous about the intruders to hang around her daughter's house, even outside. I finished pulling on jeans and a sweatshirt, and then, not too happily, went to the little wall safe I'd built into the bedroom closet and took out the Smith & Wesson.

I don't make a habit of carrying a gun—if you do, you get dependent on them and your wits slow down. But I'd been jumpy enough already between Nancy's murder and the threat to send me into the swamp after her. Now this housebreaking. I supposed it could have been local punks casing the place and seeing that no one was home. But tearing the furniture apart. It could have been a druggie coked so far out of his mind that he'd torn the furniture apart looking for money. But it could also have been her killers looking for something she had that might incriminate them. So I stuck a second clip into my handbag and pushed the loaded gun into my jeans waistband; my wits were not fast enough to stop a speeding bullet.

The Cleghorn house looked remote and bedraggled in the gray mist. Even the turret that had been Nancy's bedroom seemed to be drooping a little. Mrs. Cleghorn was waiting for me on the front walk, her normally pleasant, round face gaunt and strained. She gave a tremulous smile and climbed into my car.

"I'll ride with you if you don't mind. I'm shaking so badly I don't even know how I got home."

"You can just give me her house keys," I said. "You don't need to come along if you'd be happier staying here."

She shook her head. "If you went by yourself, I'd only spend the time worrying that someone was waiting in ambush for you."

While I followed her directions for the quickest way up, along South Chicago to Yates, I asked if she'd called the police.

"I thought I'd wait. Wait until you saw what happened. Then"—she gave a twisted little smile—"maybe you could do it for me. I think I've done all the talking to police that I can stand. Not just for now, but forever."

I reached across the gearshift to pat her hand. "It's okay. Happy to be of service."

Nancy's house was up on Crandon, near Seventy-third Street. I could see why Mrs. Cleghorn called it a white elephant—a big wooden monster, its three full stories filled an outsize lot. But I could also see why Nancy had bought it—the little cupolas at the corners, the stained-glass windows, the carved wooden banister on the stairwell inside, all evoked the comfort and order of Alcott or Thackeray.

It wasn't immediately obvious that someone had been in the house. Nancy had apparently put everything she had into buying it, so the front hallway had no furniture. It wasn't until I went up the oak stairs and found the main bedroom that I saw the damage. I sympathized fully with Mrs. Cleghorn's decision to wait for me in the entryway.

Nancy had apparently made the main bedroom her first rehab project. The floor was finished, the walls plastered and painted, and a working fireplace, with a tiled mantel and gleaming brass fittings, was set in the wall opposite the bed. The effect would have been charming, except that the furniture and bedding had been thrown about the room.

I tiptoed gingerly through the rubble. I was violating all possible police rules—not calling to report the destruction, walking through it and disturbing the evidence, adding my detritus to that of the vandals. But it's only in rule books that every crime gets detailed lab inspection. In real life I didn't think they'd pay too close attention, even though the homeowner had been murdered.

Whatever the vandals had been looking for didn't take up much space. Not only had they ripped the mattress cover away and slashed through the stuffing, but they had taken up the grate in the fireplace and removed several bricks. Either money, if I stayed with the coked-out-addict theory. Or papers. Some kind of evidence Nancy had of something so hideous, people were willing to kill to keep it a secret.

I went back downstairs, my own hands shaking a little. The destruction of a house is such a personal violation. If you can't be safe within your home base, you feel you have no security anywhere.

Mrs. Cleghorn was waiting at the bottom. She put a motherly arm around my waist—seeing me upset helped her gain some composure.

"The dining room is the only other room Nancy really had fixed up. She was using the built-in cupboards as a little home office until she had the time and the money to fix up the study."

I suggested that Mrs. Cleghorn continue to stay in the hall. If the marauders hadn't found what they were looking for upstairs, I had an unwilling vision of what the cupboards might look like.

The reality was far worse than anything I had brought myself to imagine. Plates and tableware lay scattered on the floor. The seats had been ripped from the chairs. All the shelves in the walnut cupboards that formed the far wall of the room were splintered. And the papers that made up Nancy's personal life were strewn about like ticker tape the day after a big parade.

I compressed my lips tightly, trying to hold my feelings in while I picked through the rubble. By and by Mrs. Cleghorn called to me from the doorway: I'd been away so long she'd gotten worried and braced herself to face the destruction. Together we culled bank statements, picked an address book from the heap, and took anything relating to mortgage or insurance for Mrs. Cleghorn to go through later.

Before leaving I poked around in the other rooms. Here and there a loose floorboard had been pried up. The fireplaces—there were six altogether—were missing their grates. The old-fashioned kitchen had come in for its share of damage. It probably hadn't looked too good to begin with, its fixtures dating from the twenties, old sink, old icebox, and badly peeling walls. In typical vandal style the intruders had dumped flour and sugar on the floor and pulled all the food from the refrigerator. If the police ever caught up with them, I'd recommend a year spent fixing up the house as the first part of their sentence.

They'd come in through the back door. The lock had been jimmied and they hadn't bothered to shut it properly behind them. The backyard was so overgrown, no one passing in the alley would be able to see that the place was open. Mrs. Cleghorn dug a hammer and nails out of the workshop

Nancy had set up next to the pantry; I hammered a board across the back door to keep it shut. There seemed to be nothing further we could do to restore wholeness to the place. We left wordlessly.

Back at the house on Muskegon, I called Bobby to tell him what happened. He grunted and said he'd refer the matter to the Third District, but for me to stand by in case they wanted to ask me anything.

"Yeah, sure," I muttered. "I'll stick by the phone for the rest of the week if it'll keep the police happy." Perhaps it was just as well that Bobby had already hung up.

Mrs. Cleghorn busied herself with coffee. She brought it to me in the dining room, with leftover cake and salad.

"What were they looking for, Victoria?" she finally asked after her second cup.

I picked moodily at some spice cake. "Something small. Flat. Papers of some kind, I suppose. I don't think they can have found them, or they wouldn't have been prying up the bricks in the other fireplaces. so where else would Nancy have left something? You're sure she didn't drop anything off here?"

Mrs. Cleghorn shook her head. "She might have come in while I was at work. But—I don't know. Do you want to look at her old bedroom?"

She sent me alone up the attic stairs to old turret where Nancy and I had waited for Sister Anne or battled pirates. It was an unbearably sad room, the remains of childhood sitting forlornly on the worn furniture. I turned over teddy bears and trophies and a worn poster of the early Beatles with studied indifference, but found nothing.

The police arrived when I got back downstairs and we spent an hour or so talking to them. We told them I'd gone over with Mrs. Cleghorn to help her find Nancy's papers—that she didn't want to go alone and I was an old friend and that we'd found the chaos and called them. We talked to a couple of junior grade detectives who wrote everything down in slow longhand but didn't seem any more concerned about this break-in than that of any other South Side householder. They left eventually without giving us any special instructions or admonitions.

I got up to leave shortly after they did. "I don't want to alarm you, but it's possible that the people who were looking at Nancy's place will come here. You should consider going to stay with one of your sons, however much you may dislike it."

Mrs. Cleghorn nodded reluctantly; the only one of her sons who didn't have children lived in a trailer with his girlfriend. Not the ideal guesthouse.

"I suppose I should get Nancy's car put away safely too. Who knows where these insane creatures will strike next?"

"Her car?" I stopped in my tracks. "Where is her car?"

"Out front. She'd left it by the SCRAP offices and one of the women who works there brought it over for me after the funeral. I had a spare set of car keys, so they must . . ." Her voice trailed off as she caught my expression. "Of course. We ought to look in the car, oughtn't we? If Nancy really did have something a—a killer wanted. Although I can't imagine what it could be."

She'd said the same thing earlier and I repeated my own meaningless reassurances: that Nancy probably didn't know she had something someone else wanted so badly. I went out to Nancy's sky-blue Honda with Mrs. Cleghorn and pulled the heap of papers from the backseat. Nancy had dumped her briefcase there along with a stack of files too big to fit into the case.

"Why don't you just take them, dear?" Mrs. Cleghorn smiled tremulously. "If you can look after them, get her work papers back to SCRAP, it would be a big help to me."

I hoisted the heap under my left arm and put my right arm around her shoulders. "Yeah, sure. Call me if anything else happens, or if you need help with the cops." It was more work than I wanted, but it seemed the least I could do under the circumstances.

21

Mama's Boy

I sat in my car with the heater on, flipping through Nancy's files. Anything that had to do with routine SCRAP business I put to one side. I wanted to drop the lot at the office on Commercial before leaving South Chicago.

I was looking for something that would tell me why Alderman Jurshak was opposing the SCRAP recycling plant. That was what Nancy had been trying to find the last time I talked to her. If she'd been killed because of something hot she knew on the South Side, I assumed it was in connection with the plant.

In the end I did find a document with the Jurshak name on it, but it had nothing to do with the recycling proposal—or any other environmental issue. It was a photocopy of a letter, dated back in 1963, to the Mariners Rest Life Assurance Company, explaining that Jurshak & Parma were now fiduciaries for Humboldt Chemical's Xerxes plant. Attached to it was an actuarial study showing that Xerxes losses were in line with those of other comparable companies in the area and asking for the same rate consideration.

I read the report through three times. It made no sense to me. That is, it made no sense as being the document that could have gotten Nancy killed. Life and health insurance are not my specialty, but this looked like perfectly ordinary, straightforward insurance stuff. It wouldn't even have seemed out of place to me except that it was so old and so unconnected to anything Nancy worked on.

There was one person who could explain the significance to me. Well, more than one, but I didn't feel like going to Big Art with it. Where did you find this, young lady? Oh, blowing around the street, you know how these things happen.

But young Art might tell me. Even though he was clearly on the periphery of his father's life, he might know enough about the insurance side to explain the document. Or, if Nancy had found it and it had meant something to her, she might have told him. In fact, she must have: that was why he was so nervous. He knew why she'd been killed and he didn't want to let on.

That seemed like a good theory. How to get Art to reveal what he knew was another question altogether. I contorted my face in an effort to concentrate. When that didn't produce results I tried relaxing all my muscles and hoped that an idea would float to the top of my mind. Instead I found myself thinking about Nancy and our childhood together. The first time I'd gone to her house for dinner, in fourth grade, when her mother had served canned spaghetti. I'd been afraid to tell Gabriella what we'd eaten —I thought she wouldn't let me go back to a house where they didn't make their own pasta.

It was Nancy who got me to try out for the junior high basketball team. I'd always been good at sports, but softball was my game. When I made the team my dad tacked a hoop to the side of the house and played with Nancy and me. He used to come to all our games in high school, and after our last game in college, the one against Lake Forest, he'd taken us to the Empire Room for drinks and dancing. He'd taught us how to fade, how to fake the pass then turn and dunk, and I'd won the game in the last seconds with just that move. The fake and the dunk.

I sat up. Nancy and I had worked it so many times in the past, why not now? I didn't have any proof, but let young Art think I did.

I pulled Nancy's most recent diary from the stack on the seat next to me. She had entered three phone numbers for him in her crabbed handwriting. I made my best guess at deciphering them and went to the public phone outside the beach house.

The first number turned out to be the ward office, where Mrs. May's syrupy tones denied knowledge of young Art's whereabouts while trying to probe me for who I was and what I wanted. She even offered me to Art, Sr., before I could end the conversation.

I dialed the second number and got the Jurshak, Parma insurance offices. There a nasal-toned receptionist told me at length that she hadn't seen young Art since Friday and she'd like to know since when she'd been hired to baby-sit for him. The cops had been around this morning looking for him and she was supposed to get a contract typed by noon and how could she possibly do it if—

"Don't let me keep you," I said shortly, and hung up on her.

I dug in my pockets for change but I'd used my last two quarters. Nancy had penciled an address next to the third number, down on Avenue G. That had to be Art's home. Anyway, if I got the kid on the phone, he'd probably hang up. Better to confront him in person.

I got back in the car and drove back down to East Side, to 115th and Avenue G. The house was halfway up the block, a new brick place with a high fence around it and an electronic lock on the gate. I rang the bell and waited. I was just about to ring again when a woman's voice came uncertainly through the squawk box.

"I'm here to see young Art," I bellowed. "My name is Warshawski."

There was a long silence and then the lock clicked. I pushed the gate open and moved into the estate. At least it looked more like an estate than it did your typical East Side bungalow. If this really was Art's home, I presumed it was because he still lived with his parents.

However modestly Big Art kept his office, he hadn't stinted on his home comforts. The lot to the right had been annexed and converted into a beautifully landscaped yard. At one end stood a glass building that might have housed an indoor swimming pool. Since a forest preserve ran along the back of the property, one had the sensation of being out in the country while only half a mile from some of the world's busiest manufacturing sites.

I trotted up the flagstone walk to the entrance, a porticoed porch whose columns looked a little incongruous against the modern brick. A faded blond woman stood in the doorway. The setting had some claim to grandeur but she was pure South Side in her crisply ironed print dress and the starched apron covering it.

She greeted me nervously, without trying to invite me in. "Who—who did you say you were?"

I pulled a card from my bag and handed it to her. "I'm a friend of young Art's. I wouldn't be bothering him at home but they haven't seen him at the ward offices and it's pretty important that I get in touch with him."

She shook her head blindly, a movement that gave her a fleeting resemblance to her son. "He—he's not home."

"I don't think he'd mind talking to me. Honestly, Mrs. Jurshak. I know the police are trying to get in touch with him, but I'm on his side, not theirs. Or his father's," I added with a flash of inspiration.

"He really isn't home." She looked at me wretchedly. "When Sergeant McGonnigal came around asking for him Mr. Jurshak got really angry, but I don't know where he is, Miss—uh. I haven't seen him since breakfast yesterday morning."

I tried to digest that. Maybe young Art hadn't been fit to drive last night after all. But if he'd been in an accident, his mother would have been the first to know. I shook away an unwelcome vision of Dead Stick Pond.

"Can you give me the names of any of his friends? Anyone he trusts enough to spend the night with uninvited?"

"Sergeant McGonnigal asked me the same thing. But—but he never had any friends. I mean, I liked him to stay here at night. I didn't want him running around the way so many boys do these days, getting involved in drugs and gangs, and he's my only child, it's not like there are others if you lose one. That's why I'm so worried now. He knows how upset I get if I don't hear from him and yet here he is, gone all night."

I didn't know what to say, since none of the comments I wanted to make would have kept her speaking to me. I finally asked if it was the first time he'd ever stayed away from home.

"Oh, no," she said simply. "Sometimes he has to work all night. On important presentations to clients or something. He's been doing a lot of those in the last few months. But never without calling me."

I grinned a little to myself: the kid was more enterprising than I would have suspected. I thought a minute, then said carefully, "I'm involved in one of those important cases, Mrs. Jurshak. The client's name is Nancy Cleghorn. Art is looking for some papers from her. Will you tell him that I have them?"

The name didn't seem to mean anything to her. At least she didn't turn pale and faint or cower back in alarm. Instead she asked me if I could write it down since she had a terrible memory, and she was so worried about Art she didn't think she'd get the names straight if she had to. I scribbled Nancy's name and a brief message about having her files on the back of my card.

"If something comes up, Mrs. Jurshak, you can leave a message for me at that number. Anytime, day or night."

When I got to the gate she was still standing in the doorway, her hands wrapped in her apron.

I wished I'd been more persistent with young Art last night. He was scared. He knew whatever it was that Nancy knew. So either my coming had been the last turn of the screw—he'd fled to avoid her fate. Or he'd met her fate. I should go to McGonnigal, tell him what I knew, or rather what I suspected. But. But. I really didn't have anything concrete. Maybe I'd give the kid twenty-four hours to show up. If he was already dead, it wouldn't matter. But if he was still alive, I should tell McGonnigal so he could help keep him that way. Round and round I went with it.

In the end I postponed a decision by driving back down to South Chicago, first to drop Nancy's files at SCRAP, then to visit Louisa. She was delighted to see me, using the remote-control button to turn off the tube, then gripping my hand with her brittle fingers.

When I edged the conversation around to Pankowski and Ferraro and their unsuccessful suit, she seemed genuinely surprised.

"I didn't know them two was so sick," she said in her raspy voice. "I saw 'em both off and on before they died and they never said word one about it. Didn't know they was suing Xerxes. Company's been real good to me—maybe the boys got themselves in some kind of trouble. Could see it with Joey—he was always a problem for someone. Usually a girl who didn't have her head screwed on right. But old Steve, he was your original straight arrow, if you know what I mean. Hard to see why he wouldn't get his benefits."

I told her what I knew about their illnesses and death and about the harried life that Mrs. Pankowski led. That brought her cough-racked laugh.

"Yeah, I could've told her a thing or two about Joey. We girls on the night shift all could of, come to that. I didn't even know he was married the first year I was working there. When I found that out you'd better believe I gave him his walking papers. None of that being the other woman for me. Course there was others who wasn't as picky, and he could make you laugh. Awful to think of him going through what I'm doing these days."

We talked until Louisa fell into her gasping sleep. She clearly knew nothing of Caroline's worries. I had to hand it to the little brat—she did protect her mother.

22

The Doctor's Dilemma

Mr. Contreras was waiting anxiously on the front walk when I came home. The dog, picking up his worried state, yawned nervously at his feet. When they saw me each expressed his joy: the dog leapt around me in little circles while the old man scolded me for not leaving him my day's route.

I put an arm around him. "You aren't going to start breathing down my neck are you? Repeat twenty times a day—she's a big girl, she can fall on her butt if she wants to."

"Don't joke about it, cookie. You know I shouldn't say this, I shouldn't even think it, but you're more family to me than my own family. Every time I look at Ruthie it beats me how Clara and I coulda had a kid like that. When I see you it's like looking at my own flesh and blood. I mean that, doll. You gotta look after yourself. For me and her royal highness here."

I gave a wry smile. "I guess I take after you, then—I'm real hardheaded and stubborn."

He thought it over a minute. "Okay, doll," he agreed reluctantly. "You gotta do things your way. I don't like it but I understand."

When I went in the front door I heard him saying to the dog, "Takes after me. You hear that, princess? She gets it from me."

Despite my bravado with him, I'd been watching my back off and on all day. I also checked my apartment carefully before sitting down with my mail, but no one had tried getting past the reinforced steel in the front door or the sliding bars on the back.

I couldn't face another evening of whiskey and peanut butter. Nor did I want my downstairs neighbor feeling he had the right to hover over me. Carefully locking up once more, I headed over to the Treasure Island on Broadway to stock up.

I was sautéeing chicken thighs with garlic and olives when Max Loewenthal phoned. My first thought on hearing from him out of the blue was that something had happened to Lotty.

"No, no, she's fine, Victoria. But this doctor you asked me about two weeks ago, this Curtis Chigwell—he tried to kill himself. You didn't know that?"

"No." I smelled burning olive oil and reached my left hand the length of the cord to turn off the stove. "What happened? How do you know?"

It had been on the six o'clock news. Chigwell's sister had found him when she went to the garage for some gardening tools at four.

"Victoria, I feel most uncomfortable about this. Most uncomfortable. Two weeks ago you ask for his address and today he tries to commit suicide. What was your role in this?"

I stiffened immediately. "Thanks, Max. I appreciate the compliment. Most days I don't feel that powerful."

"Please don't turn this off with your flippancy. You involved me. I want to know if I contributed to a man's despair."

I tried to control my anger. "You mean did I go throw his ugly past in his face to the point where he couldn't stand it and turned on the monoxide?"

"Something like that, yes." Max was very grave, his strong Viennese accent heavier than usual. "You know, Victoria, in your search for the truth you often force people to face things about themselves they are better off not knowing. I can forgive you for doing it with Lotty—she's tough, she can take it. And you don't spare yourself. But because you are very strong you don't see that other people cannot deal with these truths."

"Look, Max—I don't know why Chigwell tried to kill himself. I haven't seen a medical report so I don't even know that he did—maybe he had a stroke as he was turning on the car engine. But if it was because of the questions I was asking, I don't feel one minute of remorse. He's involved in a cover-up for Humboldt Chemical. What or why or how serious I don't know. But that has nothing to do with his personal strengths and weaknesses—it has to do with the lives of a lot of other people. *If*—and it's a mighty big if—if I'd known two weeks ago that my seeing him would make him turn on the gas, you'd better believe I'd do it again." By the time I finished speaking I was breathing hard, my mouth very tight.

"I do believe you, Victoria. And I have no wish to talk to you in such a mood. But I do have one request—that you not think of me the next time you need help in one of your chases." He hung up before I could say anything.

"Well, damn you anyway, you righteous bastard," I shouted at the dead phone. "You think you're my mother? Or just the scales of justice?"

Despite my rage I felt uneasy—I'd sicced Murray Ryerson on the guy in the middle of the night. Maybe they'd hounded him and his imagination had converted a minor peccadillo to murder. Hoping to ease my conscience, I tracked the crime editor down at the *Herald-Star*'s city desk. He was indignant—he'd sent reporters out to question the doctor about Pankowski and Ferraro, but they'd never been allowed in.

"Don't give me hounding, Miss Wise-ass. You're the one who talked to the guy. There's something you're not telling me, but I'm not even going to speculate on what it is. We've got some gofers down at that Xerxes plant and we'll get on it faster without mixed signals from you. We're running a lovely human-interest story on Mrs. Pankowski tomorrow, and I expect to have something from that lawyer Manheim who represented them."

Murray did finally part grudgingly with more details about Chigwell's attempted suicide. He had disappeared after lunch, but his sister didn't miss him since she was busy around the house. At four she decided to go to the garage to check over her gardening gear so she'd be ready for spring. Her comments to the press did not include any mention of me or Xerxes, just that her brother had been troubled the last several days. He was prone to depression and she hadn't thought much about it at the time.

"Is there any doubt he did it himself?"

"You mean did someone come into the garage, bind and gag him, strap him into the car, then undo the ropes when he was unconscious, assuming he'd die and it'd look like suicide? Give me a break, Warshawski."

When I finally finished the conversation I was in a worse mood than I'd been at the start. I'd made the cardinal sin of giving Murray far more information than I'd received in exchange. As a result he knew as much about Pankowski and Ferraro as I did. Since he had a staff who could follow a range of inquiries, he might well untangle what lay behind Humboldt's and Chigwell's lies before I did.

I'm as competitive as the next person—more than many of them—but it wasn't just fear of finishing behind Murray that upset me. It was Louisa's right to privacy—she didn't deserve the press pawing through her past. And it kept bugging me—irrationally, I agree—that I'd never been home when Nancy tried calling the day she died.

I looked balefully at the partly cooked chicken. The only scrap I hadn't given Murray was the letter to Mariners Rest I'd found in Nancy's car. And now that young Art had gone missing I wasn't sure who I could talk to about it. I poured myself a drink (one of the ten warning signs—do you turn to alcohol when you're upset or frustrated?) and went into the living room.

Mariners Rest was a large life and health insurer based in Boston, but they had a big branch office in Chicago. I'd seen their TV ads a million times, with a confident-looking sailor leaning against a hammock—rest with the mariners and sleep with their peace of mind.

It would be tricky explaining to a corporate actuary where I'd gotten the data. Almost as hard as trying to explain it to Big Art. Insurance companies guard their actuarial data with the care usually associated with the Holy Grail. So even if they'd accept my word on having a right to the documents, it would be hard to get them to tell me if they meant anything —like were the data accurate. They'd have to get clearance from their home office in Boston and that could take a month or more.

Caroline might know what the document meant, but she wasn't speaking to me. The only other person I could think of to ask was Ron Kappelman. The insurance information didn't look as though it had anything to do with the SCRAP recycling plant, but Nancy had liked Ron, she worked closely with him. Maybe he'd see the same exciting possibilities in the letter that she had.

By a mercy his home number was listed, and—greater miracle still—he was in. When I told him what I had he seemed most interested, asking a lot of sharp questions about how I'd come to have it. I responded vaguely that Nancy had bequeathed me responsibility for some of her private affairs, and I got him to agree to stop by at nine the next morning before he went to work.

I looked again at the mess in the living room. There was no way putting away back issues of *The Wall Street Journal* would make my place look as good as his gleaming house on Langley. I stuck the skillet with the chicken into refrigerator—I'd lost interest in cooking, let alone eating. I called an old friend of mine, Velma Riter, and went to see *The Witches of Eastwick* with her. By the time I got home I'd gotten enough of Chigwell and Max out of my brain to be able to sleep.

23

End Run

I was in the Chigwells' garage. Max had his hand around my wrist in a fierce grip. He forced me to go with him to the black sedan where the doctor sat. "You will kill him now, Victoria," Max said. I tried fighting him, but his grip on my hand was so fierce that he forced my arm up, forced me to pull the trigger. When I fired Chigwell's face dissolved, turning into the red-eyed dog at Dead Stick Pond. I was thrashing through the swamp grasses, trying to escape, but the feral dog hunted me remorselessly.

I woke up at six drenched with sweat, panting, fighting an impulse to dissolve into tears. The swamp dog in my dream had looked just like Peppy.

Despite the early hour, I didn't want to stay in bed any longer—I would only lie there sweating, my head filled with grit. I took the sheets off, bundled them together with my dirty sweats, put on jeans and a T-shirt, and padded down to the washing machine in the basement. If I could find something to run in, I'd be able to take the dog out. A run and a cold shower would get my head cleared for Ron Kappelman.

After a long search I found my old college warm-up pants stuffed in the bottom of a box in the hall closet. The elastic was loose—the drawstring would barely keep them on—and the maroon had faded to a washed-out pink, but they'd do for one morning. I weighed the gun, but my dream was too much with me—I couldn't bear to carry it just now. No one was going to attack me in front of all the joggers crowding the lakefront. Especially if a large dog accompanied me. I hoped.

Mr. Contreras had already let Peppy out by the time I finished my stretches. I met her on the stairs outside my kitchen door and the two of us set off.

It was another misty morning, about forty degrees, the skies leaden. No matter what the weather, the dog was ecstatic to be out in it. I left her at the lagoon, her tail waving like a golden pennant, and headed on to the lake.

A handful of fishermen stood along the rocks, hopeful even in this dreary weather. I nodded at a trio of black slickers who were seated on the seawall in front of me and headed out to the harbor entrance. I stood at the end of the promontory for a moment, watching the sullen water break against the rocks, but in the chilly mist my sweaty clothes started clinging to me uncomfortably. I retied the loose drawstring on the sweats and turned back.

The fierce storms earlier in the winter had washed boulders across the seawall all along the edge of the harbor; I had to leave the path more than once to keep from tripping on the loose rocks. By the time I got back to the land end of the harbor my legs were sore from broken field running; I slowed to a jog.

The trio of slickered fishermen had been watching my approach. They didn't seem to be doing much fishing. In fact, they didn't seem to have any gear. As I came to the end of the seawall they got up and formed a casual barrier between me and the road. A lone jogger passed behind the men.

"Hey!" I called.

The runner was deep in his Sony earphones. He paid no heed to us.

"Give it up, girlie," one of the men said. "We're just fishermen stopping a pretty girl for the time."

I was moving away from them, trying frantically to think. I could head back up the seawall to the lake. And get trapped between boulder and water trying to get past someone's Walkman for attention. Maybe if I went sideways—

A shiny black arm swung out and grabbed my left wrist. "The time, girlie. We'll just look at your watch here."

I swung quickly in the circle of his arm, bringing myself in and chopping hard, upward on his elbow. He was well padded with slicker and sweater, but I got enough on the bone that he grunted and loosed his grip. As his fingers slackened slightly I wrenched myself free and tore off across the park, yelling for help. None of the few people who'd ventured out in the mist were close enough to hear me over their earphones.

I usually just follow the seawall in and out. I didn't know this stretch of the park, what hiding places it might hold, where it would take me. I hoped to land at Lake Shore Drive, but I might be dead-ending on a driving range.

My assailants were weighed down by their heavy clothes. Despite my fatigue, I put some distance between us. I could see one of them working his way across to my left. The other two were presumably coming around the top, trying to set up a pincer. It all depended on how fast I could reach the road.

I put out a burst of energy, cutting at an angle to the direction I'd been going. I'd surprised the man I could see—he gave a shout of warning to the two I couldn't. It gave me confidence and I started running all out. I was going at top speed when I saw water in front of me.

The lake. It stuck a finger into the park here. The end of the inlet lay about thirty yards to my left. The man I'd hit had moved down there, blocking my exit. On my right I could see the other two slickers, moving behind me at a casual jog.

I waited until they were within fifteen yards, getting my breath, getting my courage. When they were close enough that they could start calling to me—"It's no use running—Give it up, girlie—No point in fighting"—I jumped.

The water was nearly ice. I took in a frozen filthy mouthful and spat. My lungs and heart banged in protest. My bones and head began to ache. My ears rang and light spots danced in my eyes. Yards. It's only yards. You can do it. One arm after the other. One foot up, one down, don't worry about the weight of the shoes, you're almost across, you're almost out, there's a boulder, slide across it, now you can walk, now you can climb up this bank.

The drawstring on my warm-up pants gave up completely. I wrestled myself free of them and lumbered toward the road. The wet cold was making me dizzy; inky shapes floated in front of me. I couldn't focus, couldn't see if the man at the bottom of the inlet had been able to move across the end before I'd swum over, couldn't see the size or shape of my pursuit. In my wet shoes, with my teeth chattering, I could hardly move, but help lay ahead. I pushed myself doggedly.

I would have made it if it hadn't been for the goddamn boulders. I was just too tired, too disoriented to see. I tripped over a giant rock and fell heavily. I was taking great gasps of air, trying to get to my feet, and then I was writhing in black-slickered arms, kicking, flailing, even biting, when all the floating inky spots gathered to a giant ball and fire exploded in my brain.

After a time I knew I was very sick. I couldn't breathe. Pneumonia. I'd waited outside in the rain for my daddy. He promised to pick me up during a break on his shift and the break didn't come—he never thought

I'd wait that long. Lie under this tent, breathe slowly, watch for Mama, she says everything will be all right and you know she never lies. I tried opening my eyes. The movement stabbed great fingers of pain into my brain, forcing me back into darkness.

I woke again, rocking helplessly back and forth, my arms tied, a boulder pushing into my side. I was wrapped in something heavy, something that pushed into my mouth. If I threw up, I'd suffocate myself. Lie as still as possible. Not the time to struggle.

I knew who I was this time. V. I. Warshawski. Girl detective. Idiot *extraordinaire*. The heavy stuff was a blanket. I couldn't see, but I imagined it—green, standard Sears issue. I was wedged against the backseat of a car. Not a boulder, but the drive shaft. When I got out of here I'd get City Council to make front-wheel drive mandatory for all Chicago criminals. Get stopped with a drive shaft in your car and you'd do time, like the IRS getting Al Capone. When I got out of here.

My slickered friends were talking but I couldn't make out their words through the buzzing in my ears and the thickness of the blanket. I thought at first the buzzing was left over from my cold-water bath, but by and by my tired brain sorted it into the sound of wheels on the road coming through the floorboard. The rocking and the warmth of my cocoon sent me back to sleep.

I woke up to feel cold air on my head. My arms were numb where they'd been tied behind me, my tongue thick with suppressed nausea.

"Is she still out?"

I didn't know the voice. Cold, indifferent. The voice of the man who'd called in the threat? Only two days ago? Was that all? I couldn't tell, either of time or the voice.

"She isn't moving. Want me to open her up and check?" A black man's thicker tones.

"Leave her as she is." The cold voice again. "An old carpet we're dumping. You never know who may see you, even down here. Who might remember seeing a face."

I kept myself as limp as possible. I didn't need another blow to the skull. I was pulled roughly from the car, banging my poor head, my aching arms, my sore back on the door, clenching my numb fingers to keep from crying out. Someone slung me over his back like an old roll of carpet, as though a hundred and forty pounds was nothing to him, as though I was nothing more than a light and careless load. I could hear twigs snapping underfoot, the swishing of the dead grasses. What I hadn't noticed on my previous trip here was the smell. The rank stench of putrifying grasses, mixed with the chemicals that drained into the marsh. I tried not to choke, tried not to think of the fish with their rotting fins, tried to suppress the well of nausea that grew with the pounding in my head as it bounced against my bearer's back.

"Okay, Troy. X marks the spot."

Troy grunted, slid me from his shoulder, and dropped me. "Far enough in?"

"She isn't going anyplace. Let's split."

The rank grasses and soft mud broke my fall. I lay against the chill earth. The cool mud soaking through the blanket brought a moment's relief to my sick head, but as I lay there my body's weight caused water to ooze up through the mud. I felt the dampness in my ears and panicked, thrashing uselessly. Alone in this dark cocoon, I was going to drown, black swamp water in my lungs, my heart, my brain. The blood roared in my head and I cried tears of utter helplessness.

24

In Grimpen Mire

I had passed out again. When I slowly came to I was wet all through. Water had oozed into my hair and was tickling my ears. My shoulders felt as though someone had stuck iron bars into them to separate them from my breastbone. Somehow, though, the sleep and the cold muddy water had healed my head a little. I didn't want to think—it was too scary. But minute by minute I could still make it if I used a little sense.

I rolled to one side, the blanket heavy with mud. Using every ounce of strength, I pushed myself to a sitting position. My ankles were bound together and my hands were tied behind me at the wrist—there was no way I could work them to the front of my body. But by pushing them down at my tailbone I could brace myself enough to inch forward with my legs.

I had to assume they'd taken me down the same track where they'd dumped Nancy—it was the farthest from the road, anyway. After some time of trial and error, which left me gasping for breath inside my muddy cocoon, I reckoned that the water lay to my right. I carefully made a one-hundred-eighty-degree turn so that my inching motion would take me back toward the road. I tried not to think of the distance, tried not to compute my probable speed. Forced thoughts of food, baths, bed away and imagined myself on a sunny beach. Maybe Hawaii. Maybe Magnum would appear suddenly and cut me out of my prison.

My legs and arms were shaking. Too much exertion, too little glucose. I had to stop every few pushes and rest. The second time I stopped I fell asleep again, waking only as I fell over into the grasses. After that I forced myself to a counting pattern. Five shoves, count fifteen, five shoves, count fifteen, five shoves, count fifteen. Legs wobbling, brain turning, fifteen. My fifteenth birthday. Gabriella had died two days before. The last breath in

Tony's arms while I was at the beach. Maybe there really was a heaven, Gabriella with her pure voice in the angelic choir waiting for me with wings outstretched, her arms opened in boundless love, waiting for my contralto to blend with her soprano.

A dog's bark brought me back to myself. The red-eyed hound. This time I couldn't help it: I was sick, a little trickle of bile down my front. I could hear the dog coming closer, breath heaving, short, sharp barks, then a nose pushing into the side of the blanket, knocking me over. I lay on my side in a helpless tangle of mud and blanket, kicking uselessly in the air, and felt paws press heavily into my arm.

I kicked helplessly at the blanket, trying to force the hound away. Little tears of fear slid into my nose. All the while on the other side fangs pulled at my head, my arms. When it had bit through the blanket how would I protect my throat? My arms were behind me. It wasn't minding my feeble thrashing.

Panic roared in my ears, turned my useless legs to water. Over the roaring I heard a voice. With the tiny energy left in me, I tried to cry out.

"You got her? You found her? Is that you, doll? Are you in there? Can you hear me?"

Not the hound of hell after all, but Peppy. With Mr. Contreras. My euphoria was so great that my sore muscles felt momentarily healed. I grunted feebly. The old man wrestled feverishly with the knots, talking to himself all the while.

"I mighta known to bring a knife instead of this wrench. Should have guessed that, you stupid old man, why do you want to go carrying pipe wrenches when a knife is what you need? Steady in there, doll, we almost got it, don't give up the ship now, not when we're this close."

He finally managed to rip the blanket away from my head. "Oh my, this is bad. Let's get you out of here."

He worked frantically, clumsily on the knots behind my back. The dog looked at me anxiously, then started to lick my face—I was her long-lost puppy found in the nick of time. All the while that Mr. Contreras freed my hands, rubbing some semblance of circulation back into my arms, she kept washing my face.

He was shocked to see me in my underwear, afraid I'd been raped, could hardly take in my assurances that it was just drowning my assailants had been after. Leaning heavily on his shoulder, I let him guide me, half carrying me, back to the road.

"I got some young hotshot here. Some lawyer, he says. Didn't believe you could really be down here, so he waited at the car. When her royal highness came back from the lake without you, I got kinda worried. Then this snot-nose shows up, says you was going to meet with him at nine and where was you, he can't wait all day. I know you don't want me breathing down your neck, doll, but I was there when the guy called, I heard that little friend of yours say they was going to dump you in the marsh, so I made him drive us down here. Me and her highness, you know, I figured we could find the place after you showed it to me on the map and all."

He went over and over it on the way to the road. Ron Kappelman stood there, leaning on his beat-up Rabbit, whistling lightly, looking at nothing. When he saw the three of us coming he leapt upright and sprinted across the road. He helped Mr. Contraras lift me over the fence and into the backseat of the car. Peppy gave a little bark and shoved past them to push her heavy body next to mine.

"Damn, Warshawski. You miss an appointment, you do it in a big way. What the hell happened to you?"

"You leave her alone, young man, and don't go talking dirty like that. There's plenty other words in the English language without going around swearing all the time. I don't know what your mother would think if she could hear you, but what we gotta do is get this lady to a doctor, get her patched up, then you want to butt your nose in and find out how she got where she was, maybe she'll feel like talking to you."

Kappelman stiffened as if to fight back, then realized the futility of it and got into the driver's seat. I was unconscious before he had the car turned around.

I don't remember anything of the rest of the day. How Kappelman flagged down a state patrol car and got us an eighty-mile-an-hour escort to Lotty's clinic, Mr. Contreras stubbornly insisting he wouldn't let them take me to a hospital without her say-so. Or how Lotty, taking one look at me in the back of the car, summoned an ambulance to take me to Beth Israel at top speed. Or even how Peppy wouldn't relinquish me to the paramedics. She apparently seized a wrist in her strong jaw and refused to let go. They tell me they woke me up long enough to make her drop the guy's arm, but I don't have any memory of it, not even as a dream fragment.

I finally resurfaced around six Thursday morning. After a few puzzled minutes I realized I was in a hospital bed, but I couldn't imagine what I was doing there or how I'd come to be there. As soon as I tried sitting up, though, my shoulders sent out so severe a message of pain that memory came flooding back.

Dead Stick Pond. That horrible cocoon of death. I held my arms out in front of me, despite the agony moving them brought. My wrists and hands were wrapped in gauze; my fingers looked like bright red sausages emerging from the white bandages. An IV needle was taped to my left forearm above the gauze. I followed it to a series of bags overhead and squinted at the labels. D5.45NS. That told me a lot.

I touched my fingertips gently together. They were swollen, but I could feel. I lay back again, filled with a peaceful satisfaction. I had survived. My hands were all right. They had tried to kill me, tried to humiliate me at the moment of my death, but I was alive. I fell back into sleep.

When I woke again it was to the full bustle of morning hospital routine —blood pressure, temperature, rounds—and no questions answered: doctor will tell you. After the nurses came a brisk intern who looked at my eyes and stuck pins into my feet. The pin seems to be neuroscience's most advanced piece of technology. Another intern was busy with my roommate, a woman my age who'd just had cosmetic surgery. After they'd finished Lotty herself swept in, dark eyes bright with nonclinical feeling. My intern hovered at her elbow, anxious to tell her his findings on my body. She listened for a minute, then dismissed him with an imperious wave.

"I'm sure your reflexes are all in perfect order, but let me see for myself. First let's have your chest. Breathe. Hold it. Exhale. Yes." She listened to me fore and aft, then had me shut my eyes and touch my hands together, get out of bed—a slow, lurching process—and walk on my heels, then my toes. It wasn't much compared to my usual workout, but it left me panting.

"You really should have children, Victoria—you could produce a whole new breed of superheroes. Why you are even alive at this point is a medical miracle, let alone that you can walk."

"Thank you, Lotty. I'm pretty pleased myself. Tell me how I got here and when I can leave."

She gave me the details of Peppy and the ambulance men. "And your friend Mr. Contreras is waiting anxiously down the hall. He stayed here all night, with the dog, totally against hospital policy, but the two of you are well matched—stubborn, pigheaded, with only one allowable way to do things—your own."

"Pot calling the kettle black, Lotty," I said unrepentantly, lying down. "And don't tell me the dog didn't stay here with your connivance. Or at least Max's."

I frowned and bit off my words, remembering my last conversation with the hospital's executive director. Lotty looked at me sympathetically.

"Yes, Max also wants to talk to you. He is feeling a bit remorseful. And that is no doubt why the dog spent the night in the hospital. But she must go home now, so if you will tell your tiresome neighbor you're going to live to tilt at more windmills, we'll get them to leave. Meanwhile, since your brain is no worse than usual, I'll get someone to take that needle out of you."

She whirled off at her usual forty knots. Mr. Contreras came in a minute or two later, his eyes filled with tears, his hands shaking a little. I swung my feet over the side of the bed and held out my arms to him.

"Oh, cookie, I'm never gonna forget the way we found you yesterday. More dead than alive, you was. And that young snot not believing you could be down there and me having to practically knock him out before he'd drive us. And then I couldn't get the nurses here to tell me anything about how you was doing, I kept asking and asking and they wouldn't say because I wasn't family. Me, not your family. Who has more right, I'd like to know, I says to them, some cousin in Melrose Park who don't even send her a Christmas card, or me who saved her life. But Dr. Lotty showed up and straightened it all out, her and Mr. Loewenthal between them, and put me and the dog in an empty room down the hall from you, but we had to promise not to disturb you."

He pulled a giant red handkerchief from a back pocket and blew his nose loudly. "Well, all's well that ends well, and I gotta take her highness home and feed her, but don't go telling me to mind my own business anymore, cookie, not when you got guys like this on your case."

I thanked him as best I could, giving him a tight hug and a kiss. After he left I lay back down again, cursing my lack of stamina. Lotty wanted me to stay here another day—she said I wouldn't rest if I went off on my own. She was right: I was already in a pretty fretful state, made more irritable by my sore shoulder muscles. But she'd thrown out all my clothes and wasn't going to bring me any more until Friday morning.

As it turned out most of the people I would have tried to see came to visit me, along with a few I could just as well have done without, such as the police. Lieutenant Mallory arrived in person, a sign not of my importance but of his angry concern—angry because I should have stayed clear of police business, concern because he'd been close to both my parents.

"Vicki, put yourself in my place for a change. One of your oldest friends dies and every time you turn around his only kid is thumbing her nose at you. How do you think I feel?"

"I know how you feel; you've told me six billion times," I said churlishly. I hate having to talk to people in a hospital gown—it's like you're a kid in bed and they're tucking you in for the night.

"If you'd been killed, I would have carried that responsibility to my grave. Can't you understand that? Can't you see when I give you orders it's out of concern for your safety, because of what I owe Tony and Gabriella? What will it take to pound some sense into you?"

I glowered at the bedclothes. "I'm self-employed just so I don't have to take orders from anyone. Anyway, Bobby, I did agree not to go to the state's attorney about Nancy Cleghorn. And I agreed to tell you if I ran into anything that looked like a lead into her death. I didn't."

"You obviously did!" he shouted, pounding the bedside table so hard that the water pitcher fell over. That put the cap to his anger—he yelled out the door for an orderly, then shouted at the man until the floor was cleaned to his satisfaction. My roommate turned off *The Dating Game* and scurried out to the lounge.

When the place was dry again Bobby made an effort to smother his anger. He took me through the details of the episode, waiting patiently at the spots that were hard for me to talk about, prompting me professionally when I couldn't remember something. The fact that I had a name, even just a first name, cheered him slightly—if Troy was a pro tied to any known organization, the police would have a file on him.

"Now, Vicki"—Bobby was genial—"let's get to the heart of the matter. If you didn't know anything about Cleghorn's death, why did someone try to kill you in the same manner, and in the same place that they murdered her?"

"Gee, Bobby, the way you put it, I guess I must know who killed her. Or at least why."

"Exactly. Now let's have it."

I shook my head, gingerly, since the back was still on the sore side. "It's just the way *you* put it. The way I look at it, I must've talked to someone who thinks I know more than I really do. The trouble is, I've talked to so many people the last few days and all of them have been so unpleasant that I don't know which I'd choose as my grade-A suspect."

"Okay." Bobby was determinedly patient. "Let's have who you've talked to."

I looked at the water stains on the ceiling. "There's young Art Jurshak. You know, the alderman's son. And Curtis Chigwell, the doctor who tried killing himself in Hinsdale the other day. And Ron Kappelman— SCRAP's counsel. Gustav Humboldt, of course. Murray Ryerson—"

"Gustav Humboldt?" Bobby's voice went up a register.

"You know, the chairman of Humboldt Chemical."

"I know who you mean," he said bitingly. "You want to share with me why you were talking to him? In reference to the Cleghorn woman?"

"I wasn't really talking to him about the Cleghorn woman at all," I said earnestly, turning to look at Bobby's clenched jaw. "That's what I meant —I didn't talk to any of these people about Nancy. But since they were all more or less unpleasant, any of them might have wanted to dump me in the swamp."

"For two cents I'd get someone to put you back there. It'd save a lot of time. You know something and you think you're going to be a hotshot again, go looking without saying squat to me about it. They almost got you this time. Next time they will, but until they do I have to waste city money by having someone keep an eye on you."

His blue eyes glittered. "Eileen's all upset about you being in here. She wanted to send over flowers, she wanted to take you home with her and fuss over you. I told her you just ain't worth it."

25

Visiting Hours

After Bobby left I lay back down. I tried to sleep, but the pain in my shoulders had moved to the foreground of my mind. Angry tears prickled under my eyes. I had almost gotten killed, and all he could do was insult me. I wasn't worth the bother of looking after, just because I wasn't a blabbermouth who would tell him everything I knew. I'd tried mentioning Gustav Humboldt's name, and all I'd gotten for my pains was an incredulous shout.

I twitched uncomfortably. The knot in the hospital gown was digging into my sore neck muscles. Of course I could have given him chapter and verse on all my activities for the last week. But Bobby just wouldn't have believed that a bigshot like Gustav Humboldt could be involved in bonking young women on the head. Although maybe if I'd tried giving it to him straight . . . Was he right? Was I just hotdogging, hoping to thumb my nose at him one more time?

As I lay still, letting images flow through my mind, I realized that this time, at least, wanting to give the powers-that-be a Bronx cheer wasn't what had kept me quiet. I was well and truly scared. Every time I tried sending my mind back to the three black-slickered men I shied away from the memory like a horse frightened by fire. There were a lot of parts of the assault I hadn't told Bobby, not because I was trying to hold back on him but because I couldn't bear to touch the memories. The hope that some forgotten phrase or cadence would give me a lead to who they worked for wasn't enough to force the memory of that terrifying near-suffocation.

If I spilled everything I knew to Bobby, turning the whole tangled mess over to him, it was a way of saying it out loud. Hey, guys, whoever you are, you got me. You didn't kill me but you got me so scared that I'm abdicating responsibility for my life.

Once I'd let that little piece of self-knowledge float to the top of my mind, a terrible rage began to seize hold of me. I would not be turned into a eunuch, be driven to living my life in the margins designed by someone else's will. I didn't know what was going on in South Chicago, but no one, be it Steve Dresberg, Gustav Humboldt, or even Caroline Djiak, was going to keep me from finding out.

When Murray Ryerson showed up a little after eleven, I was pacing the room in my bare feet, my hospital gown flapping around my legs. I'd vaguely seen my roommate stand uncertainly in the door and move away again, and I mistook Murray's presence for her return until he spoke.

"They told me you were fifteen minutes from death, but I knew better than to believe that."

I jumped. "Murray! Didn't your mother teach you to knock before barging in on people?"

"I tried, but you weren't anywhere near planet earth." He straddled the chair next to my bed. "You look like that Siberian tiger in that great open area at Lincoln Park Zoo, V.I. You're making me nervous. Sit down and let me have an exclusive on your brush with death. Who tried to do you in? Dr. Chigwell's sister? The folks down at the Xerxes plant? Or your pal Caroline Djiak?"

That stopped me. I pulled up my roommate's chair to face Murray. I had hoped to keep Louisa's affairs out of the papers, but once Murray started digging he'd find out pretty much anything.

"What'd little Caroline tell you—that I'd come by my ill deserts honestly?"

"Caroline's a bit confusing to talk to. She says you were looking into Nancy Cleghorn's death for SCRAP, although no one else down there seems to know anything about it. She claims she knows nothing about Pankowski or Ferraro, although I'm not sure I believe her."

Murray poured himself a glass of water from the pitcher the orderly had replaced. "The people at Xerxes keep referring us to counsel if we want to hear about those two. Or about their suicidal doctor. And it does always kind of make you wonder when people only talk to you through their lawyers. We're working on the plant secretary, the gal who works for the accountant-cum-personnel administrator. And one of my assistants is hanging out at the bar where the shift goes after work, so we'll get something. But you could sure make it easier, Miss Marple."

I slid from the chair back to bed and pulled the covers up to my chin. Caroline was protecting Louisa. Of course. That was what lay behind her song and dance. A threat to her mother was the only thing that would scare her, the only explanation consistent with her fierce terrier personality. She didn't care anything for her own safety—and certainly not enough for mine to grow hysterical over my failure to drop the investigation.

It was hard to imagine how they could menace a woman in Louisa's condition. Maybe blasting the private affairs she so ardently desired to keep secret out into the open—perhaps her most important concern in the last months of her life. Although Louisa hadn't seem worried when I saw her on Tuesday. . . .

"Come on, Vic. Give." Murray's voice had an edge that brought me back to the room.

"Murray, it wasn't two days ago you were looking haughtily down that elephant-child snout of yours telling me you didn't need anything from me and wouldn't do anything for me. So give me a reason why I should suddenly help you out."

Murray waved his hand around the hospital room. "This, baby doll. Someone wants you dead awful bad. The more people who know what you know, the less likely they'll be to try to take you out a second time."

I smiled sweetly—at least that was the goal. "I talked to the police."

"And told them everything you know."

"That would take more time than Lieutenant Mallory has. I told him who I spoke with the day before the—the assault. That included you—you weren't very pleasant, and he wanted to know about anyone who seemed hostile."

Murray's eyes narrowed above his red beard. "I came here prepared to be sympathetic, maybe even to rub ointment into the sore spots. You have a way of destroying people's tender feelings, kiddo."

I made a sour face. "Funny—Bobby Mallory said much the same thing."

"Any reasonable man would. . . . Okay. Let's have the assault story. All I have is the sketch the hospital reported to the cops. You made all four TV news spots last night, if that makes you feel more important."

It didn't. It made me feel more exposed. Whoever had tried to dump me into the South Chicago swamp had plenty of access to the news that I'd managed to crawl away. There wasn't any point to asking Murray to keep a lid on it: I gave him as much as I could bear to reveal about the experience.

"I take it back, V.I.," he said when I finished. "That's a harrowing story even with most of the details missing. You're entitled to thrash your tail awhile."

Even so he tried wheedling more information from me, stopping only when the lunches were brought in, chicken and overcooked peas, followed nervously by the woman recovering from plastic surgery. I was chewed out rather sternly by the floor head for having visitors who frightened my roommate out of her own bed. Since Murray takes up about as much space as a full-grown grizzly, she devoted enough of her remarks to him that he fled in some embarrassment.

After lunch a petite Asian underling came to inform me that Dr. Herschel had ordered deep heat for me down in physical therapy. She found a hospital robe for me. Even though I was twice her size, she helped me solicitously into a wheelchair and pushed me down to the PT unit, deep in the bowels of the hospital. I spent a pleasant hour getting wet packs, deep heat, and a massage, finishing with ten minutes in the whirlpool.

By the time my attendant had brought me back to my room, I was drowsy and ready for sleep. It was not meant to be, however: I found Ron Kappelman sitting in the visitor's chair. He put away a folder of papers when he saw me and offered me a pot of geraniums.

"You sure seem better today than I would've believed twenty-four hours ago," he said soberly. "I'm most sorry I didn't take your neighbor seriously—I just assumed something important had come up and you'd taken off. I still can't figure out how he bullied me into driving him all the way down there."

I slid back into bed and lay down. "Mr. Contreras is a little excitable, at least about my well-being, but I'm not exactly in the mood to fight it today. You find anything out about that insurance report? Or why Jurshak was appointed the fiduciary?"

"You look as though you should be convalescing, not worrying about a bunch of old files," he said disapprovingly.

"Has their status changed? Tuesday you were pretty excited about them. What turned them into old files?" Lying down wasn't a good idea—I kept drifting. I cranked the bed so I could sit up.

"The way you looked when that old man dragged you up to the fence. They didn't seem worth that much trouble."

I scanned his face for signs of menace or lies or something. All he showed was manly concern. What did that prove?

"Is that why I was dumped into the marsh? Because of the report to Mariners Rest?"

He looked startled. "I guess I assumed—because we'd talked about them and then you didn't show up for our meeting."

"You tell anyone about my having that letter, Kappelman?"

He leaned forward in his chair, his mouth set in a thin line. "I'm beginning to dislike the turn this conversation is taking, Warshawski. Are you trying to imply that I had anything to do with what happened to you yesterday?"

This made the third well-wisher whose mind I'd changed within minutes of entering the room. "I'm trying to make sure that you didn't. Look, Ron, all I know about you is that you had a brief fling with an old friend of mine. That doesn't tell me anything—I mean, I was once married to a guy I wouldn't trust with a kid's piggy bank. All it proves is that hormones are stronger than brains.

"I talked to you and to one other person about those documents. If they're the reason I was dumped into that swamp yesterday—and that's a big question mark—because I just don't know—it had to be because of one of you guys."

He made a sour face. "Okay. I guess I can buy that—just. I don't know how to convince you I didn't hire those thugs—other than on my honor as a Boy Scout. I was one once, thirty years ago or so. Will you take that as evidence of probity?"

"I'll take it into account." I lowered the bed again—I was too tired to try to push him any further. "They're springing me tomorrow. Want to try again on these papers?"

He frowned. "You really are a cold-blooded bitch, aren't you? Near death one day and hot on the trail the next. Sherlock Holmes didn't have anything on you. I guess I still want to see those damned documents—I'll stop by around six if they've let you go home."

He got up and pointed at the geraniums. "Don't eat those—they're just for the spirit. Try to enjoy them."

"Very funny," I muttered to his back. Before he'd disappeared I was deep in sleep.

When I woke again around six Max was sitting in the visitor's chair. He was reading a magazine with peaceful absorption, but when he realized I was awake he folded it neatly and stuck it in his attaché case.

"I would have been here much sooner, but my day was spent in meetings, I fear. Lotty tells me you are fine, that you need nothing but rest to be completely healed."

I ran a hand through my hair. It felt matted and sticky, which made me feel at a disadvantage. I eyed Max warily.

"Victoria." He took my left hand and held it between his two. "I hope you can forgive my cold words of a few days ago. When Lotty told me what had happened to you, I felt truly remorseful."

"Don't," I said awkwardly. "You weren't responsible for anything that happened to me."

His soft brown eyes looked at me shrewdly. "Nothing is without connection in our lives. If I hadn't goaded you about Dr. Chigwell, you might not have acted so fiercely as to get yourself into trouble."

I started to answer him, then stopped. If he hadn't goaded me, I might not have felt so reluctant to take my gun with me on my run yesterday. Maybe I even exposed myself unconsciously to danger to assuage my guilt.

"But I did have something to feel guilty about," I said aloud. "You weren't that far off the mark, you know—I only pressured Chigwell because he made me angry. So maybe I gave the final turn to his screw."

"So maybe we can both learn a little from this, to look before we leap." Max stood up to reveal a magnificent array of flowers in a Chinese porcelain bowl. "I know you leave tomorrow, but take these with you for some cheer while your poor muscles heal."

Max was an expert on oriental porcelain. The pot looked as though it had come from his personal collection. I tried to let him know how much the gesture pleased me; he accepted my thanks with his usual cheerful courtesy and left.

26

Back to Home Base

I had a new roommate in the morning, a twenty-year-old named Jean Fishbeck whose lover had shot at her and hit a shoulder before she got him in the stomach. The cosmetic surgery patient had moved three rooms down the hall.

I got the whole shooting story, with loud-pitched expletives, at midnight when Ms. Fishbeck came in from postop. At seven, when the morning shift came in to see if we'd expired in the night, she vented her rage at being awakened in the clarion nasal of the northwest side. By the time Lotty showed up at eight-thirty I was ready to go anywhere, even the psychiatric wing, just to get away from the obscenities and cigarettes.

"I don't care what shape I'm in," I told Lotty irritably. "Just sign my discharge and let me out of here. I'll leave in my nightgown if I have to."

Lotty cocked an eye at the crumpled chewing-gum wrappers and cigarette pack on the floor. She raised both eyebrows as a stream of profanity poured from behind the closed curtain while an intern tried to conduct an exam.

"The floor head told me you'd been rough on your roommate yesterday and that they were giving you someone more suited to your personality. Did you vent your anger by handing her a few punches?" She started probing my shoulder muscles.

"Ow, damn you, that hurts. And the word you want is *throw,* not *hand.* Or *land,* maybe."

Lotty used her ophthalmoscope on my eyes. "We gave you X rays and a CT scan after we stabilized you on Wednesday. By some miracle you don't have any cracks or breaks. Some more physical therapy over the next few days should help your sore muscles, but don't expect them to recover overnight—tissue tears can take as long as a year to heal if you don't rest the muscles properly. And yes, you can go home—you can do the therapy as an outpatient. If you give me your keys, I'll have Carol bring you some clothes at lunchtime."

I'd tied the keys through the laces of my running shoes before setting out on Wednesday. Lotty had rescued them before giving orders to trash what clothes I'd still been wearing on arrival at Beth Israel.

She stood up and looked at me gravely. When she spoke again her Viennese accent was pronounced. "I would ask that you not be reckless, Victoria. I would ask it except that you seem to be in love with danger and death. You make life very hard for those who love you."

I couldn't think of anything to say. She stared at me for a long moment, her eyes very dark in her angular face, then gave her head a little shake and left.

My twenty-four-hour character summary wasn't too appealing: a coldhearted bitch in love with death and danger who drove timid cosmetic surgery patients to the nursing staff for refuge. When an orderly came by an hour or so later to take me down for physical therapy, I went along morosely. The normal hospital routine, which depersonalizes patients at its expense, usually drives me into a frenzy of uncooperative sarcasm. Today I took it like a good little lump.

After my physical therapy I myself took refuge from my vituperous roommate, waiting in the lounge for my clothes with a stack of old *Glamour*s and *Sports Illustrated*. Carol Alvarez, the nurse and chief backup at Lotty's clinic, arrived a little before two. She greeted me warmly, with a hug, a kiss, and little exclamations of horror over my ordeal.

"Even Mama has been praying to the Blessed Mother for your safety, Vic." That was something, indeed—Mrs. Alvarez usually looked on me with silent contempt.

Carol had brought jeans, a sweatshirt, and a pair of boots. The clothes and underwear seemed unnaturally clean. I'd forgotten leaving them in the laundry on Wednesday. Apparently one of my downstairs neighbors had dumped them in a wet heap outside my apartment door with an angry note —Carol had generously taken the time to run them back through the machine.

She helped me quickly with the discharge routine. Since she knew a lot of the nurses on the floor, their hostility toward me cooled a little when they saw me with her. With me carrying Max's oriental bowl and Carol the geraniums, we made our way through the long corridors to the staff parking lot behind the hospital.

My head seemed stuffed with cotton, remote not just from my body but from the day around me. It had been only two days since my ill-fated run, but I felt as though I'd been away from the world for months. My boots felt new and strange and I couldn't get used to the sensation of the jeans zipped close to my body. At that they weren't as close as they used to be—the last few days seemed to have taken a good five pounds off me.

Mr. Contreras was waiting for me when we got to my apartment on Racine. He had tied a big red ribbon around Peppy's neck and groomed her auburn hair until it shone in the dull gray day. Carol turned me over to them with another kiss and left us at the door.

I would have much preferred to be alone to order my thoughts, but he had earned the right to fuss. I submitted to his ushering me into the armchair, pulling off my boots and tucking a blanket tenderly around my legs and feet.

He'd fixed an elaborate tray of fruit and cheese, which he set next to me along with a pot of tea. "Now, cookie, I'm leaving her highness here to keep you company. You want anything, you just call me. I printed my number next to the phone so you don't have to look it up. And before you go off sticking your head into trouble, you let me know. I ain't gotta hover over you—I know you hate that—but someone's gotta know where to come looking for you. You promise me that or I'm going to have to hire me a detective just to follow you around."

I held out a hand. "It's a deal, Uncle."

The honorary title moved him so much that he spoke sternly to the dog, outlining her duties to me, before slapping me on my sore shoulder and moving off down the stairs.

I'm not much of a tea drinker, but it was pleasant to stay where I'd been planted. I poured myself a cup, mixed it with a lot of heavy cream, and alternately fed grapes to myself and the dog. She sat on her haunches watching me with unwavering eyes, panting slightly, taking her guard duties seriously, assuring herself that I wasn't going to disappear again without her.

I forced my weary mind back to the time before my assault. Only three days earlier, but the neurons moved as though they'd been rusted over for years. When every muscle aches it's hard to remember feeling whole.

I'd been warned out of South Chicago Monday night. On Wednesday I'd been dispatched most efficiently. That meant something I'd done Tuesday had brought an immediate reaction. I frowned, trying to remember what all happened that day.

I'd found Jurshak's insurance report and talked to Ron Kappelman about it. I'd also left a message for young Art implying I had the material.

These were tangible documents and it was tempting to think they showed something so damaging that people would kill to keep them secure. It might be difficult to pry the truth from Kappelman if he was concealing something, but Jurshak was such a fragile young man, I ought to be able to pound the facts from him. If only I could find him. If he was still alive.

Still, I shouldn't concentrate on those two at the expense of the other people involved. Curtis Chigwell, for example. Early Tuesday I'd sicced Murray Ryerson on him and twelve hours later he'd tried to kill himself. And then there was the big shark, Gustav Humboldt himself. Whatever Chigwell knew, whatever they were concealing about Joey Pankowski and Steve Ferraro, Gustav Humboldt had full knowledge of. Otherwise he would never have sought me out to try to get me to swallow lies about two insignificant workers in his worldwide empire. And the insurance report Nancy had found dealt with his company. That must mean something—I just didn't yet know what.

Finally, of course, there was little Caroline. Now that I'd worked out that she was protecting Louisa, I figured I could get her to talk. She might even know what Nancy had seen in the insurance report. She was my best starting point.

I took the blanket from my legs and got up. The dog immediately sprang to her feet, waving her tail—if I stood up, it was clearly time to go running. When she saw me just move to the phone, she flopped down in depression.

Caroline was in a meeting, the SCRAP receptionist told me. She was not to be disturbed.

"Just write the following on a note and take in into her—'Louisa's life story on the front page of the *Herald-Star?*' And add my name. I guarantee she'll be on the phone within nanoseconds."

I had to cajole a little more, but the woman finally agreed. I carried the phone back over to the easy chair. Peppy eyed me in disgust, but I wanted to be sitting down for the coming blast.

Caroline came on the line without preamble. I let her rant at me unchecked for some minutes, shredding my character, expressing remorse that I'd risen unchastened from the swamp, even lamenting that I didn't now lie buried in the mud.

At that I decided to interrupt. "Caroline, that was vile and offensive. If you had any imagination or sensitivity, you would never have thought such a thing, let alone said it."

She was silent for a minute, then said gruffly. "I'm sorry, Vic. But you shouldn't have sent me messages threatening Ma."

"Right, kiddo. I understand. I understand that the only reason you've been behaving more like a horse's rear end than usual is because someone was gunning for Louisa. I need to know who and why."

"How do you know?" she blurted.

"It's your character, sweetie. It just took me awhile to remember it. You're manipulative, you'll bend the rules any old way to get what you want, but you're no chicken. You'd run scared for only one reason."

She was silent for another long moment. "I'm not going to say if you're right or wrong," she finally said. "I just can't talk about it. If you're right, you can understand why. If you're wrong—I guess it's because I'm a horse's rear end."

I tried to will my personality into the phone. "Caroline, this is important. If someone told you they'd hurt Louisa unless you got me to stop hunting for your father, I need to know it. Because it means there's a tie-in between Nancy's death and my looking at Joey Pankowski and Steve Ferraro."

"You'd have to sell me and I don't think you can." She was serious, more mature than I was used to hearing her.

"At least let me give it a shot, babe. Come up here some time tomorrow? As you can imagine, I'm not too fit right now or I'd zip down to see you tonight."

She finally, reluctantly, agreed to come by in the afternoon. We hung up in greater amity than I'd have thought possible ten minutes earlier.

27

The Game's Afoot

An annoying lassitude gripped my body. Even the short conversation with Caroline had tired me out. I poured some more tea and flicked on the tube. With spring training still two weeks away, there wasn't much doing during the day. I moved from soap to soap to a tearful prayer meeting—Tammy Faye's sobbing successor—to *Sesame Street* and turned the set off in disgust. It was too much to expect me to sort papers or pay bills in my enfeebled state; I wrapped myself in my blanket and lay down on the sofa for a nap.

I woke up about twenty minutes before Kappelman was due and stumbled into the bathroom to rinse my face with cold water. Someone had stolen all the dirty towels, scrubbed the sink and bathtub, and tidied up odds and ends of toiletries and makeup. Peeping into my bedroom, I was staggered to see the bed made and clothes and shoes put away. I hated to admit it, but the tidy rooms were cheering to my sore spirits.

I'd hidden Nancy's documents in the stacks of music on the piano. The elves had carefully put the music inside the piano bench, but the insurance material lay undisturbed between the *Italienisches Liederbuch* and Mozart's *Concert Arias*.

I was picking my way through *"Che no sei capace"*— whose title line seemed admirably apt, in that I understood nothing—when Kappelman rang the bell. Before I could get to the intercom Mr. Contreras had bounded out to the lobby to inspect him. When I opened my door I could hear their voices in the stairwell as they came up together—Mr. Contreras trying to tamp down the suspicions he felt toward any man who visited me, Kappelman trying to suppress his impatience with the escort.

My neighbor started talking to me as soon as his head cleared the last turn and he caught sight of me. "Oh, hi there, cookie. You have a good rest? I'm just coming to pick up her highness here, get her some air, a little food. You weren't feeding her cheese, were you? I meant to tell you—she can't tolerate it."

He came into the room and started inspecting Peppy for signs of illness. "You don't want to go walking her alone, now, nor going off by yourself on one of your runs. And don't let this young guy here keep you going past when you've got yourself worn out. And you want any help with anything, me and the dog'll be at the ready; you just give us a holler."

With this thinly veiled warning, he collected Peppy. He hovered at the door with more admonitions until I finally thrust him gently onto the landing.

Kappelman looked at me sourly. "If I'd known the old man was going to investigate my character, I'd've brought my own attorney along. I'd say you were safe if you kept him with you—anyone attacks you he'll talk them to death."

"He just likes to imagine I'm sixteen and he's both my parents," I said with more indulgence than I felt. Owing my life to Mr. Contreras didn't keep me from finding him a little wearing.

I offered Kappelman a drink. His first choice was beer, which I rarely have in the house, followed by bourbon. I finally unearthed a bottle of that from the back of my liquor cupboard.

"An old South Sider like you ought to be ready with a shot and a beer," he grumbled.

"I guess it's just one more sign of how much I've abandoned my roots." I took him into the living room, folding up the blanket I'd left on the couch so he could sit there. My place was never going to be the equal of his Pullman showcase, but at least it was neat. I didn't get any compliments, but then he couldn't be expected to know how it usually looked.

After a few polite nothings about my health and his day, I handed Nancy's packet to him. He pulled a pair of glasses from the breast pocket of his shabby jacket and carefully went through the document a page at a time. I sipped my whiskey and read the day's papers, trying not to fidget.

When he'd finished he put his glasses away with a little gesture of puzzled helplessness. "I don't know why Nance had these. Or why she thought they might have been important."

I gritted my teeth. "Don't tell me they're completely meaningless."

"I don't know." He hunched a shoulder. "You can see what they are as easily as I can. I don't know that much about insurance, but it looks as though Xerxes might have been paying more than these other guys and Jurshak was trying to persuade the company"—he looked at the document searching for the name—"Mariners Rest to lower their rates. It obviously meant something to Nancy, but it sure doesn't to me. Sorry."

I scowled horribly, causing the kind of wrinkles they warn starlets against. "Maybe the point isn't the data but the fact that Jurshak handled the insurance. Maybe still does. He wouldn't be my first choice as either an agent or a fiduciary."

Ron smiled a little. "You can afford to be superior—you aren't trying to do business in South Chicago. Maybe Humboldt felt it was easier to go with the flow on Jurshak than use an independent agent. Or maybe it was genuine altruism, trying to give business to the community where he set up his plant. Jurshak wasn't very big in South Chicago, let alone the city, back in '63."

"Maybe." I swirled my glass, watching the golden liquid change to amber as it picked up the lamplight. Art and Gustav doing good for the good of the community as a whole. I could see it on a billboard, but not so easily in real life. But I'd grown up around Art so I followed revelations about him—deals that made him or his partner, Freddy Parma, a director —and insurance provider—for a local trucking company, a steel firm, a rail freight hauler, and other outfits. Campaign contributions flowed from these companies in a most gratifying stream. Mariners Rest Assurance Company might not know these things, but Ron Kappelman ought to.

"You're looking awfully sinister." Kappelman interrupted my reverie. "Like you think I'm an ax murderer."

"Just my coldhearted bitch expression. I was wondering how much you know about Art Jurshak's insurance business."

"You mean stuff like Mid-States Rail? Of course I do. Why do you—" He broke off mid-sentence, his eyes widening slightly. "Yes. In that light going to Jurshak for fiduciary assistance doesn't make much sense. You think Jurshak has something on Humboldt?"

"Could be the other way around. Could be Humboldt has something to cover up and he figures Jurshak is the man to do it for him."

I wished I knew if I could trust Kappelman—he shouldn't have needed me to spell that out for him. I took the documents back and looked at them broodingly.

After a pause Kappelman smiled at me quizzically. "How about dinner before I head south? You fit enough to go out?"

Real food. I thought I could make the effort. Just in case Kappelman was leading me back to my pals in the black raincoats, I went into the bedroom to get my gun. And make a call on the extension by my bed.

Young Art's mother answered the phone; her son still hadn't shown up, she told me in a worried whisper. Mr. Jurshak didn't know yet that he had disappeared, so she'd appreciate my keeping it quiet.

"If he shows up, or if you hear from him, make sure he gets in touch with me. I can't tell you how important it is that he do so." I hesitated, not sure whether melodrama would make her totally nonfunctional or guarantee her giving my message to her son. "His life may be in danger, but if I can talk to him, I think I can keep anything from happening to him."

She was starting to hiss questions at me in a strained whisper, but Big Art cut in behind her, wanting to know who she was talking to. She hung up hurriedly.

The longer young Art stayed away, the less I liked it. The kid didn't have any friends and he didn't have any street sense. I shook my head uselessly and stuck the Smith & Wesson into the waist of my jeans.

Kappelman was calmly reading *The Wall Street Journal* when I came back to the living room. He didn't look as though he'd been monitoring me on the phone, but if he was truly an evil creep, he'd be able to appear innocent. I gave up chewing on it.

"I have to tell Mr. Contreras I'm going out—otherwise, when he realizes I'm not up here he's going to call the cops and have you arrested for murdering me."

He made a fatalistic gesture. "I thought I'd left that kind of crap behind when I moved out of my mother's house. That's why I'm in Pullman—it was as far as I could reasonably get from Highland Park."

As I locked the dead bolt the phone started to ring. Thinking it might be young Art, I excused myself to Ron and went back into the apartment. Much to my astonishment it was Ms. Chigwell, in extreme distress. I braced myself, thinking she had called to upbraid me for driving her brother to attempt suicide. I tried a few awkward apologies.

"Yes, yes, it was very sad. But Curtis was never a strong character—it didn't surprise me. Nor that he wasn't able to do it successfully. I suspect he meant to be found—he left all the lights on in the garage, and he knew I would come in to see why. After all, he believes I drove him to it."

I blinked a little at the indulgent contempt in her voice. She surely wasn't phoning to assuage any putative guilt on my part. I asked an exploratory question.

"Well, really, it's just something—something very strange happened this afternoon." She was suddenly stumbling, losing her usual gruff assurance.

"Yes?" I said encouragingly.

"I know it's inconsiderate of me to bother you, when you just had such a terrible ordeal yourself, but you are an investigator, and it seemed to me you were a more proper person to go to than the police."

Another long pause. I lay down on the couch to ease the soreness between my shoulders.

"It's—well, it's Curtis. I'm sure he broke in here this afternoon."

That was sufficiently startling that I sat up again. "Broke in? I thought he lived with you!"

"He does, of course. But, well, I rushed him to the hospital when I found him on Tuesday. He wasn't very sick and they released him on Wednesday. He was terribly embarrassed, didn't want to face me over the breakfast table, and said he was going to stay with friends. And to be frank with you, Miss Warshawski, I was just as happy to be rid of him for a few days."

Kappelman came over to where I was sitting. He waved a note under my nose—he would be down with Mr. Contreras getting permission for my outing. I nodded abstractedly and asked Ms. Chigwell to continue.

She took a breath, audible across the lines. "Fridays are my day at the hospital, you know. I do volunteer work with elderly ladies who no longer —well, you don't want to hear about that now. But when I got back I knew the house had been broken into."

"And you called the police and stayed with a friend until they arrived?"

"No. No, I didn't. Because I realized almost immediately it had to be Curtis. Or that he had let someone in who wouldn't have known the house well enough not to create a disturbance."

Confusion was making me impatient. I interrupted to ask if any valuables were gone.

"Nothing like that. But you see, Curtis's medical notebooks are missing. I'd hidden them from him after he tried burning them, and that's why—" She broke off. "I'm explaining this so badly. It's why I hoped you would come, even though it's a great distance and you are most tired yourself. I feel sure that whatever Curtis was involved with down at the Xerxes plant that he didn't want to tell you is in those notebooks."

"Which are missing," I interjected shortly.

She gave the ghost of a laugh. "Only his copies. I kept the originals. I typed his notes up for him over the years. That's all that's missing. I never told him I kept all the original notebooks.

"You see—he had put the data in Father's old leather diaries, the ones he he had custom-bound for himself in London. It seemed—a kind of desecration to throw them out, but I knew Curtis would be horribly angry to think I was keeping them out of memory for Father. So I never told him."

I felt a little prickling along the base of my neck, that primitive adrenaline jolt that lets you know you're getting close to the saber-toothed tiger. I told her I'd be at her house within the hour.

28

The Golden Notebooks

Kappelman and Mr. Contreras had struck an uneasy truce over the grappa bottle. Ron got quickly to his feet when I came in, putting a stop to a long anecdote about how Mr. Contreras knew when he first saw him what a lightweight one of my old lovers had been. I explained glibly that I'd had an urgent SOS from an aunt of mine in the suburbs, one I couldn't ignore.

"Your aunt, doll? I thought you and her—" Mr. Contreras caught the look of steel in my eyes. "Oh, your aunt. Is she in some kind of trouble?"

"More just panicking over me," I said firmly. "But she's my mother's only surviving relative. She's old and I can't leave her hanging." It seemed wrong somehow to confuse the redoubtable Ms. Chigwell with my mother's mad Aunt Rosa, but you have to work with what's at hand.

Kappelman agreed with me politely—whether he believed me was another matter. He finished his grappa in a long swallow, winced as the raw alcohol hit his esophagus, and said he'd see me to my car. "Relatives are a trial, aren't they?" he added sardonically.

He waited patiently while I looked around the car for any obvious signs of bombs, then shut the door for me with an old-fashioned courtesy at variance with his bedraggled clothes.

The temperature had dropped some ten degrees, just below freezing. After the dull fog of the last few weeks, the sharper air braced me. A few snowflakes drifted into the windshield, but the roads were clear and I had a quick run out the Eisenhower to York Road.

Ms. Chigwell was waiting for me at the door, her gaunt fierce face unchanged for the trying events of the last few days. She thanked me unsmilingly for making the trip, but I was beginning to know her and could tell her rough manner wasn't meant to be as unfriendly as it appeared.

"I'm having a cup of tea. My brother keeps telling me it's a sign of weakness, turning to stimulants when one feels troubled, but I think I've proved to be tougher than him. Would you like a cup?"

One serving of tea a day was all the stimulus I could handle. Declining as politely as I could, I followed her into the living room. It presented a scene of cozy domesticity worthy of Harriet Beecher Stowe. A fire burning cleanly in the grate refracted rich colors in the silver tea service on a low table nearby. Ms. Chigwell gestured me to one of the chintz armchairs facing the fireplace.

"In my day young ladies did not have lives of their own outside the household," she said abruptly, pouring tea into a translucent china cup. "We were supposed to marry. My father was a doctor out here, when it was really a separate little town, not part of the city at all. I used to help him out. By the time I was sixteen I could've set a simple fracture, treated a lot of the fevers he saw. But when it came time for college and medical training, that was Curtis's role. After Father died in 1939, Curtis tried keeping up the practice. He wasn't much good at it, though; patients kept going elsewhere until finally he had to take a position at that plant."

She looked at me fiercely. "I see you're an active young woman, you do what you want, you don't take no for an answer. I wish I'd had your backbone at your age, that's all."

"Yes," I said gently. "But I had help. My mother ended up on her own in a strange country—she couldn't speak the language; the only thing she could do was sing. She almost died as a result, so she swore I would never be as helpless and scared as she was. Believe me, that makes a big difference. You're asking too much of yourself to think you should have done it all on your own."

Ms. Chigwell swallowed her tea in large gulps, her throat muscles working, her left hand clenching and unclenching. Finally she felt enough in command of herself to speak again.

"Well, as you can tell, I never married. My mother died when we were seventeen. I kept house for my father and then for Curtis. I even learned to type so I could help them with their work."

She smiled mirthlessly. "I didn't try to follow what Curtis did at that company he worked for. My father had been a great country doctor, a master diagnostician. I suspect all Curtis did was take people's temperatures when they felt ill to see if they had a legitimate excuse to leave work early. By 1955, when he started in with these detailed records of his, I no longer knew anything of what went on in the medical world—the changes were too vast from my childhood days. But I still knew how to type, so I typed whatever he brought home for me."

Her story made me shiver a little. And mutter a little word of thanks to my mother's spirit. Fierce, intense, prickly, she'd been difficult to live with, but my earliest memories included her strong belief in me and what I could achieve with my life.

Ms. Chigwell must have seen some of the thought in my face. "Don't pity me. I've had many fine moments in this life of mine. And I never indulge in self-pity—a far greater weakness than tea, and one Curtis is most subject to."

We sat quietly for a while. She poured herself a second cup and drank it in slow, measured sips, staring sightlessly into the fire. When she had finished she put the cup down with a decisive snap and moved the tray to one side.

"Well, I mustn't keep you with my maundering. You've come a great distance and I can tell you're in a fair amount of pain, even though you're trying to hide it."

She stood upright with only a slight effort. I copied her slowly and stiffly and followed her up the carpeted stairs to the second floor. The upper landing was lined with bookshelves. Clearly a great many of Ms. Chigwell's fine moments had come from books—there were easily a thousand of them, all neatly dusted and carefully aligned on their shelves. How she'd ever known something was amiss among this orderly infantry was amazing. It took someone axing my front door to bits for me to know I'd suffered a home invasion.

Ms. Chigwell nodded toward an open door on my right. "Curtis's study. I came in here last Monday evening because I smelled fire. He was trying to burn his notebooks in his waste can. An appalling idea, since the waste can was leather, and it, too, began to burn with a terrible odor. I knew then that whatever was bothering him had to do with those records. But I thought it would be most wrong of him to back away from the facts by destroying them."

I felt an uneasy sympathy for Curtis Chigwell, living with this battalion of rectitude. It would drive me to stronger stimulants than tea.

"Anyway, I took them, and hid them behind my boating books. Obviously a foolish mistake, since boating has always been my great love. It is the first place Curtis would have thought to look. But I believe he felt so humiliated by my catching him in the act, or perhaps so frightened about not being able to get rid of his guilty secret, that the next afternoon he tried killing himself."

I shook my head. So Max had been right in a way. By stirring up the Xerxes pot I'd put so much pressure on Chigwell that he'd felt he had no options left. It made me feel a little seasick. I followed Ms. Chigwell quietly down the hall, my feet sinking in the soft gray pile.

A room at the end held a profusion of flowering plants that absorbed the eye. This was Ms. Chigwell's sitting room, with a rocking chair, her knitting basket, and a serviceable old Remington on a small table. The books continued in here, in shelves that were built only to waist level, serving as platforms for the red and yellow and purple flowers.

She knelt in front of the shelf next to the typewriter and started pulling leather-bound volumes from it. They were old-fashioned diaries, bound in rich green, with Horace Chigwell, M.D., tooled in gold on each cover.

"I hated Curtis using Father's personal diaries, but there seemed no good reason for him not to. Of course the war—Hitler's war—put a stop to things like personally bound diaries, and Curtis never had his own. He coveted these terribly."

There were twelve altogether, covering a period of twenty-eight years. I flipped through them curiously. Dr. Chigwell had written in a prim, spidery hand. It looked neat on the page, all the letters carefully aligned, but it proved tough to read. The books seemed to be an inventory of the medical history of the Xerxes employees. At least I presumed the names spelled out in the difficult script were the employees'.

Sitting in a wicker straight-backed chair, I rummaged among the volumes until I found 1962—the year Louisa had started at Humboldt. I thumbed slowly through the names—they weren't presented in alphabetical order—but didn't see hers. In 1963, after she'd been there a year, she showed up near the end of the list as a white female, age seventeen, address on Houston. My mother's name leapt out at me—Gabriella Warshawski was the person to be notified in case of an emergency. Nothing about the baby, nothing about its father. Of course that didn't prove Chigwell hadn't known about Caroline—just that he hadn't put the information in his notebooks.

The rest of the entry seemed to be a series of notes in medical shorthand: "BP 110/72, Hgb 13, BUN 10, Bili 0.6, CR 0.7." I assumed "BP" was blood pressure but couldn't even begin to guess what the other letters meant. I asked Ms. Chigwell, but she shook her head.

"All this technical medicine is long after my time. My father never did any blood work—they didn't even know about typing blood in his day, let alone what they can do with it now. I suppose I was too bitter about not becoming a doctor to want to know anything."

I puzzled over the entries a few more minutes, but this was work for Lotty. I stacked the books. Time for me to do something I could understand: I asked her how the intruders had gotten into the house.

"I presume Curtis let them in," she said stiffly.

I leaned back in the chair and looked at her thoughtfully. Maybe no one had been in the house this afternoon. Maybe she was seizing the opportunity offered by her brother's disappearance to avenge herself for his bungling their father's practice all these years. Or perhaps in the confusion of the last few days she'd forgotten where she'd hidden the typed notes. She was, after all, nearly eighty.

I tried probing, but not very skillfully. She frowned ferociously.

"Young lady, please do not treat me like a senile old woman. I am in full possession of my faculties. I saw Curtis trying to burn his notes five days ago. I can even show you the spot where the wastebasket burned through to the carpet.

"Why he wanted to destroy them I have no idea. Nor why he should sneak in here to steal them. But both of these things occurred."

My face felt a little hot. I got up and told her I'd check out the premises. She was still a little frosty, but she took me on a tour of the house. Although she said she'd tidied any disarray among her books and silver, she hadn't vacuumed or dusted. After a painstaking search worthy of Sherlock Holmes, I did find traces of dried mud on the stairwell carpeting. I wasn't sure what that proved, but I could easily believe it wouldn't have come from Ms. Chigwell. None of the locks showed any sign of forcing.

I didn't think she should stay the night here alone—anyone who came in once in such a way could easily return, with or without her brother. And if they had seen me arrive, they might easily come back to demand why in ways that an old lady—however tough she might be—would be unable to withstand.

"No one is forcing me from my home. I grew up in this house and I am not leaving it now." She scowled at me fiercely.

I tried my best to dissuade her, but she was adamant. Either she was scared and didn't want to admit it, or she knew why her brother was so desperate to get his hands on the notebooks. But then she wouldn't have given the originals to me.

I shook my head in irritation. I was exhausted, my shoulders ached, my head was throbbing slightly where I'd been hit. If Ms. Chigwell wasn't telling the truth, tonight wasn't the night for me to figure it out—I needed to go to bed. As I was leaving, though, something else occurred to me.

"Who did your brother go to stay with?"

At that she looked a little embarrassed—she didn't know. "I was surprised when he said he was going to stay with friends, because he doesn't have any. He did get a call Wednesday afternoon about two hours after he got out of the hospital, and it was a little after that that he announced he was going away for a few days. But he left when I was doing my volunteer stint at the hospital, so I don't have any idea who might have come by for him."

Ms. Chigwell also had no idea who had called her brother. It had been a man, because she had picked up an extension at the same time Curtis had. Hearing a man say her brother's name, she'd immediately hung up. It was a pity, really, that her sense of moral rectitude had been too great for her to eavesdrop on her brother, but you can't have everything in an imperfect world.

It was close to eleven when I finally left. Looking back, I could see her gaunt frame silhouetted in the doorway. She lifted a hand in a formal gesture and shut the door.

29

Night Crawlers

I hadn't realized how tired I was until I got into my car. The pain in my shoulders returned in a wave that swept me back limply in the front seat. Little tears of hurt and self-pity pricked my eyelids. Quitters never win and winners never quit, I quoted my old basketball coach grimly. Play through the pain, not against it.

I rolled the car window down, my sore arm moving slowly to the commands of my brain. I sat for a while, watching the Chigwell house and the surrounding street, dozing a bit, finally deciding the indomitable old lady wasn't under surveillance before putting the car into gear and heading for home.

The Eisenhower is never really clear of traffic—trucks thunder into the city throughout the night, some people are getting off late-night shifts, others heading for the action that begins only after dark. I joined the sweep of anonymous vehicles at Hillside. The steady stream of lights, red from the cars, orange on the sides of the trucks, the rows of streetlamps stretching into the distance as far as the eye could see, made me feel isolated and alone. A little speck in the great universe of lights, an atom of dust who could merge with the mud of Dead Stick Pond without leaving a trace behind.

My fragmented mood stayed with me as I drove slowly along Belmont to my apartment on Racine. I was hoping with the bottom half of my mind that Mr. Contreras and Peppy would be up to greet me—the top half sternly said I didn't want the old man breathing down my neck all the time.

That secret yearning may have saved my life. I had paused outside Mr. Contreras's ground-floor apartment, putting down the diaries to tie my shoes, seeing if my presence might rouse the dog so that I'd have a little companionship before going to bed.

The silence on the other side of the door told me the apartment was empty. Peppy certainly would have made herself known when she heard me, and the old man would never leave her outside alone this late at night. I looked up the stairs, foolishly wondering if they might be waiting for me at the top.

My unconscious mind realized something was wrong. I forced myself to stand motionless, pushed my tired brain to thought. The upper stairwell lay in darkness. One landing light might burn out, but both in the same evening stretched coincidence too far. Since the well of the lobby was lighted, anyone coming up the steps to the second or third floor would stand well framed in a pool of light.

From the topmost landing came a faint murmuring, not the sound of Mr. Contreras talking to Peppy. Picking up the notebooks, I eased my way to the lobby floor. I tucked the stack under one arm, pulled the gun out, flipped the safety off. Turned to face the street. Crouching low, I opened the outer door and slid into the night.

No one shot at me. The only person on the street was a moody-looking young man who lived down the block. He didn't even glance at me as I hurried by him toward Belmont. I didn't want to take my car—if someone was waiting for me outside the apartment, they might be keeping an eye on my Chevy: let them think I was still hanging around. If someone was waiting. Maybe fear and fatigue were making me jump at fantastic interpretations of light and street sounds.

At Belmont I tucked the Smith & Wesson back into my jeans and flagged a cab to Lotty's apartment. It was only a mile or so away, but I was in no condition to walk that far tonight. I asked the cabby to wait until I knew whether anyone was going to let me in. In the helpful style of today's drivers, he snarled at me.

"You don't own me. I give you ride, not my service for life."

"Splendid." I pulled back the five I'd been about to hand him. "Then I'll pay you after I know whether I'm spending the night here."

He started shouting at me, but I ignored him and opened the passenger door. That prompted him to get physical; he turned full around in the seat and swung at me. I slammed the stack of journals down on his arm with all the force of the pent-up frustrations from the last few days.

"Bitch!" he snarled. "You leave. You get from my cab. I don't need your money."

I slid from the backseat, keeping a wary eye on him until he drove off with a great squealing of rubber. All I needed now was for Lotty to be away at an emergency or sleeping too soundly to hear the bell. But the gods had not ordained me to have a total season of disaster this evening. After a few minutes, while my nervous irritation grew, her voice twanged at me through the intercom.

"It's me, Vic. Can I come up?"

She met me at the door to her apartment wrapped in a bright red dressing gown, looking like a little Mandarin with her dark eyes blinking away sleep.

"I'm sorry, Lotty—sorry to wake you. I had to go out this evening. When I got home I thought there might be a reception committee waiting for me."

"If you want me to come with you to blaze away at a few muggers, the answer is emphatically no," she said sardonically. "But I am glad to see you had a little more care for your skin than to go after them by yourself."

I couldn't respond to her breezy mood. "I want to call the police. And I don't want to go back over to Racine until they've had a chance to check the place out."

"Very good indeed," Lotty said, amazed. "I begin even to think you might live to be forty."

"Thanks a bunch," I muttered at her, going to the phone. I didn't like turning tail, handing my problems over to someone else to solve. But refusing to get help just because Lotty was being sarcastic seemed stupid.

Bobby Mallory was home. Like Lotty, he was inclined to taunt me a little over going to him for help, but once he'd absorbed the facts his professional persona took over. He asked me a few crisp questions, then assured me he'd have a squad car there without lights before he left his house. Before hanging up, though, he couldn't keep from rubbing my nose in it.

"You just stay put now, Vicki. I can't believe you're letting the police handle police business, but remember—the last thing we want is for you to come bounding up and get in between us and a couple of hoods."

"Right," I said sourly. "I'll look at the morning papers to see how things turn out."

The line went dead in my ear. I spent the next hour or so moving restlessly around Lotty's sitting room. She tried at first to talk me into going to sleep in her spare bed, preparing hot milk with brandy for me, but she finally left me to myself.

"I need my sleep even if you don't, Victoria. I'm not going to lecture you on rest after your physical ordeal—if by now you don't know you should, no words of mine will have any effect. Just remember—your body is an aging organism. It will repair itself more and more slowly as time goes by, and the less help you give it, the less you will be able to rely on it."

I knew by the tone as much as the words that Lotty was truly angry, but I was too fragmented still to make any kind of response. She loves me; she was afraid I would put myself at such risk I would die and abandon her. I understood that; I just couldn't fix it tonight.

It was only when she'd shut her door with an angry snap that I remembered the Chigwell notebooks. Not the time to knock at her bedroom and ask for help in deciphering his medical shorthand. I drank some of the milk and lay down on the daybed with my boots off, but I couldn't relax. All I could think was that I had run scared from my problems, had turned to the police, and now I was waiting like some good old-fashioned damsel in distress for rescue.

It was too much. A little after midnight I pulled my boots back on. Leaving a note on the kitchen table for Lotty, I crept out of the apartment, quietly closing the door behind me. I started walking south, keeping to the main streets, hoping to find a cab. My restless energy held my fatigue at bay; when I got to Belmont I stopped looking for taxis and covered the last half mile at a brisk walk.

I'd been imagining the street filled with flashing blue-and-whites and uniformed men racing around. By the time I got home, however, any police activity had disappeared without a trace. I went cautiously into the lobby, crouching a little, hugging the walls out of range of the stairwell.

The upper-landing lights were on again. As I climbed the first half flight, going sideways with my back sliding along the wall, Mr. Contreras's apartment door opened. Peppy bounded out, followed by the old man.

When he saw me tears started streaming down his cheeks. "Oh, doll, thank God you're all right. The cops was here, they wouldn't tell me nothing, wouldn't let me into your place or tell me if they knew where you was. What happened to you? Where you been?"

After a few disjointed minutes we got our stories out. Around ten-thirty someone had called him, telling him I was down in my office and in bad shape. It didn't occur to him to summon help or ask himself who the strange phone caller was. Instead he bundled Peppy up, bullied a passing cab into taking both of them, and hurled himself downtown. He'd never been to my office, so he'd wasted some time finding the place. When he saw that the door was locked and the lights out, he'd been too impatient to find the night watchman: he'd used his trusty pipe wrench to break the lock.

"I'm sorry, doll," he said dolefully. "I'll fix it for you in the morning. If I'd been using my head, I guess I would've known it was someone trying to get me and the dog out of the way."

I nodded abstractedly. Someone was keeping close enough tabs on me to know that my downstairs neighbor would be watching if they set up an ambush. Ron Kappelman. Who else had seen Mr. Contreras at such close quarters?

"Did the police find anyone here?" I asked abruptly.

"They took a couple of guys away in a paddy wagon, but I didn't get any kind of look at them. I couldn't even do that for you. They came gunning for you and they got me out of the way with a cheap trick that wouldn't of fooled a six-year-old. And then me not knowing where'd you'd gone off to or nothing. I knew it couldn't be your aunt, not after what you told me about her and your ma, but I just didn't have any idea where you could be."

It took me awhile to get him calmed down enough that he would let me spend the night alone. After a few more rehearsals of worry and self-reproach, he finally saw me up the stairs to my apartment. Someone had tried breaking into my apartment, but the steel-lined door I'd had installed after my last home invasion had held. They couldn't cut through it, and they hadn't been able to get by my third dead bolt. Even so I made a thorough tour of the premises with Mr. Contreras and the dog. He left her with me, waiting outside until he heard the last bolt slide home before going downstairs to his own bed.

I tried calling Bobby at the Central District, but he'd disappeared—or didn't want to take my call. None of the other officers I knew were in and the ones I didn't know wouldn't tell me anything about the men they'd picked up at my place. I had to give it a rest until morning.

30

Fence Mending

I was being buried alive. An executioner wearing a black plastic hood poured dirt on me. "Just tell us the time, girlie," he said. Lotty and Max Loewenthal sat nearby eating asparagus and drinking cognac, ignoring my helpless screams. I woke from the dream sweating and panting, but every time I went back to sleep the nightmare returned.

When I finally got up for good it was late morning. I was stiff and sore, my head filled with the cotton wool an uneasy night always leaves behind. I moved on thick, ungainly legs to the bathroom. With Peppy watching anxiously from the doorway, I soaked in the tub for a long while.

It had to be Kappelman who'd arranged for last night's ambush. He was the only one who knew I was leaving my apartment, the only one who knew the anxious care Mr. Contreras lavished on me. But try as I might, I couldn't think why he'd do it.

It wasn't beyond belief to think he might have murdered Nancy. Love affairs gone awry bring at least one person a day to Twenty-sixth and California. But a crime of passion had nothing to do with me. All my machinations about Humboldt, about why Pankowski and Ferraro had sued the company, about Chigwell didn't seem to connect with Ron Kappelman. Unless he knew something he was desperate to keep hidden about Jurshak's insurance file. But what could his involvement had been with them?

It was easier to think that Art Jurshak had staged last night's aborted attack. After all, he could have drawn the old man off without knowing I wasn't at home, then decided to lie in wait until I got back. My mind churned fruitlessly. The water grew cold, but I didn't stir until the telephone began to ring. It was Bobby, brighter and more alert than I could tolerate in my febrile state.

"Dr. Herschel says you left her in the middle of the night. I thought I told you to stay away from your apartment until we gave you the all-clear."

"I didn't want to wait for the Second Coming of Christ. Who did you find at my place last night?"

"Watch your language around me, young lady," Bobby said automatically—he doesn't think nice girls should talk like hard-boiled dicks. And even though he knows half the reason I do it is to ride him, he can't resist rising to the bait. Before I could put in my two cents about not being a subaltern he could order about—there are baits I also can't resist—he hurried on.

"We picked up two guys hanging around your door. They say they'd just come upstairs for a smoke, but they both had picklocks and guns. The state's attorney got us twenty-four hours with them on concealed and unregistered felony weapons. We want you to come down to a lineup—see if you can identify either of these gents as being involved in Wednesday's attack on you."

"Yeah, I guess," I said unenthusiastically. "They had black slickers on, the kind with hoods that cover a lot of the face. I'm not sure I'd ever recognize them again."

"Great." Bobby ignored my lack of ardor. "I'll have a uniformed man pick you up in half an hour—unless that's too early for you."

"Like Justice, I never sleep," I said politely, and hung up.

Murray phoned next. They'd put the morning edition to bed before word of an arrest outside my place had come in from one of his police snitches. His boss, knowing of our relationship, had woken him with the news. Murray pumped away with tireless energy for several minutes. Finally I cut him off crossly:

"I'm going down to look at a lineup. If either Art Jurshak or Dr. Chigwell's sister is there, I'll give you a call back. Which reminds me—the good doctor has gone off with the kind of guys who like to break into other people's houses."

I hung up on his squawk. The phone rang again as I was stomping into the bedroom to get dressed. I chose to ignore it—let Murray get his news from public radio or something. As I was brushing my hair with surly ill will, Mr. Contreras brought breakfast to the door. My last night's desire for his companionship had worn off. I drank a cup of coffee ungraciously and told him I didn't have time to eat. When he started fussing over me I lost my temper and snapped at him.

A hurt look came into his faded brown eyes. He collected the dog with quiet dignity and left. I immediately felt ashamed of myself and ran after him. He'd already reached the lobby, though, and I didn't have my keys with me. I headed back up the stairs.

While I was gathering my keys and my handbag, sticking the Smith & Wesson into my jeans, the uniformed man arrived to take me down to the lineup. I carefully locked the dead bolt behind me—some days I don't bother with it—and ran down the stairs. Soonest started, soonest ended, or whatever it was Lady Macbeth said.

The uniformed man turned out to be a woman, Patrol Officer Mary Louise Neely. She was quiet and serious, holding herself ramrod straight in her fiercely pressed navy serge, calling me "ma'am" in a way that made me acutely aware of the twelve or more years between us. She opened the door for me with military crispness and ushered me down the walk to the waiting patrol car.

Mr. Contreras was out in front with Peppy. I wanted to make some gesture of reconciliation, but Officer Neely's stern presence robbed me of any words. I held out a hand, but he nodded stiffly to me, calling the dog sharply as she headed down the walk behind me.

I tried asking the patrolwoman insightful questions about her work and whether the Cubs or the Sox could worsen their abysmal performance of last season. She snubbed me completely, though, keeping her stern gaze on malefactors on Lake Shore Drive, murmuring periodically into her lapel transmitter.

We covered the six miles to the Central District at a good clip. She pulled smartly into the police lot about fifteen minutes after leaving my apartment. Okay, it was Saturday, not much traffic, but it was still an impressive performance.

Neely whisked me through the labyrinth of the old building, exchanging unsmiling greetings with fellow officers, and brought me to an observation room. Bobby was there, with Sergeant McGonnigal and Detective Finchley. Neely saluted them so sharply, I thought she might keel over backward.

"Thanks, Officer." Bobby dismissed her genially. "We'll carry on from here."

I found my palms sweating slightly, my heart beating a little faster. I didn't want to see the men who'd bundled me into that blanket on Wednesday. That was why I'd fled my place last night. They had me well and truly spooked. And now I was to perform like an obedient dog under the watchful eyes of the police?

"You got names on the two you picked up?" I asked, keeping my tone cool, trying to shade it with a little arrogance.

"Yeah," Bobby grunted. "Joe Jones and Fred Smith. They're almost as funny to deal with as you are. And yes, we've requested a print check, but these things never happen as fast as you hope they will. We can make a case on the loitering in a private building and carrying concealed unregistered weapons. But you know and I know they'll be on the street Monday unless we can back it up with attempted murder. So you're to tell me if they're your pals who sent you swimming on Wednesday."

He nodded to Finchley, a black plainclothesman I'd known when he started on patrol. The detective went to a door across the room and gave orders to unseen people beyond to start the lineup.

Eyewitness identification is not the great revelation they make of it in courtroom dramas. Under stress the memory plays tricks on you—you're sure you saw a tall black man in blue jeans and it was really a fat white man in a business suit. Stuff like that. Probably a third of my presentations as a public defender had been based on reciting remarkable instances of mistaken identity. On the other hand, stress can burn some indelible memories—a gesture, a birthmark—that come back when you see the person again. It never hurts to try.

Keeping my hands in my pockets so as to hide their tremor, I walked with Bobby to the one-way observation window. McGonnigal turned out the lights on our side and the little room beyond sprang into relief.

"We've got two sets for you," Bobby murmured in my ear. "You know the routine—take your time, ask for any of them to turn around or whatever."

Six men walked in with self-conscious pugnacity. They all looked alike to me—white, burly, somewhere around forty. I tried to imagine them with black hoods, the executioner of my nightmare this morning.

"Ask them to talk," I said abruptly. "Ask them to say 'Just tell us the time, girlie' and then 'Dump her here, Troy. X marks the spot.'"

Finchley conveyed the request to the unseen officers running the show. One by one the men obediently mumbled their lines. I kept watching the second guy from the left. He had a kind of secretive smile—he knew they'd never make a serious charge stick. His eyes. Could I remember the eyes of the man who'd come up to me at the edge of the lagoon? Cold, flat, calculating his words to find my weaknesses.

But when this man spoke I didn't recognize the voice. It was husky, with the twang of the South Side, not the emotionless tones I remembered.

I shook my head. "I think it's the second guy from the left. But I don't recognize the voice and I can't be absolutely certain."

Bobby nodded fractionally and Finchley gave orders to dismiss the lineup.

"Well?" I demanded. "Is he the one?"

The lieutenant smiled reluctantly. "I thought it was a long shot, but he's the guy we picked up outside your front door last night. I don't know if your ID is strong enough for the state's attorney. But maybe we can find out who puts up bond for him."

They brought in the second lineup, a parade of black men. I'd seen only one of my attackers close up. Even though I presumed Troy was one of the men in front of me, I couldn't pick him out, even with a voice check.

Bobby was in high good humor with my ID of the first man. He ran me genially through the paperwork and got Officer Neely to take me home, sending me off with a pat on the arm and a promise of telling me when the first court date would be.

My own mood wasn't nearly as pleasant. When Neely had dropped me at my apartment I went up to change into running shoes. I wasn't up for a run yet, but I needed a long walk to clear my brain before seeing little Caroline this afternoon.

First, though, I had to mend a few fences. Mr. Contreras received me coolly, trying to mask his hurt feelings under a veneer of formality. But subtlety wasn't really part of his makeup. He unbent after a few minutes, told me he would never come up to my apartment again without phoning first, and fried up some eggs and bacon for lunch. I sat talking with him afterward, curbing my impatience at the long flow of irrelevant reminiscence. Anyway, the longer he talked the longer I could put off facing a tougher conversation. At two, though, I figured I'd avoided Lotty long enough and set off for Sheffield.

Lotty wasn't as easy to kiss and make up with. She was home in between her morning clinic hours and an afternoon concert with Max. We talked in the kitchen while she whipped tiny stitches into the hem of a black skirt. At least she didn't slam the door on me.

"I don't know how many times I have patched you up in the last ten years, Victoria. Many. And almost every time a life-threatening situation. Why do you value yourself so little?"

I stared at the floor. "I don't want anyone solving my problems for me."

"But you came here last night. You involved me in your problems, and then you disappeared without a word. That isn't independence—that is thoughtless cruelty. You must make up your mind about what you want with me. If it is just to be your doctor—the person who patches you up when you've decided to run your head in front of a bullet—fine. We will go to such cold encounters. But if you want to be friends, you cannot behave with such careless disregard for my feelings for you. Can you understand that?"

I rubbed my head tiredly. Finally I looked at her. "Lotty, I'm scared. I've never been this frightened, not since the day my dad told me Gabriella was dying and nothing could be done for her. I knew then that it was a terrible mistake to depend on someone else to solve my problems for me. Now I seem to be too terrorized to solve them for myself and I'm thrashing around. But when I ask for help it just drives me wild. I know it's hard on you. I'm sorry for that. But I can't get enough distance right now to do anything about it."

Lotty finished pulling the thread through her hem and put the skirt down. She gave a wry little smile. "Yes. It is not an easy thing to lose one's mother, is it? Could we make a little compromise, my dear? I won't demand of you responses you can't make. But when you find yourself in this state, will you tell me, so that I am not making myself so angry with you?"

I nodded a few times, my throat too tight for me to speak. She came over to me and held me close to her. "You are the daughter of my heart, Victoria. I know it's not the same as having Gabriella, but the love is there."

I smiled shakily. "In your fierceness you're two of a kind."

After that I told her about the notebooks I'd left behind. She promised to look at them on Sunday, to see if she could make anything of them.

"And now I must dress, my dear. But why not come spend the night here? Maybe we'll both feel a little better."

31

Old Fireball

When I got back to my apartment I stopped to tell Mr. Contreras I was home and let him know Caroline would be arriving soon. My conversation with Lotty had done something to restore my equilibrium. I felt calm enough to abandon my plan for a walk in favor of a little housekeeping.

The partially cooked chicken I'd stashed in the refrigerator Tuesday night had become pretty rank. I carried it down to the garbage can in the alley, scrubbed the refrigerator with soda to deaden the smell, and bundled my newspapers out front for the recycling team to pick up. By the time Caroline arrived a little after four, I'd paid all my December bills and had organized the receipts for my tax returns. I was also feeling all my sore muscles.

Caroline came quietly up the stairs, smiling a little nervously. She followed me into the living room, turning down my offer of refreshments in a soft, breathy voice. I couldn't remember ever seeing her so ill at ease.

"How's Louisa doing?" I asked.

She made a throwaway gesture. "She seems stable right now. But kidney failure leaves you pretty depressed—it seems dialysis only gets a fraction of impurities out of the system, so you're always feeling nightmarish."

"Did you tell her about the call you got—about Joey Pankowski being your father?"

She shook her head. "I haven't told her anything. About your looking for him or—or, well, about anything. I had to let her know Nancy was dead, of course—she would have seen it on TV or heard it from her sister. But she can't take any more upsets like that."

She played nervously with the fringe on one of the sofa cushions, then burst out, "I wish I'd never asked you to find my father for me. I don't know what magic I thought you could work. And I don't know why I thought finding him would alter my life in any way." She gave a harsh little laugh. "What am I saying? Just having you look for him has changed my life."

"Could we talk about that a little?" I asked gently. "Someone called you two weeks ago and told you to chase me away, didn't they? That was when you phoned me with that incredible rigmarole about not wanting me to look for your father."

Her head was bent down so far all I could see was her wild copper curls. I waited patiently. She would not have made the trek up to Lakeview if she hadn't decided to tell me the truth—it was just taking her some time to give her courage the last screw.

"It's the mortgage," she finally whispered to her feet. "We rented for years and years. Then when I started working we could finally save enough to make a down payment. I got a call. A man—I don't know who he was. He said—he said—he'd been looking into our loan. He thought—he told me—they would cancel it if I didn't make you stop looking for my father —stop you from asking all those questions about Ferraro and Pankowski."

At last she looked up at me, her freckles standing out sharply from the pallor of her face. She held out her hands beseechingly and I moved from my chair to put my arms around her. For a few minutes she nestled against me, trembling, as though she were still little Caroline and I was the big kid who could save her from any danger.

"Did you call the bank?" I asked her presently. "See if they knew anything about it?"

"I was afraid if they heard me asking questions, they might do it, you know." Her voice was muffled against my armpit.

"What bank is it?"

She sat up at that and looked at me in alarm. "You're not going to go talk to them about it, Vic! You mustn't!"

"I may know someone who works there, or someone on the board," I said patiently. "If I find I can't ask a few questions very discreetly, I promise not to paw up the dirt. Okay? Anyway, it's a pretty good bet that it's Ironworkers Savings & Loan—that's where everyone in the neighborhood has always gone."

Her big eyes searched my face anxiously. "It is, Vic. But you have to promise, really promise, you won't do anything that will jeopardize our mortgage. It would kill Ma if something like that happened now. You know it would."

I nodded solemnly and gave my word. I didn't think she was exaggerating the affect on Louisa of any kind of major disturbance. As I thought about Caroline's frantic response to the threat on her mother, something else occurred to me.

"When Nancy was murdered you told the police I knew why she'd been killed. Why did you do that? Was it because you really wanted me to keep an eye on you and Louisa?"

She blushed violently. "Yes. But it didn't do me any good." Her voice was barely a squeak.

"You mean they did it? Cut off your mortgage?"

"Worse. They—they somehow figured out—I'd gone to you about her murder. They called me again. At least it was the same man. And said if I didn't want to see Ma's medical benefits cut off, I'd better get you away from South Chicago. So I was really scared then. I tried my best, and when this man called me back I told him—told him I couldn't—couldn't stop you, that you were on your own."

"So they decided to stop me themselves." My throat was dry; my own voice came out harshly.

She looked at me fearfully. "Can you forgive me, Vic? When I saw the news, saw what happened to you, it shattered me. But if I had to do it again, I'd have to do it the same way. I couldn't let them hurt Ma. Not after everything she went through for me. Not with all her suffering now."

I got up and paced angrily to the window. "Didn't it occur to you, if you told me I could do something about it? Protect her and you? Instead of running blind, so that I almost got killed myself?"

"I didn't think you could," she said simply. "When I asked you to find my father I was still imagining you were my big sister, that you could solve all my problems for me. Then I saw you weren't as powerful as I'd imagined you to be. It was just, with Ma so sick and everything, I needed someone so badly to look after me, and I thought maybe you'd still be that person."

Her statement dissipated my anger. I came back to the couch and smiled wryly at her. "I think you've finally grown up, Caroline. That's what it is all right—no big people to clean up all the mess around us. But even if I'm not still the kid who could whip the neighborhood to save your butt, I'm not totally ineffective. I think it's possible to tidy some of the garbage floating around on this one."

She gave a shaky smile. "Okay, Vic. I'll see if I can help you."

I went to the dining room and pulled a bottle of Barolo from the liquor cupboard. Caroline rarely drank, but the heavy wine helped steady her. We talked for a while, not about our current problems, but general things—whether Caroline really wanted a law degree if she didn't have to play catch-up with me. After a glass or two we both felt able to return to the discussion at hand.

I told her about Pankowski and Ferraro and the conflicting reports on their suit against Humboldt Chemical. "I don't know what that has to do with Nancy's death. Or with the attack on me. But it was when I found out about it and started questioning people about them that someone threatened me."

She listened to a detailed report on my encounters with Dr. Chigwell and his sister, but she couldn't shed any light on the blood work he'd kept on Xerxes employees.

"This is the first I ever heard about it. You know the kind of person Ma is—if they sent her in for a medical exam every year, she did it without thinking about it. A lot of things people told her to do on the job didn't make any sense to her, and this would be one of them. I can't believe it has anything to do with Nancy's death."

"Okay. Let's try another one. Why did Xerxes buy their insurance through Art? Is Jurshak still the fiduciary on their life-health stuff? Why was it important enough to Nancy that she was carrying it around?"

Caroline shrugged. "Art keeps a pretty tight grip on a number of the businesses down there. He might have gotten their insurance in exchange for a tax break or something. Of course when Washington was elected Art didn't have as many favors to hand out, but he still can do a lot for a company if they do something for him."

I pulled Jurshak's report to Mariners Rest from Mozart's *Concert Arias* and handed it to Caroline. She frowned over it for several minutes.

"I don't know anything about insurance," she finally said. "All I can tell you is that Ma's benefits have been first-class. I don't know about any of these other companies."

Her words triggered an elusive memory. Something someone had said to me in the last few weeks about Xerxes and insurance. I frowned, trying to drag it the surface, but I couldn't get hold of it.

"It meant something to Nancy," I said impatiently. "What? Did she collect data on health and mortality rates for any of these companies? Maybe she had some way of checking the accuracy of this report." Maybe the report didn't mean anything. But then why had Nancy been carrying it around?

"Yes. She did track all these health statistics—she was the director of Health and Environmental Services."

"So let's go down to SCRAP and check her files." I got up and started hunting for my boots.

Caroline shook her head. "Nancy's files are gone. The police impounded what she had in her desk, but someone had cleaned out her health files before the cops got them. We just assumed she'd taken them home with her."

My anger returned in a rush, fueled by disappointment: I was sure we'd reached a break in the case. "Why the hell didn't you tell the police that two weeks ago? Or me! Don't you see, Caroline? Whoever killed her took her papers. We could have been looking exclusively at people involved in these companies, instead of trailing around after vengeful lovers and all that crap!"

She heated up just as fast. "I told you at the time she was killed because of her work! You just were on your usual fucking arrogant head trip and wouldn't pay any attention to me!"

"You said it was because of the recycling plant, which this has nothing to do with. And anyway, why didn't you tell me that her files had disappeared?"

We went at it like a couple of six-year-olds, both venting our fury over the threats and humiliations of the past few weeks. I don't know how we would have extricated ourselves from the escalating insults if we hadn't been interrupted by the buzzer outside my front door. I left Caroline in the living room and stormed to the entrance.

Mr. Contreras was standing there. "I don't mean to be butting in, cookie," he said apologetically, "but this young fella's been ringing the lobby bell for the last couple of minutes and you two was so wrapped up, I thought maybe you couldn't hear him."

Young Art trailed in behind Mr. Contreras. His square, chiseled face was flushed and his auburn hair disheveled. He was biting his lips, clenching and unclenching his hands, in so much turmoil that his usual beauty was obscured. The family resemblance I saw in his distraught face staggered me so much that it muffled my surprise at seeing him.

I finally said weakly, "What are you doing here? Where have you been? Did your mother send you?"

He cleared his throat, trying to speak, but he couldn't seem to get any words out.

Mr. Contreras, his promise not to breathe down my neck still present in his mind, didn't linger to issue his usual unsubtle threats against my male visitors. Or maybe he'd summed up Art and figured he didn't need to worry.

When the old man had left Art finally spoke. "I need to talk to you. It—

things are worse than I thought." His voice came out in a squawky little whisper.

Caroline came to the living-room door to see what the uproar was about. I turned to her and said as gently as I could, "This is young Art Jurshak, Caroline. I don't know if you've ever met, but he's the alderman's son. He's got something confidential he needs to tell me. Can you call some of your pals at SCRAP, see if any of them know anything about this report Nancy was carrying around with her?"

I was afraid she was going to argue with me, but my stunned mood got across to her. She asked if I was all right, if it was okay to leave me with young Art. When I reassured her she went back to the living room for her coat.

She stopped briefly at the door on her way out and said in a small voice, "I didn't mean all those things I was saying. I came here to get back on good terms with you, not to shout like that."

I rubbed her shoulders gently. "It's okay, fireball—it goes with the territory. I said some stupid things myself. Let's forget it."

She gave me a quick hug and took off.

32

Flushed Out of the Pocket

I took Art into the living room and poured him a glass of the Barolo. He gulped it down. Water would probably have been just as good under the circumstances.

"Where have you been hiding? Do you know every beat cop in Chicago is carrying your description? Or that your mother's going crazy?" They weren't the questions I really wanted to ask, but I couldn't figure out how to frame those.

His lips stretched in a nervous parody of his usual beautiful smile. "I was at Nancy's. I figured no one would look there."

"Hn-unh." I shook my head. "You've been gone since Monday night and I was at Nancy's on Tuesday with Mrs. Cleghorn."

"I spent Monday night in my car. Then I figured no one would be bothering with Nancy's house. I—I could see it had been torn up pretty good. It's been kind of spooky, but I knew I'd be safe there since they'd already searched it."

"Who's 'they'?"

"The people who killed Nancy."

"And who are they?" I felt as though I was interrogating a jug of molasses.

"I don't know," he muttered, looking away.

"But you can guess," I prodded. "Tell me about the insurance your father manages for Xerxes. What was Nancy's interest in it?"

"How did you get those papers?" he whispered. "I called my mother this morning, I knew she'd be worried, and she said you had been by. My —my old man—Big Art had found the card you left and really blown sky high, she said. He was screaming that—that if he got his hands on me, he'd see I remembered never to betray him again. That's why I came here. To see what you know. See if you can help me."

I looked at him sourly. "I've been trying to get you to tell me a few things for the last two weeks and you've been acting as though English was your second language and you weren't too fluent in it."

He scrunched up his face in misery. "I know. But when Nancy died I was so afraid. Afraid my old man had something to do with it."

"Why didn't you run away then? Why wait until I talked to you?"

He flushed an even deeper red. "I thought maybe no one would know— know the connection. But if you saw it, anyone could."

"Like the police, you mean? Or Big Art?" When he didn't answer I said with what patience I could muster, "Okay. Why did you come here today?"

"I called my mother this morning. I knew my old man would be at a meeting, that I could count on him not being home. The slate-makers, you know." He smiled unhappily. "With Washington dead, they were all getting together this morning to plan for the election. Dad—Art—might miss a Council meeting, but he wouldn't stay away from that.

"Anyway, Mother told me about you. About how you'd been around but then you'd almost ended up the same—the same way as Nancy. I couldn't stay in her place forever, there was hardly any food anyway and I was scared to turn on the lights at night in case someone saw and came into inspect. And if they were going to go after anyone who knew about Nancy and the insurance, I figured I'd better get help or I'd be dead."

I curbed my impatience as best I could. It was going to be a long afternoon, getting information from him. The questions that were really burning my tongue—about his family—would have to wait until I could pry his story from him.

The first thing I wanted to clear up was his relationship with Nancy. Since he had let himself into her house he couldn't very well keep denying they'd been lovers. And the story came out, sweet, sad, and stupid.

He and Nancy had met a year before on a community project. She was representing SCRAP, he the alderman's office. She'd attracted him immediately—he'd always liked older women who had her kind of looks and warmth and he'd wanted to go out with her right away. But she'd put him off with one excuse or another until a few months ago. Then they'd started dating and had rapidly moved to a full-blown affair. He'd been deliriously happy. She was warm, loving—on and on.

"So why didn't anyone know about it if you were both so happy?" I asked. I could just see it, barely. When he wasn't shredding himself with misery his incredible beauty made you want to touch him. Maybe it was enough for Nancy, maybe she thought the aesthetics of it compensated for his immaturity. She might have been cold-blooded enough to want him as a conduit to the alderman's office, but I didn't think so.

He shifted uncomfortably. "My dad always raved on so much against SCRAP, I knew he'd hate it if I was dating someone who worked there. He felt they were trying to take over the ward from him, you know, always criticizing things like the broken sidewalks in South Chicago and the un-employment and stuff. It's not his fault, you know, but when Washington got in charge, you didn't see a penny going to the white ethnic neighbor-hoods."

I opened my mouth to argue the point, then shut it again. South Chi-cago had begun its demise under the late great Mayor Daley and had been assiduously ignored by Bilandic and Byrne alike. And Art, Sr., had been alderman all that time. But fighting such a war wasn't going to do me any good this afternoon.

"So you didn't want him to know. And Nancy didn't want her friends to know about you, either. Same reason?"

He squirmed again. "I don't think so. I think—she was a little bit older than me, you know. Only ten years. Well, almost eleven. But I think she was afraid people would laugh at her if they knew she was seeing someone so young."

"Okay. So it was a big secret. Then she came to you three weeks ago to see if Art was opposed to the recycling plant. What happened then?"

He reached nervously for the wine bottle and poured the last of the Barolo into his glass. When he'd gulped most of it down he started spitting out the story, a bit at a time. He knew Art was against the recycling plant. His dad was working hard to bring new industry to South Chicago, and he was afraid a recycling plant would put some companies off—that they wouldn't want to operate in a community where they had to go to the extra trouble of putting their wastes in drums for recycling instead of just dumping them into lagoons.

He'd told Nancy that and she had insisted on seeing any files about the project. Apparently, like me, she'd figured it wasn't worth arguing whether Art, Sr.'s, professed reasons were the real ones.

Young Art hadn't wanted to do it, but she'd pushed hard. They went back to the insurance office late one night and she went through Art's desk. It was horrible, the most horrible night he'd ever spent, worrying about his father or his father's secretary coming in on them, or one of the beat cops seeing a light and surprising them.

"I understand. The first time you break and enter is always the hardest. But why did Nancy choose this insurance file over something about recycling?"

He shook his head. "I don't know. She was looking for anything with the names of any of the companies involved in the recycling plant on it. And then she saw these papers and said she didn't know we—my dad's agency—handled Xerxes's insurance, and then she read through them and said this was hot stuff, she'd better copy it and take it along. So she went down the hall to use the machine. And Big Art came in."

"Your father saw her?" I gasped.

He nodded miserably. "He had Steve Dresberg with him. Nancy ran, but she scattered the originals all over the floor. So they knew she was copying them."

"And what did you do?"

His face disappeared into a little ball of such abject shame that I felt almost sorry for him. "They never knew I was there. I hid in my own office with the lights off."

I didn't know what to say. That he could have abandoned Nancy to her fate. That he knew Dresberg had been there with his old man. And at the same time the logical part of my mind began worrying about the problem: Was it the insurance papers or was it the fact that Nancy had seen Art with Dresberg? It wasn't surprising that the alderman had ties to the Garbage King. But it was understandable that he kept them quiet.

"Don't you understand?" I finally cried out, my voice close to a howl. "If you'd said something about your father and Dresberg last week, we might have gotten somewhere in investigating Nancy's death. Don't you care anything about finding her killers?"

He stared at me through tragic blue eyes. "If it was your father, would you want to know—really know—he was doing that kind of thing? Anyway, he already thinks I'm such a failure. What would he think if I turned him in to the cops? He'd say I was siding with SCRAP and the Washington faction against him."

I shook my head to see if that would clear my brain, but it didn't seem to help any. I tried speaking, but every sentence I started ended in a few sputtered words. Finally I asked weakly what he wanted me to do.

"I need help," he muttered.

"You ain't kidding, boy. But I don't know if even a Michigan Avenue analyst could do anything for you, and I'm damned sure I can't."

"I know I'm not very tough. Not like you or—or Nancy. But I'm not an imbecile, either. I don't need you making fun of me. I can't fix this myself.

I need help and I thought since you'd been a friend of hers you might . . ." His voice trailed off.

"Rescue you?" I finished sardonically. "Okay. I'll help you. In exchange for which I want some information about your family."

He looked wildly at me. "My family? What's that got to do with anything?"

"Just tell me. It's got nothing to do with you. What was your mother's maiden name?"

"My mother's maiden name?" he repeated stupidly. "Kludka. Why do you want to know?"

"It wasn't Djiak? You never heard of that?"

"Djiak? Of course I know the name. My father's sister married some guy named Ed Djiak. But they moved to Canada before I was born. I've never met them—I wouldn't even have heard of Dad's sister if I hadn't seen the name on a letter when I joined the agency—when I asked my father he told me about it—said they'd never gotten along and she'd cut the connection. Why do you want to know about them?"

I didn't answer him. I felt so nauseated that I leaned my head over onto my knees. When Art had come in with his face all flushed, his auburn hair wildly standing around his head, his resemblance to Caroline had been so strong that they might have been twins. He'd gotten his red hair from his father. Caroline took after Louisa. Of course. How simple. How simple and how horrifying. All the same genes. All in the same family. I just hadn't wanted to begin thinking such a thing when I saw them side by side. Instead I'd been trying to work out some way Art's wife could be related to Caroline.

My conversation with Ed and Martha Djiak three weeks earlier came back to me in full force. And with Connie. How her uncle liked to come around and have Louisa dance for him. Mrs. Djiak knew. What had she said? "Men have difficulty controlling themselves." But that it was Louisa's fault—that she'd led him on.

My gorge rose so violently, I thought I would choke. Blame her. Blame their fifteen-year-old daughter when it was her own brother who got her pregnant? My one thought was to get out of here, to get down to East Side with my gun and beat the Djiaks until they admitted the truth.

I got up, but the room swam darkly in front of me. I sat back down again, steadying myself, becoming aware of young Art talking frightenedly in the chair across from me.

"I told you what you asked. Now you've got to help me."

"Yeah, right. I'll help you. Come along with me."

He started to protest, to demand to know what I was going to do, but I cut him off sharply. "Just come with me. I don't have any more time right now."

My tone more than my words stopped him. He watched silently while I got my coat. I tucked my driver's license and money into my jeans pocket so I wouldn't be hampered by a purse. He started to stammer some more questions—was I going to shoot his old man?—when he saw me take out the Smith & Wesson and check the clip.

"Shoe's on the other foot," I said curtly. "Your father's buddies have been gunning for me all week."

He blushed again with shame and lapsed back into silence.

I took him down to Mr. Contreras. "This is Art Jurshak. His papa may have had something to do with Nancy's death and he isn't feeling too kindly toward his kid right now. Can you keep him here until I can make some other arrangement for him? Maybe Murray will want to take him."

The old man preened himself importantly. "Sure thing, doll. I won't say a word to anybody, and you can count on her highness here to do the same. No need to go asking that Ryerson guy to do anything—I'm perfectly happy to keep him as long as you want."

I smiled faintly. "After a couple of hours with him you may change your mind—he's not a lot of fun. Just don't tell anyone about him. That lawyer—Ron Kappelman—may come around. Say you don't know where I've gone or when I'll be back. And not a word about your guest."

"Where are you going, doll?"

I pressed my lips together in a reflex of annoyance, then remembered our truce. I beckoned him into the hall so I could tell him without Art's hearing. Mr. Contreras came quickly, the dog at his ankles, and nodded gravely to show he remembered both name and address.

"I'll be here when you come back. I won't let anyone lure me away tonight. But if you're not back by midnight, I'm calling Lieutenant Mallory, doll."

The dog padded after me to the door, but gave a little sigh of resignation when Mr. Contreras called her back. She knew I had my boots on, not my running shoes—she'd just been hoping.

33

A Family Affair

I could hear Mrs. Djiak's hurried footsteps after I rang the bell. She opened the door, drying her hands on her apron.

"Victoria!" She was horrified. "What are you doing here this late at night? I begged you not to come back again. Mr. Djiak will be furious if he knows you're here."

Ed Djiak's nasal baritone wafted down the hallway, demanding of his wife who was at the door.

"Just—just one of the neighbor children, Ed," she called back breathlessly. To me she said in a hurried undervoice, "Now go quickly, before he sees you."

I shook my head. "I'm coming in, Mrs. Djiak. We're going to talk, all three of us, about the man who got Louisa pregnant."

Her eyes dilated in her strained face. She grabbed beseechingly at my arm, but I was too angry to feel any compassion for her. I shook her hand from me. Ignoring her piteous cries, I brushed past her into the house and down the hall. I didn't take my boots off—not to add a deliberate insult to her distress, but because I wanted to be able to leave quickly if I had to.

Ed Djiak was sitting at the table in the immaculate kitchen, a little black-and-white TV in front of him, a beer mug in his hand. He didn't look up immediately, assuming it was just his wife, but when he saw me his long dark face turned a deep umber.

"You have no business in this house, young woman."

"I wish I could agree with you," I said, pulling a chair back from the table to face him. "It nauseates me to be here and I won't prolong the visit. I just want to talk about Mrs. Djiak's brother."

"She doesn't have a brother," he said harshly.

"Don't pretend Art Jurshak isn't her brother. I don't think we'd have too much trouble finding Mrs. Djiak's maiden name—I'd have to wait until Monday, when I could go down to City Hall and check your marriage license, but I expect it'll say Martha Jurshak. Then I could get copies of Art's and her birth certificates and that'd probably clinch the matter."

The umber in his face deepened to mahogany. He turned to his wife. "You damned talkative bitch! Who have you been telling our private affairs to?"

"No one, Ed. Really. I haven't said a word to anyone. Not once in all these years. Not even to Father Stepanek, when I begged you—"

He cut her off with a slice of his hand. "Who's been talking to you, Victoria? Who's been spreading slander about my family?"

"Slander implies false report," I responded insolently. "Everything you've said since I came into this house confirms that it's true."

"That what's true?" he demanded, recovering himself with a strong effort. "That my wife's maiden name was Jurshak? What if it was?"

"Just this. That her brother Art got your daughter Louisa pregnant. You told me he wasn't very strong, Martha. Did he have a history of liking little girls?"

She was wiping her hands over and over in her apron. "He—he promised he would never do it again."

"Damn you, don't say anything to her," Djiak roared, springing from his chair. He shoved past me roughly to where Mrs. Djiak stood and slapped her.

I was on my feet smashing my fist into his face before I realized what I was doing. He was thirty years older than me, but still very strong. It was only because I took him completely by surprise that I managed to hit him full force. He recoiled against the refrigerator and stood for a moment, shaking his head to recover from the blow. Then the ugly anger returned and he came for me.

I was ready. As he charged I slid a chair in his path. He crashed against it, his momentum forcing him and the chair into the table. His fall brought down the TV set and the beer in a jumbled mess of glass and fluid. He lay sprawled under the table, the chair on top of him.

Martha Djiak gave a little moan of horror, whether over the sight of her husband or the mess on the floor I couldn't know. I stood over him, panting from fury, my gun in my hand barrel-first, ready to smash it into him if he started to get up. His face was glazed—none of his womenfolk had ever fought back against him.

Mrs. Djiak screamed suddenly. I turned to look at her. She couldn't speak, only point, but I saw a little fire sparkling along the back of the television where something had mixed with the exposed wires. Maybe a jar of solvent that was kept at the ready for oil stains menacing the kitchen. I stuffed the gun back into my jeans waistband and snatched the dish towel from her apron pocket. Carefully skirting the pool of beer, I crawled under the table and unplugged the set.

"Baking soda," I called sharply to Mrs. Djiak.

The demand for a commonplace household item helped her regain some balance. I watched her feet move to a cupboard. She crouched down and handed me the box across her husband's body. I dumped the contents on the blue flames flickering around the set and watched the fire go out.

Mr. Djiak slowly untangled himself from the mess of chair and broken glass. He stood for a moment looking at the wreck on the floor, at the wet stains on his pants. Then, without saying anything, he left the room. I could hear his heavy footsteps pass down the hall. Martha Djiak and I listened to the front door slam.

She was shaking. I seated her in one of the plastic-covered chairs and heated water in the teakettle. She watched me dumbly while I rummaged through her cupboards looking for tea. When I found the Lipton bags tucked neatly into a canister, I made her a cup, mixing it well with sugar and milk. She drank it obediently in scalding gulps.

"Do you think you can tell me about Louisa now?" I asked when she'd turned down a second cup.

"How did you find out?" Her eyes were lifeless, her voice little more than a tired thread.

"Your brother's son came to visit me this afternoon. Each time I've seen him I thought he looked familiar, but I put it down to years of looking at Art on posters or TV. But today Caroline was with me. She and I were in the middle of an argument. Young Art walked in with his face flushed, all agitated, and suddenly I realized how much he resembled Caroline. They might almost be twins, you know—I just hadn't connected them before because I wasn't expecting it. Of course he's got that unearthly beauty and she's always so disheveled, it wasn't until they were both upset at the same time that you could really see it."

She listened to my explanation with her face screwed up painfully, as if I were lecturing in Latin and she was trying to make me think she could follow me. When she didn't say anything I prodded her a little.

"Why did you throw Louisa out of the house when she got pregnant?"

She looked at me directly then, some mix of fear and disgust on her face. "Keep her in the house? With that shame for all the world to know about?"

"It wasn't her shame. It was Art's, your brother's. How can you even compare the two?"

"She wouldn't have gotten—gotten in trouble if she hadn't led him on. She saw how much he liked her to dance for him and kiss him. He—he had a weakness. She should have kept away from him."

My nausea was so acute, it took all my will not to jump on her physically, to slam her body into the debris under the table. "If you knew he had a weakness for little girls, why the *hell* did you let him near your daughters?"

"He—he said he wouldn't do it again. After I saw him—playing with—with Connie when she was five, I told him I would tell Ed about it if he ever did it again. He promised. He was afraid of Ed. But Louisa was too much for him, she was too evil-minded, she led him on against his own strength. When we saw she was going to have a baby, she told us how it happened and Art explained it to us, how she led him on against his own strength."

"So you threw her out into the world. If it hadn't been for Gabriella, who knows what would have happened to her? The two of you—what a couple of sanctimonious righteous bastards you are."

She took my insults unflinchingly. She couldn't understand why I would be angry over such logical parental behavior, but she'd seen me beat up her husband. She wasn't going to risk exciting me.

"Was Art already married then?" I asked abruptly.

"No. We told him he was going to have to find a wife, start a family, or we'd have to tell Father Stepanek, tell the priest, about Louisa. We promised we wouldn't say anything if she moved away and he started a family."

I didn't know what to say. All I could think of was Louisa at sixteen, pregnant, out on her own, the holy ladies of St. Wenceslaus parading in front of her door. And Gabriella riding in on her white horse to the rescue. All the old insults from the Djiaks about Gabriella's being a Jew came back to me.

"How can you pretend to call yourselves Christians? My mother was a thousand times the Christian you ever were. She didn't go around blathering a lot of sanctimonious bullshit; she lived charity. But you and Ed, you let your brother seduce your child and you call her wicked. If there really was a god he would annihilate you for daring to come to his altar, babbling about your righteousness. If there is a god, my only prayer is that I never have to be within a mile of you again."

I lurched to my feet, my eyes hot with furious tears. She shrank back in her chair.

"I won't hit you," I said. "What good would it do either of us?"

Before I'd reached the hall she was already on her hands and knees cleaning up the broken glass.

34

Bank Shot

I staggered from the house to the car, my stomach heaving, my throat tight and tainted with bile. All I could think of was to get to Lotty, not to stop for anything, for a toothbrush or a change of underwear. Just go straight to sanity.

I made it there on luck. A blaring horn at Seventy-first Street brought me briefly to myself. I skirted my way carefully through Jackson Park, but I almost hit a bicyclist darting across the Drive at Fifty-ninth. Even after that I kept finding the speedometer needle around seventy.

Max was drinking cognac in Lotty's sitting room when I got there. I smiled jerkily at him. With a great effort, I remembered the two had gone to a recital together and asked how they'd enjoyed the music.

"Superb. The Cellini Quintet. We knew them in London when they were just getting started after the war." He reminded Lotty of an evening in Wigmore Hall when the power had gone off, and how the two of them had stood holding flashlights over the music so their friends could continue the concert.

Lotty laughed and was adding a memoir of her own when she broke off. "Vic! I hadn't seen your face in the light when you came up. What is the matter?"

I forced my lips to the form of a smile. "Nothing life-threatening. Just a strange conversation that I'll tell you about sometime."

"I must be off anyway, my dear," Max said, rising. "I've stayed far too long drinking your excellent cognac."

Lotty saw him to the door, then hurried back to me. "What is it, *Liebchen?* You look like death."

I tried smiling again. To my dismay, I found myself sobbing instead. "Lotty, I thought I'd seen every horrible thing people could do to each other in this town. Men killing each other for a bottle of wine. Women pouring lye on their lovers. Why this should upset me so much I don't know."

"Here." Lotty put some brandy to my mouth. "Drink this and settle yourself a bit. Try to tell me what happened."

I swallowed some of the cognac. It washed the taste of bile from my throat. With Lotty holding my hand, I blurted out the story. How I'd seen the resemblance between young Art and Caroline, and thought his mother must have been related to Caroline's father. Only to learn that it was his father who was related to Caroline's grandmother.

"That part wasn't so awful," I gulped. "I mean, of course it's awful. But what made me so sick is their horrible scrubbed piety and the way they insist Louisa was to blame. Do you know how they raised her? How strictly those two sisters were watched? No dates, no boys, no talk about sex. And then her mother's brother. He molested the one girl and they let him stay around to molest the other. And then they punish her."

My voice was rising; I couldn't seem to control it. "It can't be, Lotty. It shouldn't be. I should be able to stop something that vile from going on, but I don't have any power."

Lotty took me in her arms and held me without speaking. After a time my sobbing dried up, but I continued to lie against her shoulder.

"You can't heal the world, *Liebchen*. I know you know that. You can only work with one person at a time, in a very small way. And over the individuals you help you have much effect. It's only the megalomaniacs, the Hitlers and their ilk, who think they have the answer for everyone's life. You are in the world of the sane, Victoria, the world of the limited."

She took me into the kitchen and fed me the remains of the chicken she'd cooked for Max. She continued to pour brandy into me until I was ready for sleep. After that she took me to her spare room and undressed me.

"Mr. Contreras," I said thickly. "I forgot to tell him I was spending the night here. Can you call him for me? Otherwise he'll have Bobby Mallory dragging the lake for me."

"Certainly, my dear. I'll do it as soon as I see you're sleeping. Just rest and don't worry."

When I woke Sunday morning I felt light-headed, the result of too much brandy and tears. But I'd had my first thorough sleep since my attack; the soreness in my shoulders had diminished to the point where I no longer noticed it every time I moved.

Lotty brought in *The New York Times* with a plate of crisp rolls and jam. We spent a leisurely morning over papers and coffee. At noon, when I wanted to start talking about Art Jurshak—about some way to get past his ubiquitous bodyguards to speak to him—Lotty silenced me.

"This will be a day of rest for you, Victoria. We're going to the country, get fresh air, turn the mind off completely from all worries. It will make everything seem more possible tomorrow."

I gave in with as good grace as I could muster, but she was right. We drove into Michigan, spent the day walking at the sand dunes, letting the cold lake air whip our hair. We dawdled around in the little wineries, buying a bottle of cherry-cranberry wine as a souvenir for Max, who prided himself on his palate. When we finally returned home around ten that night, I felt clean throughout.

It was a good thing I'd had that day of rest. Monday turned into a long, frustrating day. Lotty was gone when I woke up—she makes rounds at Beth Israel before opening her clinic at eight-thirty. She left me a note saying she'd looked at Dr. Chigwell's notebooks after I went to bed, but didn't feel confident in interpreting the blood values he'd been recording. She was taking them to a friend who specialized in nephrology for a reading.

I called Mr. Contreras. He reported a quiet night, but said that young Art was getting restless. He'd loaned him a razor and a change of underwear, but he wasn't sure how long he could keep the boy at the apartment.

"If he wants to leave, let him," I said. "He's the one who wanted protection. I don't really care too much if he doesn't want to accept it."

I told him I'd be by to pack a small suitcase, but that I was going to stay with Lotty until I felt more secure against midnight marauders. He agreed, wistfully—he'd much rather I sent young Art to Lotty and stayed with him and Peppy.

After stopping at my place for a shower and a change of clothes, I went downstairs to spend a few minutes with Peppy and Mr. Contreras. The strain of the last few weeks was starting to etch hollow lines in young Art's face. Or maybe it was just thirty-six hours spent with Mr. Contreras.

"Do you—have you done anything?" His uncertain voice had faded to a pathetic whisper.

"I can't do anything until I've talked to your old man. You can help make that happen. I don't see how I can get past his security guards to see him alone."

That alarmed him—he didn't want Art, Sr., to know he'd come to me; that would really get him in hot water. I reasoned and cajoled to no avail. Finally, getting a little testy, I headed for the door.

"I'll just have to call your mother and tell her I know where you are. I'm sure she'd be glad to set up a meeting between me and your old man in exchange for knowing her precious baby was safe and sound."

"Goddamn you, Warshawski," he squeaked. "You know I don't want you talking to her."

Mr. Contreras took umbrage at the young man's swearing at me and started to interrupt. I held up a hand, which mercifully stopped him.

"Then help me get in touch with your dad."

At last, fulminating, he agreed to call his father, to say he needed to talk to him alone and to set up a meeting in front of Buckingham Fountain.

I told Art to try to set the appointment for two today—that I'd call back at eleven to check on the time. As I left I could hear Mr. Contreras upbraiding him for talking so rudely to me. It sent me southward with my only laugh of the day.

My parents had banked at Ironworkers Savings & Loan. My mother had opened my first savings account for me there when I was ten so I could stash stray quarters and baby-sitting earnings against the college education she long had promised me. In my memory it remained an imposing, gilt-covered palace.

When I walked up to the grimy stone building at Ninety-third and Commercial, it seemed to have shrunk so with the years that I checked the name over the entrance to make sure I was at the right place. The vaulted ceiling, which had awed me as a child, now seemed merely grubby. Instead of having to stand on tiptoe to peer into the teller's cage, I towered over the acned young woman behind the counter.

She didn't know anything about the bank's annual report, but she directed me indifferently to an officer in the back. The glib story I'd prepared to explain why I wanted it proved unnecessary. The middle-aged man who spoke to me was only too glad to find someone interested in a decaying savings and loan. He talked to me at length about the strong ethical values of the community, where people did everything to keep their little homes in order, and how the bank itself renegotiated loans for its longtime customers when hard times hit them.

"We don't have an annual report of the kind you're used to examining, since we're privately owned," he concluded. "But you can look at our year-end statements if you want."

"It's really the names of your board I'd like to see," I told him.

"Of course." He rummaged in a drawer and pulled out a stack of papers. "You're sure you don't want to inspect the statements? If you were thinking of investing, I can assure you we are in extremely sound condition despite the death of the mills down here."

If I'd had a few thousand to spare, I would have felt obligated to give it to the bank to cover my embarrassment. As it was I muttered something noncommittal and took the directors list from him. It held thirteen names, but I knew only one of them: Gustav Humboldt.

Oh, yes, my informant told me proudly, Mr. Humboldt had agreed to become a director back in the forties when he first started doing business down here. Even now that his company had become one of the largest in the world and he was a director of a dozen Fortune 500 companies, he still stayed on the Ironworkers board.

"Mr. Humboldt has missed only eight meetings in the last fifteen years," he finished.

I murmured something that could be taken for extravagant awe at the great man's dedication. The picture was becoming tolerably clear to me. There was some problem with the insurance on the work force at the Xerxes plant that Humboldt was determined not come to light. I couldn't see what that had to do with the lawsuit or the deaths of Ferraro and Pankowski. But maybe Chigwell knew what the actuarial data I'd found meant—perhaps that was what his medical notebooks would reveal. That part didn't bother me too much. It was Humboldt's personal role that both scared and angered me. I was tired of being jerked around by him. It was time to beard him directly. I extricated myself from the Ironworkers' hopeful officer and headed for the Loop.

I wasn't in the mood to waste time hunting out cheap parking. I pulled into the lot next to the Humboldt Building on Madison. Stopping just long enough to comb my hair in the rearview mirror, I headed into the shark's cove.

The Humboldt Building housed the company's corporate offices. Like most manufacturing conglomerates, the real business went on in the plants spread across the globe, so I wasn't surprised that their headquarters could be squeezed into twenty-five stories. It was a strictly functional building, with no trees or sculptures in the lobby. The floor was covered with the utilitarian tile you used to see in all skyscrapers before Helmut Jahn and his pals started filling them with marble-lined atria.

The old-fashioned black notice board in the hallway didn't list Gustav Humboldt, but it told me the corporate offices were on twenty-two. I summoned one of the bronze-doored elevators and made my slow way up.

The hall that I entered from the elevator was austere, but the tone had changed subtly. The lower half of the walls was paneled in a dark wood that also showed on either side of the pale green carpet. Framed prints of medieval alchemists with retorts, toads, and bats hung above the paneling.

I headed down the green pile to an open door on my right. The green carpeting continued past the door, where it spread into a large pool. The dark wood was picked up in a polished desk. Behind it sat a woman with a phone bank and a word processor. She was impeccably polished herself, her dark hair pulled back in a smooth chignon to show the large pearls in her shell-shaped ears. She turned from the word processor to greet me with practiced courtesy.

"I'm here to see Gustav Humboldt," I said, trying to sound authoritative.

"I see. May I have your name please?"

I handed her a card and she turned with it to the phones. When she'd finished she smiled apologetically.

"You don't seem to be in the appointment calendar, Ms. Warshawski. Is Mr. Humboldt expecting you?"

"Yes. He's been leaving messages for me all over town. This is just my first opportunity to get back to him."

She returned to the phones. This time when she finished she asked me to take a seat. I lowered myself into an overstuffed armchair and flipped through a copy of the annual report thoughtfully placed next to it. Humboldt's Brazil operations had shown a staggering growth last year, accounting for sixty percent of overseas profits. Their capital investment of $500 million in the Amazon River Project was now paying handsome dividends. I couldn't help wondering how much capital development it would take before the Amazon looked like the Calumet.

I was studying the breakdown of profits by product line, feeling a proprietary pleasure in the good performance of Xerxine, when the polished receptionist summoned me—Mr. Redwick would see me. I followed her to the third in a series of doors in a little hallway behind her desk. She knocked and opened the door, then returned to her station.

Mr. Redwick got up from his desk to hold out a hand to me. He was a tall, well-groomed man about my own age, with remote gray eyes. He studied me unsmilingly while we shook hands and uttered conventional greetings, then gestured me to a small sofa set against one wall.

"I understand you think Mr. Humboldt wishes to see you."

"I *know* Mr. Humboldt wishes to see me," I corrected him. "You wouldn't be talking to me if that weren't the case."

"What is it you think he wants to see you about?" He pressed his fingertips together.

"He's left a couple of messages for me. One at the insurance offices of Art Jurshak, the other at the Ironworkers bank in South Chicago. Both messages were most urgent. That's why I came here in person."

"Why don't you tell me what he said, and then I can evaluate whether he needs to talk to you himself or whether I can handle the matter."

I smiled. "Either you are totally in Mr. Humboldt's confidence, in which case you know what he said, or you're not—in which case he would much prefer that you not find it out."

The remote eyes grew colder. "You can safely assume that I'm in Mr. Humboldt's confidence—I'm his executive assistant."

I yawned and got up to study a print on the wall across from the sofa. It was a Nast cartoon of the Oil Trust, and as nearly as my inexpert eye could tell, it seemed to be an original.

"If you aren't willing to talk to me, you're going to have to leave," Redwick said sharply.

I didn't turn around. "Why don't you just check with the big guy—let him know I'm here and getting restless."

"He knows you're here and he asked me to meet with you."

"How hard it is when strong-willed people disagree so vehemently," I said mournfully, and left the room.

I walked fast, trying each of the doors I came to, surprising a succession of hardworking assistants. The door on the end opened to the great man's cove. A secretary, presumably Ms. Hollingsworth, looked up in surprise at my entrance. Before she could utter a protest, I'd gone into the inner chamber. Redwick was on my heels, grabbing at my arms.

Behind the mahogany door, in the midst of a collection of antique office furnishings, sat Gustav Humboldt, a document unopened on his knees. He looked beyond me to his executive assistant.

"Redwick. I thought I made it clear this woman was not to disturb me. Have you come to think that my decisions no longer carry authority?"

With a considerable diminution in his cool poise, Redwick tried explaining what had happened.

"He really did do his best," I chimed in helpfully. "But I knew that deep down you would be sorry forever if you didn't talk to me. You see, I just came from the Ironworkers Savings and Loan, so I know you're the person who pressured Caroline Djiak into firing me. And then there's the matter of the life and health insurance that Art Jurshak's been handling for you. Not my idea of a proper fiduciary, a man who pals around with guys like Steve Dresberg, and the state insurance commissioner would probably agree with me."

I was on thin ice there, since I wasn't sure what the report meant. Obviously it had rung a thousand bells with Nancy, but I could only guess at why. I danced my way through possibilities, throwing in references to Joey Pankowski and Steve Ferraro, but Humboldt refused to rise to the bait. He strode to his desk and picked up the phone.

"Why did you lie to me about that lawsuit?" I continued conversationally when he had hung up. "I know a big ego is a sine qua non for success on the scale you've achieved, but you must really be myopic if you thought I'd take your unsupported word on that suit. Too many things had been happening in South Chicago for me not to be suspicious of a high-powered CEO who—"

I was interrupted by some new arrivals—three security guards. I couldn't help being flattered that Humboldt thought it would take so many men to get me out of his building—one of that size and apparent conditioning would have done the trick given the shape I was in. I didn't feel up to a bravado display but went along without a fuss.

As they ushered me from the room—with more force than was really necessary—I called over my shoulder, "You gotta get better help, Gustav. The guys who dumped me in Dead Stick Pond are in custody and it's only a matter of time before they cop a plea by telling the police who hired them."

He didn't answer me. As Redwick shut the door behind us, though, I heard Humboldt say, "Someone has got to shut that meddlesome bitch up for me."

Alas, this seemed to put paid to the idea of my ever drinking his remarkable brandy again.

35

Changing Words at Buckingham Fountain

It was a little after eleven when the great apes finished escorting me from the zoo, time for me to check in with young Art. I was within walking distance of my office, but I wanted to get clean away from the Humboldt Building. I paid my eight dollars for the privilege of parking next to it for an hour and moved the car to the underground garage.

I'd forgotten Mr. Contreras's forcible entry to my office Friday night. He'd done a thorough job on the door. First he'd smashed in the glass in the hopes of being able to reach in and turn the lock. When he'd found it was a key-operated dead bolt, he'd methodically broken all the wood around it and pulled it from the frame. I ground my teeth at the sight, but didn't see any point in mentioning it when I called the old man. It would be easier to arrange for someone else to repair it than to go through his long string of remorse—and far easier to get outside help than to go through the agony of watching Mr. Contreras fix it.

Art came uneasily to the phone. He had spoken with his dad, but he wanted me to know that I really owed him. It had been pure hell having to negotiate with Big Art. Oh, yes, he'd gotten the old man to agree to come to the fountain, although he said he couldn't make it before two-thirty. It had taken a lot of cajoling; his father had pressured him unbelievably to be told where he was staying. If I had any idea how hard it was to stand up to Big Art, I might treat him with a little more respect.

"And can't you think of some place better for me than here? This old man can't leave me alone. He treats me like I'm some kind of child."

I replied more soothingly than I felt, "And if you really want to go someplace else, I don't have any objection. I'll see if I can arrange something with Murray Ryerson at the *Herald-Star* when I talk to him this afternoon. Of course he'll want some kind of story in exchange."

I hung up on his shrieking that I had to promise not to go to the papers about him, but I did forbear to mention his name to Murray when I called.

"You know, Warshawski, you're a fucking pain in the ass," he greeted me. "Don't you ever check in with your answering service? I left about ten messages for you over the weekend. What did you do to the Chigwell woman? Hypnotize her? She won't talk to the press—she says you can handle any queries we have about her brother."

"It's a course I took by mail," I said, surprised and pleased. "You send in all these matchbooks and they ship you a set of lessons on how to make yourself invisible, how to enter the thoughts of another person—all that kind of stuff. I just never had a chance to try it before."

"Right, wise-ass," he said resignedly. "Are you now prepared to reveal all to the people of Chicago?"

"You told me you didn't need me—that you were getting all your info direct from the people at Xerxes. I want to talk to you about something much more exciting—my life. Or its possible termination."

"That's old news. We already covered it last week. You'll have to go all the way this time for us to get excited about it."

"Well, stay tuned—you may get your wish. I've got some heavy guys gunning for me." I watched a handful of pigeons vying for space on the windowsill. Tough dirty urban birds—better decor for my office than original prints by Nast or Daumier.

"Why are you telling me this now?" he demanded suspiciously.

A train rattled by on the Wabash el tracks. The pigeons fluttered momentarily as the vibrations shook the window, then settled back on the sill.

"In case I don't live through the night I want someone who'll follow my trail to know where it's been taking me. I'd like that person to be you, since you're better able to think ill of the gods than the cops are, but the hitch is, I need to talk to you before one-thirty."

"What happens at one-thirty?"

"I strap on my six-guns and walk alone down Main Street."

After some more poking, to see if matters were as urgent as I claimed, Murray agreed to meet me near the newspaper for a sandwich at noon. Before leaving the Pulteney I sorted my mail, tossed everything but a check from one of the clients I'd done a financial search for, then called a friend to replace my office door. He said he'd get to it by Wednesday afternoon.

Since it was close to twelve already, I headed north to the river. The air had thickened to a light drizzle. Despite Lotty's dire words, my shoulders felt pretty good. Another couple of days—If I stayed a jump ahead of Gustav Humboldt—and I could start running again.

The *Herald-Star* faces the *Sun-Times* from the south side of the Chicago River. A lot of that area is getting trendy, with racquet courts and chichi little restaurants springing up, but Carl's still serves a no-nonsense sandwich to the newspaper people. Its scarred booths and deal tables are packed into a dingy stone building on Wacker where it runs under the main road next to the river.

Murray swept into the tavern a few minutes after me, raindrops making his red hair glint under the dim lights. Lucy Moynihan, Carl's daughter, who took over the place when he died, likes Murray. She let us jump the crowd to take a booth at the back and stayed for a few minutes to kid with Murray about the money he'd lost to her in last week's basketball pool.

Over a hamburger I told him much of what I'd been doing the last three weeks. For all his flamboyance and conceit, Murray is an intent listener, absorbing information through every pore. They say you remember only thirty percent of what anyone tells you, but I've never had to repeat a story to Murray.

When I'd finished he said, "Okay. You got a mess. You have your old childhood brat wanting you to find who croaked your teammate, an indigestible young Jurshak, and a strangely behaving chemical company. And maybe the Garbage King. You be careful if Steve Dresberg is really involved. That boy plays very much for keeps. I can see him being tied in with Jurshak, but what's Humboldt got to do with it?"

"I wish I knew. Jurshak handles his insurance, which isn't a crime as much as a misdemeanor, but I can't help wondering what Jurshak's doing for Humboldt in return." The elusive memory I'd been trying to force since Saturday swam across the surface of my mind again and disappeared.

"What?" Murray demanded suspiciously.

"Nothing. I thought I remembered something but I can't quite get it. But I wish I knew why Humboldt is lying about Joey Pankowski and Steve Ferraro. It's got to be something really important because when I went to his office today to ask him about it, I got hefted out by some enormous security apes."

"Maybe he just doesn't like you buzzing around him," Murray said maliciously. "There are times when I wish I had security apes to kick you out too."

I faked a punch at him but he took hold of my hand and held it for a minute. "Give, Warshawski. There's no story here yet. Just speculations that I can't put in print. Why are we having lunch together?"

I pulled my hand away. "I'm doing some research. When I have some results I may have a better idea of why Humboldt's lying, but right now I'm off to meet with Art Jurshak. I've got a major club to use on him, so I hope he'll cough up what he knows. So that's what I want from you. If I somehow die, talk to Lotty, to Caroline Djiak, and to Jurshak. Those three are the key."

"How serious are you about being in danger?"

I watched Murray drain his stein and signal for a third. He weighs two-forty, maybe two-fifty—he can absorb it. I stuck with coffee—I wanted my head as clear as possible for Jurshak.

"More than I like. Someone left me for dead five days ago. Two of the same hoods were waiting outside my apartment on Friday. And today Gustav Humboldt sounded strangely like Peter O'Toole trying to get his barons to do in Becket. It's pretty real."

Of course Murray wanted to know the club I had on Jurshak, but I was absolutely determined not to let that get public. We fought about it until one-fifteen, when I got up and laid a five on the table and headed out. Murray hollered after me, but I hoped to be on a southbound bus before he could extricate himself and follow.

A 147 bus was just closing its doors as I reached the top of the stairs. The driver, a rare humanitarian, opened them again when he saw me running for the curb. Art had said two-thirty instead of two—I just wanted to make sure he didn't show up early with some kind of armed escort. I hardly knew young Art and I sure didn't trust him—he might have lied to me about fooling his father. Or maybe Big Art didn't trust his kid, either, and discounted the story. Just in case, I wanted to get there ahead of a trap.

I rode down to Jackson and walked the three blocks east to the fountain. In the summer Buckingham Fountain is the showpiece of the lakefront. Then it's shrouded by trees and crowded with tourists. In the winter, with the foliage dead and the water turned off, it makes a good spot to talk. Few people visit it, and those who do can be seen a good way off.

Today Grant Park was desolate under the dull winter sky. Empty potato-chip bags and whiskey bottles mixed in with the dead leaves provided the only signs of human presence in the area. I retreated to the rose garden on the fountain's south side and perched on the base of one of the statues at its corners. I stuck the Smith & Wesson in my jacket pocket with my thumb resting on the safety.

A light drizzle kept up intermittently during the afternoon. Despite the relative warmth of the winter air, I was chilled through from sitting still in the damp. I hadn't worn gloves so that I could handle the gun more readily, but by the time Jurshak showed up my fingers were so numb, I'm not sure I could have fired.

Around a quarter to three a limo stopped on Lake Shore Drive to deposit the alderman and a companion. The limo moved on up the drive to Monroe, where it circled and came to a halt about a quarter mile from the fountain. When I was sure no one was getting out to take a bead, I scrambled down from my perch and made my way back to the park.

Jurshak was looking around, trying to find his son. He paid only passing attention to me until he realized I was planning to talk to him.

"Art won't be able to make it, Mr. Jurshak—he sent me instead. I'm V. I. Warshawski. I think you've heard my name from your wife. Or from Gustav Humboldt."

Jurshak was wearing a black cashmere coat that buttoned up to his chin. With his face set off by the black collar, I could see an overwhelming resemblance to Caroline—the same high round cheeks, short nose, long upper lip. Even his eyes were the same gentian, a bit faded with age, but that true blue that you rarely see. In fact, he looked more obviously like her than he did young Art.

"What have you done with my son? Where are you holding him?" he demanded in a forceful, husky voice.

I shook my head. "He came to me on Saturday afraid for his life—said you'd told his mother he was as good as dead for letting me get that report you filed for Xerxes with Mariners Rest. He's someplace safe. I don't want to talk to you about your son, but your daughter. You may want to ask your friend to step aside while we speak."

"What are you talking about? Art's my only child! I demand that you take me to him at once, or I'll get the police along quicker than you can blink." His mouth set in the angry stubborn line I'd seen on Caroline's face a thousand times.

Art had been a power in Chicago since before I'd started college. Even without his clique controlling the City Council, there were plenty of police who owed Jurshak favors and would be happy to run me in if he wanted them to.

"Think back a quarter century," I said softly, trying not to let anger turn my voice ragged. "Your sister's daughters. Those luxurious afternoons when your niece danced for you while your brother-in-law was away at work. You can't have forgotten how important you were in the lives of those two girls."

His expression, as mobile as Caroline's, changed from rage to fear. The wind had whipped color into his cheeks, but beneath the red his face looked gray.

"Take a walk, Manny," he said to the stocky man at his side. "Go wait in the car. I'll be over in a couple of minutes."

"If she's threatening you, Art, I oughta stay."

Jurshak shook his head. "Just some old family problems. I thought this was going to be business when I asked you and the boys to come along. Go ahead—one of us oughta stay warm."

The stocky man looked at me narrowly. He apparently decided the bulge in my pocket must be gloves or a notebook and headed back to the limo.

"Okay, Warshawski, what do you want?" Jurshak hissed.

"A whole bunch of answers. In exchange for answers I will not let the fact that you are a child molester with a daughter who is also your great-niece get into the papers."

"You can't prove anything." He sounded mean, but he didn't try moving away.

"Screw that," I said impatiently. "Ed and Martha told me the whole story the other night. And your daughter looks so much like you, it'd be an easy make. Murray Ryerson at the *Herald-Star* would be on it in a minute if I asked him, or Edie Gibson at the *Trib*."

I moved to one of the metal benches at the edge of the paving around the fountain. "We've got a lot to say. So you might as well make yourself comfortable."

I saw him looking over at the limo. "Don't even think it. I've got a gun, I know how to use it, and even if your boys finished me off, Murray Ryerson knows I'm meeting with you. Come sit down and get it over with."

He came over, his head down, his hands jammed into his pockets. "I'm not admitting anything. I think you're full of hot air, but once the press got their teeth into a story like that, they'd ruin me just with the innuendoes."

I gave what was meant to be an engaging smile. "All you'd have to do is say I'm blackmailing you. Of course I'd run Caroline's photo, and they'd interview her mother and all that stuff, but you could give it a shot. Now let's see—we've got so much old family business to talk about, I don't even know where to begin. With Louisa Djiak's mortgage, or me in the mud at Dead Stick Pond, or Nancy Cleghorn."

I spoke musingly, watching him out of the corner of my eye. He seemed a little jumpier at Nancy's name than Louisa's.

"I know! That report you sent to Mariners Rest for Xerxes. You're running a fiddle on the insurance, aren't you? What are they doing—paying a higher rate than they're charged so you can pocket the difference? And what difference does it make if someone finds out? It ain't exactly going to ruin you in the neighborhood. You've been charged with worse and been reelected."

Suddenly the memory that had been eluding me since I talked to Caroline on Saturday popped to the surface. Mrs. Pankowski standing in her doorway, telling me her financial woes, saying Joey didn't leave her any insurance. Maybe he hadn't signed up for the group plan. But that was a Xerxes benefit, I thought, noncontributory life insurance. Only maybe it was term; since he hadn't been with the company when he died, he wouldn't be covered. Still, it was worth asking.

"When Joey Pankowski died, why didn't he get any life insurance?"

"I don't know what the hell you're talking about."

"Joey Pankowski. He used to work at Xerxes. You're the fiduciary on their LHP business, so you must know why an employee doesn't collect life insurance when he dies."

He looked suddenly as though he'd collapsed through the middle. I thought frantically, trying to follow up my advantage with piercing questions. But he was an old hand at taking the heat and he could tell I didn't really have anything. He recovered enough poise to keep up a front of stubborn denial.

"Okay. Let it go. I can figure it out fast enough when I talk to the carrier. Or some other employees. Let's go back to Nancy Cleghorn. She saw you and Dresberg together at your office, and you know as well as I do that no insurance commissioner will let you keep your license if you hang around with the mob."

"Oh, knock it off, Warshawski. I don't know who this Cleghorn girl is, other than reading in the papers that she got herself killed. I may talk to Dresberg from time to time—he does a lot of business in my ward and I'm the alderman for the whole ward. I can't afford to be a dainty lady holding her nose when she smells garbage. The insurance commissioner isn't going to think once about it, let alone twice."

"So it wouldn't bother you to let it be known that you and Dresberg met in your office late at night?"

"Prove it."

I yawned. "How do you think I even heard about it? There was a witness, of course. One who's still alive."

Even that didn't shake him enough for me to be able to pry anything from him. When the conversation ended I not only felt frustrated but too young for the job. Art just had too much more experience than I. I felt like grinding my teeth and saying "Just you wait, Black Jack, I'll get you in the end." Instead I told him I'd be in touch.

I walked away from him toward Lake Shore Drive. Sprinting across in front of the traffic, I watched him from the far side. He stood for a long moment looking at nothing, then shook himself and headed back toward his limo.

36

Bad Blood

I retrieved my car and headed back to Lotty's. All I'd really gotten from seeing Jurshak was information that he'd been working some kind of fraud with the Xerxes insurance. And something major, based on his expression. But I didn't know what it was. And I needed to find out quickly, before all the people who were mad at me converged once and for all and sent me to my permanent rest. The urgency tightened my stomach and congealed my brain.

Rush-hour traffic was already thickening the main streets downtown. The menace in Humboldt's voice this morning lingered in my ears. I drove cautiously through the February twilight, trying to make sure no one was tailing me. I drove all the way up to Montrose and exited at the park, doubling around twice before figuring I was in the clear and heading back to Lotty's.

It didn't surprise me that I got there before she did—to accommodate working mothers Lotty keeps the clinic open until six most evenings. I went out for some food—the least I could do in thanks for her hospitality was to have dinner ready. I started again on the chicken with garlic and olives I'd been trying to make the night before my attack, hoping that if I kept the front of my mind occupied, the back would begin to sprout ideas. This time I prepared the whole dish without interruption and set it to simmer over a low flame.

By then it was close to seven-thirty and Lotty still hadn't returned. I began to get worried, wondering whether I should check the clinic or with Max. A late emergency might have detained her, either at the clinic or hospital. But she'd also be an easy target for anyone bent on getting revenge on me.

At eight-thirty, when I'd tried both clinic and hospital without results, I headed out to search for her. Her car pulled up in front of the building just as I was locking the lobby door.

"Lotty! I was getting worried," I cried, dashing over to meet her.

She followed me back into the building, her pace lagging, most unlike her usual brisk trot. "Were you, my dear?" she asked tiredly. "I should have remembered how nervous you've been the last few days. It's not like you to be in such a fret over a few hours."

She was right. Another sign that I had moved beyond any semblance of rationality in dealing with the issues at hand. She moved slowly into her apartment, taking off her coat with careful movements and stowing it methodically inside a carved walnut wardrobe standing in the hallway. I led her to an armchair in her sitting room. She let me pour her a small brandy—the only alcohol she drinks, and then only when under severe strain.

"Thank you, my dear. That's most helpful." She slipped her shoes off; I found her slippers laid neatly next to her bed and brought them out for her.

"I spent the last two hours with Dr. Christophersen. She's the nephrologist I mentioned showing your chemical company notebooks to."

She finished the brandy but shook her head when I offered her the bottle. "I suspected something when I looked at the records, but I wanted a specialist to do a thorough interpretation." She opened her briefcase and pulled out a few pages of photocopies. "I left the notebooks locked in Max's safe at Beth Israel. They are too—too frightening to be floating around the city streets where anyone could lay hands on them. This is a summary of Ann's—Dr. Christophersen's—notes. She says she can do a thorough analysis if it's needed."

I took the pages from her and looked at Dr. Christophersen's square, tiny writing. She was citing the blood work reported in the pages of Chigwell's notebooks, using Louisa Djiak's and Steve Ferraro's records as an example. The blood chemistry details made no sense to me, but the summary at the bottom of the page was in plain English and appallingly clear:

These records show blood history for Ms. Louisa Djiak (white unmarried female, one parturition) from 1963 to 1982, the last year for which data were taken; and for Mr. Steve Ferraro (white unmarried male) from 1957 to 1982. Records also exist for approximately five hundred other employees at Humboldt Chemical's Xerxes plant covering the period 1955 to 1982. These records show changes in the values of creatine, blood urea nitrogen, bilirubin, hematocrit, and hemoglobin, and white blood count consistent with the development of renal, liver, and bone marrow dysfunction. Conversation with Dr. Daniel Peters, Ms. Djiak's attending physician, confirm that the patient first came to him in 1984, only at her daughter's insistence. At that time he diagnosed chronic renal failure, which has now progressed to an acute stage. Other complications kept Ms. Djiak from being a good candidate for transplant.

The blood work indicates that noticeable renal damage occurred as early as 1967 (CR = 1.9; BUN = 28) and severe damage by 1969 (CR = 2.4; BUN = 30). The patient herself began experiencing typical diffuse symptoms—itching, fatigue, headaches—around 1979 but thought perhaps she was experiencing "change of life" and did not deem it necessary to consult a physician.

The report went on to give a similar summary of Steve Ferraro, ending with his death from aplastic anemia in 1983. The rest of the precise script detailed the toxic properties of Xerxine, and showed that the changes in blood chemistry were consistent with exposure to Xerxine. I read the document through twice before putting it down to stare, appalled, at Lotty.

"Dr. Christophersen did a lot of work, calling Louisa's and Steve Ferraro's doctors and doing all that checking," was the only comment I could get out at first.

"She was horrified—most horrified—at what she was seeing. I gave her the names of two patients I knew could be checked on and she did the follow-up this afternoon. At least in the case of your friend and Mr. Ferraro, it seems abundantly clear that they had no idea what was happening to them."

I nodded. "It makes a hideous kind of sense. Louisa starts having vague symptoms that she thinks are menopause—at thirty-four?—but then she never had any sex education to speak of, maybe it's not so incredible. Anyway, she wouldn't blab it around the plant. A lot of them come from the kind of background she did—where anything having to do with private body functions was shameful and never to be discussed."

"But, Victoria," Lotty burst out, "what is the sense of all this? Who besides a Mengele is so cold, so calculating in keeping these kinds of records, and saying nothing, not one word, to the people involved?"

I rubbed my head. The spot where I'd been hit was pretty well healed, but now that my brain was so stressed out, the injury was throbbing in a dull way, the pounding drum in the jungle of my mind.

"I don't know." Lotty's enervated state had infected me. "I can see why they don't want any of it coming out now."

Lotty shook her head impatiently. "Not so I. Explain, Victoria."

"Damages. Pankowski and Ferraro sued for indemnity payments they believed were rightfully theirs—they tried to build a case saying their illnesses were the result of exposure to Xerxine. Humboldt defended himself successfully. According to the lawyer who handled their suit, the company had two workable defenses—the first was that these guys both smoked and drank heavily, so no one could prove that Xerxine had poisoned them. And the second, which seemed to do the trick, was that their exposure had taken place before Xerxine's toxicity was known. So that . . ."

My voice trailed off. The problem with Jurshak's report to Mariners Rest became staggeringly clear to me. He was helping Humboldt hide the high mortality and illness rates at Xerxes to get favorable rate consideration from the insurance carrier. I could imagine a couple of different ways they could work it, but the likeliest seemed to be that they'd buy a better package from Mariners Rest than they offered the employees. Employees would be told that they didn't have coverage for certain tests or certain amounts of hospital stay. Then when the bills came in they'd go through the fiduciary and he'd fix them before sending them to the insurance company. I thought about it from several different angles and it still looked good. I got up and headed for the phone extension in the kitchen.

"So that what, Vic?" Lotty called impatiently behind me. "What are you doing?"

Turning off the chicken for starters: I'd forgotten the dinner I'd left simmering happily on the back of the stove. The olives were little charred lumps while the chicken seemed to have welded itself to the bottom of the pan. Definitely not the most successful recipe in my repertoire. I tried scraping the mess into the garbage can.

"Oh, never mind the dinner," Lotty said irritably. "Just put it in the sink and tell me the rest of your thinking. The company argued that they couldn't be responsible for the illness of anyone who worked for them if it took place before 1975 when Xerxine's toxicity was established by Ciba-Geigy. Is that it?"

"Yeah, except I didn't know about Ciba-Geigy or that 1975 was the critical year. And my bet is that they claimed to have lowered their ppm of Xerxine to whatever the decreed standard was, and that that's what their reports to Washington show. The ones that Jurshak sent out for Humboldt. But that the analysis SCRAP did at the plant shows much higher levels. I need to call Caroline Djiak and find out."

"But, Vic," Lotty said, absently scraping charred chicken from the skillet, "you still don't explain why they wouldn't tell their workers their bodies were being damaged. If the standard wasn't set until 1975, what difference did it make *before* then?"

"Insurance," I said shortly, trying to find Louisa's number in the directory. She wasn't listed. Snarling, I went back to the spare room to dig my address book out of my suitcase.

I returned to the kitchen and started dialing. "The only person who might tell us definitely is Dr. Chigwell, and he's missing right now. I'm not sure I could make him talk even if I could find him—Humboldt scares him much more than I do."

Caroline answered the phone on the fifth ring. "Vic. Hi. I was just putting Ma to bed. Can you hold? Or should I call back?"

I told her I'd wait. "But you see," I added to Lotty, "those notebooks mean bankruptcy now. Not for the whole company necessarily, but certainly for the Xerxes operation. A good lawyer gets hold of that stuff, contacts the employees or their families, and really goes to town. They've got all those Manville settlements to use by way of precedent."

No wonder Humboldt had been desperate enough to seek me out personally. His little empire was being threatened by the Turks. Frederick Manheim had been right—it must have seemed incredible to all of them that a detective could start nosing around Pankowski and Ferraro and not be looking for evidence of the blood work.

Why had Chigwell tried to kill himself? Overcome by remorse? Or did someone threaten him with a fate worse than death if he told Murray or me anything? The people he'd pranced off to on Friday might well have killed him by now if they thought he was going to crack on them.

I didn't think I'd ever find out exactly what happened. Nor did I see a way of bringing Nancy's death back to the great shark. The only hope would be if the two thugs Bobby had in custody spilled their guts and somehow managed to implicate Humboldt. But I didn't pin much hope on that. Even if they did talk, someone like Humboldt knew too many ways of insulating himself from the direct consequences of his actions. Just like Henry II. I shivered.

When Caroline came back on the line I asked her if Louisa had a brochure describing her Xerxes benefits.

"Christ, Vic, I don't know," she said impatiently. "What difference does it make?"

"A lot," I answered shortly. "It could explain why Nancy was killed and a whole lot of other unpleasant stuff."

Caroline gave an exaggerated sigh. She said she'd ask Louisa and put the phone down.

Nancy would have known about Xerxes's real loss experience because she was monitoring that as SCRAP's environment and health director. So when she'd seen the letter to Mariners Rest and found the company's rate structure, she'd seen at once that Jurshak was handling some kind of fiddle for them. But who had taken her files out of her office at SCRAP? Or maybe she'd had them on her, preparing for a confrontation with Jurshak, and he'd seen they were found and destroyed. But she'd left the other stuff in her car and he hadn't looked there.

When Caroline came back on the line she told me that Louisa thought she'd brought a flyer home with her but it would be buried in her papers. Did I want to wait while she looked? I asked her just to find it and leave it out for me to pick up in the morning. She began a barrage of questions. I couldn't deal with the insistent pressure in her voice.

"Give my love to Louisa," I interrupted tiredly, and hung up on her indignant squawks.

Lotty and I went out for a sober supper at the Dortmunder. Both of us felt too overwhelmed by the enormity revealed by the Chigwell notebooks to have much appetite, or to want to talk.

When we got home I checked in with Mr. Contreras. Young Arthur had taken off. The old man had locked front and back doors when he took Peppy out for her evening walk, but Art had opened a window and jumped out. Mr. Contreras was miserable—he felt he'd let me down the one time I'd actively sought his help.

"Don't worry about it," I said earnestly. "You couldn't possibly watch him twenty-four hours a day. He came to us for protection—if he doesn't want it, it's his neck, after all. You and I can't spend our lives looking around for scissors if he wants to keep sticking his head into nooses."

That cheered him slightly. Although he apologized several times more, he was able to talk about something else—like how lonely Peppy was with me away.

"Yeah, I miss both of you," I said. "Even your hot breath down my neck when I want to be alone."

He laughed delightedly at that and hung up much happier than I was. Although I really didn't give a damn what happened to young Art, I wasn't sure how much he'd learned of what I was figuring out. I didn't relish the thought of his taking any of it back to his father.

My answering service told me Murray had been trying to reach me. I tracked him down and told him nothing had jelled yet. He didn't really believe me, but he didn't have any way to prove I was wrong.

37

The Shark Puts Out Bait

My brain was in that numbed, feverish state where you sleep as though you are drugged—heavily but without getting any rest. The tragedy of Louisa's life kept playing itself out in my dreams, with Gabriella scolding me harshly in Italian for not having taken better care of our neighbor.

I woke for good at five and paced restlessly around Lotty's kitchen, wishing I had the dog with me, wishing I could get some exercise, wishing I could think of a way to force Gustav Humboldt to listen to me. Lotty joined me in the kitchen a little before six. Her drawn face told the tale of her own sleepless night. She put a strong hand on my shoulder and squeezed it gently, then went wordlessly to make coffee.

After Lotty had taken off for her early morning rounds at Beth Israel, I headed south once more to see Louisa. She was glad to see me, as always, but seemed tireder than the previous times I'd been there. I questioned her as gently and subtly as I knew how about the onset of her illness, when she'd first started feeling bad.

"You know those blood tests they used to take—old Chigwell the Chigger?"

She gave a scratchy laugh. "Oh my, yes. I saw where the old chigger tried to kill himself. It was on all the TV stations last week. He always was a weak little man, scared of his own shadow. Didn't surprise me he wasn't married. No woman wants a little shrimp like that who can't stand up for himself."

"What did he tell you when he took your blood?"

"One of our benefits, they called it, getting a physical every year like that with the blood work and everything. Not the kind of thing I would of thought of doing. Didn't know people went in for that sort of thing. But it was okay with the head of the union and the rest of us didn't care. Got us off the floor with pay one morning every year, you know."

"They never gave you any results? Or sent them to a doctor for you?"

"Go on, girl." Louisa flapped her hand and coughed loudly. "If they'd a gave us results, we wouldn't of known what they meant anyway. Dr. Chigwell showed me my chart once and I'm telling you, it was like Arab scrawl as far as I was concerned—you know those wiggly lines they put on their banners and all? That's about what medical tests look like to me."

I forced myself to laugh a little with her and sat talking awhile. She wore out quickly, though, and fell asleep in the middle of a sentence. I stayed with her while she slept, haunted by Gabriella's accusations in my dreams.

What a life. Growing up in that soul-killing house, raped by her own uncle, poisoned by her employer, and dying slowly and painfully. Yet she wasn't an unhappy person. When she'd moved next door she was frightened but not angry. She'd raised Caroline with joy and had taken pleasure in the freedom to lead her own life away from her parents. So maybe my pity was not only misplaced but condescending.

While I watched Louisa's chest rise and fall with her stertorous breath, I wondered what I should tell Caroline about her father. Not telling her was a form of control, a seizing of power in her life I had no right to. But telling her seemed unreasonably cruel. Did she deserve so heavy a knowledge?

I was still chewing it over in my mind when she dashed in at noon to fix Louisa's lunch, a light little meal with no salt and precious little food. Caroline was glad to see me but in a hurry, racing between meetings.

"Did you find the flyer? I left it by the coffeepot. I wish you'd tell me why you're so excited about it—if it concerns Ma I have a right to know."

"If I knew exactly how it concerned her, I'd tell you in a flash—I'm just picking my way through the forest right now."

I found the flyer and studied it while she took Louisa's lunch in to her. It left me more baffled than I'd been originally: all kinds of benefits Louisa got regularly were excluded. Outpatient care, dialysis, home oxygen. When Caroline came in I asked her who paid for all those things, wondering if she was somehow scraping the money together.

She shook her head. "Xerxes has been real good to Ma. They pay all these bills without asking. If you can't tell me what's going on with my own mother, I'm heading back to the office. And maybe I can find someone there who'll tell me. Maybe I'll hire my own investigator." She stuck out her tongue at me.

"Try it, brat—all the PI's in town have been informed that you're a bad risk."

She laughed and left. I stayed until Louisa had eaten her meager lunch and fallen asleep once more. Leaving the television on as white noise, I tiptoed out and returned the spare key to the ledge over the back porch.

I wished I understood the point of doing all that blood work years before anyone was interested in suing the company. Presumably it tied in with the insurance fiddle, but I couldn't see the exact connection. I didn't know anyone at Xerxes who might talk to me. Ms. Chigwell might, but her connection had been tenuous and not exactly sympathetic. She was all I had, though, so I made the long drive to Hinsdale.

Ms. Chigwell was in the garage painting her dinghy. She greeted me with her usual abrupt gruffness, but since she invited me in for tea I presumed she was glad to see me.

She had no idea why they had started doing the blood work down at the Xerxes plant. "I just remember that Curtis was in a flurry about it because they had to send all those specimens to some lab and then keep separate records of them, giving the employees numbers and so on. That's why he kept his own notebooks, so he could follow them by name and not have to worry about the numbering scheme."

I sat in the chintz armchair for over an hour, eating a large pile of cookies, while she discussed what she would do if she couldn't find her brother.

"I always wanted to go to Florence," she said. "But I'm too old now, I guess. I've never been able to get Curtis to agree to travel outside the country. He always suspects he'll get some terrible disease from the food or the water, or that foreigners will cheat him."

"I've always wanted to go to Florence, too—my mother came from a little town in southeastern Tuscany. My excuse is, I never have enough money together to pay for the airfare." I leaned forward and added persuasively, "You gave your brother most of your life. You don't have to spend the rest of it waiting at the window with a candle burning. If I was seventy-nine and in good health and had some money, I'd be at O'Hare with a suitcase and a passport in time for tonight's flight."

"You probably would," she agreed. "You're a brave girl."

I left soon after and headed back to Chicago, my shoulders aching again. Talking to Ms. Chigwell had been a long shot. I could've done it by phone if I didn't enjoy seeing her, but the fruitless errand at the end of a long week left me worn out. Maybe it was time to give the police what I had. I tried imagining how I'd tell Bobby my story:

"You see, they'd been doing all these blood tests on their employees and now they're afraid someone will find out and sue them for suppressing evidence of how toxic Xerxine really was."

And Bobby smiling indulgently and saying, "I know you took a liking to the old lady, but it's obvious she had a grudge against her brother all these years. I wouldn't take her reports at face value. How do you even know those notebooks were his? She has some medical training—she might have faked them just to get him in hot water. Then he disappears and she wants to unload them. Hell"—no, Bobby wouldn't use bad language in front of me—"Heck, Vicki, maybe they had one fight too many and she popped him on the head and then panicked and buried his body in Salt Creek. Then she calls you to say he's disappeared. You're high on the lady; you'll believe the story the way she wants to tell it."

And who was to say it hadn't happened that way? At any rate I was pretty sure that Bobby would look at it like that before he'd go after someone as important in Chicago as Gustav Humboldt. I could give Murray the whole story, but far from sharing Bobby's reluctance to go after Humboldt, Murray would leave a swath like General Sherman's through the lives of the people involved. I just didn't want to give him anything that would make him go after Louisa.

I stopped at my own apartment to cheer Mr. Contreras up over the loss of young Art and to see the dog. It was too dark for me to feel comfortable about going out with her, but she was clearly developing the restlessness an active animal feels when she doesn't get enough exercise. Another reason to get Humboldt off my back—so I could run the dog.

Once more I checked the roads around me, but my tail still seemed clear. In a way this made me less cheerful rather than more. Maybe my pals were just waiting for Troy and Wally to make bail. But maybe they'd decided that an ordinary hit wouldn't do and were looking for something more decisively spectacular, like a bomb in my car or at Lotty's apartment. Just in case, I parked some distance from her building and rode the bus back down Irving Park.

I made a frittata for dinner, a greater success than the chicken, since it wasn't scorched, but whether it had any taste I couldn't have said. I told Lotty my various dilemmas, about how to bring matters home to Jurshak and Humboldt, and about whether to tell Caroline I'd found her father.

She pursed her lips. "I can't advise you about Mr. Humboldt. You will have to think of a plan. But about Caroline's father, I must tell you that in my experience it is always better for people to know. You say it is horrible news, and it is. But she is not a weakling. And you cannot decide for her what she can know, what she is better off not learning. For one thing, she may discover it in a more terrible way from someone else. And for another, she can easily imagine things that seem more hideous to her. So in your place I would tell her."

It was a more articulate way of stating my own thoughts. I nodded. "Thanks, Lotty."

We spent the rest of the evening silently. Lotty was going through the morning's papers, the light making little prisms on the half-glasses she wore for reading. I did nothing. I felt as though my mind were encased in lead shielding—protective covering to keep any ideas from entering. The residue of my fear. I kept nipping at the big shark but I was afraid to find a harpoon and attack him directly. I hated knowing he'd been able to intimidate me, but knowing it didn't make a stream of ideas gush forth.

The phone startled me from my somber reverie around nine. One of the house staff at Beth Israel wasn't sure what to do with a patient of Lotty's. She talked to him for a while, then decided she'd better handle the delivery herself and left.

I'd bought a bottle of whiskey yesterday along with the groceries. After Lotty had been gone half an hour or so, I poured myself a drink and tried to get interested in John Wayne's televised antics. When the phone rang again around ten I turned off the set, thinking the caller might be one of Lotty's patients.

"Dr. Herschel's residence."

"I'm looking for a woman named Warshawski." It was a man's voice, cold, uninterested. The last time I'd heard it it had told me that the person hadn't been born who could swim in a swamp.

"If I see her, I'll be glad to give her a message," I said with what coolness I could muster.

"You can ask her if she knows Louisa Djiak," the cold voice went on flatly.

"And if she does?" My voice wobbled despite every effort I put into controlling it.

"Louisa Djiak doesn't have much longer to live. She could die at home in her bed. Or she could disappear in the lagoons behind the Xerxes plant. Your friend Warshawski can make the choice. Louisa is down at Xerxes now. She's well sedated. All you have to do—all you have to tell your friend Warshawski to do is go down and take a look at her. If she does, the Djiak woman will wake up in her bed tomorrow without knowing she ever left it. But if any police come along with Warshawski, they'll have to find some frogmen who like diving in Xerxine before they can give the Djiak woman a Christian burial." The line went dead.

I wasted a few minutes on useless self-recrimination. I'd been so focused on myself, on my closeness to Lotty, I'd never imagined Louisa's being in danger. Despite the fact that I'd told Jurshak I knew her secret. If she and I were gone, no one would remain to speak about it and he would be safe.

I forced myself to think calmly—cursing myself not only wasted time, it would cloud my judgment. The first thing to do was get moving—I could wait for the long drive south to develop some brilliant strategy. I loaded a second clip and stuck it in my jacket pocket, then scribbled a note for Lotty. I was amazed to see my handwriting flow in the same large dark strokes as always.

I was just locking Lotty's door when I remembered the ruse that had gotten Mr. Contreras away from our building a few nights ago. I didn't want to walk into a trap here. I went back inside to make sure that Louisa really was missing from the bungalow on Houston. No one answered the phone. After a few frantic calls—first to Mrs. Cleghorn to get the names and numbers of some other people at SCRAP—I learned Caroline had come back to the office around four. She was closeted now with some EPA lawyers downtown in what was likely to be an all-night session.

The woman I talked to had the number of the people living in my parents' old house, a couple named Santiago. Caroline had given their home phone number to everyone she worked with in case of some emergency. When I called Mrs. Santiago she obligingly told me that Louisa had been taken away in an ambulance around eight-thirty. I thanked her mechanically and hung up.

It had been almost half an hour since I'd gotten the call. It was time to move. I wanted company for the trip but it would be wanton to bring Mr. Contreras along—for him and Louisa both. I thought of friends, of police, of Murray, but of no one whom I could ask to go with me into such extreme danger.

I looked carefully around the hallway when I left Lotty's. Someone had known to phone me here—they might take the easy route and just shoot me as I walked down the stairs. I kept my back pressed against the stairwell wall, crouching low. Instead of going out the front door, I went on down to the basement. Carefully picked my way across the dark floor, fumbling cautiously with Lotty's keys for the one that undid the double lock on the basement door. Made my way down the alley to Irving Park Road.

A bus pulled up just as I got to the main road. I dug in my pocket to find a token under the spare clip and finally pried one out without having to flash my ammunition to the world at large. I rode the eight blocks down Irving Park standing, seeing nothing either of passengers or the night. At Ashland I hopped down and found my car.

The bus's grinding diesel had somehow provided the background I needed to relax my mind completely, for ideas to flow. If an ambulance had come for Louisa, if she was completely sedated, they must have found a doctor. And there could be only one guess as to what doctor would be involved in such an infamous scheme. So there was one person who shared my involvement whom it would not be criminal to ask to share my risk. For the second time today I headed out the Eisenhower to Hinsdale.

38

Toxic Shock

Veils of fog rose from the drainage ditches lining the tollway, covering the road in patches so that other cars appeared only as shrouded pricks of red. I kept the speedometer pointed at eighty, even when the thick mist drowned the road in front of us. The Chevy vibrated noisily, prohibiting conversation. Every now and then I rolled the window down and put up a hand to feel the ropes. They'd loosened a bit but the dinghy stayed on top.

We exited at 127th Street for the trek eastward. We were about eight miles west of the Xerxes plant, but no expressway connects the east and west sides of Chicago this far south.

It was getting close to midnight. Fear and impatience gripped me so strongly, I could scarcely breathe. All my will went into the car, maneuvering around other vehicles, squeaking through lights as they turned, keeping a weather eye cocked for passing patrol cars as I managed to do fifty in the thirty-five-mile zones. Fourteen minutes after leaving the tollway we were turning north on the little track that Stony Island becomes that far south.

We were on private industrial property now, but I couldn't cut the headlights on the rutted, glass-filled track. I'd chosen a run-down looking plant in the hopes that they wouldn't run to a night watchman. Or dog. We pulled to a stop in front of a large cement barge. I looked at Ms. Chigwell. She nodded grimly.

We opened the car doors, trying to move quietly but more concerned with speed. Ms. Chigwell held a strong pencil flash for me while I cut the ropes. She folded a blanket across the hood so that I could slide the dinghy down as noiselessly as possible. We then laid the blanket on the ground to make a little cradle for the dinghy. I pulled it over to the cement barge while she followed, holding the flash and carrying the oars.

The barge was tied up next to a set of iron rungs built into the wall. We lowered the dinghy over the side, then I held its painter while Ms. Chigwell climbed briskly down the ladder. I followed her quickly.

We each took an oar. Despite her age, Ms. Chigwell had a strong, firm stroke. I matched mine to hers, forcing my mind from the incipient throb in my healing shoulders. She had to use both hands to row, so I held the pencil flash. We hugged the left bank; I periodically shone the light so we could avoid barges and keep track of the names on the slips as we rowed past. The bank had long since been cemented over; company names were painted in large letters next to the steel ladders that led to their loading bays.

The night was silent except for the soft clop of our oars breaking water. But the thick mist carrying the river's miasmas was a pungent reminder of the industrial maze we were floating through. Every now and then a spotlight broke the fog, pinpointing a giant steel tube, a barge, a girder. We were the only humans on the river, Eve and her mother in a grotesque mockery of Eden.

We rowed north past the Glow-Rite landing, beyond steel and wire companies, plants that did printing, made tools or saw blades, glided by the heavy barges tied up next to a rebar mill. Finally Ms. Chigwell's penetrating little flash picked up the double X's and the giant crown gleaming black in the fog.

We banked the oars. I looked at my watch. Twelve minutes to cover the half mile or so. It had seemed much longer. I grabbed a steel rung as we slid by and carefully pulled the dinghy up next to it. Ms. Chigwell tied the painter with practiced hands. My heart was beating hard enough to suffocate me, but she seemed utterly calm.

We pulled dark caps down low on our foreheads. We clasped hands for a moment, her compulsive squeeze showing what her impassive face hid. I pointed at my watch in an exaggerated movement and she nodded calmly.

Pulling my gun out and releasing the safety, I scrambled up the ladder, my right hand bare so that I could feel the trigger of the Smith & Wesson. I slowed down at the top, cautiously raising my dark-hatted head so that just my eyes came above the bank. If I cried out, Ms. Chigwell would row as fast as she could back to the car and raise an alarm.

I was at the back of the plant, at the concrete platform where the barge had been tied the last time I'd visited the place. Tonight the steel doors surrounding the loading bay were rolled shut and padlocked. Two spotlights at the corners of the building cut the haze around me. As nearly as I could tell no one was anticipating a river approach.

I slid my gun hand over the top of the bank and kept the Smith & Wesson in front of me as I hoisted myself onto land. I rolled over and lay still for a count of sixty. That was Ms. Chigwell's signal to start the climb herself. I could just make out the change in the darkness as her head popped over the edge of the bank—anyone farther away wouldn't be able to see her. She waited another count of twenty, then joined me on the loading platform.

The steel doors lay in a shadow cast by the projecting roof. We moved close to them, trying not to touch them—the sound of arms or gun brushing on steel would vibrate like a reggae band in the still night.

In front of us the spotlights turned the fog into a heavy curtain. Using its draperies as a shield, we moved slowly around to the north end of the plant where the clay-banked lagoons lay. Ms. Chigwell moved with the practiced silence of a lifelong second-story woman.

As soon we rounded the corner we moved into thicker fog and danker smells. No lights shone on the lagoons. We sensed their pungent presence to our right but didn't dare use the flash. Ms. Chigwell stayed close to me, holding my muffler, feeling her way cat-footed behind me in the dark. After an eternity of careful steps, moving slowly through ruts, sidestepping metal scraps, we reached the front end of the plant.

The fog was thinner here. We crouched behind some steel drums and peered cautiously around them. A single light burned at the gate leading into the yard. After looking for a long moment I could make out a man standing near the entrance. A sentry or lookout. An ambulance was in the center of the drive. I wished I knew if Louisa was still in it.

"Is she going to show up or not?"

The unexpected voice near my left startled me so much, I almost knocked myself against the steel drum. I recovered, trembling, trying to control my breathing. Next to me, Ms. Chigwell remained as impassive as ever.

"It's been a little over two hours. We'll give her until one. Then we'll have to decide what to do with the Djiak woman." The second voice belonged to my anonymous phone caller.

"She'll have to go into the lagoon. We can't afford any more traces."

Now that my heart had settled to a less tumultuous pace, I recognized the first speaker. Art Jurshak, showing a strong family feeling for his niece.

"*You* can't." The second man spoke with his usual uninterested coldness. "The woman's going to die soon anyway. We'll just get the doctor to give her a little shot and return her to her bed. Her daughter will find she died in the night."

At the mention of the doctor it was Ms. Chigwell's turn to tremble a little.

"You're losing it," Art said angrily. "How're you going to get her back into the house without the daughter seeing you? Anyway, she'll know her mother's gone—she's probably roused the neighborhood by now as it is. Better just dispose of Louisa here and set a trap for Warshawski someplace else. It'd be best if they were both gone."

"I'll do it for you," the cold voice said flatly. "I'll get rid of them both and the daughter, too, if you want. But I can't if I don't know why you're so desperate to see them put away. It wouldn't be ethical." He used the last word without any hint of irony.

"Damn you, I'll take care of things myself," Art muttered furiously.

"Fine," the voice said irritatingly. "Either way it's fine. You tell me what they know and I'll have that, or you kill them yourself and I'll have that. It's a matter of complete indifference to me."

Jurshak was silent for a minute. "I'd better see how the doc is making out."

His footsteps echoed and disappeared. He'd gone inside. So Louisa wasn't in the ambulance. Presumably one of the flat-voiced man's side-kicks was waiting in its interior instead of Louisa—they'd left it temptingly in the middle of the yard so I'd head straight to it.

How to get past the cold-voiced man standing at the entrance was a tougher question. If I sent Ms. Chigwell out as a diversion, she'd be a dead diversion. I was wondering if we could jimmy a door or a window around the side when the man solved the problem for us. He strolled out to the center of the yard, where he stopped to knock on the back of the ambu-lance. The rear door opened a crack. He stood talking through the open-ing.

I tapped Ms. Chigwell on the shoulder. She stood up with me and we sidled slowly to the shadow of the wall. While we watched, the ambulance door shut again and the cold-voiced man wandered on out to the gate. As soon as he was on the far side of the vehicle, I crouched low and sprinted around the corner to the plant entrance. Ms. Chigwell's footsteps sounded softly behind me. The ambulance shielded us from the view of the gate sentry and we made it inside without hearing any outcry.

We were on a concrete apron outside the plant floor. The sliding steel curtain that separated the manufacturing area from the main entrance was shut, but a normal-sized door next to it stood ajar. We quickly darted through it, shutting it softly behind us, and found ourselves immediately in the plant.

We walked on tiptoe, although the noises around us would have drowned any sounds we made. The pipes let out their intermittent belches of steam and the cauldrons bubbled ominously under the dull green safety lights. Fritz Lang had invented this room. Presently we would come to the end and find only cameramen and laughing actors. A drop of liquid fell on me and I jumped, convinced I'd been poisoned with a toxic dose of Xerxine.

I glanced at Ms. Chigwell. She was looking straight ahead, ignoring the spitting from above as assiduously as she avoided the obscene graffiti crawled on the huge "No Smoking" signs. Suddenly, though, she bit back a cry. I followed her eyes to the far corner of the room. Louisa lay there on a stretcher. Dr. Chigwell stood on one side of her, Art Jurshak on the other. The two of them stared at us, slack-jawed.

Dr. Chigwell found his voice first. "Clio! What are you doing here?"

She marched forward fiercely. I held her arm to keep her from getting within Jurshak's grabbing range.

"I came to find you, Curtis." Her voice was sharp and carried authoritatively over the hissing pipes. "You've gotten yourself involved with some very nasty people. I presume you've spent the last week or so with them. I don't know what Mother would say if she were alive to see you, but I think it's time you came back home again. We'll help Miss Warshawski get this poor sick woman back into the ambulance and then you and I will return to Hinsdale."

I had my gun leveled at Art. Sweat stood out on his round face, but he said pugnaciously, "You can't shoot. Chigwell here has a needle ready to inject Louisa. If you shoot me, it's her death warrant."

"I'm overcome, Art, by your family feeling. If this is the first time you've seen your niece in twenty-seven years or so, your reaction would move even Klaus Barbie to tears."

Art made a violent gesture. He tried shouting at me, but the messages—guilt over his long-forgotten incest, fear of others finding it out, rage at seeing me alive—kept him from getting out anything coherent.

"Is this woman his niece?" Ms. Chigwell demanded of me.

"Yes, indeed," I said loudly. "And she has closer ties to you than that, doesn't she, Art?"

"Curtis, I will not tolerate your killing this unfortunate young woman. And if she is your friend's niece, it is absolutely unthinkable that you do so. It would be unethical and totally unworthy of you as the inheritor of Father's practice."

Chigwell looked at his sister dejectedly. He shrank a little inside his overcoat and his hands hung loosely at his sides. If I acted now, he wouldn't do anything to Louisa.

I was bracing myself to take a flying leap at Art when I saw malice replace the frustration in his face—he was watching someone come up behind us.

Without glancing around, I seized Ms. Chigwell and rolled with her behind the nearest vat. When I looked up I saw a man in a dark overcoat stroll into the area where we'd been standing. I knew his face—I'd seen it on TV or the papers or in court when I'd been a public defender—I just couldn't place it.

"You took your fucking time, Dresberg," Jurshak snapped. "Why'd you let that Warshawski bitch in here to begin with?"

Of course. Steve Dresberg. The Garbage King. Majestic slayer of little flies buzzing around his trash empire.

He spoke in the cold flat voice that made the hairs prickle along my spine. "She must've cut her way under the fence and come in when I was out talking to the boys. I'll get them to go take care of her car when we're done here."

"We're not done here yet, Dresberg," I announced from my nook. "Too much success has gone to your head, made you careless. You should never have tried to kill me the same way you did Nancy. You're getting soft, Dresberg. You're a loser now."

My taunts didn't move him. He was a pro, after all. He lifted his left hand from his coat pocket and pointed a large gun—maybe a Colt .358— at Louisa. "Come out now, girlie, or your sick friend here will be dead a few months before her time." He didn't look at me—a message that I was too trivial for direct attention.

"I listened to you and Art out front," I called. "The two of you agreed she's as good as dead already. But you'd better get me first, because if you shoot at her, you're dead meat."

He swung so fast, I didn't have time to drop before he fired. The bullet went wide as the shot boomed in the cavernous room. Ms. Chigwell crouched, white but stern, on the floor next to me. Unbidden, she took her keys from her sweater pocket. While she moved to one side of our protective vat, I slid to the other. When I nodded she darted around the end of the vat and hurled her keys at Dresberg's face.

He fired at the movement. From the corner of my eye I saw Ms. Chigwell drop. I couldn't go to her now. I got behind Dresberg and fired at him. The first shot went by him, but as he turned to face me I got him twice in the chest. Even then he fired two more rounds before collapsing.

I ran to him and jumped on his gun arm with all my force. His fingers loosened on the revolver. Jurshak was moving up on me, hoping to wrestle Dresberg's gun away before I could get to it. Fury was riding me, though, choking the breath from me, covering my eyes with a hazy film. I shot Jurshak in the chest. He gave an enraged cry and fell in front of me.

Chigwell had stood next to Louisa's stretcher throughout the fracas, his hands flaccidly at his side, his head hunched into his coat. I went over to him and slapped his face. I meant at first just to rouse him from his stupor, but my rage was consuming me so that I found myself pounding him over and over, screaming at him that he was a traitor to his oath, a miserable worm of a man, on and on, over and over. I might have kept at him until his body joined Jurshak and Dresberg on the floor, but through the haze I felt a tug on my arm.

Ms. Chigwell had staggered over, trailing blood on the dirty concrete. "He's all of that, Miss Warshawski. All that and more. But let him be. He's an old man and not likely to change at this time of life."

I shook my head, exhausted and sick. Sick of the stench in the plant, of the foulness of the three men, of my own destructive rage. My gorge rose; I skipped behind a vat to throw up. Wiping my face with a Kleenex, I returned to Ms. Chigwell. The bullet had grazed her upper arm, leaving a bloody furrow of singed flesh but no deep wound. I felt a small measure of relief.

"We've got to get into an office, someplace we can secure, and call the police. There're at least three more men outside and you and I are not taking on any more thugs tonight. We've got to move fast before they start worrying about Dresberg and come looking for him. Can you hold out awhile longer?"

She nodded gamely and helped me bully her brother into showing us the way to his old office. I pushed Louisa's stretcher behind them. She was still alive, her breath coming in short shallow gasps.

When we were inside with the door locked I moved Louisa into the tiny examining room to one side of the office. With the remaining shreds of my strength, I pushed the heavy metal desk athwart the door. I sank to the floor and pulled the phone down next to me.

"Bobby? It's me. Sorry to wake you, but I need your help. Lots of help and fast." I explained what had happened as clearly as I could. It took a few tries to get him to understand me and even then he was skeptical.

"Bobby!" My voice cracked. "You've got to come. I have an old woman with a bullet wound and Louisa Djiak with some awful drug in her and three thugs prowling outside. I need you." The anguish got through to him. He took directions to the plant and hung up before I could say anything else.

I sat for a moment with my head in my hands, wanting nothing more than to lie down on the floor and cry. Instead I forced myself to stand up, to release the half-empty clip and slip in a full one.

Chigwell had taken his sister into the little examining room to patch up her arm. I wandered in to look at Louisa. While I stood there her eyelids fluttered open.

"Gabriella?" she said scratchily. "Gabriella, I might've known you wouldn't forget me in my troubles."

39

Plant Clean-Up

Louisa went back to sleep while I held her hand. When her weak grasp had relaxed I turned to Chigwell and demanded fiercely what he had given her.

"Just—just a sedative," he said, licking his lips nervously. "Just morphine. She'll sleep a lot for the next day, that's all."

From her seat at the desk Ms. Chigwell gave him a look of scalding contempt, but seemed too exhausted to put her feelings into words. I fixed a pallet for her in the examining room, but she came from a generation too modest to lie down in public. Instead she sat upright in the old office chair, her eyelids drooping in her white face.

Fatigue was combining with the tension of waiting to drive me into a frenzy of nervous irritation. I kept checking my barricades, moving into the examining room to listen to Louisa's shallow, gasping breaths, back to the office to look at Ms. Chigwell.

Finally I turned on the doctor, putting all my feverish energy into prying his story from him. It made a short, unedifying tale. He had worked so many years with the Xerxes blood tests that he'd managed to forget one niggling little detail: He wasn't letting people know he thought they might be getting sick. When I showed up asking questions about Pankowski and Ferraro, he'd gotten scared. And when Murray's reporters had shown up he'd become downright terrified. What if the truth came out? It would mean not just malpractice suits but terrible humiliation at Clio's hands—she'd never let him forget that he hadn't lived up to their father's standard. That comment brought him the only fleeting sympathy he had from me—his sister's fierce ethics must be hell to live with.

When the doctor's suicide attempt failed he didn't know what to do. Then Jurshak had called—Chigwell knew him from his workdays in South

Chicago. If Chigwell would give them a little simple help, they would arrange for any evidence against him to be suppressed.

He'd had no choice, he muttered—to me, not his sister. When he learned all they wanted was for him to give Louisa Djiak a strong sedative and look after her down at the plant for a few hours, he was happy to comply. I didn't ask him how he felt about going one step further and giving her a fatal injection.

"But why?" I demanded. "Why go through that charade to begin with if you weren't going to give employees their results?"

"Humboldt told me to," he mumbled, looking at his hands.

"I could have guessed that part!" I snapped. "But why in God's name did he tell you to?"

"It—uh—it had to do with the insurance," he muttered in the back of his throat.

"Spit it out, Curtis. You're not leaving until I know, so say it and get it over with."

He stole a look at his sister, but she sat white and still, lost in her own cloud of exhaustion.

"The insurance," I prompted.

"We could see—Humboldt knew—we had too many health claims, too many people were losing work time. First our health insurance began going up, way up, then we were dropped by Ajax Assurance and had to find another company. They'd done a study, they told us our claims were too high."

My jaw dropped. "So you got Jurshak to act as your fiduciary and screw up the data so you could prove you were insurable to another carrier?"

"It was just a way of buying time until we could figure out what the problem was and fix it. That was when we started doing the blood studies."

"What was happening on the worker's comp side?"

"Nothing. None of the illnesses were compensable."

"Because they weren't work related?" My temples ached with the effort of following his convoluted tale. "But they were. You were proving they were with all that blood data."

"Not at all, young lady." For a moment his pompous side reasserted itself. "That data did not establish causality. It merely enabled us to project medical expenses and the probable turnover of the work force."

I was too appalled to speak. His words came out so glibly that they must have been spoken hundreds of times at committee meetings or before the board of directors. Let's just see what our work-force costs will be if we know that X percent of our employees will be sick Y fraction of the time. Run different cost projections tediously by hand in the days before computers. Then someone has the bright idea—get hard data and we'll know for sure.

The enormity of the whole scheme made me murderous with rage. Louisa's harsh breath in the background added fuel to my fury. I wanted to shoot Chigwell where he sat, then ride off to the Gold Coast and plug Humboldt. That bastard. That cynical, inhuman murderer. Anger swept through me in waves, making me weep.

"So no one got their proper life or health coverage just to save you guys a few miserable stupid dollars."

"Some of them did," Chigwell muttered. "Enough to keep the wrong people from asking questions. This woman here did. Jurshak said he knew her family so he was obligated to look after her."

At that I thought I really would commit murder, but a movement from Ms. Chigwell caught my attention. Her gaunt face was unchanged, but she'd apparently been listening despite her seeming remoteness. She tried holding out a hand to me, but her strength wasn't up to the task. Instead she said in the thread of a voice:

"What you're describing is too heinous to discuss, Curtis. We'll talk tomorrow about our arrangements. We can't go on living together after this."

He deflated again, shrinking inside himself without speaking. He probably couldn't think beyond tonight, with its threat of arrest and prison. Perhaps other horrors were adding to the gray pallor around his mouth, but I didn't think so—I didn't think he had enough imagination to picture what he'd really been doing as the Xerxes doctor. Maybe being booted into the cold by the sister who had always protected him was punishment enough—maybe it would hurt him worse than anything I could do.

Exhausted, I returned to the examining room to look at Louisa again. Her shallow breathing seemed unchanged. She muttered in her sleep—something about Caroline, I couldn't make out what.

It was then that the shots started. I looked at my watch: thirty-eight minutes since I'd called Bobby. It had to be the police. Had to be. I forced my weary shoulders into action, moving the desk back from the door. Telling my charges to stay put, I turned out the room lights and crept back to the plant. Another five minutes passed, and then the place was filled with boys in blue. I moved out from the cover of one of the vats to talk to them.

It took awhile to get things sorted out—who I was, why an alderman was lying in his own blood next to Steve Dresberg on a factory floor, what Louisa Djiak and the Chigwells were doing there. You know—all the usual stuff.

When Bobby Mallory showed up at three we started moving faster. He listened to my worries about Louisa for about thirty seconds, then had one of the men send for a fire department ambulance to take her to Help of Christians. Another ambulance had already carted Dresberg and Jurshak to County Hospital. Both were still alive, their futures uncertain.

I snatched a minute in the confusion to call Lotty, let her know the bare bones of what had happened and that I was unhurt. I told her not to wait up, but in my secret heart I begged her to.

When the state police arrived they assigned a car to ferry the Chigwells home. They'd wanted to send Ms. Chigwell to a hospital for observation, but she was adamant about returning to her own home.

Before Mallory came I'd been telling everyone that Jurshak had lured Chigwell down to the plant with a tale about finding a half-dead employee on the premises. Ms. Chigwell hadn't let him go alone this late at night and the two found themselves caught in the cross fire. Bobby looked narrowly at me, but finally agreed to my version when it was clear he wasn't going to get anything else from the doctor or his sister.

Bobby left me squatting wearily against a pillar on the plant floor while he conferred with the Fifth District commander. The light winking from uniform jackets and hardware made me dizzy; I shut my eyes, but I couldn't keep out the clamor, or the murky Xerxine smell. What would my creatine level be after tonight? I pictured my kidneys filled with lesions —blood-red with black holes in them, oozing Xerxine. Someone shook me roughly. I opened my eyes. Sergeant McGonnigal was standing over me, his square face displaying unusual concern.

"Let's get you outside—you need some fresh air, Vic."

I let him help me to my feet and stumbled after him to the loading bay, where the police had rolled back the steel doors leading to the river. The fog had lifted; stars showed little yellow pricks in the polluted heavens. The air was still pungent with the scent of many chemicals but the cold made it fresher than it was inside the plant. I looked down at the water glinting black in the moonlight and shivered.

"You've had a pretty rough night."

McGonnigal's voice held just the right level of concern. I tried not to imagine him learning how to talk to difficult witnesses like that at a seminar in Springfield—I tried to think he really cared about the horrors I'd been through. After all, we'd known each other six or seven years.

"A little exhausting," I admitted.

"You want to tell me about it, or do you want to wait to talk to the lieutenant?"

So it was role-playing from a seminar. My shoulders sagged a bit farther. "If I tell you, will I have to repeat it to Mallory? It's not a story I feel like going over more than once."

"You know the cops, Warshawski—we never take any story just once. But if you'll give me the outline tonight, I'll make sure that does for now—get you home while there's still a little left of the night to sleep in."

Maybe there was a little personal concern mixed in. Not enough to make me tell the whole truth and nothing but—I mean, I wasn't going to explain about the doctor's medical texts. And certainly not Jurshak's relations with Louisa. But after I'd pulled a crate over to the water's edge and sat on it, I gave him more details than I'd originally planned to.

I started with the call from Dresberg. "He knew Louisa was important to me—my mother had looked after her when she was pregnant and they'd been pretty good friends. So they must have realized she was one person I'd come out here to help."

"Why didn't you call us then?" McGonnigal asked impatiently.

"I didn't know how you'd manage a quiet assault. They had her in the back of the plant here—they'd simply have murdered her if they figured they were under attack. I wanted to sneak in here myself."

"And just how did you manage that? They had a lookout where the road turns off to here and another guy at the gates. Don't tell me you sprayed some amnesiac in the air and slid by them."

I shook my head and pointed at the dinghy floating below us. The floodlights overhead picked up the incredulity in McGonnigal's face.

"You rowed up the river in that? Come on, Warshawski. Get real."

"It's the truth," I said stubbornly. "Believe it or not. Ms. Chigwell was with me—it's her boat."

"I thought you said they'd come here together."

I nodded. "I knew if I told you the truth, you'd keep her and her brother here all night and they're too old for that. Besides, she got shot in the arm, even if it did just graze her—she should have been in bed hours ago."

McGonnigal pounded the crate with the flat of his hand. "You don't have an armlock on empathy, Warshawski. Even the police are capable of showing concern for a couple as old as the Chigwells. Can't you drop your sixties 'Off the Pigs' mentality for five minutes and let us do our job? You could have been killed and gotten the Djiak woman and your elderly friends knocked off in the bargain."

"For your information," I said coldly, "my father was a beat cop and I never in my life referred to the police as pigs. Anyway, no one got killed, not even those two pieces of shit who deserved it. Do you want to hear the rest of my story or would you rather get up in your pulpit and preach at me some more?"

He sat stiffly for a moment. "I guess I can see why Bobby Mallory shows up at his worst around you. I was bragging to myself that I was going to show the lieutenant what a younger officer with sensitivity training could do with a witness like you, and I blew it in five minutes. Finish your story—I won't criticize your methods."

I finished my story. I told him I didn't know how Chigwell had gotten hooked up with Jurshak and Dresberg, but that they'd forced him to come along tonight to look after Louisa. And that Ms. Chigwell was worried about him, so when I showed up with my crazy suggestion that we row up the Calumet and sneak up on the plant from the rear, she jumped at the chance.

"I know she's seventy-nine, but sailing's been her hobby since she was a kid and she sure handled her oar splendidly. So then we got here, and we had a lucky break—Jurshak went into the plant and Dresberg walked off to check on the people in the ambulance. Who was in it? Is that who shot at you guys when you showed up?"

"No, that was the sentry," McGonnigal explained. "He tried making a run for it. Someone got him in the abdomen."

I suddenly realized that Caroline Djiak didn't know where her own mother was. I explained the problem to McGonnigal. "She's probably roused the mayor by now. I should call her if I can get back into one of the offices."

He shook his head. "I think you've done enough running around for one evening. I'll send a uniformed man over to her house—then she can get an escort down to the hospital if she wants. I'll run you home."

I thought it over. Maybe I'd just as soon not include a close encounter with Caroline in the night's strains.

"Could we go pick up my car? It's down on Stony a half mile or so."

He pulled out his walkie-talkie and summoned a uniformed officer—my pal Mary Louise Neely. She saluted him smartly, but I could see she was eyeing me curiously. So maybe she was human after all.

"Neely, I want you to drive Ms. Warshawski and me down the road to pick up her car. Then go to the address she gives you on Houston." He sketched the situation with Caroline and Louisa.

Officer Neely nodded enthusiastically—it's a break to be signaled out for a special assignment from among so many. Even though it was just chauffeuring duty, it gave her a chance to make an impression on a senior man. She trailed behind us as McGonnigal went to tell Bobby what we were doing.

Bobby agreed reluctantly—he wasn't going to contradict his sergeant in front of me or a uniformed officer. "But you're talking to me tomorrow, Vicki, whether you like it or not. You hear?"

"Yeah, Bobby. I hear. Just wait until the afternoon—I'll be a lot more cooperative if I get some sleep."

"Yeah, princess. You private operators work when you feel like it and leave the garbage for the cops to sweep up. You'll talk to me when I'm ready for you."

The light was dancing in my eyes again. I had moved beyond fatigue to a state where I'd start hallucinating if I wasn't careful. I followed McGonnigal and Neely into the night without trying to respond.

40

Night Shakes

When Officer Neely had dropped us at my car, I dug the keys from my jeans pocket and handed them wordlessly to McGonnigal. He turned the car in the rutted yard while I leaned back in the passenger seat, releasing it so it was almost horizontal.

I was sure I'd fall asleep as soon as I lay back, but images from the night kept exploding in my head. Not the silent trip up the Calumet—that had already faded to the surreal world of half-remembered dreams. Louisa lying on the cart at the end of the plant, Dresberg's cold indifference, waiting for the police in Chigwell's office. I hadn't been afraid at the time, but the recurring pictures gave me the shakes now. I tried clenching my arms against the sides of the seat to control the shaking.

"It's aftershock." McGonnigal's voice came clinically in the dark. "Don't be ashamed of it."

I pulled the seat back to its upright position. "It's the ugliness," I said. "The horrible reasons Jurshak had for doing it, and the fact that Dresberg isn't a man anymore, he's an unfeeling death machine. If they'd just been a couple of punks jumping me in an alley, I wouldn't feel this way."

McGonnigal reached out an arm and groped for my left hand. He squeezed it reassuringly but didn't speak. After a minute his fingers stiffened; he withdrew them and concentrated on turning onto the Calumet Expressway.

"A good investigator would take advantage of your fatigue and get you to explain what Jurshak's horrible reasons were."

I braced myself in the dark, trying to prepare my wits. Never speak without thinking. A cardinal rule to my clients in my public defender days. First the cops wear you out, then they show you some sympathy, then they get you to spill your guts.

McGonnigal tried taking the Chevy up to eighty, but slowed to seventy when it started vibrating. Police privilege.

"I expect you have some cover story ready," he went on, "and it'd really be police brutality to force you to keep it up when you're this tired."

After that the temptation to tell him everything I knew became nearly irresistible. I forced myself to watch what aspect of landscape one could see from the expressway canyons, to push away the picture of Louisa's disoriented gaze confusing me with Gabriella.

McGonnigal didn't speak again until we were passing the Loop exits and then it was only to ask for Lotty's address.

"Would you like to come back to Jefferson Park with me instead?" he asked unexpectedly. "Have a brandy, unwind?"

"Spill all my secrets in bed after the second drink? No—don't get upset, that was supposed to be a joke. You just couldn't tell in the dark." It sounded appealing, but Lotty would be anxiously awaiting me—I couldn't leave her hanging. I tried explaining this to McGonnigal.

"She's the one person I never lie to. She's—not my conscience—the person who helps me see who I really am, I guess."

He didn't answer until he'd pulled off the Kennedy at Irving Park. "Yeah, I understand. My grandfather was like that. I was trying to picture myself in your situation with him waiting up for me; I'd have to go back too."

They didn't teach that in any seminar in Springfield. I asked about his grandfather. He'd died five years ago.

"The week before my promotion came through. I was so mad I almost resigned—why couldn't they have given it to me when he was still alive to see it? But then I could hear him saying, 'What do you think, Johnnie— God runs the universe with you in mind?' " He laughed a little to himself. "You know, Warshawski, I've never told that to another soul?"

He pulled up in front of Lotty's place.

"How're you going to get home?" I asked.

"Umm, I'll summon a squad car. They'll be glad to have an excuse to leave the mayhem in Uptown for a chance to drive me."

He held the keys out to me. Under the sodium light I could see his eyebrows lift in inquiry. I leaned across the seat divider and put my arms around him and kissed him. He smelled of leather and sweat, human smells that made me wriggle closer to him. We sat like that for several minutes, but the ashtray in the divider was digging into my side.

I pulled away. "Thanks for the ride, Sergeant."

"A pleasure, Warshawski. We serve and protect, you know."

I invited him to come up and call a squad car from Lotty's but he said he'd do it from the street, that he needed the night air. He watched while I undid the lobby locks, then sketched a wave and walked off.

Lotty was in her sitting room, still in the dark skirt and sweater she'd put on for the hospital seven hours earlier. She was flicking the pages of *The Guardian,* making only a pretext of interest in Scottish economic woes. She put the paper down as soon as she saw me.

It felt like home to nestle in her arms; I was glad I'd decided to come back here instead of going off with McGonnigal. While she bathed my face and fed me hot milk, I told her the night's tale, the strange ride up the river, my fears, Ms. Chigwell's indomitable courage. She frowned deeply over Chigwell's betrayal of his medical vows. Lotty knows there are unethical doctors but she never likes to hear about them.

"The worst part in a way was when Louisa woke up and thought I was Gabriella," I said as Lotty led me into the spare room. "I don't want to be back there, you know, back in South Chicago cleaning up behind the Djiaks the way my mother did."

Lotty slid my clothes off with practiced medical fingers. "A little late to be worrying about that, my dear—it's all you've been doing this last month."

I made a face—maybe I would have been better off with the sergeant after all.

Lotty pulled the covers over me. I was asleep before she'd turned out the light, falling deep into dreams of mad boat journeys, of scaling cliffs while being attacked by eagles, of Lotty waiting at the top for me saying, "A little late to be worrying, isn't it, Vic?"

When I woke at one the next afternoon I was unrefreshed. I lay for a bit in a drowsy lethargy, stiff both mentally and physically. I wanted to lie there indefinitely, to drift to sleep until Lotty came home and took care of me. The last few weeks had taken from me any ability to find pleasure in what I did for a living. Or indeed any reason for continuing it.

If I had been able to follow my mother's dreams, I'd be my generation's Geraldine Ferrar, sharing intimate moments across a concert stage with James Levine. I tried imagining what it would be like, to be talented and pampered and wealthy. If someone like Gustav Humboldt came after me, I'd have my press agent whip up a few paragraphs for the *Times* and call the police superintendent—who would be my lover—to knock him down a few pegs.

And when I was worn out some other person would stagger to the bathroom on badly swollen feet to try to clear her head under a cold-water tap. She would make my phone calls, run my errands, suffer hideous hardships for me. If I had time, I would thank her graciously.

In the absence of this selfless Bunter, I called my answering service myself. Mr. Contreras had phoned once. Murray Ryerson had left seven messages, each progressively more emphatic. I didn't want to talk to him. Not ever. But since I'd have to eventually, I might as well get it over with. I found him steaming at the city desk.

"I've had it with you, Warshawski. You cannot get help from the press without delivering your side of the bargain. This fight in South Chicago is old news. The electronic guys already have it. I helped you out on the understanding you'd give me an exclusive."

"Stick it in your ear," I said nastily. "You did sweet nothing for me on this case. You took my leads and gave me back zero. I beat you to the finish line and now you're pissed. The only reason I'm calling at all is to keep the communications lines open for the future, because believe me, I'm not too interested in talking to you in the present."

Murray started to roar back, but his newspaper instincts won out. He put on the brakes and began asking questions. I thought about describing my midnight boat ride up the misty, acrid Calumet, or the utter fatigue of soul I felt after talking to Curtis Chigwell. But I didn't want to justify myself to Murray Ryerson. Instead I gave him everything I'd told the police, along with a vivid description of the fight around the solvent vats. He wanted me to join a photographer down at the Xerxes plant to show where I'd stood and got indignant at my refusal.

"You're a fucking ghoul, Ryerson," I said. "The kind of guy who asks disaster victims how they felt when they saw their husbands or children go up in smoke. I am not going into that plant again, not even if they gave me the Nobel Peace Prize for doing it. The faster I forget the place the happier I'll be."

"Well, Saint Victoria, you go feed the hungry and tend to the sick." He slammed the receiver in my ear.

My head still felt leaden. I went out to the kitchen and made myself a pot of coffee. Lotty had left a note in her thick black script next to the pot —she'd turned off the phone before she left, but both Murray and Mallory had called. I knew about Murray, of course, but Bobby had mercifully not hounded me after the one message. I suspected McGonnigal had intervened and was grateful.

I poked around the refrigerator but couldn't get interested in any of Lotty's healthy food. Finally I settled at the kitchen table with the coffee. Using the extension on the counter, I called Frederick Manheim.

"Mr. Manheim. It's V. I. Warshawski. The detective who came to see you a few weeks ago about Joey Pankowski and Steve Ferraro."

"I remember you, Ms. Warshawski—I remember everything connected with those men. I was sorry to read about the attack on you last week. That didn't have anything to do with Xerxes, did it?"

I leaned back in the chair, trying to find a comfortable spot for my sore shoulder muscles. "By a strange set of coincidences, yes. How would you feel about getting a cartload of material implying that Humboldt Chemical knew the toxic effects of Xerxine as early as 1955?"

He was silent for a long moment, then he said cautiously, "This isn't your idea of a joke is it, Ms. Warshawski? I don't know you well enough to figure out what you think is funny."

"I never felt less like laughing. I'm looking at such an incredible display of cynicism that every time I think of it I get consumed by rage. My old neighbor in South Chicago is dying right now. At the age of forty-two she looks like a war-ravaged grandmother." I checked myself.

"What I really want to know, Mr. Manheim, is whether you're prepared to organize and manage action on behalf of hundreds of former Xerxes employees. Maybe present ones as well. You should think about it carefully. It would be your entire life for the next decade. You couldn't handle it alone in your storefront—you'd have to take on researchers and associates and paralegals, and you'd have to fight off the big guns who'd want to cut you out because they smelled the contingency fees."

"You make it sound real attractive." He laughed quietly. "I told you about the threat I got when I was preparing to appeal. I don't think I have much choice. I mean, I don't see how I could live with myself if I had a chance now to win that case and passed it up just so I wouldn't have to give up my quiet practice. When can I get your cartload?"

"Tonight, if you can drive up to the North Side. Seven-thirty okay?" I gave him Lotty's address.

When he'd hung up I phoned Max at the hospital. After a few minutes on my late-night adventure—which had made the morning papers in skeleton form—he agreed to get the Chigwell documents copied. When I said I'd come by at the end of the day for the originals, he protested graciously: it would be his pleasure to bring them to Lotty's for me.

After that I really couldn't delay a heart-to-heart with Bobby. I tracked him down by phone at the Central District and agreed to meet him there in an hour. That gave me time for a soak in Lotty's tub to limber up my sore shoulders and a call to Mr. Contreras assuring him I was alive, moderately well, and would return home in the morning. He started a long, anxious dump about how he'd felt when he saw the news this morning; I cut him off gently.

"I've got a date with the police. I'll be pretty well tied up today, but we'll have a late breakfast tomorrow and catch up."

"Sounds good, doll. French toast or pancakes?"

"French toast." I couldn't help laughing. It got me down to police headquarters in a light enough mood to deal with Bobby.

His pride was badly wounded by my nailing the Emperor of Trash. Dresberg had been dancing rings around Chicago's finest for years. For any private investigator to have caught him dead to rights would have hurt Mallory. But that it had to be me so upset him that he kept me downtown for four hours.

He interrogated me himself, while Officer Neely took notes, then sent in relays of people from the Organized Crime Division, followed by the Special Functions Unit, finishing with an escorted interview with a couple of feds. By then my fatigue had come back full force. I kept dropping off between questions and it was getting hard for me to remember what I was revealing and what I'd decided belonged to me alone. The third time the feds had to poke me awake they decided they'd had enough of a good time and urged Bobby to send me home.

"Yeah, I guess we've got everything we're going to get." He waited until his office was empty, then said edgily, "What'd you do to McGonnigal last night, Vicki? He made it real clear he wasn't going to be present while I talked to you."

"I didn't do anything," I said, raising my eyebrows. "He turn into a boar or something?"

Bobby frowned at me. "If you're trying to level any charges against John McGonnigal, who is one of the finest—"

"Circe," I cut in hastily. "That's what she did to Odysseus's crew. I assumed you were thinking of that. Or something like it."

Bobby narrowed his eyes but all he said was, "Go on home, Vicki. I don't have the energy for your sense of humor right now."

I was at the door when he lighted his last squib. "How well do you know Ron Kappelman?" His voice had a studied casualness that warned me to be careful.

I turned to look at him, my hand still on the doorknob. "I've talked to him three or four times. We're not lovers, if that's what you're asking."

Bobby's gray eyes measured me steadily. "You know Jurshak did a few favors for him when he signed on as SCRAP's counsel?"

I felt the bottom fall out of my stomach. "Like what?"

"Oh, cleared the way for him to do all the renovation work on his house. That kind of thing."

"And in exchange?"

"Information. Nothing unethical. He wouldn't jeopardize his clients' standing. Just let the alderman's office know what moves they might make. Or what moves a smart PI like you might be making."

"I see." It was an effort to get words out, let alone keep my voice steady. I braced myself against the door. "How do you know all this?"

"Jurshak talked a lot this morning. Nothing like the fear of death to get someone babbling. Of course the courts will throw it all out, information obtained under duress. But watch who you talk to, Vicki. You're a smart girl—smart young lady. I'll even agree you've done some good work. But you're one person alone. You just can't do the job the cops are paid to do."

I was too tired and soul-sick to argue. I felt too bad even to think he was wrong. My shoulders slumped, I slogged my way down the long corridors to the parking lot and headed back to Lotty.

41

A Wise Child

When I got to Lotty's, Max was already there. I felt so down after my talk with Mallory that I would have preferred canceling my meeting with Manheim: What could one person do alone, anyway? As it was I only had time to explain to Lotty who Frederick Manheim was and why I'd invited him when he showed up. His round solemn face was flushed with excitement, but he shook hands politely with Max and Lotty and offered Lotty a bottle of wine. It was a '78 Gruaud-Larose. Max raised his brows appreciatively, so I assumed it was a good bottle.

As we talked in the kitchen my drooping self-confidence began to revive. After all, I had been worried about Kappelman's role all along. It wasn't a failure on my part. Bobby just was trying to skewer me because I'd stopped Steve Dresberg when he and his thousands of backups hadn't been able to touch him.

I whipped up omelets while Max opened the wine, reverentially letting it breathe. While we ate at Lotty's kitchen table we talked about general topics—the wine was too splendid to pollute with Xerxine.

Afterward, though, we moved into Lotty's sitting room. I spelled out the story for Max and Manheim. Lounging on the daybed, I explained what I'd learned from Chigwell—that they'd done the tests because they could see their high rates of illness as early as 1955.

"You should see if you can talk to Ajax. They were handling Xerxes's life and health insurance at the time. I know they went to Mariners Rest in 1963 with evidence of how good and pure they were, but if you find out why Ajax dropped them back in the fifties you may get some inside dope on why they decided to look at blood instead of—I don't know, some other choice."

Manheim, propped on his elbows on the floor, was naturally most interested in what lay in Chigwell's notebooks. Lotty sketched the data for him, but warned him he would have to get an array of specialists.

"I am only a perinatologist, you know. So what I'm telling you is only what I've learned from Dr. Christophersen. You will need many people—blood specialists, a good renal pathologist. And above all, you will need a team in occupational health."

Manheim nodded soberly at all their advice. His rosy cherub's cheeks glowed deeper red as he filled legal pads with notes. Every now and then he asked me a question about the plant and the employees.

Lotty finally put a halt to the discussion—she had to get up early, I was her patient and wasn't fit for another all-night session, and so on. Manheim stood up reluctantly.

"I'm not going to do anything in a hurry," he warned me. "I want to double-check the data, find the lab that did the blood work for them, all that kind of stuff. And I'm going to have to consult with a specialist in environmental law."

I held up my hands. "It's your baby now. You do what you want with it. You just need to keep in mind that Gustav Humboldt isn't going to lie down with his legs up in the air while you're gathering facts—for all I know he's already figured out a way to put the clamps on the lab. You want one last chance to back out?"

He thought for a short minute, then grinned reluctantly. "I've spent enough time on my tush in Beverly—I can't turn down this one. As long as you agree to provide moral support every now and then."

"Yeah, sure, why not," I agreed as positively as I could—I didn't want tentacles from South Chicago to keep reaching out to strangle me.

When Manheim had gone I headed off to bed, leaving Max in the sitting room with a bottle of Lotty's cognac. Lotty came in for a minute after I'd brushed my teeth to tell me Caroline had phoned while I was with the police.

"She wants you to call her. But as she was angry and became rather rude, I thought it wouldn't hurt her to wait."

I grinned. "That's my Caroline. She say anything about Louisa?"

"I gather since she slept through her ordeal she's none the worse for it. Sleep well, my dear."

She was gone when I got up in the morning. I puttered aimlessly around the kitchen, drinking coffee. I started to make toast, then remembered my promise to eat breakfast with Mr. Contreras. I slowly packed my overnight bag. The longer I stayed at Lotty's the less interested I seemed to be in looking after myself. It was time to go before I slipped into unconquerable lassitude.

In deference to Lotty's tidy spirit, I took the sheets from the guest bed and bundled them up with the towels I'd used. I wrote a note telling her I'd taken them home with me to launder. I straightened up the other signs of my presence as best I could and headed over to Racine.

Mr. Contreras's delight at seeing me was equaled only by the dog's. Peppy jumped up to lick my face, her golden tail thumping the door hard enough to swing it shut. My neighbor took the laundry from me.

"These Dr. Lotty's things? I'll wash 'em for you, doll. After breakfast you'll want to unwind, look at your mail, do whatever. So the case is over? Everything locked up with those two villains in the hospital? I mighta known you'd take care of those guys, doll. I shouldn't of worried so much about you. No wonder you got teed off."

I put an arm around him. "Yeah, it all looks swell now that the battle's nearly over. But shooting someone in that kind of situation is just luck—you can't aim. I could be in intensive care instead of Dresberg if the luck had gone the other way."

"*Nearly* over?" His faded brown eyes showed concern. "You mean those guys still have someone gunning for you?"

"Other way around. There's a big old white shark thrashing around in the water. Dresberg and Jurshak were his allies. Who knows what else he's got stashed in his cove." I tried to keep my tone light. "Anyway, I came back here for French toast. Got any?"

"Sure, doll, sure. Everything's ready—just waiting for you before I turn on the griddle." He rubbed his hands together and bustled me inside.

Somewhere from the recesses of his life he'd dug up a white linen tablecloth. He'd cleared the dining-room table of the magazines and bric-a-brac that usually cluttered it and covered it with the cloth. A vase in the middle held red carnations. I was touched.

He swelled with pride at my compliments. "These were Clara's things. They never meant so much to me but I couldn't bring myself to give them to Ruthie when she died; Clara kind of treasured them and I just couldn't quite see Ruthie prizing them like she should."

He hurried off to the kitchen and came back with a glass of fresh orange juice. "Now you sit here, doll, and I'll have breakfast out to you in two shakes."

He fried up tall mounds of bacon and gargantuan stacks of French toast. I ate what I could and repaid him by telling the tale of my midnight trip up the Calumet. He was caught between awe at the exploit and jealousy that I hadn't picked him to go with me, pipe wrench and all.

I gallantly suppressed a shudder at the idea. "I didn't think it would be fair to Peppy," I explained. "If we both got killed or laid up, who would look after her?"

He accepted that grudgingly—and a bit suspiciously—and asked me to tell him again how I'd shot Dresberg. Finally, around noon, I felt I'd stayed long enough and made my escape upstairs. The old man had stacked my mail neatly inside my apartment door, letters in one pile, newspapers in another. I flipped through the letters quickly—nothing personal. Not one thing. Just bills and solicitations. In irritation I tossed the lot, including my home phone bill. The papers would keep—I'd go through them later and see how they'd covered Xerxes.

My rooms had that strange appearance of a place you haven't visited for a while—they seemed somehow unfamiliar, as though I'd heard them described but hadn't ever actually seen them. I moved around restlessly, trying to reestablish myself in my own existence. And trying not to wonder what Humboldt might next attempt. I wasn't entirely successful. At two when the doorbell rang I jumped a little. This has got to stop, Victoria, I admonished myself. I walked purposefully to the intercom and pressed it.

Caroline's voice came tinnily through. If anything were needed to restore my self-confidence, it would be a little roughhousing with her. I prepared myself for battle and buzzed her in.

I could hear her moving up the stairs with a slow, heavy tread most unlike her usual canter. When she made the last turning and came into view, I could see that she looked somber. My heart contracted. Louisa. Tuesday night's escapade had been too much for her weak system and she'd died.

"Hello, Caroline. Come on in."

She stood in the doorway. "Do you hate me, Vic?"

My eyebrows went up in surprise. "Why on earth do you ask that? I thought you'd shown up to chew me out for exposing Louisa to so much abuse two nights ago."

"It wasn't your fault. It was mine. If I'd told you what was going on . . . You almost got killed because of me. Twice. But all I could do was scream at you like the spoiled little brat you kept telling me I was."

I put an arm around her and dragged her into the apartment—the last thing I wanted was for Mr. Contreras to hear us and come bounding up. Caroline leaned against me and let me take her over to the couch.

"How's Louisa?"

"She's back home." Caroline hunched her shoulders. "She actually seems a little better today. She doesn't remember anything that happened, and whatever they shot her full of gave her a better sleep than she usually gets."

She picked up a copy of *Fortune* and started twisting it around. "The police came by right after I'd gotten home and found her missing. I'd been at a marathon meeting downtown, you know, going over the recycling stuff with some of the local EPA attorneys. I thought Ma'd had a bad turn, that the neighbors or Aunt Connie had taken her to the hospital. Then when the cops came for me I went a little crazy."

I nodded. "Lotty told me you'd called yesterday with an angry message. I just didn't have the strength to get back to you."

She looked at me directly for the first time since she'd arrived. "I don't blame you—I was mad enough to spit blood and then some. I was screaming my head off at you while I drove to Help of Christians. But when I got there all I could think of was you and your mother looking after Ma and me all those years. And then I thought of what you'd been through for the two of us just these last three weeks. And I felt terribly ashamed. It never would have happened if I hadn't pushed you into looking for my father when you didn't want to do it."

I took her hand and squeezed it. "I've been plenty mad at you—probably cursed you worse than you did me. And I'm not exactly wearing a halo —if I'd bugged out when you asked me to I'd never have been left for dead in the swamp and Louisa wouldn't have been kidnapped."

"But I don't think the police would ever have found out the truth," she objected. "They never would have found Nancy's killer, and Jurshak and Dresberg would still be ruling South Chicago. I shouldn't have been such a chicken—I should have told you about the threats to Louisa to begin with, so you wouldn't get blindsided."

I knew I needed to tell her about discovering who had gotten Louisa pregnant, but I couldn't seem to find the words. Or maybe it was just the courage. While I was fishing around for it Caroline said abruptly:

"I bought Ma some cigarettes. I remembered what you said that first night you came by, how they wouldn't make her any worse and they might cheer her up. And I could see all I was trying to do was have power over her, keeping her from having one thing that might bring her a little pleasure."

Her last words brought back Lotty's advice most strongly. I took a breath and said, "Caroline, I have to tell you—I did find out who your father was."

Her blue eyes turned very dark. "Not Joey Pankowski, right?"

I shook my head. "I'm afraid not. There isn't any easy way to say this, or to hear it, but it would be really wrong for me not to tell you—a most noxious way of controlling your life."

She looked at me solemnly. "Go ahead, Vic. I—I think I'm more grown up than I used to be. I can take it."

I took both her hands and said gently, "It was Art Jurshak. He was your—"

"Art Jurshak!" she burst out. "I don't believe you. Ma never would have come across him in a million years! You're making this up, aren't you?"

I shook my head. "I wish I were. Art—he—uh—your Grandmother Djiak is his sister. He used to spend a lot of time with Connie and Louisa when they were little, and the Djiaks chose not to notice that he was abusing them. Your grandparents are both terrified of sex, and your grandfather especially is frightened of women, so they made up a vile fairy tale for themselves that it was your mother's fault when she got pregnant. Although they did stop seeing Art, it was Louisa they punished. They're a pretty loathsome couple, Ed and Martha Djiak."

Her freckles stood out like polka dots against the pallor of her face. "Art Jurshak. He's my father? I'm related to him?"

"He gave you some chromosomes, babe, but you're not related to him, not by any manner of means. You're your own person, you know, not his. Not the Djiaks', either. You've got guts, you've got integrity, and, above all, you have valor. None of that has any relationship to Art Jurshak."

"I—Art Jurshak—" She gave a little bark of hysterical laughter. "All these years I thought your father had got Ma pregnant. I thought that was why your mother did so much for us. I thought I was really your sister. Now I see I don't have anyone at all."

She got up and ran for the door. I ran after her and caught her arm, but she wrenched herself free and jerked the door open.

"Caroline!" I tore down the stairs after her. "This doesn't change that. You will always be my sister, Caroline!"

I stood on the sidewalk in my shirt sleeves, watching helplessly as she drove recklessly down the street toward Belmont.

42

Humboldt's Gift

I think the last time I felt this bad was the day after my mother's funeral, when her death suddenly became real to me. I tried calling Caroline, both at her house and at SCRAP. Both Louisa and a secretary agreed to take messages, but wherever Caroline was she didn't want to talk to me. A thousand times or so I thought of calling McGonnigal, asking the police to keep an eye out for her—but what could they do about one distraught citizen?

Around four I borrowed Peppy from Mr. Contreras and drove her over to the lake. I wasn't up to running, although she certainly was, but I needed her silent love and the expanse of sky and water to soothe my spirit. It wasn't out of the question that Humboldt, a sore loser if ever there was one, had some kind of backup to Dresberg, so I kept a hand on the Smith & Wesson in my jacket pocket.

I threw sticks left-handed for the dog. She didn't think much of the distance they went, but fetched them anyway to show she was a good sport. When she'd worked off some of her excess energy, we sat looking at the water while I kept my right hand on the gun.

In some remote part of my mind I knew I should think of a way to take the initiative with Humboldt, so that I didn't have to walk around with one hand in my pocket for the rest of my life. I could go to Ron Kappelman and force the issue with him, see how much he'd been feeding Jurshak about my investigation. Maybe he'd even know how to reach Humboldt.

The whole prospect of action seemed so impossible that just thinking about it made my eyelids feel leaden, my brain fogged over. Even the idea of getting up and walking to the car would take more effort than I could manage. I might have sat staring at the waves until spring if Peppy hadn't gotten fed up and started pushing me with her nose.

"You don't get it, do you?" I said to her. "Golden retrievers don't feel guilty about their neighbors' puppies. They don't feel obligated to look after them till death."

She agreed happily, tongue lolling. Whatever I said was fine as long as action accompanied it. We walked back to the car—or I walked and Peppy danced in a spiral around me to make sure I didn't stray or go back into catatonia.

When we got home Mr. Contreras came bustling out with Lotty's clean sheets and towels. I thanked him as best I could, but told him I wanted to be alone.

"I'd like to keep the dog awhile too. Okay?"

"Yeah, sure, doll, sure. Whatever you say. She misses your runs, that's for certain, so she'd probably be glad to stay with you, make sure you haven't forgotten her."

Back in my own place, I tried Caroline again, but she was still either gone or refusing to talk to me. Disheartened, I sat at the piano and picked my way through *"Ch'io scordi di te."* It had been Gabriella's favorite aria and it suited my mood of melancholy self-pity to play it through, then work at singing it. I felt tears of bathetic sorrow pricking my eyelids and went back to the middle, where the soprano line is most melodic.

When the phone rang I jumped up eagerly, sure it was Caroline willing finally to talk to me.

"Miss Warshawski?" It was the quavering voice of Humboldt's butler.

"Yes, Anton?" My voice was calm but an adrenaline surge cleared my lethargy like sunlight on fog.

"Mr. Humboldt would like to speak with you. Please hold." The voice held frosty disapproval. Perhaps he thought Humboldt wanted to make me his mistress and he feared I was too low class for the tone of the Roanoke.

A minute or so went by. I tried to get Peppy to come to the phone and act as my secretary but she wasn't interested. Finally Humboldt's rich baritone vibrated the earpiece.

"Ms. Warshawski. I would be most grateful if you would pay me a visit this evening. I have someone with me whom you would be sorry not to meet."

"Let's see," I said. "Dresberg and Jurshak are in the hospital. Troy is under arrest. Ron Kappelman isn't of much interest to me anymore. Who you got left?"

He gave his hearty chuckle to show that Monday's contretemps was just an unhappy memory. "You're always so direct, Ms. Warshawski. I assure you there will be no gunplay if you will pay me the courtesy of a visit."

"Knives? Hypodermics? Vats of chemicals?"

He laughed again. "Let us just say you would regret it forever if you did not meet my visitor. I'll send my car for you at six."

"You're very kind," I said formally, "but I prefer to drive myself. And I will bring a friend with me."

My heart was pounding when I hung up, and wild surmises flashed through my mind. He had Caroline hostage, or Lotty. I couldn't check on Caroline, but I did phone Lotty at the clinic. When she came to the phone, surprised at my urgency, I explained where I was going.

"If you don't hear from me by seven, call the police." I gave her Bobby's home and office numbers.

"You're not going alone, are you?" Lotty asked anxiously.

"No, no, I'm taking a friend."

"Vic! Not that meddlesome old man! He'll cause more trouble than he'll save you."

I laughed a little. "No, I agree with you totally. I'm taking someone who's silent and reliable."

Only after I promised to call her as soon as I got away from the Roanoke would she agree to my going without a police escort. When she'd hung up I turned to Peppy. "Come on, babe. You're going to the haunts of the rich and powerful."

The dog expressed herself interested as always in any expedition. She watched, her head cocked, while I checked the Smith & Wesson one last time to make sure a bullet was chambered, then bounded down the stairs ahead of me. We managed to make it outside without a checkup by Mr. Contreras—he must have been in the kitchen making supper.

I looked around cautiously to make sure I wasn't walking into an ambush, but no one was lying in wait. Peppy jumped into the backseat of the Chevy and we headed south.

The doorman at the Roanoke greeted me with the same avuncular courtesy I'd had on my first visit. Apparently Anton hadn't told him I was a menace to society. Or the memory of my five-dollar tip outweighed any nasty messages from the twelfth floor.

"The dog is accompanying you, ma'am?"

I smiled. "Mr. Humboldt is expecting her."

"Very good, ma'am." He turned us over to Fred at the elevator.

I moved with practiced grace to the little bench at the rear. Peppy sat alertly at my feet, her tongue hanging out, panting a little. She wasn't used to elevators, but she took the uncertain flooring with the cool poise of a champion. When we'd been decanted she sniffed around the marble floor of Humboldt's lobby, but came to attention at my side when Anton opened the ornate wooden door.

He looked coldly at Peppy. "We prefer not having dogs up here, as their habits are difficult to predict or control. I'll ask Marcus to keep her in the lobby until you're ready to leave."

I grinned a little savagely. "Uncontrollable habits sound as though they should mesh perfectly with your boss's style. I'm not coming in without her, so make up your mind how bad Humboldt wants to see me."

"Very good, madam." The frost in his voice had moved into the low Kelvin range. "If you will follow me?"

Humboldt was seated in front of his library fire. He was drinking out of a heavily cut glass—whiskey and soda as nearly as I could tell. My stomach twisted as I watched him, my anger returning and jolting my system.

Humboldt looked severely at Anton when Peppy came in at my left heel, but the majordomo said aloofly that I refused to see him without her. Humboldt immediately switched personae, genially asking the dog's name and trying to make much of her beauty. She'd picked up his antagonism, though, and didn't respond. I ostentatiously walked around the room with her, inviting her to sniff in corners. I flicked back the heavy brocade curtains, but the view was of the lake—there was no place for a sniper to hide.

I dropped the curtain. "I was kind of expecting a burst of machine-gun fire. Don't tell me my life is going to settle into monotony."

Humboldt gave his rich little chuckle. "Nothing affects you, does it, Ms. Warshawski? You really are a most remarkable young woman."

I sat in the armchair facing Humboldt; Peppy stood in front of me, looking from him to me with concern, her tail down. I patted her head and she went down on her haunches without relaxing.

"Your mystery guest hasn't arrived yet?"

"My guest will keep." He chuckled gently to himself. "I thought you and I could have a little chat first. It might not be necessary to produce my visitor. Whiskey?"

I shook my head. "Your rarefied cellars are giving me ideas above my income, I can't afford to get used to them."

"But you could, Ms. Warshawski. You could, you know, if you would stop going around with that outsize chip on your shoulder."

I leaned back in the chair and crossed my legs. "Now that is really unworthy of you. I expected a much grander, or at least more subtle, approach."

"Now, now, Ms. Warshawski. You're too hasty to react much of the time. You could do worse than listen to me."

"Yeah, I guess I could follow the Cubs on a road trip. But you might as well spit it out now so I'll know if I have to dodge your minions' bullets for the rest of my life."

He refused to let himself get ruffled. "You've paid a great deal of attention to my affairs recently, Ms. Warshawski. So I've returned the compliment and paid much attention to yours."

"I bet my researches were a lot more exciting than yours." I kept my hand on Peppy's head.

"Perhaps we have different ideas of what might prove exciting. For instance, I was most intrigued to learn that you owe a balance of fifty thousand dollars on your apartment and that your mortgage payments are not easy for you to meet."

"Oh, God, Gustav. You aren't going to pull the old I'll-get-the-bank-to-cut-off-your-mortgage routine, are you? That's getting pretty boring."

He continued as though I hadn't spoken. "Your parents are both dead, I understand. But you have a good friend who stands toward you as sort of a mother, I believe—this Dr. Charlotte Herschel. Yes?"

I tightened my fingers so strongly in Peppy's hair that she gave a little yelp. "If anything happens to Dr. Herschel—*anything*— from a flat tire to a bloody nose—you will be dead within twenty-four hours. That's a cast-iron prophecy."

He gave his hearty chuckle. "You're so active, Ms. Warshawski, that you imagine everyone must be as energetic as yourself. No, I was more concerned about Dr. Herschel's medical practice. Whether she would be able to keep her license."

He waited for me to react again, but I'd managed to regain enough self-control to keep quiet. I picked up *The New York Times* from the little table that lay between us and flipped to the sports section. The Islanders were on a roll—how disappointing.

"You're not curious, Ms. Warshawski?" he finally asked.

"Not especially." I turned to a discussion of the Mets' prospects going into training camp. "I mean, there're so many creepy things you might do it'd be a waste of energy wondering which particular one you've lighted on this time."

He put his whiskey glass down with a snap and leaned forward. Peppy growled a little in the back of her throat. I put what looked like a restraining hand on her—it's hard to imagine a golden retriever attacking someone, but if you don't like dogs, you might not know that.

He kept an eye on Peppy. "So you are prepared to sacrifice your home and Dr. Herschel's career to your stubborn pride?"

"What do you want me to do?" I said irritably. "Lie on the floor and kick and scream? I'm prepared to believe you have much more in the way of power, money, whatever than I do. You want to rub my nose in it, be my guest. Just don't expect me to act real excited about it."

"Don't jump so quickly to conclusions, Ms. Warshawski," he said plaintively. "You're not without options. You just don't want to hear what they are."

"Okay." I smiled brightly. "Tell me."

"Get your dog to lie down first."

I gave Peppy a hand signal and she obediently dropped to the floor, but she kept her back haunches tensed, ready to jump.

"I'm only offering possibilities. You mustn't be so quick to react to the first one. It's just one scenario, you see, your mortgage, Dr. Herschel's license. There are others. You might be able to pay off that debt with enough money left to get yourself a car more suited to your personality than that old Chevy—you see, I have been doing my research. What would you drive if you had the opportunity?"

"Gosh, I don't know, Mr. Humboldt. I haven't thought a lot about it. Maybe I'd move up to a Buick."

He sighed like a disappointed father. "You should listen to me seriously, young lady, or you will soon find yourself out of options."

"Okay, okay," I said. "I'd like to drive a Ferrari, but Magnum's already doing that. Maybe an Alfa . . . So you'll give me my co-op and a sports car and Dr. Herschel's license. What would you like from me as a show of gratitude for such generosity?"

He smiled: everyone can be pressured or bought. "Dr. Chigwell. A willing, hardworking man, but not, alas, of great ability. Unfortunately, to have a doctor at an industrial location does not give one access to physicians of Dr. Herschel's caliber."

I put the paper down and stopped petting the dog to prove I was all attention.

"He kept some notes over the years on our employees at Xerxes. Without my knowledge, of course—I can't keep on top of all the details of an operation the size of Humboldt."

"You and Ronald Reagan," I murmured sympathetically.

He looked at me suspiciously, but I kept an expression of intent interest on my face.

"I only recently learned about these notes. The information in them is useless because it's totally inaccurate. But in the wrong hands it might look most damaging to Xerxes. It could be difficult for me to prove that all the data he collected were wrong."

"Especially over a twenty-year period," I said. "But if you could get those notebooks, you would give me my mortgage? And withdraw any threat to Dr. Herschel?"

"There would also be a bonus for you because of the amount of trouble you've been subjected to by some of my overly zealous friends."

He reached inside his jacket pocket and held out a piece of parchment for me to look at. After glancing at it casually I dropped it on the little table between us. My coolness took an effort—the document represented two thousand preferred shares of Humboldt Chemical. I picked up the *Times* again and looked at the stock summaries.

"Closed at 101 3/8 yesterday. A two-hundred-thousand-dollar bonus with no brokerage fees. I'm impressed." I leaned back in the chair and looked at him squarely. "Trouble is, I could double that just by shorting Humboldt. If money was that important to me. It just isn't. And you're shit out of luck on the notebooks, anyway—they've already gone both to an attorney and to a team of medical specialists. You're dead. I don't know what the value of the coming lawsuits is, but half a billion probably isn't too far off the mark."

"You'd rather put your friend, the woman who has stood as a mother to you, out of practice, for the sake of some people you never met and who aren't worth your consideration anyway?"

"If you've been doing research on me, you know that Louisa Djiak isn't a casual acquaintance," I snapped. "And I defy you to think of any threat to Dr. Herschel that her reputation for probity wouldn't be equal to."

He gave a smile that made him look very like a shark. "Really, Ms. Warshawski. You must learn not to be so hasty. I would not make any threat I didn't feel competent to execute."

He rang a bell tucked into the mantel. Anton appeared so quickly, he must have been hovering in the hallway.

"Bring our other visitor, Anton."

The butler inclined his head and left. He returned a moment or two later with a woman of about twenty-five. Her brown hair was permed around her head in tight little corkscrews that exposed too much of her blotchy neck. She had obviously made an effort over her appearance; I supposed the ruffled acetate dress was her best, since the boxy high heels had been dyed a matching aqua. Under the thick pancake covering her acne she looked belligerent and a little frightened.

"This is Mrs. Portis, Ms. Warshawski. Her daughter was a patient of Dr. Herschel's. Isn't that right, Mrs. Portis?"

She nodded vigorously. "My Mandy. And Dr. Herschel did what she should have known better than to do, a grown woman with a little girl. Mandy was crying and screaming when she came out of the examining room, it took me days to get her settled down again and find out what went on. But when I found out—"

"You went to the state's attorney and made a full report," I finished smoothly, despite a rage that was making my cheeks flame.

"She was naturally too disturbed to know what do to," Humboldt said with an unctuousness that made me what to shoot him. "It's very difficult to bring charges against a family doctor, especially one who can summon the support that Dr. Herschel can. That's why I feel grateful for my own position, which enables me to help out a woman like this."

I stared incredulously at him. "You really think you can take someone with Dr. Herschel's reputation to court with a woman like this as your witness? An expert lawyer will shred her. You're not just an egomaniac, Humboldt—you're stupid with it."

"Be careful whom you call stupid, young lady—an expert lawyer can make anyone break down. Nothing turns a jury hostile faster. And besides, what would the publicity do to Dr. Herschel's practice? Not to mention the state licensing board? Especially if Mrs. Portis is joined by other worried mothers whose daughters Dr. Herschel has treated. After all, Dr. Herschel is almost sixty and has never married—a jury would be bound to suspect her sexual preferences."

The pulse in my neck was throbbing so violently, I could hardly breathe, let alone think. The dog was whimpering a little at my feet. I forced myself to stroke her gently; it helped slow my heartbeat a little. I got up and moved to a phone on a corner table, Peppy close on my heels.

Lotty was still at the clinic. "Vic! You're all right? It's nearly seven now."

"I'm okay physically, Dr. Herschel. But mentally I'm slightly deranged. I need to explain something to you and get your reaction. Do you have a patient named Mrs. Portis?"

Lotty was puzzled but didn't ask any questions. She came back to the phone quickly. "A woman who saw me once two years ago. Her daughter Amanda was eight at the time and throwing up a lot. I suggested psychological problems and it drove her away in a huff."

"Well, Humboldt has dug her up out of some ditch. And gotten her to agree to claim you abused her daughter. Sexually, you understand. Unless we turn Chigwell's notebooks over to him."

Lotty was silent a moment. "My license for the notebooks in other words?" she finally said. "And you thought you had to call to get my answer?"

"I didn't feel able to speak for you on such a matter. He's also offering me two hundred K in stock shares, just so you know the size of the bribe. And my mortgage."

"Is he with you? I will speak to him myself. But you should know I will tell him that I did not see my parents killed by Fascists only to bow down to them in my old age."

I turned to Humboldt. "Dr. Herschel would like to talk to you."

He pushed himself out of his armchair. Almost the only sign of his age was the effort it took when he got up. I stood next to him as he spoke to Lotty, my breath coming in short noisy pants. I could hear her concise alto going on at length, lecturing him as she might a failing student, although I couldn't make out the exact words.

"You are making a mistake, Doctor, a most serious error," Humboldt said heavily. "No, no, I will not be insulted further on my own phone, madam."

He hung up and glared at me. "You will be very sorry. Both of you. I don't think you appreciate how very much power I have in this town, young lady."

The pulse in my neck was still throbbing. "There are so many things you don't appreciate, Gustav, that I hardly know where to start. You're dead. You're through in this town. The *Herald-Star* is working on your connection to Steve Dresberg and believe me, they'll find it. You may think you have it buried fifty layers deep, but Murray Ryerson is a good archaeologist and he's burning right now.

"But more than that, your company is through. Your little chemical emporium just ain't big enough to absorb the shock when those Xerxine suits start pouring in. It may be six months, it may take two years, but you're looking at half a billion in claims, easy. And it's going to be like shooting rats in a barrel to prove malicious intent on your part—Humboldt's part. That company you built up—it's going to be like Jonah's gourd—grew in a night and withered in a night. You're dead meat, Humboldt, and you're so crazy you can't even smell the rot."

"You're wrong, you little Polish bitch! I'll show you how wrong you are!" He hurled his whiskey glass across the room where it smashed into one of the bookcases. "I'll break you just as easily as that glass. Gordon

Firth will never hire you again. You'll lose your license. You'll never get another client again. I'll see you on West Madison with the other drunks and has-beens and I'll laugh at you. I'll roar with laughter."

"You do that," I said fiercely. "I'm sure your grandchildren will be much entertained by the spectacle. In fact, I bet they'd like to hear the whole story of how you poisoned people to maximize your goddamned bottom line."

"My grandchildren!" he roared. "If you dare come near them, neither you nor your friends will ever know another night's sleep in this city!"

He kept shouting, his threats escalating to include not just Lotty but other friends whose names his researchers had dredged up. Peppy's hackles rose and she growled menacingly. I kept one hand on her collar and pressed the buzzer in the mantel with the other. When Anton came I pointed at the shattered glass.

"You may want to clean that up. And I think Mrs. Portis would be more comfortable if you'd send her down to Marcus to get a cab. Come, Peppy." We left as quickly as we could, but it seemed I could hear that maniacal bellow all the way to the lobby.

43

Bringing It All Back Home

Lotty and I spent the next few days with my lawyer. I don't know if it was Carter Freeman's efforts, or Anton's, or just that the scene at the Roanoke had terrified her, but Mrs. Portis lost interest in bringing charges against Lotty. We had a tougher time over my mortgage—for a few weeks it looked as though I might have to find a place to rent. But Freeman managed to settle that somehow, too. I've always suspected that he put up a guarantee himself, but he only raises his brows and feigns ignorance and changes the conversation when I try asking him.

After a bit my life regained its normal flow—running Peppy, spending time with friends, breaking my heart over Chicago's sports teams—the Black Hawks at that particular season. I returned, too, to my normal workload, looking at industrial fraud, doing background searches on candidates for sensitive financial positions, that kind of thing.

I worked hard to keep thoughts of Humboldt and South Chicago at bay. In the normal course of things I wouldn't let loose ends drift away at the end of a case, but I just couldn't take any more involvement in the old neighborhood. So I decided to leave Ron Kappelman's role in the mess as an unanswered question. If Bobby's accusation was true, that he'd been feeding Jurshak news of my whereabouts, I should by rights go down to Pullman and confront him. I just didn't have the mental energy to pursue it any further, though. Let the state's attorney figure it all out when Jurshak and Dresberg came to trial.

Sergeant McGonnigal was another loose end that never got tied up. I saw him with Bobby a couple of times while going over endless statements and interrogations. He acted pretty cold until he realized I wasn't going to blow the whistle on his late-night lapse from policeman decorum. Over time I knew I was better off not getting too cozy with a cop, however empathic, but we never talked about it.

By May, with the Cubs already vying for last place, Humboldt Chemical was trading in the high fifties. Frederick Manheim had consulted enough experts in law and medicine that whispers of possible trouble had followed the trade winds east to Wall Street. Manheim came to consult with me a couple of times, but I was weary to the depths of my spirit of Humboldt.

I told Manheim I'd testify at any trials about my role in learning of the cover-up, but not to count on me for any other support. So I didn't know what Humboldt was doing to prepare a counterattack. A blurb in the papers a few days after our final encounter said he was being treated for stress at Passavant, but since the *Herald-Star* ran a photo of him throwing out the first pitch for the Sox on opening day, I guess he'd gotten over it.

Round about that time, as the Cubs moved north from Tempe, I got a postcard from Florence. "Don't wait until you're seventy-nine to see it," ran the brief message in Ms. Chigwell's spidery hand. When she returned home a few weeks later she called me.

"I just wanted to let you know that I'm not living with Curtis anymore. I bought his share in the house from him. He's gone to a retirement home in Clarendon Hills."

"How do you like living alone?"

"Very much. I just wish I'd done it sixty years ago, but I didn't have the courage to do it then. I wanted to tell you, because you're the one who made it possible, showing me how a woman can live an independent life. That's all."

She hung up on my incoherent protest. I smiled a little—gruff to the end. I hoped I was that tough forty years ahead.

The only thing that really troubled me was Caroline Djiak; I couldn't get her to talk to me. She'd resurfaced after a day's absence, but she wouldn't come to the phone, and when I drove down to Houston Street she shut the door on me, not even letting me in to see Louisa. I kept thinking I'd made a terrible mistake—not just in telling her about Jurshak, but in keeping up my dogged search when she'd been trying to call me off.

Lotty shook her head sternly when I fretted about it. "You're not God, Victoria. You can't pick and choose what's best for people's lives. And if you're going to spend hours in lachrymose self-pity, please do it someplace else—it's not an appetizing spectacle. Or find another line of work. Your dogged searches, as you call them, spring from a fundamental clarity of vision. If you no longer have that sight, you no longer are suited to your job."

Her bracing words didn't kill my self-doubts, but in time even my worries over Caroline receded. When she called in early June to tell me Louisa had died, I could accept her abrupt conversation with relative equanimity.

I went to the funeral at St. Wenceslaus, but not to the house on Houston for food afterward. Louisa's parents were running the event, and whether they aped pious grief or murmured sly animadversions on divine providence I would be hard put to control my desire to decimate them.

Caroline made no effort to speak to me at the service; by the time I got home my lachrymose self-pity over her had been replaced by an older, more familiar feeling—irritation at her brattiness. So when I found her waiting on my doorstep a month or so later, I didn't exactly welcome her with open arms.

"I've been here since three," she said without introduction. "I was afraid you'd gone out of town."

"Sorry I didn't leave my schedule with your secretary," I replied sardonically. "But then, of course, I wasn't anticipating the pleasure."

"Don't be mean, Vic," she begged. "I know I deserve it—I've been a horse's rear end the last four months. But I need to apologize or explain or —well, anyway, I don't want you only to be mad when you think about me."

I unlocked the lobby door. "You know, Caroline, I'm reminded irresistibly of Lucy and Charlie Brown and the football. You know how she always promises *this* time she won't pull it away just as he's kicking—and she always does, and he always lands smack on his butt? I have a feeling I'm about to end on my ass one last time, but come on up."

Her ready color came. "Vic, please—I know I deserve anything you want to say to me, but I've come here to apologize. Don't make it harder on me than it already is."

That shut me up, but it didn't quiet my suspicions. I led her silently to my apartment, fixed her a Coke while I had a rum and tonic, and took her to the little ledge that serves as my back porch. Mr. Contreras waved at us from his tomatoes, but stayed below. The dog came up to join the party.

After she'd fondled Peppy's ears and drunk her soda, Caroline took a deep breath and said, "Vic, I really am sorry I ran out on you last winter, and—and avoided you afterward. Somehow—somehow it's only since Louisa died that I could see it from your viewpoint. See that you weren't making fun of me."

"Making fun of you!" I was astonished.

She turned crimson again. "I thought, you see, you had such a wonderful father. I loved your dad so much, I wanted him to be my father too. I used to lie in bed and imagine it, imagine how much fun we'd have when we were all together as a family, him and me and Ma and Gabriella. And you'd be my real sister, so you wouldn't feel pissed off at having to look after me."

It was my turn to be embarrassed. I tried muttering something and finally said, "No eleven-year-old wants to be saddled with looking after a baby. I expect if you'd really been my sister, I would have been more annoyed instead of less. But I wasn't laughing at you for having a—a different father than mine. It never once crossed my mind."

"I know that now," she said. "It just took me a long time to figure it out. It was me that felt humiliated at the idea of Art Jurshak being—well, doing that to Ma. You know. Then when she died I suddenly saw what it must have been like for her. And it made me realize what a remarkable woman she was, because she was such a good mother, she was so lively, and really loved life and everything. And it would have been so easy for her to be angry and bitter and take it out on me."

She looked at me earnestly. "Then last week I went—went to see young Art. My brother, I guess he is. He was pretty good about it, even though I could see it was just hell for him. Having to talk to me, I mean. It was awful for him growing up. Art wasn't any kind of father. He only got married to keep the Djiaks from spoiling his political career, and after young Art was born he moved into the spare bedroom. He never wanted to have anything to do with his own son. So in a crazy kind of way I can see I was better off. You know, just with Ma. Even if—even if he hadn't been her uncle, it would have been so much worse living with him than it was growing up without a father."

My throat was a little tight. "I've been full of self-recriminations these last four months, thinking I made the colossal mistake of an egomaniac in keeping on the case when you asked me to quit. And then in telling you about him."

"Don't," she said. "I'm glad to know. It's better to find out for sure, rather than imagine it in my head, even if what I made up was a hell of a lot nicer than what reality turned out to be. Besides, if Tony Warshawski had really been my father, he'd seem like a pretty big sleaze moving Ma and me next door to you and Gabriella."

She laughed, but I took her hand and held it. After a bit she said hesitantly, "I—this next part is hard to tell you, after all the insults I shouted at you about leaving the neighborhood. But I'm leaving, too. I'm moving away from Chicago, actually. I always wanted to live out in the country, the real country, so I'm going to Montana to study forestry. I never admitted it to anyone, because I thought if I wasn't like you, doing social activism stuff, you know, that you would despise me."

I gave an inarticulate squawk that made Peppy jump.

"No, really, Vic. But all these things I've been thinking about, well, I see you never wanted me to be like you. It was just part of my head trip, how I thought if I did the same things you did, you would like me well enough to let me really be part of your family."

"No way, babe—I want you doing what's good for you, not what's right for me."

She nodded. "So I applied out there and rushed everything through and I'm leaving in two weeks. I'm making Ma's folks buy the house on Houston and that's giving me the money to go. But I wanted to tell you in person, and I hope you meant it, that you'll always be my sister, because, well, anyway, I hope you meant it."

I knelt next to her chair and put my arms around her. "Till death do us part, kid."